Augustus Jessopp, Roger North

The Lives of the Right Hon. Francis North, Baron Guilford

The Hon. Sir Dudley North; and the Hon. and Rev. Dr. John North. Together with the autobiography of the author. Vol. III

Augustus Jessopp, Roger North

The Lives of the Right Hon. Francis North, Baron Guilford
The Hon. Sir Dudley North; and the Hon. and Rev. Dr. John North. Together with the autobiography of the author. Vol. III

ISBN/EAN: 9783337012359

Printed in Europe, USA, Canada, Australia, Japan

Cover: Foto ©Raphael Reischuk / pixelio.de

More available books at **www.hansebooks.com**

THE LIVES OF THE NORTHS.

THE HON. ROGER NORTH

THE LIVES OF THE

[RI]GHT HON. FRANCIS NORTH, BARON GUILFORD; THE HON. SIR DUDLEY NORTH; AND THE HON. AND REV. DR. JOHN NORTH.

BY THE HON.

ROGER NORTH,

TOGETHER WITH

THE AUTOBIOGRAPHY OF THE AUTHOR.

EDITED BY

AUGUSTUS JESSOPP, D.D.

IN THREE VOLUMES.

VOL. III.

LONDON: GEORGE BELL AND SONS, YORK STREET, COVENT GARDEN.

1890.

CHISWICK PRESS:—C. WHITTINGHAM AND CO., TOOKS COURT,
CHANCERY LANE.

CONTENTS.

VOL. III.

THE AUTOBIOGRAPHY OF THE HON. ROGER NORTH.

CHAPTER I.

NOTES OF ME.

THE onely felicity, which came at my nativity attended me to this hour and will to that of my last breath, and after all leav a perfume in a reasonable good Name at parting, is that of being descended from Religious, vertuous, wise, and sound parents. That they were so is granted by all that knew them, and that I am happy from their vertues I know and can affirme. And if I should goe about to trace up all the stepps by which I perceiv it, I must make a journall of my life, but that is too much at this time of the day. I lay it downe for a truth, Quasi Evangelicall, that the best legacy parents can leav to their children is good principles and sound bodys. And to prove it shall alledg some few passages of my oune experience, who ascribe all the good I know and the many deliverances I have had, next to Almighty Providence, (which for ought I know wrought by such means) to the Caracter of My parents.

2. Our childhood past, as usuall, under the Mother's governement. Wee were taught to Reverence our father, whose care of us then consisted cheifly in the Gravity and decorum of his comportment, order and sobriety of life, whereby no Indecent or Mischevous Impressions took place with us from his example, and when he deposed his temper, and condescended to entertein the little credulous Imper-

tinents, it was with an agreable as well as moral Effect, tending either to Instruct or Encourage what was good, and to defie the Contrary; which is not onely a care but a skill in parents to doe, without Relucting the tender minds of children by the austerity of comands and threats. The constant reward of Blessing,[1] which was observed as sacred, was a petit Regale in his closet, and that allwais came as a reward of what was to be encouraged, and denyed when demerited; whereby it appears that great use may be made of that fondness which disposeth parents to gratifie children's litle craving appetites, by doing it with an adjunct of precept, as a reward of obedience and vertue, such as they are capable of, and at the same time being kind, and tender in Gratifiing them. This makes yong Creatures thinck that their will is not enough, without other means, to obtein their desires, and knowing that, they will Conforme, which breeds an habit of order in them and lasts to the end. The Contrary is seen, when fondness makes parents Indulg all things to children, upon their Importunate demands, and oftentimes without it, whether wholsome or not, as in giving them wine, and strong drinks. Than which nothing more destroys Nature in children. And in this particular, our parents were kind and happy to us. For wee never tasted any wine or strong drink, nor did wee know that there was anything desirable in it. For there was no such thing in the family as cracking of botles, sitting whole afternoons and nights drinking and roaring, to stirr us up to a curiosity of knowing what it was that made such sport, and doing the like. For at the table there was litel, and that fell not much in discours to catch our attention, which was quick enough, as where there is tasting, and giving Judgment of wine, with a consequence of Healths that setts children on fire; and raiseth a porpos In them to do the like, when they can, which they seldom faile to execute. And that drinking

[1] " .... So posting from Dover to London, and finding his father's door open, he entered the house in his Spanish habit. His father seeing one in that garb *kneeling and begging his blessing*, demanded who he was? for he did not know him."—*Jebb's Life of Nicholas Ferrar*, § 19. " .... children kneel to ask blessing of parents in England; but where else ? "—*Donne's Sermon on Genesis i.* 26.

that was among the servants of the first rank called gentlemen, would often be too much; but ordinarily in their
conversation at home, there was a liberty but no Excess.
Wee observed nothing from hence to tempt us, especially
when there was scarce a draught between meals above
stairs, where our greatest Regards lay; and sometimes
tasting of the old strong beer, which the gentlemen drunk,
it was so disgustfull to our tender pallats, that wee hated
the thought of strong drink; and for my owne part, I can
affirme, that untill the conversation in London had after
many years a litle broke me to it, I could not with pleasure tast a glass of clarret, tho of the best, and continually
prest to keep pace with those I had the honour to converse
with.

3. This as to drinking, to which I shall onely add, that
wee were Indulged full liberty of drinking small beer, as
often as wee had a mind. For which end, there was alwais
a stone-botle kept going in our quarters, for every one to
Resort too, and when empty, a servant replenish't it;
which thing I mention, to shew the prudence used in
giving appetite in ordinary and fitting things its full swing.
For certeinly Nature calls for that which is good for itself.
And setting aside wantoness, which is easy to be perceived and may be as easily checked in children, their
appetites are the best Indications of what is good for them.
But there was another use made of this botle, for our
Mother would steal into it slices of Rubarb, and other
Medicinall things she thought fitt for us, and wee came by
use to like it so better then when plaine; which saved the
ungratefull Importunity and Reluctance between parents
and children about phisick, which generally is extream
odious to them; but this way, it was stole upon us, and
not tainted with aversions, which I am perswaded, does
more hurt than the medicin profits.

4. Our dyet was very plaine, and rather short than
plentyfull, but often. Never indulged with bitts and
curiositys. I have seen some so treated with seeming
dayntys, as the medullas, braines and the like, that nothing ordinary would doune with 'em. This tends to deprave
not onely the appetite, but the fancy, and makes children
grow meer fopps in eating. We must be contented with

what was assigned us or fast, and consequently never were tormented with vaine expectations of Dayntys, and the crying expostulations about what was not to be had, whereby yong things are cast into more paines, when they cannot be gratified, than can be compensated by any thing to be thought of or given them. So much is fondness mistaken, which oftener is the caus of paine then pleasure, where it is unreasonably applyed.

5. The Govement of us was In generall severe, but tender; our mother maintained her authority, and yet condiscended to Entertein us. She was learned (for a lady) and Eloquent. Had much knowledg of history, and readyness of witt to express herself, especially in the part of Reproof, wherein she was fluent and pungent. And not onely her children but servants dreaded her Reproof, knowing how sensibly she would attag them, and in the most nice and tender articles that Concerned them. But without occasion given to the Contrary, she was debonair, familiar, and very liberall of her discours to entertein all, and ever tending to goodness, and morality. This saved us that were children, and of Stubborne spirits, as such usually are, the trouble and Inconvenience of contesting points with her, for we knew beforehand, from the steddy conduct of her authority, that submission was the best cours, and Comported accordingly. It is not to be Imagined how Ill customes at first breed trouble to parents, when children have by some Instances found their parents yeild, it breeds such a willfullness, that it becomes almost desperate to cross them; and they will persevere in crying, till they are bursten, or fall in fitts, all which is prevented by early caution. We had, as I sayd stubborne spirits, aud would often set up for ourselves, and try the experiment, but she would reduce us to termes by the smart of correction; and which was more grievous, would force us to leav crying, and condiscend to the abject pitch of thanking the Good Rail, which she sayd was · to breake our spirits, which it did effectually, I need not hint the perpetuall care she took wee should contract no ill habits by conversing with servants, especially lying, which she allwais preach't against, as well as hardly forgave, when discovered. And for the part of learning to Read, and

bringing us to it at sett hours, leaving the Intervalls to Remission, which is absolutely necessary to yonglings and making all possible Impressions in the way of Religion, by discoursing and answering wisely, when wee were talkative and to show how vertue may be mixt with delight, she used to tell us tales, allways concluding in Morality, to which, as children use, wee were most attentive. On Sundays also she would comply, when wee sollicited for a story, but it must be a sunday one, as she called it, and then would tell some scripturall history, which was more pleasing to us becaus more admirable and extraordinary then others. Nothing could be more apropos, then this method, for forming the minds of children to a prejudice In favour of what was good.

6. As to instinct or Inclination, some is comon to all or most men, others peculiar to some onely. The former may be Reduc't to the generall account of pleasure, and consequently aversion to labour and Industry. This Induceth Idleness, and its traine of pleasures, which lett runn on, as an Ulcer to a gangreen, become debauchery and all manner of vice. The other is, when some are propens to women, gluttony, false dealing, lying, violence, ill nature, and the like, which in some will appear very early, and as I conceiv may happen either *ex traduce*,[1] which I call Instinct, or some accident of forme or constitution of the body, most commonly the former. Those generall Inclinations which tend to deprave mankind, are well enough obviated in youth, by the comon Methods used in Education of children; For That case which allways happens in a concerne so universall as breeding children, must needs be provided for by a traditionall method of proceeding in it. And this with carefull parents is constantly done, by Impressing In their tender minds duty to parents, inforc't by the universall custome of asking blessing, learning to read, being putt to scool, and kept to it all their youth, and then handed into manly Imployments, as they become capable, without allowing any vacancy or Idle time. And

---

[1] Alluding to the question discussed among the schoolmen, whether the soul was *propagated* like the body, or in every case infused and *created* anew. The maintainers of the first view were called *Traducionists*. Their opponents were *Creationists*.

the more these methods are neglected, or borne downe by Feminine vanity and fondness, the more profligate and debauch't the age prooves. And I wish the present were not a sad example of it, which by a generall defection of all principles of vertue, declares that The last was not so carefull as it should have bin.

7. But it is an happyness that wee had, That our parents destined all but our elder, who was to succeed in the honour and estate, to Imployments, and wee were without Remission held close to the Methods proper to Fitt us for them. And wee were given to understand early, that there was no other means of living to be expected, then what came out of our Industry. Wee saw what was to be had, and knew there was no more, and so were forc't to be contented. Wee were not deluded by a vaine pompous way of living, which in strait circumstances accelerates Ruin, or taught accomplishments proper for such a way of living, But with all the parsimony Imaginable, with necessarys but no superfluitys; and what learning in philosophy and arts we had it came cheap, being pick't up by our owne care, and not the charg of our parents, who could not have assigned so much as had bin necessary for such purposes. This as to generall Instinct or nature comon to all or most men, provided against as I sayd, by the traditionall methods of education.

8. I shall note but one thing more, as a Great failing in ordinary Education, which is that parents and curators will choos rather to descend to children's capacity in their conversation, then Indeavour to rais them up to a better forme, by presenting them with patternes, as If the child speaks broken, the nurs will too, whereas there were need of being more articulate then In conversing with adult persons, for so the child, Instead of knowing how it errs, and the way to amend, is establish't as much as in the nurs lys, in its defects. And so also for things, which is much more material then language. If a child asks an Idle question, they will make as Idle answer, whereas In prudence that opportunity should be taken to Instill some Religious or Morrall principle, or Informe the Judgment in some usefull knowledg, Removing such childish mistakes as are ordinary to them, For then the child's attention is

awake, and it Imbibes greedily what is sayd much more then when a precept or lesson is obtruded. And also, however Idle and loos persons of age may converse, it is not fitt to doe so among children, who are more observing and Retentive then is Imagined, from the quickness of their apprehensions more then malice. And they have an Implicite faith in all men and women say and do, and it will cast a prejudice on their principles, if it be ill, and mend them if good; Therefore actions and speeches afore children should be allways exemplary.

Maxima Reverentia debetur pueris.

[The foregoing is printed exactly as it stands in the original manuscript. It has not been thought advisable to continue giving the author's exact spelling and punctuation.]

CHAPTER II.

SCHOOL DAYS AND UNIVERSITY LIFE.

THUS far is an account of our education to the next step, which is to school. My first launching was to a country minister[1] in the neighbourhood. After that to the Free School at Bury St. Edmund's, though very young and small,. during which time nothing considerable happened, unless it were that I first there perceived two great articles of happiness—liberty and the use of money. For at usual times we had our latitude of ramble in play with equals, which was a most agreeable variety; and in a small purchase of fruit, to which our family were most extremely addicted, I was sensible of greater plenty than I ever yet knew, or hope ever in this world to be again sensible of. I had frequent indispositions then, and after a year an acute fever, which endangered a consumption. At first I was followed with heartening things,[1] but at length, by advice (most cruelly given in my hearing, who had a Garagantua stomach), put in a way of starving as the only cure, but my impatience was entertained with great supplies of money, which I extorted from every one, so that none made me a visit free of cost, and in this I was as rigorous of pecuniary respects as any judge or Minister of State, until I was deluded of all my running cash by a fraudulent proposition of purchasing a calf, in hopes of a belly full. My weak side was known, and there the deceitful friend applied and gained the point, without doing violence to the avaricious devil that had entered, and was not to be thrust out of such a crazy house as might fall in the convulsion. But I gained little of my aim, my allowance proceeded by the same rule of diminution, and I had only the compliment of being asked what joint, and then persuaded to what was resolved on. So great states are by necessity constrained to quit

---

[1] Rev. Ezekiel Catchpole.

realities for form, which the victor will allow as a silly salve to honour. Upon recovery from this sickness I was sent again to my old parson, where by the liberty I took of eating their plain food, which was mostly bread and cheese, and sporting abroad in a good air, I was in a fortnight recovered to a full vigour and colour, though very pale and weak when I came.

10. I shall never forget the frugal way of living that old man, with his family, had. They kept a maid, a ploughman, and one team; the parish clerk did all the task work, and the rest the old woman did. Nay, the parson himself and his son wrought hard in harvest, and none was so inconsiderable as to stand out; in short, it was a direct farmer's economy, which I think I profited much by seeing, for otherwise I should never have had a notion of it, nor the knowledge of so much rustic variety as that let me into. I will say this for the honour of the old man, that notwithstanding he was very penurious, yet the loaf, cheese, and small beer were always free to his family to come to, and eat and drink when and what they pleased, and never was any poor man whatever that asked an alms by right-down begging, or with fiddle or pipe as often is done, who went away without, the relief of that sort, and broken meat when there was any, but that was but seldom. I believe many of the opulent clergy, who puff with housekeeping, cannot say so much, and it seems to have been a most reasonable way of living, such as one could not in modesty ask of God Almighty a better, while we are commanded to pray for daily bread. The town was then my grandfather's, consisting of tillage farms, and small dairies, so that business was usually done by noon, and it was always the custom for the youth of the town, who were men or maid servants, and children, to assemble, after horses baited, either upon the green or (after haysel) in a close accustomed to be so used, and there all to play till milking time, and supper at night. The men to football, and the maids, with whom we children commonly mixed, being not proof for the turbulence of the other party, to stoolball, and such running games as they knew. And all this without mixing men and women, as in dancing with fiddle, but apart. No idle or lascivious frolics between

them, and at last all parting to their stations. I mention this because it seems to me to have been a better condition of country living than I ever observed anywhere else, and being at those years free from all cares, made a happier state than all honour and wealth can boast of. Here I stayed two or three years, and then was removed to the Free School of Thetford, which was a most excellent air for health; and then furnished with an agreeable master. He was scholar enough, and withal mild and discreet. He had no fault but too much addicted to drinking company, which at last made him a sot and ended his days. But he used not to neglect his school, but take his cups when we took our liberty. Here I stayed till I was ready for the University, and first began here to be sensible of some tolerable capacity; for I came away with a school-boy's conscience undefiled, never being assisted in any school exercise, but performed all myself. And though not of the prime of my rank, yet not contemptible, and might, as my master used to say, have been better, were I not lazy, which he often laid in my dish. I must confess, in English, I have borrowed from books whole sets of verses; but my luck was such that I had none but very mean ones to steal out of, such as Poor Robin and Quarles, which not being in my master's library, I was never discovered. Once, I remember, on a Restoration Day I had filched a copy from Poor Robin, which at last concluded with a highflown passage—

But I,
In perfect loyalty will live and die.

at which my master exclaimed and said I should be trusty Roger.

11. I was not very athletic, yet stood not out in any such exercise, but pleased myself more in manufactures and gimcracks, which was an indication of an inclination which ever did and will follow me. I had several manufactures going, as lanterns of paper, balls, and thread purses, which brought in some money. I had got a trick to make fireworks, as serpents, which being strong bound, and the composition little abated with coal, would act very impetuously; but I could not make a rocket hold, for want of the skill to temper and take down the composition, but

all I offered at broke, yet I could make the serpents, being small and so bearing the force with a wand bound to them, rise as rockets. I got acquainted with artificers, and learnt to turn, which was a great diversion to me, because it produced somewhat neat, and well accommodated to several of the plays we had. There was lewd company among us, but I was not forward enough to be taken into their gang, though I, like others, was very desirous to come up to the state of manhood most shewed, as I thought, by the conversation of women.

12. There was a navigable river [1] in the town, which above the bridge branched into many brooks and scattered streams. This made us all expert boatmen, swimmers, and fishers. We used to pass whole days naked; and once going down to a sandy place to swim, a frolic carried us to Brandon,[2] where, after example, I got drunk, and in the return must needs go swim again, but at first step fell over all into the water, being not in a condition to stand. The cold of the water made us all instantly sober, and after our pastime we returned home in good order.

13. There is a Saxon castle hill and three great ramparts round it, built, as I suppose, to defend the pass against the Mercian inroads. I had acquired a habit to run down from the summit of this hill to the bottom, and to stop or go swift as I would, which was done by keeping the body always perpendicular and using the point of the right heel to stop upon, which sometimes would slide till it met a rub, but if not I kept the upright posture, which was always secure. This I could never teach any, and wondered at myself for it, being a sleight not ordinary.

14. Here it was that I began (as I said) to have a sense of myself. I was aspiring enough, and would have been in the league with the capital boys, but had not a tour of address and confidence to be admitted, but kept in a middle order, and had my equals and inferiors, as well as superiors. I conceived a strange apprehension that I should prove a weak man, if not a fool, which shewed I aimed at more than I found I could reach, and in this despondence I had no comfort but performing exercises

[1] The Little Ouse.
[2] Brandon Ferry, about seven miles by water.

without help. That did almost persuade me I should shift in other stations as well as that. I had, by the benefaction of several relations, a better cash than others, which made me an envy to the rest. This went partly in trade, which I hinted, and most in fruit, of which I was a most insatiable helluo. If fruit had been in any way hurtful, I had been poisoned. There was seldom a night when I did not eat a pennyworth of apples (and no small one) in bed before I slept, but this was in time of ripe apples, for green fruit I never could like, and surely ripe fruit is the best food for young folks.

15. Here I first knew what debt was, for this ingordigiousness of fruit having exhausted our stock, being good customers we found credit, and once was upon the score 2*s.* 6*d.*, which was a burden so heavy to a little man of honour, that he declined ever after to be in like circumstances, and having cleared this by an expedient of old clothes, was firmly resolved in the matter.

16. This gives me occasion to note the benefit of public schools to youth, beyond private teaching by parents or tutors. For there they learn the pratique of the world according to their capacities. For there are several ages and conditions, as poor boys and rich, and amongst them all the characters which can be found among men, as liars, cowards, fighters, dunces, wits, debauchees, honest boys, and the rest, and the vanity of folly and false dealing, and indeed the mischiefs of immorality in general may be observed there. Besides, the boys enter into friendships, combinations, factions, and a world of intrigues, which though of small moment, yet in quality and instruction the same as among men. And further, boys certainly league with equals, which gives them a manage and confidence in dealing ; teaches them to look before they leap ; being often cuffed and put to cuff again ; laugh at others' follies and are laughed at themselves ; I need not press the advantage this brings to youth, in their learning to be men at little cost. I knew the torment of debt for 2*s.* 6*d.* ; others make their first experiment with their whole fortune, which wit bought cannot be worth the price, because coming too late is good for nothing. Whereas in private teaching, their company is either superiors, inferiors, and

if equals, but a few, without the liberty and variety of pratique as in a populous school. If superiors, the youth is overawed and sneaks, if inferiors he grows insolent, being taught by the freedom of abusing such companions to insult all the days of his life, and in either of these ways of breeding, never gets a true weighed habit of converse ; and besides, wants the spur which is raised by emulation, upon others' performances, than which nothing conduceth more to make a youth sedulous and industrious. But, after all, fondness of parents will prevail, and against the greatest reason in the world with respect to private good, and policy with respect to the public, parents [keep] their children near them, or rather near their ruin.

17. I know they pretend danger, want of looking after, and the like. As for danger, none can live free from accident, and such are most obnoxious as are bred least in the way of it, for they are ignorant, and suffer for want of common precautions. Such as are bred in action (as in public schools) generally know all dangers that are not very extraordinary and avoid them ; as for instance, swimming, which if learnt (as I did in such a school), is a precaution against all accidents of surprise by water ; and if they have not such exquisite looking after as mothers expect with respect to cleanliness, there is generally a reasonable care because it is one thing which recommends, and not the school, but others who board youths to it, and of such there is a choice.[1] And after all, if there be any defect, the youths themselves will often supply it by their own application, which is still a profitable learning. But enough of this.

18. After having finished the course here, my next step was to the University, but an interval of about a year interposed, while I stayed at home, and my father read to me *Molineux's Logic.* I do suppose it was under deliberation what profession I should embark in. I often heard the Civil Law spoke ; but that was not so flourishing to invite. The Common Law prevailed, by the advice of

---

[1] I understand the passage to mean " A reasonable care of the boys is one thing that recommends a school, not the mere name of the school, but the good word of others who have youths as boarders at the school, and of such schools there is always a choice."

my brother, who was then well advanced in it, for he had got an ascendant in circuit practice, which let in all the rest by degrees.[1] I am inclined to think that this profession [is] not good for brothers bred together, because one will certainly overtop, and like over-forward plants drip and mortify the other. All the business which comes for respect, which is not a little, will go to him that is thought most capable, and the other shall be discouraged and pine to nothing. But one much above the other helps him, by steering his under business through his hand, and so leads him forward without any damage to himself.

19. At Cambridge I lived a year, in which time nothing extraordinary happened to me, unless it were that I was forced to live in the quality of a nobleman, with a very strait allowance. I was not capable to conduct myself, but had a brother who was in the place of tutor, and provided all things for me. Besides the first cost of a gown which was not over rich, few of ordinary quality spent less than I did. And it chiefly lay in not going in company, for I had not confidence, nor money, and very seldom on my own account made or received a visit.[2]

20. This way of living with a brother, for I had the same chamber, engaged me to spend my time in reading, as he did, who was a most strict student. But I am sensible that if I had not been under such restraint (it was not of force, but a sort of grave silent authority, with which I could not for shame contend) I should have been very idle. I did most extremely envy the common scholars for the joy they had at football, and lament my own condition, that was tied up by quality from mixing with them, and enjoying the freedom of rambling which they had. And not having either money or assurance to mix with my equals, who were wild and extravagant enough, was obliged to walk with grave seniors, and to know no other diversion. This infelicity, as I then thought it, was

---

[1] Francis, afterwards Lord Guilford. He was called to the Bar, 28th June, 1661, and succeeded so rapidly that he was made a Bencher of the Middle Temple, 5th June, 1668, *i.e.*, while his brother Roger was an undergraduate at Cambridge.

[2] He entered at Jesus College as Fellow Commoner under the tutorship of his brother John, 30th October, 1667. Cf. *Life of Hon. and Rev. Dr. John North*, § 12.

in truth the greatest felicity I could have. For by the common liberty I was inclined to follow, I should have been in great danger of being hardened in some sort of vice, idleness for certain, and carried it to London with me, and then improved it to very ill purposes. So that I must owe much of my preservation to the strait fortunes of my family, which put such a bridle on my propensities of youth, which are at best to idleness and liberty, that I could not make any dangerous excursions.

21. As to study there, I followed my own appetite, which was to natural philosophy, which they call physics, and particularly Descartes, whose works I dare say I read over three times before I understood him. The third time my brains were enlightened, and I gained the notions of his vortices, vapours, and striata. I had this labour for want of a tutor, for my brother was but so in name for protection, and answering the college, but never read any lectures to me, nor cared to answer my impertinent silly questions, which came upon him so thick that I perceived his temper disturbed at it; for he was a most thoughtful indefatigable man. Therefore I forbore. And at that time new philosophy was a sort of heresy, and my brother cared not to encourage me much in it. I had the old physics, as Magirus[1] and Senectutus,[2] but could not thresh so at them. I read most of the latter, but without content; for I was not satisfied to understand what motion was . . . . [*sic*] and transparency the act of a clear body, and the rainbow the sun's reflection in a concave cloud, with much of the like nature. I had a book of atomical philosophy, after Democritus, which entertained me better, but I found such a stir about Descartes, some railing at him and forbidding the reading him as if he had impugned the very Gospel. And yet there was a general inclination, especially of the brisk part of the University, to use him, which made me conclude there was somewhat extraordinary in him, which I was resolved to find out, and at length did so, wherein the *nitimur in vetitum* had no small share. I

---

[1] Johannis Magiri, *Phisiologiæ Peripateticæ, Libri Sex, cum Commentariis* . . . . . . Printed at the University Press, Cambridge, 1642, 8vo.

[2] Query, Sennertus.

had not been so furiously fond if the author had been obtruded; but shewn and then withdrawn, made us more deviously prosecute him. I joined with this study some mathematics, to which also I had an inclination. And having read Fournier on Euclid,[1] I wondered at the emptiness of that study, and used to say what a stir is here to prove that one line is equal to another—to what end is it? And troubling my brother often with such talk, he used constantly to say that it was a rule I might depend on in the study of the mathematics, that if I were not pleased I did not understand. This at last set me on work again, and when I once got hold of the thread, and found it come, that is, perceived the drift of the many (seeming) useless propositions, tending to prove others of consequence, I devoured the science with great greediness; and this illumination I had upon consideration of the forty-seventh proposition, which is that in all [right angled] triangles the square of the greater [side] is equal to those of the two others. This entered me alive, as I may say, and I digested it with great satisfaction, and having got Barrow, which is much the best,[2] I launched farther and made myself master of so much as served to common practical geometry, but the more abstruse secrets tending to algebra I was not a match for. I had books of ethics and metaphysics also to peruse, but my delight was in philosophy and mathematics, which my brother did not interrupt, being glad that I was employed, and so long did not disturb him with prattle and idle questions. Logic I did not touch upon there, having had enough at home, but I improved that by seeing the practice of disputation in the public school and college, and never thought of performing any exercises in public. Logic is a very dull science, especially that which relates to disputation, and must be driven by a tutor well versed in it, as a smith hammers iron out of a lump into a bar. And to say truth an age more advanced than ordinary youths fresh in the university is most proper for the study

[1] George Fournier, S.J., *Euclidis sex priores Elementorum Geometricorum libri demonstrati* . . . . Paris, 1644, 12mo.

[2] Dr. Isaac Barrow was Lucasian Professor of Geometry at this time. His *Euclidis Elementa* had been published in 1655, the *Euclidis Data* in 1657.

of logic. But in regard that is a time when somewhat must be learnt, and the rules of logic regulate the mind and make it more just to weigh other learning, and although the person neither is delighted nor thoroughly understands the drift nor perhaps the force of what he reads, yet it is fit to be learnt early; for when the mind is more advanced, and comes to work critically upon points of other learning and hath need, memory brings into use the former dull rules, and they are a great help, which else would not at such pinch be at hand. My brother used to recommend to me translating, and accordingly I englished Sallust's *Catiline* with some essay of paraphrase, intending to season the style, which is in bare translation dull, with somewhat of English quickness. But this was far from being considerable enough to preserve: however it is a most useful exercise, and fit to be recommended to all students. This is a mixture of language and invention. Exercises which are only of invention torment young minds too much, and after all are not [so] useful as the exercise of language, the readiness and neatness of which prevails more than deep sense.

III.   C

CHAPTER III.

LONDON LIFE.

AT the last I was sent home with a fen ague, such as will be busy thereabouts, and returned no more, but stayed at home until the Parliament called my father to London in the year 1669,[1] and with him and the rest of our family came to London, was admitted of the M[iddle] Temple, had a small chamber poorly furnished, and a little law library, and so was first left in full title and power to shift for myself.[2] This was a dangerous crisis of life. For in this town of London there are such company, and such temptations to idleness and disorder, that youth cannot wholly resist it.

23. I shall discourse more of that anon. In the meantime, let me state my circumstances as to money. First, to furnish my chamber, purchase a gown and necessaries to enter in commons in the Temple, I had allowed me £10, which was far from sufficient, yet with that and other accidental acquests it served, and my yearly Exhibition was £40 and no more at first. And our careful mother, who had made up a stock (as she called it) by small legacies, accounted with interest, answered £30, which bought the stock of law books I began with. This was my equipage, with which, without the aid I had from my brother, who died Lord Keeper, I could not have subsisted, and must have fallen ; but his goodness, shewed in too many instances to be particularised, preserved me : so great a happiness is it in a family when the elders have got good hold on the world before the youngers come in play. In this state I jogged on for divers years, wherein I shall note some

---

[1] His father Dudley, fourth Lord North, had succeeded to the title in December, 1667.

[2] He was admited at the Middle Temple, *Specialiter*, 21 April, 1669; admitted to Chambers 1st November following.

things. But, first, I shall make a few transient observations of myself.

24. And first, with respect to the public. I know not by what influence or means I took very early to the loyal side; and even at school, where, even amongst boys, high matters are ventilated in their childish way, I used to stand up for the Crown and its power. So also at home, as soon as my father would permit that freedom, I used to manage news, and censures on that side. And I cannot to this hour discover or tell from what spring this humour arose, unless it were that universal alacrity which was upon the King's return, while I was a very boy; the discourse of which, though not much minded by me, might sink and make an impression so as to determine my early inclination, and that goes a great way in the future conduct of life. It cannot be that we at those years should know any differences relating to public government, for such are built upon experience, either from books or observation; and few, even of men adult, ever settle their minds right, from such means: then how should we? But so it was, and I believe from that accident, which was not by me perceived, that I thought a king to be a brave thing, and those that killed him base men, and consequently the coming back of his son a glorious triumph. Such little accidents, when placed on men that come forwarder in the world than I could pretend to, have great influence in the great revolutions and troubles of the world. With me this happened right, for my brother the Keeper, though bred under the puritanical anti-monarchical party, took to the loyal party, and it was the true cause and means of all his preferments. And this prejudice of mine was, by conversation with him and hearing his discourses and reasonings with others, confirmed into an inexpugnable fidelity to the Crown. It is strange that he should not be biassed by his breeding the other way, but I have these thoughts of it.

25. He was not bred when disloyalty had credit, as in the beginning of Cromwell's wars, for then hypocrisy had seized on all the public appearances of things, and godliness in their sense grew up to such a credit that there was never enough fasting, praying, and preaching. This, at first, was thought to be purity of mind and zeal; that no-

thing lay under it but religion and the public good. Whoever lived in those times was more or less tainted, according to the degrees of their sincerity and want of means to know better; which was my poor father's case, who went along as the saints led him, till the army took off the mask and excluded him from the Parliament. Then he found himself deceived, retired, and candidly owned his being deluded, even in print after the Restoration, which was not done either for fear or hopes of preferment,—for neither took place or could so do with him at those years, —but purely conviction of mind and desire of arming others against the like deceits for the future. But those who came in when the saints had fallen out one with another, and made spoil and havoc of the public, and preaching in their way was grown contemptible, if not ridiculous, and generally understanding men sighed for their prince again, when the experiment of reformation had proved a deformation of all that was good; and religion so furious as was before held out, found to be mere hypocrisy, to serve as an engine of power and tyranny; and all the pretensions of public [advantage] found to cover nothing but private wealth; and various forms of tyranny succeeding one another, and every one fleecing the people with taxes and oppressions, the best of the nation (being the loyal gentry and clergy) undone;—this led a young man in a way different, nay, opposite to that which was commonly walked in at the beginning. This advantage my brother had; and his being grown to full maturity of reason and policy [was the cause that he] was established, and never after to be moved or shaken by those brutal storms which sedition in the time of King Charles II. raised. And it was my felicity who could not boast of so clear and firm judgment, that his company kept me steady, else perhaps the itch of opposition, delusion of faction, or lechery of politics, the averse way might have made ill impressions and made me deviate towards faction with the rest; but I had the good providence to be so armed by a long conversation, and the judgment cultivated by it, as to be armed against the time of trial which is now upon me, and enables me to defy the world and all its temptations, and to hold my honour and fidelity, as well as constant and real judgment and principle, unshaken, as I hope I shall do till the last moment of breath.

26. Next, I have observed in myself somewhat of confusion and disorder of thought. And although I had always a forwardness to attempt anything, I never could succeed to my content. And this did not appear to me more in speaking than in writing. For I was ever pleased to be writing somewhat or other, and striving at method and clearness, but could not attain so as to perfect any one design. My great aim hath been at a system of nature, upon the Cartesian or rather mechanical principles, believing all the common phenomena of nature might be resolved into them; and it would appear strange if I should tell how many offers I have made to express what I thought I clearly knew, and to do it in due order. But I had from all that pains no other profit than a discovery that I did not understand so much as I thought I did, and that my style (if it might be called such) was unnatural, affected, and obscure. I have been most sensible of my defects of this kind, and particularly in the practice of my profession; for it took away my assurance, and often when I have made a motion I could have gladly received an arquebusade for an answer. And nothing but utmost necessity could make me persevere, as I have done, in it. I find my knowledge to have had a share of everything, but not very deeply of anything. This has made me propense to talk and babble, and for want of true judgment, being confident of my sentiments, dispute with others with an arrogance or *opiniâtreté* not becoming the state I was in; which was for the most part inferior, which should, if not satisfied, have submitted. And all the content I have in the remembrance of these things is that I used all along a sincere mind; and, busy as I was, it was in prosecution of truth, and no false unjust projects.

27. Now, to reflect on what may be the cause of such imperfect command of thought, as I have lamented in myself, and which I cannot describe better than by styling it an aptness to oversee,—I ascribe the main reason to the cruel fit of sickness I had when young, wherein, I am told, life was despaired of, and it was thought part of me was dead; and I can recollect that warm cloths were applied,

which could be for no other reason, because I had not
gripes, which commonly calls for that application. It is
easy to imagine that this great violence to nature weakened
the faculties of the body as well as of the mind ; and the
other supposed, this follows. For the mind cannot work
without the actions of the body, which are its immediate
instruments. This I rather guess because I am not altogether so salacious as others of my family, which I repute
unhappiness, for [it is better] to have those faculties so
far as to know and enjoy what is gcod, and not be so
driven by them as to precipitate into diseases, troubles,
and cares, such as are well known to attend those who are
not able to govern those emotions of the body.

28. And for this happy temper I esteem myself indebted
to the sickness, and it balanced the accounts of other
matters; for if I was weakened in my memory and capacity of thinking I was eased of infinite cares which others
struggle with, and perhaps might have been insuperable to
me. And surely, if care hath anything, it is when it proceeds from wife and children, and then its venom is torment irrelievable.

29. I can judge of this defect of my memory, or rather
judgment, by comparison of my own performances with
those of others ; for I have observed in some so steady a
faculty of discharging their minds by speaking as if all
their matter were prepared and produced like wares to be
shewn with greatest advantage, and no emotion or passion,
interruption, or any outward disturbance, puts them by,
but [they] can immediately resume the thread and proceed ;
whereas I could never, though dealing in things of perfect
familiarity to my mind, relate without omissions and over-
sights of considerable articles. And therefore the defect
could not be want of instruction ; for well instructed or
not, was the same thing, my discourse was confused, and
from thence I inferred my thinking was so too. And that
is a great truth ; men's words, as to clearness or obscurity,
declare the justness or confusion of their thoughts. And,
generally speaking, men who think well either speak or
write well, and that according to the power and measure
of justness in their thinking,

30. It is a happiness I have admired and envied that

some will speak or write, and at the same time be contriving forwards to compose what is to succeed in form, and
beating about for new matter, till there is a full persuasion nothing considerable is omitted, and not be disturbed,
but pursue the method proposed, as if a discourse were
premeditated. So also to have such quickness of thought,
that no sooner is an objection started and understood but
a true, or, for want of that, a witty answer is uttered.
These are felicities to be admired and essayed, but not to
be acquired, being the produce of natural strength improved
by the practice of the mind and its performances. And by
how much I have understood this in others I have so been
conscious of my own wants, but borne it with the best
patience I could muster, and strove in my way to make the
best of my part, and be contented with the success that
would follow.

31. I have often weighed with myself whether this im-
perfection might be conquered or not, and observing some
historiettes of persons who, by industry, have attained per-
fections against nature, as for instance Demosthenes, with
stones in his mouth to cure an impediment, and talking to
the sea to habituate himself to a rabble, the worst of
noises; but I am inclined to think that a man's faculties
may be mended, but not made, by industry and practice.
His nature, as a statue or picture, may receive a polishing
or neatness from the statuary or painter. But if the
draught of the figure be naught, all the labour will not
mend it; and at last, however finished, it shall be but a
lame piece. Thus I have thought of my own faculties,
and believed that if I could make myself an arrant drudge
and slave to study and pedantism, I might perhaps attain
more readiness of words, and be better armed with matter;
but yet the incurable confusion, which I have naturally,
would remain, and if I should pass with some of the more
ignorant a little better, the sagacious would still have the
same notion of me, and I should not be much better satisfied with myself. Therefore I have been contented as the
monk, *dicere officium taliter qualiter*, and not drudge to
meliorate a bad plant, which might perhaps be so determined very much by laziness, of which my schoolmaster so
long since accused me. However, I do not repent it, since

my fortune is made, falling by Providence into an advantageous post; and I am not convinced that I could, with all the industry I could use, have mastered it by strength of parts and performances as others, not so circumstanced as I have been, have done: all which makes me still admire the blessing I have had by these advantages out of defects. As first to be preserved from the cancerous affairs of a family, and next from accident more than my merit, be established in a competent fortune, honourable in my case, and that which arms me from auy abject unwarrantable actions.

32. As to the practical diversions I have used, they are reducible to two heads : one is mathematics and the other music. As for the former, I have dipped in all sorts, so as to be informed of and understand the riddle even in the more abstruse points ; but this regards the study, for the mastery of which I have declared myself incompetent. But the practical, which is much easier, I dealt in : as geometry and its coherent arithmetic. I was an early artist at dialling, beginning to dabble in it about leaving school, and since attained a perfect notion of it, with which I have for the most part contented myself, not being much concerned in projection. I remember once I made a gentleman conceive the matter thus. Suppose an apple, or round part, divided into twenty-four parts, as the globe usually is by twelve circles, stained so as to pierce into the body and quite through, whereby the body would be divided into twenty-four parts by twelve planes made by such stain. Then cut the body in such a plane as your dial is to be upon, and the stains upon the surface of the section are the straight hour lines ; and the body being placed according to the position of the sphere, the intersection of the twelve planes is the axis and style of the dial. This is the notion of all dials, which one may easier conceive if he can iu his thoughts reduce the whole sphere of the world into the form of a glass sphere upon its axis divided as usual, and with a sun in its place on one side and the shadow of the axis on the other, to shew the hours and what planes may be placed from the centre outwards opposite to the sun, so that lines from the centre upon the plane directed to the several horary divisions upon the

sphere, the hour lines, and style are presented to the imagination. All the rest of this art is the practice, with which any man may busy himself as he sees occasion. The notion of all [dials] is but what I have described, whatever form the projection be cast into. This conceit of dialling I fell into early, and it was the first attempt above boys' play. Next, my brother F. N. furnished me with a ruler and a pair of compasses, and *Speidell's Geometry,*[1] which was of great benefit in the practical part, all which I had in common things before I went to the University, when I entered upon formal studying the theoretic.

33. After my coming to London I had *Dr. Wilkins' Dædalus*[2] to peruse. This gave me a full insight into the theory of mechanical powers, which I drove as far as I was capa[ble] of doing, resolving not to own any position of natural philosophy which did not quadrate with the general laws of mechanism. And I reviewed all the philosophy I had, and considered it with peculiar regard to them. For I concluded that whatever laws governed body, prevailed throughout, and if any observation seemed to thwart them it was not rightly understood. As for instance that the same body in a swifter motion hath more force, or in other terms, that time is equivalent to quantity in the measure of powers. Whereby it is found that if it can be contrived that a less quantity shall work in opposition to a greater in an even proportion of celerity, it shall, though of itself the weaker, being so circumstanced, prevail. This appearing to be the measure of all opposed powers, which is the subject of mechanics, I conceived to take place in all cases of collision of body, and so satisfied myself in the reason of the laws of impulses, which have of late, from the hints of M. Descartes, been improved by *Mr. Pardies*[3]

[1] *A Geometrical Extraction, or a compendious Collection of the chiefe and choyse Problemes, collected out of the best and latest Writers . . . . .* By John Speidell, practitioner in the Mathematics, and professor thereof in London . . . . are to be sold at the Author's house in the fields betweene Princes' Street and the Cockpit. 1617.

[2] Wilkins, *Mathematical Magick: or, the Wonders that may be performed by Mechanical Geometry.* In two Books. The first Book is called *Archimedes: or Mechanical Powers.* The second, *Dædalus, or Mechanical Motions.* First published in 1648.

[3] *La Statique, ou la Science des Forces Mondaines.* Par le P. Ignace Gaston Pardies, de la Compagnie de Jésus. Paris, 1673.

and others to a refined height; and I think I have carried the doctrine farther than they, I mean to cases of all irregular bodies and their unaccountable collisions, shewing that those are governed by as steady laws as the most regular, and by this have explained the windmill, ship sailing to windward, and other exotic forces, clearer than they, for which I must refer to my mechanics.

34. But while I was a dabbler in mechanics, I fell into that disease that all tyros in that art do, a conceit of having found a perpetual movement, and was wonderfully earnest and positive in it, and half wild to be putting it to experiment. This made sport for my brother F. N., who had been sick of the same infirmity, and would undertake, in whatever invention I could propose, to shew me wherein it should fail, and so he let me consider so long as I would. He was such an adept in all ingenious arts, and particularly this of mechanics, that he was master of the demonstration, which I arrived to at last, that such motion was impossible to be made by any mechanism. For if you will move the work continually, it must be done by a rotation or succession of equal powers, which shall take an advantage by the contrivance of the machine to work more on one side than on the other. If they are not equal in power, then the continual equal concern of all in place as they come cannot be maintained, as must be if it be perpetual, which must suppose a rotation. Then, if you will give to an equal a mechanical force above its equal, to weigh it down, it cannot be done but by conveying it farther from the centre of rotation, so as it may move in a greater circle in the same time; and if so, it must fall lower into the perpendicular, which to reduce to the horizon again others must be sent out still farther, and be still lower, and so *ad infinitum*, till the limits of the work puts a stop, and there is an end of the movement. My invention, of which I was so fond, was two wheels on different centres, in the horizontal line, almost contiguous, which should discharge balls out of the one into the other, which, after a demonstration that it is impossible, is needless to explain.

35. Another of my mathematical entertainments was sailing. I was extremely fond of being master of any-

thing that would sail, and consulting Mr. John Windham[1] about it, he encouraged me with a present of a yacht, built by himself, which I kept four years in the Thames, and received great delight in her. That gentleman is not to be named without a mark of honour, being such a master of all ingenious and mechanical arts, as joined with a plentiful fortune, integrity, and great application and industry, hath not been matched in any ages.

36. This yacht was small, but had a cabin and a bedroom athwart-ships, aft the mast, and a large locker at the helm; the cook-room, with a cabin for a servant, was forward on, with a small chimney at the very prow. Her ordinary sail was a boom-mainsail, stay-foresail, and jib. All wrought aft, so we could sail without a hand a-head, which was very troublesome, because of the spray that was not (sailing to windward) to be endured. My crew was a man and a boy, with myself and one servant, and, once, making a voyage to Harwich, a pilot. She was no good sea-boat, because she was open aft, and might ship a sea to sink her, especially before the wind in a storm, when the surge breaks over faster than her way flies; but in the river she would sail tolerably, and work extraordinarily well. She was ballasted with cast lead. It was a constant entertainment to sail against smacks and hoys, of which the river was always full. At stretch they were too hard for me; but by, I had the better; for I commonly did in two what they could scarce get in three boards. And one reason of the advantage they had at stretch was their topsail, which I could not carry.

37. The seasons of entertainment were the two long vacations, Lent and autumn, especially towards Michaelmas, for the summer is too hot and calm; unless by accident, those times are cool and windy, without which the sea is a dull trade. But these were for long voyages, as down below bridge to Gravesend, Sheerness, &c., which lasted for the most part five or six days. But for turning up the river, and about the town above bridge, I could, giving time, have the yacht at any stairs for an afternoon's

---

[1] Youngest son of Thomas Windham of Felbrigg, co. Norfolk. He was of Lincoln's Inn, and died of the small-pox 2nd June, 1676.— *Blomefield's Norf.*, viii. p. 115.

entertainment, as I saw occasion and found the tide serve. Once on the last seal day, we top practicers in Chancery, as usual, made merry together, and in a frolic would go to sea, as I used to call it. I sent for the yacht, which had lain all Trinity term in the heat uncaulked, so that her upper work was open, though her bottom was as tight as a dish. We went aboard, and when the vessel began to heel the water came in at her seams and flowed into the cabin, where the company was, who were too warm to perceive such an inconvenience, till at last they were almost up to the knees, and then they powdered out. We called for boats and went ashore, and the yacht was run ashore to prevent sinking downright. This made much merriment when we came together again, discovering what a present we had like to have made to our friends at the Bar by sinking and drowning the premier practicers, and so making way for the rest.

38. I used to make frequent visits at Bellhouse [1] to my relations there, because it lay near Purfleet, from whence I could walk thither. And this I did more out of respect to a lady, then Mistress A. Barrett als. Lennard, daughter of Mr. Barrett, my cousin-german, than any diversion his company afforded, who, though ingenious, and in general of a very good understanding, was of such a morose wilful spirit that it was very fastidious to be in his company, especially considering his infirmities, which had disabled him as to all action; and he spent his whole time either in bed or in a chair, and was carried from one to the other. But his daughter was bred with my Lady Dacre's own aunt, who was a lady of an extraordinary character, but particularly well bred, and of an undaunted spirit, one whom I would choose to breed a young lady and to give the tour of honour. Here she stayed till her father, like a beast, took her away, to be buried with him alive in the country; where, by the tyranny of his temper, being always cross and perverse, especially to his children, he

---

[1] Bellhouse was the seat of Lord Dacre of the South. Richard, Lord Dacre, had married as his second wife Dorothy North, the writer's aunt. Richard Barrett Lennard, son of Lord Dacre and Dorothy North, was therefore (as we should say) first cousin to Roger North. The daughter here mentioned married Carew Mildmay, Esq., of Marles Hall, Essex.

had broke her to the greatest degree of submission and obedience that I ever observed. Although she was there for the most part alone, or without company fit for her, she found ways to entertain herself so that her time was not lost. For she mastered that puzzling instrument the lute, and having a good voice, and the instruction of an Italian, one Signor Morelli, she acquired to sing exceeding well, after the Italian manner, to her own playing upon the lute or guitar. She was also addicted to books, and was mistress of French and Italian, as well to speak as read; and withal of an exceeding obliging temper, which, with the advantage of her first breeding and the assurance by that, softened by her mortified life in the country, together with a more than ordinary wit and fluency of discourse, made her as good company as one would desire in a relation.

39. It was believed that I made addresses to her, in order to a match with her, and I do not wonder at it, because it was notorious that I took frequent and great pleasure in her company. For I must profess myself a lover of virtue in anyone, either with or without the -osi, but she had both. However, if she had not been so near a relation I could not in honour have done so without a justification that way; and it will also be believed that such constructions did not escape my thoughts, and I had well considered the matter. Whereupon I must own I should have esteemed myself happy in a settlement with so worthy a person, and despair (out of my too near relation) to meet with the like within the sphere of my pretensions. But her fortune and mine were not enough to support that outward form of honour, in the way of living, according to the esteem of the world, which I thought became the quality I should take her into. And whatever philosophy I might pretend to, and by the strength of it to defy the censure of small or great vulgar, I could not expect that a woman should cordially concur with me, but on the contrary it was reasonable to believe she should retain the little emulations and pride incident to her nature, which, however prudent to conceal it, would, if not gratified by outward splendour of living, inwardly grieve her. I knew it would me, to think, as I certainly should,

that it did so.   Therefore I never made any experiment to know if my service that way would be accepted by her; but applied myself to serve and oblige her all other ways that fell in my power.   But I may perhaps speak more of the case of matching elsewhere.   In the meantime I cannot omit one passage in the history of this lady, for whom I had so much honour, to shew that virtue, early or late, will find a reward beyond what never fails to attend it, I mean (besides a quiet mind) a happy settlement.   The old man, upon the revolution of some unaccountable perverseness (for he never was friends with all his children at once) fell out with this daughter and her poor weak sister.   It was thought his reason was, that they had mutually given to each other their fortunes (which had been secured to them) and not to him.   But notwithstanding the merit of so many years' slavery to his humour, and an unmatched obedience, he was implacable, and would by all means turn her out of his house to shift for herself as well as she could.   And, concurrent with this displeasure, an overture of an honourable match came, which grew up with it, and as the one was desperate the other took place, as if Providence had provided a husband to succeed a father.   This match I treated for her, adjusted a full jointure and provision for children, and, as a father, gave her [away], and within a few years an estate fell to her husband in Somersetshire of £600 per annum. She has several sons, and lives happily, and is able to protect her sister, who was to be discarded with her.   This I look upon as a happy catastrophe after a desolate life, and should be glad for the sake of the world (if they deserved so much mercy), that all instances of virtue and vice were as conspicuously remunerated according to their deserts.

40. When I prepared for one of these voyages I used to victual my vessel with cold meats in tin cases, bottles of beer, ale, and for the seamen brandy.   And I mention this because I was sensible from it that all the joy of eating which gluttons so much court, consists in appetite, for that we had in perfection, and though our meat was coarse (beef for the most part) yet no epicure enjoyed that way so much as we did.   Once being bound for Suffolk, I

layed in a pilot at Greenwich, who understood the North course out of the river well, being used to carry lampreys into Holland. I thought it a strange trade. It seems they fish for cod with them. They are a small lamprey, having nine holes on each side in lieu of gills. These they put in flat wooden vessels of water, and carry over alive. If dead, they are unfit for use. And the keeping them alive on board employs many hands, for they must be perpetually stirred in the water by putting in cords, and then drawing them along the bottom, else they die. With a good gale I got in one tide as low as the Ooze Edge and there anchored, and lay for the next tide. This is a great way below the Nore, opposite to Thanet. There is a small sand that lies within the river, above the Nore, called the Middle Ground; and a small thread runs from that to the Ooze Edge, where is a buoy, to warn sailors of it, whereby it notes that the current is there a little divided, but upon the sands themselves a great deal, so that it does not set with that force as elsewhere. And I observe that all those shelves have a manifest cause from the coast, for where a place is sheltered from the current, as at the point between Thames and Medway, there a shelf, as at the Nore, grows. The windmill point above bridge is a visible instance of the same. For there the current sets straight from Lambeth one way, and from the bridge the other way, on the shore opposite to the point; so for want of a stream to scour, a shelf grows there, and is dry at low water. In the evening the wind slackened, and the surge yet wrought, which was a most uneasy condition, to lie stamping and tossing without a breath of wind to pay our sail, which wrought and flapped about most uneasily.

41. Here I observed that there was wind aloft, though I was too humble to enjoy it. For empty colliers came down with topsails out, full-bunted, and bows rustling, which did not a little provoke me, but patience is a seaman's capital and necessary virtue.

42. I met also with an observation which agreed with a relation I had formerly received from one John Lampett that lived at Edge Hill. It was that at the latter end of the summer the ants in the valley begin to come out with wings, and are very busy climbing up the grass, and

at the summits of the spires divert themselves with practising their wings; and at length by one unanimous consent they rise, and go up towards the high country in such
infinite numbers as take the form of a cloud and darken
the sun.   We were always apt to wonder what became of
these clouds of insects, and when I lay at the Ooze Edge I
perceived the surface of the water full of them, so that it
is plain that they flew with a westerly wind, till they
perished in the sea, and possibly some might fall short at
land, and some get over, but it is probable most met with
their fate as I saw there.

43. Next morning it was hazy, and an inward bound
vessel hailed us to know where they were.   We answered,
at the Ooze Edge.   They immediately dropped anchor, for
fear of the sand, till the day should clear enough to discover the buoy.   When the tide was made we weighed,
and the wind freshened, and we stood down the king's
channel, and the gale holding, we stemmed the neap tide
coming in, and it being high water at the Spits, we ran
over all past the Gunfleet, so that the neap ebb by evening
carried us into Harwich, where we anchored, and went on
shore to refresh.

44. At the point of the low country between the Thames
and Malden waters there is a very ugly shelf for many
over [*sic*] there were several wrecks upon it, and a great
mast is set down at the point which they call the Shoe
(that is the name of the shelf) beacon.   The Naze, or Nose
point, before we make into Harwich, appeared to us at
noon, for it is high land, and we saw it at great distance.
There was little remarkable in this day's voyage, only that
I, with my friend Mr. Chute, sat before the mast in the
hatchway, with prospectives and books, the magazine of
provisions, and a boy to make a fire and help broil, make
tea, chocolate, &c.   And thus, passing alternately from
one entertainment to another, we sat out eight whole hours
and scarce knew what time was past.   For the day proved
cool, the gale brisk, air clear, and no inconvenience to
molest us, nor wants to trouble our thoughts, neither business to importune, nor formalities to tease us; so that we
came nearer to a perfection of life there than I was ever
sensible of otherwise.

45. At Harwich we were asked if we had left our souls
at London, because we took so little care of our bodies.
For our vessel was not storm proof, and if that had come
we must have run for it, not without danger, but that is
pleasure to the eagerness of youth. After our visit in the
country we returned on board at Ipswich, having tided up
the yacht. We rode sixteen miles in the night to take the
head of the tide, and used a boat down to the first broad,
where the yacht was fallen down. It was cold in the boat,
and strange to see what invincible sleep seized us; all
dropping like so many dead things. We had a fierce gale,
about S.W., wherefore we were forced to turn it out of the
harbour; but then made but one run to the Spits, and
came to anchor, intending to put through in the night by
the soundings, without sight of the buoy, as we did, it
being tide of low ebb. And, keeping in two and three
fathoms, we succeeded well, and anchored again in deep
water, expecting the tide. The reason of our putting
through in the night, as the pilot told me, was to have a
consort, or a resort in case of distress; for there lay in the
King's Channel, above the Spits, four great East Indiamen, and if a storm had rose we could not have rode it out
in the Wallet where we lay, nor safely put through to
come at the great ships, much less shifted in the night by
making to any port. As soon as the tide of flood was
made, we sailed, turning up the King's Channel, ahead of
these Indiamen, that weighed not till the morning, and,
being ahead, we dropped again, not to lose our friends, if
need should be, and lay till broad day. I could not but
concern myself in all this important naval conduct, though
most of my crew, except the sailors, slept. And at midnight, in the air, the eating cold meat and bread, and
drinking small beer, was a regale beyond imagination. I
can say, I scarce ever knew the pleasure of eating till
then, and have not observed the like on any occasion
since.

46. Work being over, I took a nap, but before I lay
down the pilot asked, "Master, if the ships send us a bale
of goods, shan't we take them in?" I answered, "No,"
considering that if I was caught smuggling, as they call it,
I should be laughed at for being condemned to forfeit my

vessel at the custom-house, where my own brother was a ruling commissioner,[1] as he had certainly done. It was not ill advised to resolve against such a temptation, for next morning a custom-house smack came aboard us, and searched every cranny, supposing we had been dabbling. It was not unpleasant to observe the desperate hatred the seamen had to these water waiters. One vowed he could scarce forbear to run his knife in their guts, for he was at his breakfast; and they would snarl and grin, like angry dogs, upon all such searches, which frequently happened to us in the river, but durst not bite, or scarce bark at them, by which I see the trade which such men drive upon the river.

47. In the morning when we weighed we had only the tide to carry us up, for it was a dead calm, and no glass was ever so perfectly smooth as the surface of the sea; the reflection of the heavens was as bright and distinct from the water as above, scarce a sensible horizon; and there was everywhere about us much small craft bearing up in the tide. This posture was dull, and if it had been hot weather would have been very painful. We found we had good way by assaying the lead, but otherwise we could scarce know we moved. After a considerable space we found the buoys begin to enlarge, which the pilot called raising the buoy, which was an indication we had advanced. About nine of the clock the seaman called out a wind was coming. I looked out as sharp as I could to see this wind, wondering what it should be like; at length, with my glass I could perceive in the horizon at E. as it were a thread, almost imperceptible, whereby only the horizon was a little more sensible than in other places. It was always strange to me that the seamen would descry by their bare eyes things at a distance as well as I could by my glass, though a good one. And I often proved this by asking what a vessel was, how she stood, and what tack she had aboard, and the like: all which they would plainly describe when I could scarce with my bare eyes perceive anything. But looking and distinguishing or

[1] Sir Dudley North was not appointed Chief Commissioner of Customs till 1685. This fixes the date of this yachting voyage approximately. It must have taken place between 1685 and 1688.

judging by the eye is an art made by practice as other
arts grow; by being used to sea views they sooner spy
little extraordinaries than they to whom all is unusual.
Criticism of all kinds is a habit of nicety, for when much
time is spent in being acquainted with the ordinary instances any little thing extraordinary appears. The
coming of this wind due east was great joy, because so
favourable, and it was a great diversion to observe among
the craft, which had it and which not; now this, and
then another, for it came with much uncertainty, as one
might imagine supposing it had been visible as smoke is,
and we laid our sails as fair for it as we could, and at
last it came and fluttered us a good space, for, as I said,
upon the edge it was very rolling and uncertain, till at
last we were full paid, and stood in with wind and tide
and stemmed good part of the ebb. At last, the wind
failing, we came to an anchor within the middle ground,
upon the coast of Kent, above St. James' Point. And
there shall end the relation of this voyage, which I
have made more largely than pertinently, supposing it
might, at least, shew the strong inclination I had to
action and the pleasure it gave me; for, otherwise, I
could not have had such an impression from it as not
to forget one circumstance. And I must needs recommend it to all persons that are fond of pleasure to gratify
all inclinations this way, which makes health the chief
good we know, rather than those which weaken nature
and destroy health, and, by that, with vain shadows deprive us of the substantial part of life,—ease, and freedom
from pain.

48. This I have related as one of my mathematical
entertainments, for the working of a vessel, its rigging,
and position of the sails, do exercise as much of mechanics, as all the other arts of the world. And I shall
not set down my knowledge of it here, because I intend
an essay for the nonce. So also for the art and practice of perspective, which I have reduced to writing, and
was extreme delight to me, because it made my notions
just and firm, which will not be so if only kept in loose
thought.

49. Lastly, I am not to omit the access which by acci-

dent I had to the art of building, which was the burning
of the Temple ; whereof I think fit in this place to make a
description, being in my concerns a considerable crisis.
So waiving all description of the old Temple, as not worth
remembering, it fell out thus :—

CHAPTER IV.

THE FIRE AT THE TEMPLE, A.D. 1678.

ON Sunday night . . . . . .[1] about ten, being in my chamber, I heard the cry of fire. I went out, and perceived a light in a chamber, three pair of stairs next the lane out of Pump Court. This light was too fierce for anything but fire, which made me run up to see what the matter was. At the door I found such an evaporation as forced me back, and I was no sooner come down but the court was as light as day, all the smoke being turned to flame, and breaking out at the windows, as from a furnace. The like breach was made on the other side next the lane, and soon the rabble came, as usual to fires, and we were filled with them. This eruption of the fire was so sudden, that they who lodged in the staircase had scarce time to clothe themselves, much less to remove any of their goods, which, with writings, were all lost.

51. The fire was extremely furious, for it was in a hard frost, which had dried all things, and bound up the waters, which would have been employed to have stopped it, if possible. And the chambers where the fire took were all wainscotted, and cut out into small conveniences with deal, than which nothing is more combustible, and all accompanied with a strong dry wind out of the north, made such a dispatching conflagration as is rarely seen.

52. I was an observer of the progress of this fire, and perceived it to spread all ways as the combustible matter led it, and most especially up the Temple Lane and to the

---

[1] " 1678, the 26th of January, about eleven o'clock at night, broke out a fire in the chamber of one Mr. Thornbury, in Pump Court, in the Middle Temple. It burnt very furiously, and consumed in the Middle Temple, Pump Court, Elm Tree Court, Vine Court, Middle Temple Lane, and part of Brick Court. It burnt down also in the Lower Temple, the Cloisters and greatest part of Hare Court; the library was blown up . . . . . ."—*Luttrell's Diary*, vol. i. p. 7.

northward, from whence the wind came, which made some wonder that it should burn so against the wind. The reason was, the wind made the fire furious, and that made it lay hold, and within walls as it crept, it was sheltered from any wind drift of the flame, but it rather eddied with a reverberated force that way. It moved along without any leaps (as some pretended, that would then have every accident to be plot) in an oblique line from the top downwards, so that by such time as the fire was come to the bottom in one place, it was crept by the roof a considerable distance, and had taken its hold in that slope-manner, whereby I perceived plainly that, if the fire had took near the ground, it had been less apt to propagate, for then the upper floors and roof had fallen in before well on fire, and so left the adjacent buildings accessible, and the stuff falling tended to keep under the fire, and men could come over with water and abate its fury. But beginning at the top, the roofs of the adjacent buildings fired, and then it was impossible to stop either its progress, or save the lower stories; but those burnt, and wonderfully increased the fury. And the progress, as well as the beginning, were mere accident, the latter (as was said) from a flaming lump of a sea coal fire tumbling into the room upon the hot deal boards next the hearth, none being present to prevent the lighting of it. But the proprietor, who was at stake to answer damages, *quia tam negligenter custodivit ignem,* was content to translate the blame on the supposed plotters, and so joined in the cry for that, and no other cause.

53. As to the care about the matter, none was omitted that the season would permit: engines, help to lead water hand by hand from the Thames, and at last blowing up, which in case of fire is a remedy somewhat like fluxing for the pox in a natural body, doing violence in one part to preserve the whole fabric of a town from being destroyed, as happened in the great fire of London in 1666.

54. Several great men, and officers of the Guards, with soldiers, came by direction to Whitehall—where the light was seen in its most terrible posture—the Earl of Craven, who was seldom absent on such occasions, the Duke of Monmouth, who was setting up to be popular, and the

Earl of Feversham, who, by adventuring too far upon a blowing up, when it was thought the train missed, it happened to take, and a beam fell on his head, for which he was obliged to undergo the trepan, and, though dangerously wounded, recovered. I believe there is some degree of pride, and oftener affectation of popularity, but withal a certain compassion, whereof all men have a share in indifferent cases of great calamity, which induceth great men to expose themselves, in such times, when the hurry and confusion is such that without much caution they must fall in the way of mischances. Therefore the common people are ungrateful when they insult over great men, brought down by State convulsions, as they are apt to do, not considering that calamity befalls everyone in his time, and the like or worse may in some sort or other be their own case. But the brutal part of mankind have a great influence on the actions of multitudes, which are seldom or never reasonable.

55. About midnight the Lord Mayor and Sheriffs [1] came down, but the gentlemen of the Inner Temple affronted him, not owning his authority there, according to old tradition among them, and would want his help rather than connive at such a precedent to be made in derogation of their liberties, whereupon they beat down the sword, and would not permit it to be borne erect. At this he went over the way to a tavern, where some say he first got drunk, and then returned, dismissing the engine he met coming from the city. And some of his company were so kind to say, "Let's blow 'em up round, and save Fleet Street."

56. There were great endeavours to save the Middle Temple Hall, which burned had been an irreparable loss, almost to dissolve the Society. And for this end, lest the fire should creep down towards the water side, it was procured that powder should be applied to the corner of Elm Court, to lay that high building flat. For below that the buildings are so high and near that the fire must have taken across the lane, and then the hall had been lost. It happened that the floors were many and the walls thick,

---

[1] The Lord Mayor was Sir James Edwards (grocer), the Sheriffs were Richard Stow and John Chapman.

and all the stories bound together by partitions, which made the whole as one entire lump, so the powder, though twice applied, did only shake it, but did not raise it in the upright so as to let it fall down, as the manner of that operation is, and the building stands at this hour, secured by a few cramps. And it fell out that there was a double party wall and a stack of chimneys, which stopped the fire at that corner.

57. The danger was great to Fleet Street, for upwards the fire ran with irresistible force by a sort of paper buildings against the lane, and it was plain Fleet Street would take if a gap were not made by blowing up, which was done with so much precipitation that no time was allowed to the officers in the Fine Office to remove their records, but they were all confounded in the fire and rubbish, so that an Act of Parliament was made to supply them. Here it was Lord Feversham had his hurt. The gap being made, and the fuel brought under, the fire was soon stopped on that side. It appeared by the manner of this action that the care of the tradesmen was more regarded than that of the lawyers and all their implements. The thing was reasonable to be done, but it needed not such a destructive haste.

58. My concern was a ground chamber on the west side of the lane, which at last took fire, but if any had used brisk endeavours and disbursed some money it might have been saved. But everyone's business is nobody's business, especially all being employed in removing their own little concerns. I had the assistance of my brother [1] the Lord Chief Justice's family,[2] who made good riddance and saved what I had, and my chamber lay empty, to assist my friends and neighbours that had less time and help, until

---

[1] Sir Francis North was made Chief Justice of the Common Pleas 23rd January, 1673, and Lord Keeper 12th February, 1681.

[2] "We had a great rout attending, that belong to the seal, a six-clerk, under-clerks, wax-men, &c., who made a good hand of it, being allowed travelling charges out of the hanaper; and yet ate and drank in his lordship's house. I must own that, bating his lordship's illness (which was bitterness with a witness), I never was in a more agreeable *family*, for it was full as a city, and with persons of good value and conversation; all under the authority of one whom all revered."—*Life of the Lord Keeper*, § 382.

the Duke of Monmouth came to view there, in order to blow up; when it was a diverting entertainment to a proprietor to hear the discourse of the engineers about the aptness of the place for that purpose; and I remember a beam was commended for a very pretty beam. I told the Duke if he thought it for the public service to blow up there he was free to do it; and going out I heard him say he never met with people so willing to be blown up as these lawyers. So the train took, and my affair was at an end. Then I went to my Lord Chief Justice's, and lay down by him, thinking to sleep a little, for I was hot and weary; besides, I got a sprain on one foot, which made me quite lame; but when a blast went off I could not rest, but must return again to the place of action. This I attempted several times with like success, and my brother told me what dismal bounces he observed upon blowing up, which shook his house and windows like an earthquake.

59. All this while the fire went raging in all the buildings about Pump Court, the north of Elm Court, towards the cloisters and church, with an incredible fury. The chambers were small and so full of deal that a pitch barrel could not burn fiercer. I could perceive in the chambers at their first lighting a faint fire, which was still more obscured by smoke, and at last the heat melted the glass of the windows, which let in the wind, and that converted all the smoke to flame, which came issuing at the windows with a noise and fury like so many vents of hell, and at length the floors and roofs firing, the cold tiles with the suddenness of the heat would make a strange noise, crackling and snapping, till all came down together, and then such flakes of fire would rise and scatter down the wind as if all the sky were inflamed, and so drop upon the actors as well as spectators, and burnt their clothes on their backs; the horror of this fire was as great as could possibly be contrived had it been designed for wonder, and no other instance in my observation, or description of poet or painter, ever came near it. And it was no less extreme on the other side, for the cold was intense in the fiercest degree that our clime admits. The water froze in carrying and choked the engines with the ice that continually grew in it. Water

was let down from the street, but froze and stopped its own
current. Those that assisted were all wet and frozen; the
flames did not heat the air to warm such as were idle. In
short, the two extremes seemed to contend for victory.
Many got colds and knocks, but none died, so that a car-
nage was only wanting to make the Temple a perfect
Troy.

60. It is believed that houses are often fired by thieves
for opportunities of stealing; this was not so, nor was any
great execution of that kind done amongst us; for the
Templers, being sharpers, were aware, and suffered no unknown persons to meddle in their business. It is otherwise
in houses where women and children are frightened and
know not what they do, and give way to such thievish im-
positions. Here it was observed that women and children
stood in Fleet Street, ankle deep in water (for all the pipes
were cut), which in that pinching cold night could not have
been in such numbers and so pertinaciously as they did unless their husbands and friends were gone in to steal, and
they stayed expecting to carry off the booty.

61. Now was the fire stopped, save only two branches,
one was towards the church, and the other towards the
Inner Temple Hall, both which were attacked but saved.
For all the buildings immediately contiguous were laid flat
by gunpowder, but, before this could be done the fire aloft
had laid hold of the rounds of the Temple Church, but
being made accessible was quenched. The other way the
butteries and offices joining to the hall were of brick and
stone, where the fire choked itself, and the hall, though once
partly on fire, yet saved. Beyond the hall was the high new
buildings, which were made after the burning in '66, but a
low fabric of one storey interposed, which was called the
library, and if it had burnt it could not have taken upon
the other, not being high enough to reach the roof or any
window, nor could it take immediately for a thick party wall.
But some in authority, having their private concerns there,
caused gunpowder to be laid to the library, and to mend
former errors, by laying too little under a great building,
they laid too much under a small low one, and blew it with
such a vengeance as endangered the murder of many
people at great distance, for so the timbers flew, but little

hurt was done, and it had been as needful to have blown
up London Bridge as this fabric, as to danger, but one was
public and the other private, and it is well known the substance of the former must give way to the shadow or fancy
of the latter.

62. This fire lasted from eleven on Sunday eve to twelve
next day, and had opened an area of great extent, bounded
by the Middle Temple Hall and part of Elm Court south-
ward, the Palgrave buildings in old Essex Court westward,
the taverns and Hare Court northward, and the church and
Inner Temple buildings eastward, all which places lay
in view of one another. By noon there was a great assembly of all sorts spending their verdicts, which generally
turned into raillery upon the Templars. One says, "What
a world of mischief this had been had it happened anywhere else!" others, "It's no matter, the lawyers are rich
enough!" which shewed how much we were pitied. But
the best jest of this kind that fell in my way was from a
decrepid old woman, who, trudging through the Temple
when the new buildings were in some forwardness, stopped
and looked round her, and saw the scaffolding poles raised,
and men everywhere at work, "Well," said she, "I see ill
weeds will grow fast!" and returned to her posture, and
went away without more notice. It is a pity that law and
its followers, which are, at least ought to be, the fences and
guards of everyone's life and fortunes should be obnoxious
to envy and pique, as if they were the aggressors of both ;
but a common corruption of manners doth that and
worse.

63. After the fire was over, there was much inquisition
to find out the beginning of it. The best account that
I heard of from the examinations was, that the gentleman
underneath the chamber where it broke out heard the
gentleman call to his boy to bring down the link, and
about an hour before the fire broke out smelt a stink
of woollen burning, as is frequent from less accidents than
this ; but not going up to examine the matter, it increased
so that it became intolerable, and then he went up and
looked in at the keyhole and perceived all within on fire,
whereupon he gave the first notice, and shifted for himself
in the little time he had as well as he might. About half-

an-hour after the boy was gone down the laundress stayed and made a fire, which she said she left no bigger than might be covered with both her hands. So it is plain it must proceed from that fire as I observed at first. There were stories of a tall black man coming from the staircase, and saying his work was done, but denied when the party that was reported to relate it was examined on oath. And a chamber happening to smoke near the church before the fire arrived made a suspicion ; but that happened from a fire in a chamber beat about the room by the bricks of the chimney falling down. So that the plot mongers, though assisted by the voice of the concerned, to excuse himself, gained little from this business. I must confess it is a great unhappiness to be burned out of a settlement and put to provide all conveniences of life and business *de novo*, but much more when it is also the means of like ruin to others, and carries blame and future vexation by actions, if persons are so barbarous to use them. The very blame is a *crepa-cuore*. To be the unhappy means of making others unhappy is double, treble, nay almost infinite un-happiness, under which a good-natured remorseful person could not live if time did not wear off anxiety from the mind, and restore it to a tolerable peace even in the worst of calamities.

64. The losses were not great, save the fabrics (which, to say truth, were better burnt than left, being for the most part such ragged deformed stuff) the records of the Fine Office, and a great part of John Tredescant's collection of rarities, which were kept in an upper room by Mr. Elias Ashmole, and could not be all removed before the fire laid hold ; but, generally speaking, the gentlemen had time to remove all their books, writings, and such suppellectiles as they esteemed worth the trouble of carrying out.

65. Thus much of the burning, next of the building, which varies the scene and brings upon the stage, after all this tragedy, nothing but sport and comedy, which I shall introduce first by shewing the condition of the gentlemen's proprieties in their chambers.

CHAPTER V.

THE REBUILDING OF THE TEMPLE.

THE legal estate of the Temple ground was granted by James I. to trustees for the use of the Societies. It has been wondered that there was not such a grant before, but that the lawyers should buy and sell chambers, and be all the while precarious to the Crown (whose site it was) for the whole. But it seems in that reign the greediness of the Scotchmen was such that the lawyers then were afraid they should be granted (as Middle Row, in Holborn, and other such places had been) to them, who would have flayed them to the quick. This made them apply: otherwise, supposing the interest to have rested in the Crown, they had never stirred. The proprietors of the chambers have no instrument or title, but an *admissus est*, by the treasurer, whereupon they pay a fine to the Public Society. This is for the life of the person admitted. If he purchase or obtain by favour an assignment, it is a power reserved to his executors to sell and nominate another life, who shall have right to be admitted, paying a usual fine, which is small, in respect to the value. And so for two and three assignments, which import so many lives successively, to be named upon the falling of any till all are expired. And it hath been the usage, upon improvement or new building, the Society useth to grant to the proprietor, in consideration of his charge, a life and two assignments when these interests expire. The propriety falls to the public and is sold by the treasurer, and accordingly granted out. There were intermixed amongst the gentlemen a sort of chambers which they call bench chambers, and are such as the Society have reserved and not granted out, but are enjoyed by such benchers as have been at the charge of reading and served the house as a bencher, for their ease and some sort of compensation. The advantage of which is, that they may let that, or let or sell another which stands

in their own name or right, as they please. And for the
disposition of these it is in the power of the senior to
choose when any falls, if he think fit, and so the next;
whereby, if a good one falls it makes removes from the top
to the bottom, like the translation of bishops often doth
upon the death of an archbishop. This is the state and
condition of the proprieties in the Temple chambers.

67. The humour of the gentlemen is like the regents of
Cambridge, who are a pert youth, and very fond of
authority and interests, tenacious in the fancy of privilege,
and aping the prevailing powers, apt to make parties and
combinations for little advantages, and very averse to anything that seems to be imposed. The benchers are super-
cilious, and being by institution the governors of the
Society, are apt to use their authority in pinching the gentlemen, which they will not take, but oppose in the form of
what they call a rebellion. The benchers, the first and last
Friday in every term, hold their parliament, when the
treasurer presides, and all things are ordered by vote,
which the under treasurer collects, and these orders are
styled, *ad parliamentum tentum*, &c. In the vacation all
ordinary acts and directions in public matters have the
treasurer's (in his absence, the senior bencher's) sanction.
The gentlemen, that is the barristers and those under the
bar, pretend to a subordinate authority, and that allowing
the benchers to govern in terms, they have the sway in the
vacation, and on occasion of grievances, they make a parliament of themselves, even in term time; but in vacation,
to set up public gaming at Christmas, or such other disorderly purposes. And under this form, they pretend to
undo and oppose the invasions of their rights advanced by
the benchers, when they stretch their authority too far.
And young fellows got together in this manner, being pert
and witty, will, by aping the national parliament (for they
choose a speaker, and keep to the orders of the house),
togethers with jesting upon and abusing their superiors,
make excellent sport, and as it was ever a custom to
do thus, so it will be, and the wiser sort make a jest of it,
as a sort of play the young gentlemen please themselves
with. But the ill bred, sour part of the bench will be
as ridiculously in earnest, and like state politicians argue

for their own government, as if they were the Pope's Consistory, and these are they which the young gentlemen usually fall upon, and affront; either by breaking windows (which is the way of Temple distress) or threatening to pump them, or such other insolencies. But if it happen that *boute-feus* get among them, as often doth, and are for mischief in earnest, or for setting up gaming by the aid of this humour, then it grows a serious matter, and the recourse is to the judges of the Society, who have power, by directing prosecutions at law criminally or committing great offenders, to quell the rebellion, and sometimes do the young gentlemen right, wherein there is commonly more of jest than earnest.

68. And it so happened that at the time of this fire, a formidable rebellion was depending; the gentlemen were more united than had been known, even the gravest of the barristers engaged with them, which was rare, and spoke their cause just. They had been with the judges at Serjeants' Inn in Fleet Street, and the gentlemen were assembled so numerously in the hall there, filling all the benches and windows, and making such noises, that the benchers durst not come among them, but went to the judges and prevailed to have a message sent, that some select persons should attend, which was done; and the grievances set forth—the judges mediated accommodation, the managers reported time given to consider on both sides —and the fire came and parted the fray. This rebellion had mortified the benchers so as they were to submit to reason, else they had with their authority imposed excessively upon us, for this was our case, we were intermixed with them, and could not build unless the bench chambers were provided for; they had not money and were at a stand, so the whole must lay till they would have done what they pleased, and given the gentlemen what they thought fit. All this while, the fear of the benchers kept the gentlemen together, and the first thing they did was to meet together at the " Apollo " and choose a speaker, in order to consider in a parliamentary way what was to be done; but this assembly was so tumultuous, everyone being in great earnest and zeal for his interest, which had put by all jesting, as usual brought all into serious impetuous wrangle,

wherein one would have thought the Doves' Court was there, all speakers, no hearers, contrary to our intent, who by a parliament thought to preserve some sort of order, and prevent the confusion incident to a deformed multitude. Some were for passing a vote, that we would assert our right of building, because it was feared the benchers would take it out of our hands, but such of us as were more temperate were against that as factious, and thought we should adhere to our right time enough, without binding ourselves by a vote, so that was omitted.

69. Then we proceeded to nominate some one person out of every staircase as an intendant for the rest, to take care of the particular interest of that staircase, which was proper enough to be done, before we knew what would follow; but these committees were little troubled, for the benchers met at the same time, and sent to us to know if we had anything to say to them. We despatched a committee to wait upon them, with instructions only to ask of them, in the name of the gentlemen, what encouragement they would please to give them to rebuild. The committee returned with this answer, that the matter had been taken into consideration, and the gentlemen should have a resolve upon a certain day prefixed, to which time we adjourned, and being met again we appointed a committee to attend the benchers to receive their determination; which was that every gentleman who would be at the charge of rebuilding, should have a life and two assignments, the first life to be admitted without fine. Upon the report of this we entered upon the consideration whether it were sufficient or not. And two exceptions were made to it. First, that no time was set for nominating the first life, so that in case the builder died in the middle of the work, his life was spent without any enjoyment of the chamber. Second, that it was left in the liberty of the benchers to assess what fine they thought fit upon the two succeeding assignments. To have a declaration of these matters another committee was despatched, who brought us a report that the benchers would allow two years to name the first life, and set the usual fines on naming to the assignments, not exceeding £6. And, moreover, those who had assignments depending, should have the two assignments over and above. Upon

this we voted, *nemine contradicente*, that the benchers' concessions were satisfactory.

70. Here we were in possession of our main point, the steps and form of settling which I have noted, but cannot undertake to represent to the life all the apish passages we had in point of form, which being childish and mimical, carry little entertainment with them. It is enough to leave it to consideration what a sort of stir there was in a multitude of obstinate, pert, and opinionative individuals. We who had intended the point comported as we might, and steered towards the matter. And in that we had reason, for if we had not struck while the iron was hot we might have had more trouble; for, giving the benchers time to think and receive projectors' offers, they would have thought of tricks to impose upon us, to which at best they are propense enough, under the colour of acting for the good of the Society; which now, under the consternation both of the late rebellion and the instant fire, they durst not do.

71. On the other side, the benchers feared that the gentlemen might hold their terms, and do nothing effectually towards building; thereupon they made an order that everyone who claimed a burnt interest should deposit in the treasury £20, as a caution for his building, before 25th March next, or be precluded of his right. This was not pursued, being of no use as things fell out. However, some such provision was reasonable, for when cities are burnt and the good of the whole depends upon the restoration by building, it is just by laws to compel men to despatch, or yield up their interest to who will. And we were tender of our interest in this matter and would not yield that any order, however just, should touch them. Thus stood the general provision made in the Temple in order to new building.

72. But afterwards came the insuperable difficulties about the execution of a work so intricate and perplexed as this was. It was first to be determined whether we should build upon our old, or upon new, foundations, and so make an improvement of the whole, and consequently of each man's particular interest. After much consideration we concluded to new model the whole Temple, and to slight all

old foundations. For one reason was unanswerable, that
it was scarce worth the cost to build as was before the fire.
But in a new model there might be every way great advantage.

73. Then the great work was to dispose this matter to
everyone's content, for we were all Polish subjects, each
having a negative voice in the whole matter. And no
person was prepared to be contented, unless he found a
great improvement; nay, he was not content to be improved
so long as others were more improved, for he thought he had
as good a title as the others, saying, "If he or they, why
not I?" But where there was to be a deterioration, as in
some few cases it must needs happen upon alterations, be
as just and careful as you will, then it was fire and tow;
and they would fight knee high to hinder such a proceeding.
The projecting builders were very busy, and made their
applications, some to one and some to another; brought
their models, which were perused and argued upon, everyone looking with hawks' eyes to see whether he was to get
or not. If not, he battled it forthwith. Then was dimen-
sion, situation, and lights, which might be different from
their former condition, and if any of these did not answer
expectations, all was naught. And a greater difficulty than
all this was to get the benchers their chambers again. For
although they left us to negotiate and dispute the matter,
and were most of opinion that no design could be made
practicable that varied from the old foundations, yet they
observed what we did, and had this hand over us, that we
could not conclude or execute anything without them;
therefore all projects that did not comprehend their chambers, who had no money, nor expected any out of the public,
and the private would advance not, to build bench chambers
* * * * So here we stuck, and if we did hearken to
projects and view models it was for diversion and exercise
of wrangle, for all was hopeless without gaining that point.
The most reasonable kept out of these troublesome meetings, and those chiefly attended who expected to profit by
hard dealing and crossgrainedness. The humour ran more
to finding fault than expedient, as if will were shewed
in satire and scepticism more than by ease and conformity.
To be judicious and reasonable is to be dull, a character

that did not become us who were to live by nicety and dispute, and to say the truth we practised on ourselves sufficiently. Everyone was positive to his point, and would not refer. If a reference had taken place the referee had not given content, as none could when the money would not be answered; and in all this, where there was nothing real, a mere fancy wrought as powerfully as the essence of the thing itself could do, for we stick to our fancies and will persevere. These humours speak strongly for an arbitrary power to make people be content, and being once controlled they will be so. It was moved that an Act of Parliament might be obtained to erect a judicature amongst us, as after the fires of London and Southwark, but this was still to submit our interests to others, which we would not do in a grain or a scruple, and I imagined the benchers were watching occasion from our disagreement to take the whole out of our hands and deal with us as they pleased.

74. The charge of the bench chambers was estimated at £2500, for the compassing of which many projects stirred. Some were for having the benchers build for themselves and take a building interest; others were against that, for perhaps a chamber would cost £200 and sell for £400, and if any advantage was by building it was fit it should come into the common treasure and not into the benchers' purses. And then there would be no public chambers to encourage readers until two or three ages hence, when the building interest should expire. Others were for charging the chambers with an income, as in the colleges, to sink by small sums to be advanced still less and less by every new comer. This would not do, because it was still to load the readers, who could not, after the expense of their reading, spare so much money. Some would borrow the money upon the chambers to be built. There were many reasons against this. One, *instar omnium*, was, that no one would lend on such a security; besides, the debt would be insupportable to the public. Lastly, it was proposed to sell the gardens and waste ground, and with the proceeds of that build the public rooms. And this was offered to be put in execution, but miscarried, as I shall next relate.

75. It happened that the then treasurer had a kinsman, who was by profession a builder about London, and it

falling out that all Hilary Term was spent, and no contract
made, or model fixed upon, the treasurer and his cousin
contrived to impose upon the Society, and struck up a bargain, whereby the builder undertook the whole, and to accommodate all the gentlemen, at rates agreed. The bench
chambers were to cost nothing, and in compensation for
that, he was to have the waste ground and gardens, to
build as he pleased, and all supernumerary chambers were to
be his own. This done, the treasurer left the town, supposing his authority, his cousin's impudence, and our disorder,
would have made the contract good, and if the undertaker
could but once ingulf and get some foundations done,
although the gentlemen were impetuous, and blustered, the
urgency of the occasion will push forward, and they will by
degrees, the matter pressing forward, be sensible of the
necessity and give way to it. But when they begin to come
in and to take their shares of the work and to settle their
interests, then, thought they, it will be helter skelter;
everyone, like Scotch Covenanters, will strive to run before
the others to come in, for it is the nature of a multitude so
to do, whereby, if one or two can be gained, especially of
the busy party, the rest follow like sheep. And it is also
the nature of projectors to bear down whatever stands
in their way, by right or by wrong, for in cases where
it was impossible to get a precedent leave, after the wrong
is done and cannot be specifically restored, people for quiet
sake, few loving the fatigue of suits, will accept of sufficient
or less amends, whence it is a maxim that pardon is easier
obtained than leave; this was the project and contrivance.
Then, as to the execution, the builder, without speaking
with the gentlemen, to satisfy them of his design and their
account in it, goes to work, begins to dig in the garden and
to cut down the trees. The alarm was first taken by
the unburnt party, whose light and prospects were to be
stopped by this new building. They got together a small
party, and denounced immediate pumping of the workmen
if they did not that instant leave off. It seems their credit
was good, and both master and workmen believed them in
earnest, and thought it best to leave off, as they did,
so this attempt ceased before it was generally known; and
if the men had stayed till about noon when the gentlemen

came together upon the walk, as they used to do to confer
and entertain themselves with discourse of this common
concern, they had not gone off without a more severe repri-
mand. Thus ended that project, which demonstrated
to us the danger we were in of being imposed upon, and
made the way smoother for the next which succeeded,
though with much difficulty, and it happened thus.

76. There was one Nicholas Barbon, son of the old sectarian, called Praise God Barbon (being christened, Unless-
Jesus-Christ-had-died-for-thee-thou-hadst-been-damned),
bred a doctor of physic, but that trade failing he fell into
that of building, and the fire of London gave him means of
doing and knowing much of that kind. His talent lay
more in economising ground for advantage and the little
contrivances of a family than the more noble aims of architecture, and all his aim was at profit. But he had like to
have lost his trade by slight building in Mincing Lane,
where all the vaults for want of strength fell in, and houses
came down most scandalously. In other places his building stood well enough, and at the upper end of Crane
Court in Fleet Street he had made himself a capital
messuage, where he lived as lord of the manor. He was
bred in the practices, as well as the knowledge, of working
the people, under his father in the late times, though he
was too young to make any figure himself; but that, with
his much dealing in building, and consequently transacting
with multitudes, he was an exquisite mob master, and
knew the arts of leading, winding, or driving mankind
in herds as well as any that I ever observed. He judged
well of what he undertook, and had an inexpugnable pertinacity of pressing it through. He never proposed to tempt
men to give way or join but by their interest, laid plainly
before them. Supposing that, however averse at first, the
humour would spend, and they would come down to profit;
all other arguments and wheedles he esteemed ridiculous
and vain loss of time. If he could not work upon all
together he would allure them singly by some advantage
above the rest, and if he could not gain all, divide them, for
which purpose he had a ready wit, and would thow out
questions most dexterously. If anyone was fierce against
him he quarrelled, then that man's objections were charged

upon the affronts that passed, and not the reason of the thing. And he would endure all manner of affronts and be as tame as a lamb. If it was proper to his end to be so, he would be called rogue, knave, damned Barbon, or anything, without being moved ; then some others, seeing him treated so scurvily, would take the man's part, which advantage he failed not to improve. I meddle not with his morals but his prudence. He never failed to satisfy everyone in treaty and discourse, and if he had performed as well he had been a truly great man. His fault was that he knowingly overtraded his stock, and that he could not go through with undertakings without great disappointments to the concerned, especially in point of time. This exposed him to great and clamorous debts, and consequently, to arrests and suits, wherein he would fence with much dexterity, with dilatories and injunctions. He had good address and could express himself cunningly, and being master of (for none is free from) passion, was never forward to speak importunely, and then made his design the centre of all he said or did. He knew that passion and heat wear off, and as he regarded it not when rashly used by others, he never used it himself but as an engine to work with. He never despaired of a design if it were sound at bottom, but would endure repulse after repulse, and still press his point. If a proposition did not relish one way he would convert it to another, and adapt himself, as well as his designs, to the caprice as well as the interest of those he was to deal with. And to conclude his general character, he was the inventor of this new method of building by casting of ground into streets and small houses, and to augment their number with as little front as possible, and selling the ground to workmen by so much per foot front, and what he could not sell build himself. This has made ground rents high for the sake of mortgaging, and others following his steps have refined and improved upon it, and made a superfætation of houses about London.

77. I had much conversation with him on the occasion of building our chambers, as well about that as other general things relating to the public. And it may be some diversion to give an account of some passages between us.

78. I once asked him why he dealt so much in building

and to overrun his stock, and be not only forced to discontent everyone, but he perpetually harrassed with suits. He said it was not worth his while to deal little ; *that* a bricklayer could do. The gain he expected was out of great undertakings, which would rise lustily in the whole, and because this trade required a greater stock than he had, perhaps £30,000 or £40,000, he must compass his designs either by borrowed money or by credit with those he dealt with, either by fair means or foul. He said his trade would not afford to borrow on such disadvantage as he must, for want of sufficient security, be at, at 10 per cent. at least ; so he was forced to take the other way of being in debt, which he said was very much cheaper to him than borrowing, for his way was to put men off from time to time by fair words, as long as they were current, and so he got one, two, and sometimes three years. And then perhaps they would begin to threaten most fiercely to arrest him, which at last they did. So he put in bail, for which end he had always a bank of credit with a scrivener and goldsmith or two. Perhaps for some carelessness of the plaintiff's attorney the suit baffled itself at first, but if it came so far as a trial he defended stoutly, if he had colour, if not let it go by default, then brought a bill in Chancery, and perhaps got an injunction, and at the last, when the injunction was dissolved, and judgment affirmed upon a writ of error (which was one delay seldom omitted) and execution ready to come out he sent to the party, and paid the money recovered, and costs, which might amount to three, four, or perhaps five per cent., and seldom more than half the charge of borrowing, and thus he maintained a gang of clerks, attorneys, scriveners, and lawyers, that were his humble servants and slaves to command.

79. Another time I asked him how he did to take off opposition when he was upon a design that concerned many, whom it would be very chargeable to buy off directly, as when a hundred or more old houses were to be pulled down to accommodate a building design. He said he never bought off all, but only some few of the leaders and most angry of them, and that his method was this. He appointed a meeting. They would certainly be early at the place, and confirm and hearten one another to stand it out,

for the Doctor must come to their terms. So they would walk about and pass their time expecting the Doctor, and inquiring if he were come. At last word was brought that he was come. Then they began to get towards the long table (in a tavern dining-room for the most part) for the Doctor was come! Then he would make his entry, as fine and as richly dressed as a lord of the bedchamber on a birthday. And I must own I have often seen him so dressed, not knowing his design, and thought him a coxcomb for so doing. Then these hard-headed fellows that had prepared to give him all the affronts and opposition that their brutal way suggested, truly seeing such a brave man, pulled off their hats, and knew not what to think of it. And the Doctor also being (forsooth) much of a gentleman, then with a mountebank speech to these gentlemen he proposed his terms, which, as I said, were ever plausible, and terminated in their interest. Perhaps they were, at this, all converted in a moment, or perhaps a sour clown or two did not understand his tricks, or would not trust him, or would take counsel, or some blundering opposition they gave; while the rest gaped and stared, he was all honey, and a real friend ; which not doing he quarrelled, or bought off, as I said, and then at the next meeting some came over, and the rest followed. It mattered not a litigious knave or two, if any such did stand out, for the first thing he did was to pull down their houses about their ears, and build upon their ground, and stand it out at law till their hearts ached, and at last they would truckle and take any terms for peace and a quiet life.

80. He hated to make up accounts with anyone, and seldom failed to sink in his own profit a considerable balance, which the interested would lose rather than go to law upon an intricate account. This article brought good profit. If he got into an undertaking he mattered not time, for some would depend many years, and if money failed he would stand stock still, whatever ruin attended his works. Bricklayers, &c., could tease for money when employed, and if not paid knock off. I have seen his house in a morning like a court, crowded with suitors for money. And he kept state, coming down at his own time like a magnifico, in *dishabille*, and so discourse with them. And

having very much work, they were loth to break finally, and upon a new job taken they would follow and worship him like an idol, for then there was fresh money; as I observed upon his undertaking the Temple. And thus he would force them to take houses at his own rates instead of money, and so by contrivance, shifting, and many losses, he kept his wheel turning, lived all the while splendidly, was a mystery in his time, uncertain whether worth anything or not, at last bought a Parliament-man's place, had protection and ease, and had not his cash failed, which made his works often stand still, and so go to ruin, and many other disadvantages grow, in all probability he might have been as rich as any in the nation.

81. He was certainly cut out for the business of the Temple, for he conversed much with those of the Society, being a neighbour and full of law, and this for many years. He had dealt before with the Society, when he undertook the building of Essex House, and added the back gate and four staircases to the Temple. He knew our way of disposing our rooms, what conveniences we had need of, and being a very good contriver could apply to serve not only our occasions but our fancies; and likewise knew the state of our interests, and the value of them, and what profit was to be made by dealing with us. And in general he knew the best way of access to the business and how to make his profit out of it.

82. He applied to the gentlemen first, which in a mob age was the right way, knowing, that if he agreed with them, they would hand it to the benchers, whose point of having their chambers for nothing was also to be complied with.

83. He once met with the gentlemen and laid before them a crude project, to this effect: that every man's interest should be rated, and a value paid for it; that in the new building provision should be made for all that were burnt, and preference of choice in the disposition of chambers should go according to value, and parity by lot; and so much as the new was worth more than the old should be paid towards the charge of building, and the surplus towards the bench chambers, which he undertook should be done with it, the house allowing him £20 a

piece. This imperfect or rather uncertain proposal none would so much as hearken to, for it was impossible to adjust the values of chambers, which the gentlemen all overvalued, and would never submit to be arbitrated. The most part would not take chance, nor anyone's determination but their own, for the new settlement; whereby the Doctor saw this would not work, and he must find some way that should answer all objections, or at least, by the terms of it, seem so to do.

84. At our next meeting he proposed that a new model should be made of the whole Temple, making the best of the ground, but preserving the courts and gardens. That a survey be taken of the dimensions of every man's interest by the old foundations, and projected in flat, so as the quantity and height might appear. That everyone should have a chamber in the new building, in the same height as the old was, and as near the situation as could be; and that if any had more dimensions than before he should pay, if less receive a certain rate. That the bench chambers should all be built for the advantage of the improvement. That there should be four floors in the building, all ten feet high except the upper, which should be nine, and every chamber have a cellar. And the charge and rates were according to this proposal for the value and distribution of it, viz. :—

	Price of ground.			Charge of building.		
Ground chamber per square .	6	0	0	12	0	0
One pair stairs . . .	6	15	0	13	10	0
Two pair stairs . . .	5	0	0	10	0	0
Upper story	3	5	0	6	10	0
In all by the square or 100 feet flat . .	21	0	0	42	0	0

85. Here was a seeming equality to answer all pretenders. If another has more he pays, if less he is paid for it; if high the charge is less than lower. Who can assign a juster rate? You shall be as near the old as the model admits, what would you have? I must confess I was at first against this design, thinking the improvement would be too much profit, as it had been if the Doctor had had money to go through. But at last I reflected that

somewhat must be done, it was late in the year, the vacations pending, next term the benchers would be upon our backs; this was equal though many would not like it, and so resolved to make the best of my way and join with as strong a party as could be made, and so drive it through. It happened that from my relation I had not a little authority amongst them, and when it was seen that I had put myself in the head I had much the better and stronger part of the gentlemen joined with me, and though there was a schismatic party arose and separated into a distinct meeting to disturb us, we gained upon them continually. In short, we agreed: I made the articles, had them engrossed, allowed by the bench, and the model annexed, and we being settled in the model went to work briskly.

86. The method of settling ourselves was this. The model lay exposed, and everyone was to write his name on the ground plot with the number of pair of stairs high, as near as could be to his old station. And it is strange to see with what ease this was done, which one would have thought the most difficult part of all, but they were either so ingenious or so fond of their old being, that they sought not so much an amendment as the proximity to their old interest. And however large the place was the better, everyone chose rather to pay for amelioration than receive for pejoration. It was my fortune to commute a ground interest for one up two pairs of stairs, for which I wrote and where I am now, and proves the best in the Society.[1] None else had a pretence to it but my relation, Mr. G. Mountagu, who was so civil as to give way to me in it. Thus was the model settled, contracted, and signed as to situation, by the best of the gentlemen which concluded them, room being left for all others who would come in, and so it was delivered into the Treasury as the act of the whole Society, and was the happiest resolution of a perplexed touchy affair that I have known, and the present prosperity of the Temple is owing to the fortunate circumstances of it. But nothing which concerns many moves

---

[1] On his retiring from the Bar, Roger North let his nephew North Foley occupy this chamber till 1717, when, Mr. Foley being called to be Bencher of the Inn, Mr. North surrendered it to Arthur Onslow, afterwards Speaker of the House of Commons.

long together smooth and uniform ; and there was here a party that was not so well pleased as the rest, and as the way was, opposed the whole proceeding, and hoped by such distress upon Barbon to get terms of him. But our party resolved to maintain the point and support him. The colour they found to mutiny upon was, that the building straitened the hall court at the further end, which is true, but not to the inconvenience of the place, for it was made to run parallel to the hall, which formerly went bevel, widening at the further end. These gentlemen met at taverns, and several times sallied down upon the buildings, and threw down what they could, and we were never safe till the walls were out of reach, and then they acquiesced.

87. And Barbon wanting money, materials were wanting, or came in very thin. It was pleasant to see how intent the gentlemen were upon their own concerns, promoting the work and expostulating at every delay, nay, sometimes scarce forbearing violence to the workmen and to one another. For they were apt to quarrel to have bricks, &c., carried to their respective works ; sometimes much of it stood still, which put the concerned out of all patience. Aud there was at length a fail (as always in Barbon's affairs) so the house was fain to take upon them the winding up of the matter, and the accounts standing out, whereby at last it was happily finished and iu the state we see.

CHAPTER VI.

ARCHITECTURAL AND MATHEMATICAL STUDIES.

THIS negotiation about building the Temple falling into a continual inspection of general models and, when the whole was settled and our lots fixed, contrivances for the disposition of our little habitations and the multitude of small conveniences we were to carve out, meeting with a disposition propense, as mine was to such matters, must needs engage my fancy to a degree of pleasure in the execution of it. And I must ascribe the future entertainment I have had in building to this beginning. I had the drawing the model of my little chamber, and making patterns for the wainscot, and from thence the practice of working from a scale, all the while exercising the little practical geometry I had learnt before, and in short found the joys of designing and executing known only to such as practise or have practised it. This was, as I said, but a beginning. Afterwards I procured some books of architecture, as Palladio and Scamozzi; but I found that the Parallel translated by Mr. Evelyn gave me most clear instruction, for there were collated several designs accommodated to ocular inspection, with critical notes upon them. Hence I had a clear notion of the five orders, with their appendices: and besides the authors named, I procured Mr. Desgodetz' *Survey of Antiquities*, which is a most exact and beautiful work. Vitruvius I had read over, as printed by Elzevir, with the notes of Daniel Barbaro, but was more pleased with the French because of the great curiosity of the cuts, as the explanations and discourses annexed to the text. And accompanying these studies, if my little cursory reading may be so called, with the practice of invention and drawing, I fell into an humour of contriving new instruments, as well as procuring those of ordinary use, and was never satisfied till I had got a plain table, with a border graduated for holding down paper, and a drawer underneath accommodated to receive all variety of instruments. And with these I did entertain myself many hours, which might have been better and more profitably employed, but I had not power to resist my genius, and flattered myself that not running into vice I was absolved. But studies are of another place, I am now in my pleasures.

*　　*　　*　　*　　*　　*　　*

*　　*　　*　　*　　*　　*

89. The practice of drawing architectonical scenes leads to the use of the art of perspective, and that I turned in my thoughts till I made myself master of the very soul and principle of it. The practice depends on use which will find out compendiums to work short, and is exceedingly helped by a true notion of the thing. I shall not enter into any account of this art, because I have in a little tract made it intelligible to any mathematical capacity. But to shew the use in general as to designs which will not admit a strict regular proceeding, such as landscapes, wherein will fall regular bodies, as houses, forts, &c., which call for a nice perspective draught, I proposed this rule for finding the points of resort by guess: 1, form an idea of the true position of your ranges, or parallel lines which concentre somewhere; then, 2, form an idea of a line passing from the eye parallel to the range whereof you would find the resort; then, 3, observe which point of the picture the eye-line would point to, and that shall be the point of resort. This thought once well impressed makes the practice of loose perspective of much easier performance than otherwise would be, and I do not know that the same has been proposed in any of the books that treat of that art. I have employed much time in proofs of perspective designs, chiefly relating to building, and particularly to represent fabrics in their nudities (if I have leave to say so), meaning so as one may imagine them divested of their walls, as for example, if a square house were viewed at the corner, and had the roof taken off, and the walls in the two obverted sides taken down, the floors being supported by props. This makes a very perplexed figure, for you must order it so as being above the top you see down into the upper rooms, and the other rooms you

see as much of as the floors do not hide. And such a draught as this, humoured with the shadows truly pointing, is not only very pleasant to the eye, but doth almost supply the place of a perfect model. And [from] the consideration of such perspectives, as also to give a sort of relief to orthographical draughts, I attained a competent knowledge of shadows, which gives a great spirit to a draught, and in perspectives is essential.

90. I found Indian ink to be a good sort of shade, but fitter for nicer shades than I dealt in, that is faces and the like. For working with it was too tedious for architecture. Then I found that ink of the common sort, which was of too hard a black to be used plain, might be abated with water and so wrought with a pencil, and succeeded well enough when the shade was not to be very tender. The like of water boiled with much wood-soot in it; for that might be tempered with water and ink to make a very natural shade, and is used for *schizzis* of painters. They call it washing, and usually they work not on a white ground, where the transparency makes the lights, as the strongest light is the paper untouched, but on darkened paper, and then the whites or lights are laid in, when proper, which they call heightening, and the prime models or *schizzis* of the great masters in painting are so washed and heightened. I have endeavoured, but for want of early practice under a good instruction, could not attain the art of designing figures as painters do, and left off all attempt towards it, saving an antique head, festoons, capitals, and such common decorations of architecture; but for the regular part of the design, so as to give the true profile in proportion all manner of ways, none were readier than myself nor more exact.

*   *   *   *   *   *   *

*   *   *   *   *   *

91. I have had much pleasure in the theory of light, which leads to optics and the other mathematical sciences derived from it, all which have their foundation from the general laws of nature, which regulate the effect of impulses of one body upon another, and consequently on the true government of reflection and refraction. It is by them we demonstrate that the angle of incidence shall

be always equal to the angle of reflection, and that refractions shall wend one way or other according as the light passeth into or from a more dense medium, which are rules so steady and also important in all the doctrine of light that they seem laws depending on the immediate will of the great Author of nature, and not derivative, as they plainly appear from the system of nature, as I have elsewhere proposed it, which still magnifies the artifice and Artificer of nature. For that a single principle or two should produce such infinitely various effects, and those be made sensible at such distances, and so plain as we find by vision, as also by hearing, is a much greater perfection than if consisting of mere contrivances, or (as the heathen fancied) if a God presided in the government of every branch of nature.

*　　*　　*　　*　　*　　*　　*

*　　*　　*　　*　　*　　*

92. As to the reason of light, I have ever admired Mr. Newton's hypothesis as new and most exquisitely thought, which is, in short, that light, generally speaking, is a blended mixture of all colours, and that these colours are the different effects of certain rays, as blue is of rays which are of that sort, and diversified from others as producing that effect; so red, green, yellow, &c.; and these coloured rays are not refrangible to the same angle, but some to a greater and some less, which makes the distinction of colours in all refractions. And they are not accidentally created by that action, but only separated, existing all. But still there wants a physical solution of this hypothesis, without which, however plausible, it will not be admitted. I have endeavoured at this work, and conceive I know the reason of light, but whether it will square with this hypothesis or not, does not positively determine. My solution is this, that when a force falls upon a fluid there are two sorts of action communicated, one progressive, as waves on the surface of water, which produces sound, the other in an instant, by reason of the perpetual contiguity of water, this is light; and our corresponding organs are fitted to receive, augment, and expose proper nerves to convey the sense of it to the seat of perception. As the ear has a broad verge to take in a large compass of

air, which must go contracting, and consequently accelerating, to the tympanum or drum within; so also the eye, by refraction, drives the whole capacity into a less compass, not unlike a burning glass, which gives a greater force upon the retina or optic nerve. Now as to light, what we observe comes, for the most part, from fire. The true understanding of that is necessary to the knowledge of light. Fire, I take it, is not found, but either in the centre of a vortex or where some atmosphere presseth; the former is the sun and fixed stars, the other our culinary fire. And it is no other but a fierce agitation of the minute parts or bodies of which combustible solids are composed. If this happen in ether, so as there is no room for the grosser matter to give way and inclose this combustion, it immediately blends in the ether, and, dispersing every way, is lost. But in our atmosphere the air presses in all bodies, and if one is disposed to ascend until the action is arrived to such a pitch as to have force to throw off the pressing atmosphere, and have free scope for the action to work, it does not take the shape of fire, that is light; for until it takes a light we call the action heat or fermentation, and not fire. Then to bring this to the purpose of seeing, an action which has force to beat off the atmosphere, is of force to make an impression on our optic nerves, but this is not done *in toto* but *particulatim*. For the stroke of each part of that fire, or burning body, upon the contiguous part of the atmosphere, is by the rule of impulses carried *in fluids* every way in right lines, so that light is composed of infinite (if I may so speak) pulses of minute parts upon the air, which perhaps, considering the variety of form and force concerned in these impulses, and that everyone has its distinct effect, this solution may quadrate with Mr. Newton's hypothesis. But I cease to prosecute these matters further, leaving them to their places in the notes I have made of my thoughts upon most physical heads; but this being a most admirable theory, I could not avoid touching upon it *en passant*.

93. Therefore I shall leave the rest that concerns my dabbling in philosophy, until I resume the thread of time again, and also pass from those joys I had in mathematical

exercises to the other I proposed, music, and therein enlarge a little.   For the very remembrance of these things
is delight, and while I write methinks I play.   All other
employments that filled my time go on account of work
and business : these were all pleasure.

CHAPTER VII.

OF MUSIC AND ITS IMPORTANCE IN EDUCATION.

AS to music, it was my fortune to be descended of a
family where it was native. My grandfather, the first
Dudley, Lord North,[1] having travelled in Italy, where that
muse is queen, took a liking to it. And when his vanities
and attendant wants had driven him into the country, his
active spirit found employment with many airy entertainments, as poetry, writing essays, building, making mottoes
and inscriptions; but his poetry called him to music, for
he would have the masters set his verses, and then his
grandchildren, my sisters, must sing them. And among
others he used to be wonderfully pleased with these, being
a chorus of Diana's nymphs—

> " She is chaste, and so are we;
> We may chase as well as she."

And having a quarrel with an old gentleman, could not
hold goading him with poetry and the chorus of a song
running thus—

> " A craven cock, untried, will look as brave.
> So will a cur, a buzzard, jade, or knave."

95. This digression to shew how a retired old fantastic
courtier could entertain himself; and much more of this
sort may be seen in his book, which he called the *Forest
of Varieties*.

96. He played on that antiquated instrument called the
treble-viol, now abrogated wholly by the use of the violin,
and not only his eldest son, my father, who for the most
part resided with him, played, but *his* eldest son Charles,
and younger son, the Lord Keeper, most exquisitely and
judiciously; and he kept an organist in the house, which

---

[1] Succeeded his grandfather Roger, second Lord North, in 1600.

was seldom without a professed music master. And the
servants of parade, as gentlemen ushers, and the steward,
and clerk of the kitchen, also played, which, with the
young ladies', my sisters, singing, made a society of music,
such as was well esteemed in those times. And the course
of the family was to have solemn music three days in the
week, and often every day, as masters supplied novelties
for the entertainment of the old lord. And on Sunday
night voices to the organ were a constant practice, and at
other times symphonies intermixed with the instruments.

97. This good old lord took a fancy to a wood he had
about a mile from his house, called Bansteads, situate in
a diluvial (*sic*) soil, and of ill access. But he cut glades
and made arbours in it, and no name would fit the place
but Tempe. Here he would convoke his musical family,
and songs were made and set for celebrating the joys
there, which were performed, and provisions carried up.
For more important regale of the company, the concerts
were usually all viols to the organ or harpsichord. The
violin came in late, and imperfectly. When the hands
were well supplied, then a whole chest went to work, that
is six viols, music being formed for it, which would seem a
strange sort of music now, being an interwoven hum-
drum, compared with the brisk *battuta* derived from the
French and Italian. But even that in its kind is well,
and it must make a great difference when music is to fill
vacant time which lies on hand, from that which hath
moderate business in it, and being harmonious, will let one
sleep or drowse in the hearing of it. Without exciting,
the ball or dance is well enough ; but when heads are brisk
and airy, hunting up entertainments, and brought to music
as the best where it is expected to be accordingly, and the
auditors have not leisure or patience to attend to moderate
things, but must be touched sensibly, brisk, and with
bon goût; then I confess this sort will not please, but it
must come with all the advantages that can be, and even
the best and most relieved harmony will scarce hold out
any long time.

98. And I may justly say, that the late improvements
of music have been the ruin, and almost banishment of it
from the nation. I shall speak more of this anon. Now

let me lament the disadvantage this age hath, and posterity will find in the discontinuance of this entertainment. And whether the now-reigning humour of running to London be more the cause that it is discontinued, than the discontinuance of it be the cause (at least in some measure) of that, I will not determine; I am sure both are true *in quanto*. The mischief is plain, that is, leaving the country, which I will not demonstrate here, but shew that want of country entertainment must be a great cause of it, and that is done by observing that vice will start up to fill the vacancy. When we know not how to pass the time, we fall to drink. If company is not at home, we go out to markets and meetings, to find such as will join in debauchery, and the country is dull for want of plentiful and exquisite debauchery. There can scarce be a full family kept, because the humour of drinking lets in all manner of lewdness. Even fathers and daughters, with servants and children, male and female, go into promiscuousness. And it is scarce reasonable to expect better unless you can provide diversion, to fill the time of the less employed part of a genteel family, which is, and when used heretofore was, of great use towards it. For young spirits put in any way will be very busy and employ themselves, but not put into a way, pant after debauchery. Now when music was kept in an easy, temperate air, practicable to moderate and imperfect hands, who for the most part are more earnest upon it than the most adept, it might be retained in the country. But since it has arrived at such a pitch of perfection, that even masters, unless of the prime, cannot entertain us, the plain way becomes contemptible and ridiculous, therefore must needs be laid aside. By this you may judge what profit the public hath from the improvement of music. I am almost of Plato's opinion, that the State ought to govern the use of it, but not for their reasons, but for the use it may be in diverting noble families in a generous way of country living.

99. Nor is this improvement come to that height with us that it should win us so to it. I grant in Italy and the Royal Chapel here it hath been extraordinary good; but look out among the celebrated entertainments that have of late been set up in this town, and we shall not find any

that deserves the character of a musical entertainment; this lets me in to consider the nature of such things.

100. There is the same rule to be observed in all sorts of composed delights formed for the regaling of mankind, whether it be fireworks, comedy, or music. As for eating, I know not what rule to propose, for all depends on appetite, which being sharp or cloyed, begins and ends the matter, so let that pass. But to instance, first in fireworks, the master must contrive that the beginning be moderate, for the least thing at first serves, and then other parts enter with a noise and fire perpetually increasing, and the greatest fury must be at the last, and then all expire at once. This draws the spectators from one degree of amazement to another, without any relapse or flagging, till it arrives at the acme and then to cease; for the least pause or abatement, nay non-progression, spoils all. The like as to comedy, which is introduced with slow, easy, and clear parts, and in the progress grows busy, perplexed, and at last dissolves in peace all at once,—*Mercurio vindice.* Tragedy is the same, for that in the way of sorrow and calamity grows up gradually into a catastrophe of woe, ending as misery itself ends, in mortality,

101. So for a musical entertainment; if there be not a continual procession of it with increase of force, and intermixed with variety of measure and parts, to set off and give lustre to each other, as light and darkness, but to stop and so the measure cease, and incoherent pieces added without design, perhaps the several parts and passages may be good in their kind, but the whole taken together cannot be a good entertainment. As a comedy may have good scenes and be a very ill play,—a song, a fugue, a solo, or any single piece,—and so all the rest may be very good in their several kinds, but for want of a due coherence of the whole the company will not be pleased. And thus it is with the music exhibited in London publicly for half-crowns : a combination of masters agree to make a concert as they call it, but do not submit to the government of anyone, as should be done, to accomplish their design. And in the performance each takes his parts according as his opinion is of his own excellence. The master violin must have its solo, then joined with a lute, then a fugue or

sonata, then a song, then the trumpet and hautbois, and so
other variety as it happens; and upon every piece ended
the masters shift their places to make way for the next;
the thorough bass ceaseth, and the company know not
whether all is ended or anything more to come and what;
which pauses, and devious accidental species of music
presented one after the other without judgment or design,
are so defective as justly to be compared to a ballad singer,
who having done one ballad begins another to a pleasant
new tune.   But this combination regulated might exhibit
very good music, for the pert forwardness of some, or
rather of all the masters, would be restrained, and they
obliged to take the parts designed, and to stick to them,
without perching forward to shew their parts and please
themselves in being admired.   And the thorough bass
should never cease but play continuously, for that holds
the audience in attention, and with the instruments (as
some must be always) accompanying, will be no ill music,
whereas the master has a latitude to bring in some
caprice, or extravagance of measure or humour, conformable to the music past or next following.   And then any
single parts of voice, violin, lute, hautbois, trumpets, or
mixtures of them, may be introduced orderly and with coherence.   So as the cessation of them before was not a
lacuna or rupture, but a pause as for breath, and when returned are a *dénouement* of the entertainment so much
prized in stage plays.   And in short the whole is of a
piece, and all the process of it considered and put together with skill and design to give advantage to each
part, and never let the audience cease attention, but continually improve and raise it, till the end, when the greatest
force ceasing speaks there is no more.   Such an entertainment I never heard composed for an hour's pastime,
which is enough, but my knowledge of the art tells me it
should be so; but for smaller time it is common, as in the
Italian sonatas, French brawls, and English fancies, which
well done are a specimen or model of what should be in
greater designs.   This is my apprehension and censure
touching these recreations, wherein the hearers are only
considered, and therefore fit only for great cities full of
idle people.

102. But as for performers, it is wholly a different case, for their entertainment is of another species from that of hearers. We know that there is a pleasure in mere action as such, witness the usual running and play of boys, who will not walk on the ground if a rail be near, but they must walk on the top of that. So sliding on skates, riding full speed upon a horse, shuttlecock, tennis (without wager), and many such things are pleasant, merely as action, and a doing of somewhat, though to no end but doing. So if a nail be to be driven, and two or three stand by, each has a mind and would be pleased to do it. Therefore it must be allowed that action itself is a pleasure, and such will be allowed to performers, which the audience cannot pretend to. Mr. Hobbes to this has affixed another, rejoicing in their own skill, which is witty, and in measure true, and also very lawful, harmless, and satisfactory. There is no reason but persons who have a skill that is not common should be pleased with it, and if discretion keep out affectation and pedantry, that happiness is without blame. It is most certain that gentlemen are not obliged to aim at that perfection as masters who are to earn their support by pleasing not themselves, for it is their day labour, but others. And therefore audiences are not so well when their own entertainment is the business, because they indulge their own defects, and are not distasted or discouraged by stops, errors and faults, which an audience would laugh at. But it is so unhappy, that gentlemen seeing and observing the performances of masters, are very desious to do the same, and finding the difficulty and the pains that are requisite to acquire it, are discouraged in the whole matter and lay it aside, which is chiefly to be ascribed to this town, which is the bane of all industry, because many other pleasures stand with open arms to receive them.

103. Whereas in the country, where there are not such variety of gay things to call young folks away, it is incredible what application and industry will grow up in some active spirits, and this voluntarily, without being incited, as where there is an inlet to music, having time and a fancy to it, some will be wonderfully resigned to master a reasonable performance in it. And for want of

this or some other virtuous, or at least harmless, employment within doors, the youth of the country fall to sports, as dogs, horses, hawks and the like, abroad, wherein they will become very exquisite artists. Which I mention only to shew how reasonable it is to have in a country family some subject of virtuous pastime or arts more useful, which if not gainful professions, may be as food to the industry of youth bred there, who will otherwise (as I noted) fall into sottishness and vice. And nothing of the unprofitable kind can be so good as music, who is a kind companion and admits all to her graces, either men by themselves, or men and women together, or the latter single, with either instruments and voices, or either alone, as the capacities are, and fail not to entertain themselves and their parents and friends with pleasures sensible to those that have found the sweets of them. And for this reason I would not have families discouraged for want of perfection, which, to say truth, is not to be had out of a trade, but to entertain their youth and give them good example, and they will be ambitious enough to improve; and if it be to be had, active spirits will find it. But after all nothing of music is so mean and ill performed which is not commendable and extreme useful in a country family.

104. This lets me in to speak a little of teaching, on which much of this depends; for men the viol, violin, and the thorough bass instruments, organ, harpsichord, and double bass are proper; for women the spinnet or harpsichord, lute, and guitar; for voices both. I cannot but commend the double bass or standing viol for plain basses especially for accompanying voices, because of its softness, joined with such a force as helps the voice very much; and the harpsichord for ladies, rather than the lute; one reason is it keeps their body in a better posture than the other, which tends to make them crooked. The other instruments—and further of these I decline to criticise, because I intend in a discourse apart to do it fully. But masters are to be first had who can reasonably answer for what they undertake, and of them I recommend the elder, rather than the younger, although the latter may be more agreeable for novelty and briskness, which is so in most things, especially music. My reason is, that the elder are better

artists in teaching the principles of music, having more
experience, and that is the main design at first; elegance
of performance is the finishing, which will be looked after
in time. First get a teacher who understands and has
experience in teaching, which is a distinct art from playing,
and few or scarce any young men have it. When they
teach it is merely by imitation, and know not the true
reason of the excellences they have; nor can obviate the
devious errors of scholars, nor so well judge of beauty or
deformity of habits, but will let them run on till past cure.
I might add other reasons, such as seducing young people
and betraying them to ruin, which they are too apt to do;
but of that I suppose parents are apt enough to take
thought for, if not, their children being fortunes, especially
daughters, are in much danger from such gamesters. But
the older men who have families of their own are safe and
will be prudent; their dullness, and perhaps humours,
must be borne with, for they trade in air altogether, which
is a light business.

105. I spoke of teaching by imitation as the worst way,
especially at first, so need say no more of that. But I
would advise that beginners should be trained as in manufacture and trades, first taught to provide the material and
then to put it together, and lastly to finish it. In music
the material is sound, which may be made well or ill, and
that difference in the first formation of it is of the greatest
importance. Good drugs are not more considerable in
medicine than the producing a good sound in music. It is
the substance and foundation, which failing, all fails, and
all this I declare abstracted from graces, or any other
accomplishment whatever. And further, that all thoughts
of grace confounds it, so that whoever is to begin and learn
to draw the sound, is not to be put out with any sort of
gracios, but to be kept from it until they attain a fitness
for it. It is rarely observed, but let it pass for a truth
upon my word, that the greatest elegance of the finest
voices is the prolation of a clear plain sound. And I may
add that in voice or instrument (whereby the hand draws
the sound) it is the most difficult part to perform. But
our devious inclinations lead as well masters to teach, as
scholars to press the learning of tricks, such as the trill,

slide, &c.   All which are good in their time, but the fabric must be raised before the carving, such as it is, is put on.

106. Therefore as to the practice, I would have a voice or hand taught, first to prolate a long, true, steady, and strong sound, the louder and harsher the better, for that will obtain a habit of filling and giving a body to the sound, which else will be faint and weak, as in those who come to sing at maturity of years, when the organs of voice are stiff and intractable; and so for a bow hand, to spend the whole bow, at every stroke, long or short. These lay a good foundation, the roughness and harshness of which will soften in time, the loud may abate, but soft voices cannot be made loud at pleasure.   These must be formed early, as the limbs to arts, by much striving and continual exercise, so as to grow, and settle into a form to fit the use and practice of them.   Then next I would have them learn to fill, and soften a sound, as shades in needle-work, in sensation, so as to be like also a gust of wind, which begins with a soft air, and fills by degrees to a strength as makes all bend, and then softens away again into a temper, and so vanish.   And after this to superinduce a gentle and slow wavering, not into a trill, upon the swelling of the note such as trumpets use, as if the instrument were a little shaken with the wind of its own sound, but not so as to vary the tone, which must be religiously held to its place, like a pillar on its base, without the least loss of the accord.

*   *   *   *   *   *
*   *   *   *   *

107. The next thing to be taught is the transition of the voice or hand from one tone to another, or the practice of the gamut.   And under this, the first care is to secure the true sound of the note passed into, whether flat or sharp, viz., semitone, or tone, and with a full prolation of each, and the managery of it, swelling and waving as I have described.   Then next the grace of passing from one to another, which in some sort connects them, though several, as if they were links in a chain, very distinct, yet connected all together; for if there be any pause between note and note, it is amiss, but with the same breath as one note ends the next begins.   And if you would take a distinct

breath to each note, it must not begin with the entrance of the next, but with the expiring of the last, otherwise there will be a stop more sensible upon the taking breath. This is that is called a slide, and in a hand instrument is done with the finger, mixing the neighbour notes a little in the transition. Even the organ and harpiscord will do the same thing, as may be observed upon any one's playing, for nature itself almost leads to it. Then lastly, the art of mixing two sounds with the same prolation of breath should be learnt, which brings the trill, and being rightly used is a great beauty, but otherwise ridiculous in music, and this ought to be strictly observed, that the trill gives way to harmony. Therefore, either in sounding an instrument to a voice, or in concert of many parts, or any full and loud music, the trill is nonsense or, worse, bad sense, and the best Italians decline it. But single parts to a ground, for delicacy, where it can be perceived, the harmony being maintained by the bass, it is an excellent grace when well performed, otherwise better altogether left out, or at least with a faint offer at it in proper places where custom, as in cadence, has made it expected. But for an accompanying part, which is to maintain the harmony, to trill, and upon the low notes, whereon it most leans, unless it be upon a little ritornell or solo, is senseless and destructive to the music; but that is the fault of our English masters, who, accompanying a voice, will clatter trills at bottom to make one wild. And it is the constant custom of ignorance to affect superficial ornaments and neglect the substance, which I have noted in other places. But even masters are to be aware of this, and lead their scholars by fit paths and steps whereby they may attain a just perfection.

108. But it will be said, this is a tedious process, and will not be pursued by those who seek pleasure and not a trade. I must confess that is true; none will so addict themselves to learn anything in fit manner if left to themselves. But parents have authority, and do exact it in these cases, to oblige their children to endure the fatigue of learning many things which they would altogether decline if left to themselves. Therefore, if there is not either compulsion or an extraordinary inclination and perseverance it is in vain for a master to pursue teaching, and one

supposed the other must be granted. But there may be mixtures to entertain a little the scholar, and to make him sensible he advances, as composed songs and lessons that have an inviting air and formed to exercise what has been taught, as well as to delight the learner ; and in these there will be a great delight, especially if brought into harmony or concert, which is the greatest perfection and pleasure music can afford to performers. And in this a master may shew his discretion and conduct, for he may engage his scholars in a deep concern for the business in hand if he will, which brings me to—

109. The next and last thing I shall observe in teaching is to let the scholars early into a sense of harmony. Some have not a nature capable of it, which is soon discovered, and I have known those who could neither understand a perspective draught to represent anything, nor mixture of sounds to contain anything more than a jar or confusion of noises. These are to be obligated to other business, they are not cut out for arts. But to return to harmony, which is that that governs all. A single part must suppose it and have a relation accordingly or it will not be well, as the draught of a head and shoulders only must suppose a whole posture, the action, place, and the position of objects about it, according to perspective, else it will not be right and moving in imitation of the life. So sounds must be such as fit a complete accord, in case it were laid to it, otherwise it is not airy and pleasing, for this reason it is that no person can perform a single part, either with voice or hand, well, unless he understand the harmony and force of it. So that the skill of harmony, which we call composition, no less necessary to all musical performances than understanding and experience is to the practice of any art whatsoever. Therefore I recommend the precepts of composition, together with the solution or rationale of them to be communicated to the scholars, together with the other steps in teaching. It may be said all this is not to be had, so in vain to attempt anything. I answer, in giving advice, it must be for the best. Perhaps it cannot be so executed, but so far as it may it is useful, and a bad dinner is better than fasting. Let us make the best of what we have,—push at the head, employ

our time and industry in virtuous exercises and arts. If we get not perfection we shall be very well pleased and never repent.

110. How little these methods are pursued is rather a subject to lament, than of hope to reform. Ladies hear a new song and are impatient to learn it. A master is sent for and sings it as to a parrot, till at last with infinite difficulty the tune is got, but with such infantine, imperfect, nay broken abominable graces, in imitation of the good, that one would split to hear it; yet this is fine, and the ladies go to teaching one another, especially if a little natural lusciousness be couched in the words, and none think that before they learn the practice they must learn the principle, and be made capable : that done, the song is learnt by note as a book is read, which is an infinite ease and satisfaction. But enough of errors, there are so much in the world, not only in these circumstantials, or as they are called, trifles, but in the body and soul of humanity, as would make one sick to think and spew to repeat.

111. Now to resume the relation of my own proceedings. I was instituted by that eminent master of his time, Mr. Jenkins. He was a person of much easier temper than any of his faculty, he was neither conceited nor morose, but much a gentleman, and had a very good sort of wit, which served him in his address and conversation, wherein he did not please less than in his compositions. He was welcome to the house of all lovers, and particularly with us, being resident in the house for divers years, and at last parted and died at Sir P. Wodehouse's seat in Norfolk. He was an innovator in the days of Alphonso, Lupo, Coperario, Lawes, &c., who were musicians of fame under King Charles I., and superinduced a more airy sort of composition, wherein he had a fluent and happy fancy.[1] And his

---

[1] JOHN JENKINS was a native of Maidstone in Kent, where he was born in 1592. Hawkins (*Hist. of Music*, ii. 583, ed. 1833) has given some account of him. He says that Jenkins "resided for a great part of his life" in the family of Hamon le Strange of Hunstanton Hall, Norfolk. This must have been previous to his being received into the house of Lord North, at Kirtling, for Sir Hamon died in 1654, and it is evident that Roger North is speaking of the time of his boyhood. At Hunstanton Jenkins must have been the teacher of Roger le Strange, son of Sir Hamon, who was so irritated in after years by being called

way took with the age he lived in, which was a great happiness to him, but he lived so long that he saw himself out-
run and antiquated.   He was a great friend to Stefkins,[1]

" Oliver's Fiddler," that he wrote a pamphlet in 1662 to justify himself
and explain the circumstances under which on one occasion he had taken
a part in a musical performance, and not left the room when Cromwell
entered it.   Jenkins died at Kimberley, 17 Oct., 1678, at the age of
eighty-six, and there is still to be seen in Kimberley Church an incised
slab with the following inscription :—

> Under this stone Rare Jenkins lie
> The Master of the Musick Art
> Whom from ye earth the God on High
> Call^d unto Him to bear his part
> Aged eighty-six October twenty-seven
> In Anno seventy-eight he went to Heaven.

Blomefield (*Hist. of Norf.* ii. 538) was in error in saying that this slab
is lost.   It may still be seen on the chancel floor.   (Farrar, *Church
Heraldry of Norfolk*, i. p. 282.)

(ii.) ALPHONSO.   Alphonso Ferabosco, born, it is said, of Italian
parents at Greenwich, one of the most famous musicians of Queen
Elizabeth's time.   He published a book of " Ayres " in 1609, with
commendatory verses by Ben Jonson, who addressed to him two of his
epigrams (Gifford's *Jonson*, viii. 237, 238.   See Hawkins' *History of
Music*, i. 479, and Nichols' *Progresses of James I.* ii. 185.)   This Alphonso
had a son of the same name, also a musician of note : the two have often
been confounded.   Roger North appears to be alluding to the son.

(iii.) LUPO.   There were four of James I.'s musicians of this name,
Joseph, Thomas senior and junior, and Peter Lupo.   (Nichols' *Progresses, James I.* i. 598.)

(iv.) COPERARIO.   Giovanni Coperario, otherwise John Cooper.   Of
him see Hawkins, ii. 504.   He taught music to the children of James I.
Both Henry and William Lawes were his pupils.

(v.) WILLIAM LAWES, son of William Lawes of Dinton, Wilts.   He
was first a chorister at Chichester.   In 1602 he became a gentleman of
the Chapel Royal, and subsequently one of the private musicians to
Charles I.   He was killed at the siege of Chester in 1645.   His brother
HENRY LAWES was much more famous.   He not only composed the
music to Milton's *Comus*, but it is even said that this beautiful
masque was written at Lawes' suggestion.   Milton certainly addressed
one of his sonnets to Lawes.   There is a good account of the brothers in
Hawkins (u. s. p. 581), but it contains inaccuracies which are corrected
by Col. Chester (*West. Abbey Registers*, p. 157.)   William Lawes died
21 Oct. 1662, and was buried in the cloisters of Westminster Abbey,
aged sixty-six, being then one of the gentlemen of his Majesty's chapel.
He composed the anthem for the coronation of Charles II.

[1] THEODORE STEFKINS is mentioned by Hawkins as one of the finest
performers on the lute in his time, but Roger North seems rather to be
alluding to one of his sons, FREDERICK or CHRISTIAN, who were of the

the famous violist, and held a constant correspondence
with him, and would often send him presents of his compositions, whereof I had the honour to be the bearer. He
much admired the books of Signor Nicola Matteis,[1] which
I brought from London and shewed him, and by that declared a candour seldom found in masters, who off-hand
despise all but themselves. I began in that interval of
time as passed between school and Cambridge, and being
at first backward and averse to the pains of a new jargon,
as the elements of music were to me, and to be learnt and
applied I knew not how or why, I fell lazy, and it was
thought inaptness, which made my father and his friend
Mr. Jenkins almost give me over. But my mother, being
for pushing me on, took opportunity to let me know that
my father took notice of my neglect of music, and I should
hear of it. This made me buckle a little closer, till I had
got so far into the business as enabled me to practise
alone, and then I had the cord by the end, and left not to
pull till I had the command of my little instrument, the
treble viol. After this, when I went to Cambridge, being
very young, and also, by reason of my character, very re-
cluse, which two agree not together, I was glad to get what
time I could to practise, which further engaged me; and
in process of time I became as fond of music as young
folks are of anything they take to, and was never so well
pleased as when I was playing or writing. This gives me
occasion to observe that the writing of music conduced as
much to my learning as anything could have done, for I
was very sedulous and industrious at it, and began very
early. I designed to write over all Mr. Jenkins' compositions, and did execute my purpose upon a great many, but
for want of good paper and good directions in making the
characters black and regular, my first papers came to little.
From the treble viol I passed to the bass viol, where I
stuck a considerable time, and the chief *rémora* to my en-

band of William and Mary, and were renowned for their performance
upon the viol. (Hawkins, u. s. pp. 725, 771.)

[1] NICOLA MATTEIS, author of two collections of airs for the violin.
"The composition and performance of Nicola Matteis had polished and
refined our ears, and made them fit and eager for the sonatas of Corelli."
—Burney, *Hist. of Music*, iv. 640.

trance into concert, which I was ambitious of, was the want of the knack of keeping time. I knew the divisions and sub-divisions well enough, and could measure the short notes, as crotchets, &c., but long notes I could not measure, and began to think it impossible for me ever to attain it, for how could I by my mind make the measure of a breve. At last, making my grief known to my brother Francis, who was then a master, he shewed me the method of doing it, which I took, and was perfect at it immediately. It was but this: play crotchets, which every one can do, in even time by an even pass of the hand, as striking on a table or drum, then play with the same bow, but distinguishing the notes, as in the Italians' tremolo, which is easy, too, in such short notes. Lastly, play without such tremulous distinction, but make the distinction in the mind, which when one attempts is as easy as the rest; so by counting in the mind even measures, that may be judged so, I found I could govern the time of the longest notes; for it is impossible to guess the time of slow notes, there must be some measure of them. Alone it is in the mind, but in concert it is done by the other parts; for observing others' play gives you a measure for your own. This notion, with a little practice, brought me into the con-cert, and then I thought I was preferred enough. Thus, from a little shewing at first, together with my own application and industry, I attained the use of the treble and bass viol.

112. But I was not to stop here, but having wrote over much music, and some in the score, I observed a little of the composition, and offered at a little of the kind, which Mr. Jenkins seeing was so kind as to correct it, and shew me the faults; then it was played, which was no small pride; but afterwards I got books, Mr. Simpson's *Division Violist* and his *Compendium.*[1] Mr. Jenkins lent me But-

---

[1] CHRISTOPHER SIMPSON. . . . . in his younger days he was a sol-dier in the army raised by William Cavendish, Duke of Newcastle, for the service of Charles I. against the Parliament; he was of the Romish communion, and patronised by Sir Robert Bolles of Leicestershire, whose son, a student in Gray's Inn, Simpson taught on the viol. . . . . . In the year 1655 Simpson published in a thin folio volume a book enti-tled *Chelys Minuritionum, in English The Division Viol*, printed in columns, viz., in Latin with an English translation . . . . In 1667

ler,[1] with a commendation of it that it was the best of the
kind. I studied that, but not without difficulty, because he
had a different character, as *de* for the and *dat* for that, and
some others. I also procured Morley's *Introduction*,[2] which
books, together with constant playing and writing, and in
London in very edifying concerts, I became, as I thought,
a master of composition, which was great pleasure, and I
essayed some compositions of three parts, which I cannot
commend. Some of two I made airy enough, which my
brother, the Chief Justice, would be content to play. I was
not out at song neither, for my father translated the Italian
old song which his daughters had learned : " Una volta
finira," &c., " Time at last will set me free," &c., and gave
it to me to set, which I did in three parts, imitating
somewhat I had heard of Italian : it was in three flats,
a solemn key, and I thought succeeded well ; my brother
gave me the encouragement to ask where I stole several
passages.

113. Here I cannot decline to recommend to all learners
the art of composition, I might call it rather the science,

Simpson published *A Compendium of Practical Music* in 5 parts, containing—i. The Rudiments of Song ; ii. The Principles of Composition ;
iii. The Use of Discord ; iv. The Form of Figurate Descant ; v. The
contrivance of Canon. The book is dedicated to William, Duke of
Newcastle.—Hawkins, u. s. pp. 707—712.

[1] CHARLES BUTLER, a native of Wycomb, in the county of Bucks,
and a Master of Arts of Magdalen College, Oxford, published a book
with this title, *The Principles of Music, in Singing and Setting, with the
twofold use thereof, Ecclesiastical and Civil.* 4to. London, 1636.—Wood,
Athenæ Oxon. (ed. Bliss) vol. iii. p. 209. Hawkins (u. s. p. 575) says
that Butler's *Principles of Music* " is a very learned, curious, and
interesting work . . . . . may be read to great advantage, and may be
considered as a judicious supplement to Morley's *Introduction.*"

[2] Before the publication of Morley's *Introduction* the precepts of
musical composition were known but to few, as existing only in manuscript treatises, which being looked upon as inestimable curiosities were
transmitted from hand to hand with great caution and diffidence ; so
that for the most part the general precepts of music, and that kind of
oral instruction which was communicated in the schools belonging to
cathedral churches and other seminaries of music, were the only foundation for a course of musical study . . . ." THOMAS MORLEY was one
of the gentleman of Queen Elizabeth's chapel. He obtained the degree
of Mus. Bac. at Oxford, 8 July, 1588. His *Plaine and Easie Introduction to Musicke* was published in 1597. See Wood's *Fasti Oxon.* i.
241, and Hawkins, u. s. pp. 489 and 567.

because it is for the judgment to know, though the execution and invention be an art, it may not seem so essential
to the playing well on a single instrument, that one whose
design goes no further need trouble himself with it.   But
I found otherwise, and that in any part I undertook I was
very much assisted by my knowledge of and acquaintance
with the air. It gave me courage as well as skill to fill and
swell where the harmony required an emphasis; so also to
know how to give the right favour to the notes, whereby
some are made a little sharper, others a little more flat, is
a matter of skill, and depends on the composition.   And
nothing is more accomplished by it than a voice.   It gives
a judgment to the owner of it which doth almost reconcile
a bad voice to a good ear, and if an ear be deficient it makes
it tolerable, for such a one will not be in the least out of
tune . nor wanting to give a proper form at every turn.
And it certainly confirms performance at sight, as understanding is a help to the reading any language, which,
whatever the character be, is difficult if the tongue is unknown.   It takes the burden from the eye, for a little cost
informs the understanding that is acquainted with it, and
the memory will carry you on many a note without a look
on the paper, as the sense guides in reading.   And as it
makes the performance easy and true, it also gives an employment to the judgment in the apprehension of the conduct of the air, and taking notice when it is well or otherwise, and noting all extraordinary passages.   In short it is
necessary to the accomplishment of all sorts of musical
performance to have a thorough and clever notion of the
composing parts, and from my own experience I can assure
no one will repent the pains bestowed upon it who resolves
to make music a pleasure either to himself or
others.

114. And I think this will appear by my giving an account of the rest of my progress in music. I used constant and weekly meetings in London, which made me
ready at hand and sight playing, and shewed me much
variety of composition; and it was my fortune to be in
that company which introduced the Italian composed
entertainments of music which they call *sonatas*, and in
old times more imitated by our masters in what they

called *fantasias*. The court about this time entertained only the theatrical music and French air in song, but that somewhat softened and variegated; so also was the instrumental more vague and with a mixture of caprice, or Scottish way, than was used by the French, but the Italian had no sort of relish. But we found most satisfaction in the Italian, for their measures were just and quick, set off with wonderful solemn graves, and full of variety. The old English fantasias were in imitation of an older Italian sort of sonata, but fell from the sprightliness and variety they had, even in those times, into a perpetual grave course of fugue, and if the fugue quickened into a little division, or an air of triple was pricked in, it was extraordinary. For this reason the old English music has passed for dull entertainment, and I must agree it is so to impatient hearers; but I ever was pleased with it, and esteemed the best of them, as Coperario and Alphonso Ferabosco, as agreeable as I desire, and chiefly for the facility and sedateness of the music. It is not like a hurry of action, as looking on a battle, where the concern for one side or other makes a pleasure, but like sitting in a pleasant cool air in a temperate summer evening, when one may think or look or not, and still be pleased. At length the time came off the French way and fell in with the Italian, and now that holds the ear. But still the English singularity will come in and have a share. It is enough that of all foreign styles the Italian most prevails. This let me in to observe the elegance of the ordinary course of discords, which with the Italians perpetually occur. But that which thoroughly filled me with the riches of air and composition, was the constant touching a viol to my brother's voice.

115. He loved the Italian songs and recitativos to fondness, and would compass sea and land to obtain anything new. He had his first *goût* that way from some books Mr. Willis lent him, which came from Rome, and were of Ricilli and others, and ever after his acquaintance with them he delighted in such airs. He had no voice, but exquisite skill. I had neither voice nor skill when he first put me upon singing little basses to notes he would sound. I took the encouragement and improved myself

only with him to a bass part, and found I had a capacity of a tolerable low voice. Then we went about getting duos, English, Italian, and Latin, with which we exercised plentifully. And it being necessary to the sound of a voice, whatever it is, to have an instrument to accompany, and I being well habituated to the viol, and the fingering, I used to touch the principal notes as well as I could, and by degrees to put in chords, and at last to full harmony, as the instrument would afford. The continual use of this, together with a solitary practice, which my brother allowed me even in company (that I avoided to sit with for the wine sake) which he had sometimes at his house, their talk (too wise for me), and my viol, which did not (being soft) offend them, made an entertainment for us all, and me a complete, ready, and dexterous thorough bass man. And nothing less than being so hackneyed to it could have given me that readiness and fulness of parts which I acquired, and which is the greatest delight to practise, insomuch, that it encouraged me to finger the harpsichord and organ, whereby, notwithstanding I am (through age) incapable of hand, I can yet touch a ready thorough bass of plain notes, true, full, and classic harmony to voices or concert ; and I have added to my pleasures of this kind the use of my own voice to almost any instrument, which, not from nature or teaching, is tolerable, but only from the knowledge of music itself. And it is not a little diverting to observe that although I have no grace of a voice, and no hand upon a harpsichord, yet from the true sound and easy transitions from note to note, joined with a proper and full though plain harmony, I am thought both to sing and play well by such as are not masters, which confirms what I said, that gracing is like lace on a garment, which doth not give a beauty without a handsome contour of the whole. And such effect is there from the true though plainest music, which may be wholly spoiled by offering at graces, which lose the sound without giving any compensation for it, but is not much mended by the best gracing, because the delicacy lies in the true harmony of sound, which is the substance, the rest is pretty but trifling, and of little weight. To close this, I add only, that in the business of gracing, judgment of harmony still governs, for it is in truth but missing those elegances in the performance which the master might set down in the composition, but in common cadences and passages it is left to the performer, who is supposed to understand so much. And most of our ordinary graces are but the interspersing of discords in proper places. The trill is the sound of two notes, seconds together; the beat the same, only that mixes the lower, as the trill the upper note, as the accessory. For the principal note that bears the weight must have its chief emphasis, the other is but accessional. So the falling upon a second, or hanging upon a seventh, which is the way of sliding grace, is the same which the rule of discords prescribes. And there is no greater grace than breaking the time in the minutes, and still holding it punctually upon the main, to conserve the grand beat or measure. For this sprinkling of discord, or error, is like damask, grotesque, or any unaccountable variegation of colours, that renders a thing agreeable; and yet we discern not the distinction of parts, but only a pretty sparkling, such as the painters observe nature hath, which art cannot altogether imitate. And a plain sound not thus set off is like a dull plain colour, or as a bad copy of a good picture, that wants the spirit and life which a sparkling touch gives it. Thus a life and warmth in the colouring of a picture are well resembled to graces in music, which are not the body but the soul that enlivens it, or as the animal spirits that cannot be seen or felt, but yet make that grand difference between a living and a dead corpse.

116. Now, to look a little back, I cannot but wonder at the accidents of life, considering how very desirous and at what charges some are, and withal of a good capacity to learn music, and cannot attain it, and without much formal teaching, and that only of the viol, it is my lot to master the art in such a degree as I have here discoursed. I neither esteem myself more capable, industriously inclined, or ingenious, but on the contrary much less than others, but ascribe it wholly to the accident of family and company. My quality and relation gave me respect and admittance where others could not so well have come; and not only so, but a forward place in performances, which, joined with a genius and inclination, was my advantage. But before I

leave this subject I must apologise for the long discourse I have made upon it, which seems as if I valued myself upon what, collated with business and profit, is esteemed trivial and mean. As I am discoursing of my own life, I cannot but dwell long on those things which have had a great share of my time; but I never made music a minion to hinder business. It was a diversion, which I ever left for profit, and laid it down and resumed it as time enlarged or straitened with me. If I had built any vainglory upon it I should have been more an author in the way of composition, and have valued myself upon it, and had a name in print, perhaps, at the foot of some foolish song, as others with as little title have done. I ever declined this vanity, though perhaps, if seriously attempted, I might have succeeded reasonably well. I considered that it is not versifying makes a poet, and mediocrity is as contemptible in music. I left that to the professors. Perhaps one in my station might have met with a reward of flattery for vulgar composition, but my aspiring was above that. I must confess that I was always a friend to the publishing of compositions, because it led to prepare company (for all are not perfect sights' men) to perform who could not without possession of the copies and practice well do it. And I hated the humour of engrossing and secresy which most affect—masters for profit, wherein they are excusable, others for vanity, to enjoy the sole possession of a jewel in their opinion, than which no vanity is more childish.

117. This made me encourage the masters to print, and always encouraged it by subscription and buying, for it is money makes all things move. And farther, I attempted to shew them that without the charge of a graver or composing characters they might print by buying copperplates grounded, and etching themselves their music upon them, and a little habit would perfect them in the reverse writing, which seemed the hardest part. The copper so prepared, that is polished and ground, might be bought for 1s. 6d. per lb. and sold again after it was done with for 1s. 2d., which was but a small charge. And to give a demonstration of this, I bought a plate, etched a sonata or two upon it in score, and entitled it "Tentamen calcographicum." This miscarried a little by the fury of the aquafortis, that

made the character too coarse, but might have been prevented by tempering it with water. But this I thought
might shew how practicable the thing was, and I gave the
plate to Carr,[1] but found none to follow the industry of my
example.

118. It may be I might have run too much into the
sottish resignation that some shew to this slight entertainment, music, if my brother, with whom I was used to converse and very much revered his authority, had not sometimes given me a gentle check for hunting of music, as he
called it, which made me a little ashamed of owning too
much of it. Whatever may be thought of it, as ordinarily
used, we had a title to a better character than fiddlers, for
we had the philosophy as well as the practice of it among
us, and used to dispute, as of other ingenious subjects,
very earnestly of the reason of harmony. And my brother,
who rode Admiral in all things, thought it worth his time
to put his sentiments in writing, which were printed, and
titled " A Philosophical Essay of Music." I intend to enlarge a little upon these matters in some notes upon the
treatise, if it be printed again, so pass them by here and
resume the thread of relation, broke off at the building of
the Temple, which was one considerable epoch of my life.

[1] JOHN CARR, a printer and publisher of music. He was the first to
use copperplates in printing music.—Hawkins, chap. 152, vol. ii. p. 735.

CHAPTER VIII.

EARLY LIFE AT THE BAR.

ABOUT the time of the fire I had been and was a practiser at the common law, my first entrance to which I
will speak of. I had studied about five years, whilst my
brother was king's counsel, solicitor, and attorney general.
And although I was not a regular student, to proceed in
order and take in all the year-books, but read the more
modern reports, I digested them well by commonplace,
which was a good foundation and preparative for me to
build upon, which I afterwards learnt in practice. And I
must own to that, more of my skill in the law than from
hard reading; but without a competency of the latter the
others would not have done, no more than bare reading
without practice, which pedantiseth a student, but never
makes him a clever lawyer. During my time of study I
was not without my excursions, but a short purse, and regard for my brother kept me from fatal extravagances. I
was all the while under great diffidence of my success in
the profession, and looked on my fortune to depend on my
brother's life, and that if he should die I were lost. Sure
I felt in myself defects to cause this despondence, and I
could not work my mind to a better courage, which diffidence even to despair sat on me, even within my practice
and after I had got a sum of money. My brother observing it, to keep up my spirits, sold me an annuity of £200
for £1600, for life, with a clause of re-purchase. And
when I had mastered about £8000 he executed the power
and took in his grant. I feared nothing so much as being
precarious and servile from necessity. And, to say truth,
I had always an ambition to honourable freedom, and could
scarce brook the many mortifications, by little contempts
my brother, sometimes in jest and often in earnest, would
put upon me. He had somewhat of humour that way of
raising his own by depressing others' characters. But I

am satisfied it did me good, and worked off much vanity and self conceit I should otherwise have had. But I at length broke out in resentment of it to him, after he had the Seal, and I remember I said I had endured patiently for ten years. He wondered at the expression, which was more passionate than prudent, but ever after he was tender of my countenance.

120. When Lord Chief Justice Vaughan died my brother was advanced to the Common Pleas in his place of Chief Justice, which was a most happy preferment, and what his heart wished. It was no less a preferment to me, for the favourite's place, as they term it in Westminster Hall, was considerable. I was immediately called to the bar, *ex gratiâ*, not having standing, although I had performed such exercises as the house required, save a few. My first flight in practice was the opening a declaration at Nisi Prius in Guildhall, under my brother, which was a crisis like the loss of a maidenhead ; but with blushing and blundering I got through it, and afterwards grew bold and ready at such a formal performance, but it was long ere I adventured to ask a witness a question. The next engagement was the circuit, which proved very commodious to me, because I was hardy and painful, and never was absent from my opportunities. One Mr. Henry Montagu, an acquaintance and companion, as well as a relation of my brother, thought to profit by going, but my name and relation so much nearer carried all from him; besides, he was idle and I was diligent, and never absent from my brother in his retirements, and I kept so close to him that I can safely say I saw him abed every night without intermission for divers years together, which enables me to contradict the malicious report a relation raised of him, that he kept a mistress, as the mode of that time was. But at length Mr. Montagu desisting, I had the sole advantage of the respect usually paid the judge's friend. My brother used to say he supposed none thought him partial on any such account, his justice was known to be above it ; but it was a common civility and respect both counsel and attorneys used to pay to the judge, by retaining his friend, though clients were so weak as to think more.

121. At London I constantly attended the King's Bench,

where motions were short and matter of practice, which was easy and very often only of course. I endured crowding and writing at the bar for divers years, which is a fatigue unknown to all that have not been practisers there; for such is the heat, sweat, and pain of standing, especially with fulsome persons, such as Saunders, afterwards Lord Chief Justice, that I am sure the galleys for a time is not greater pain. Now I have mentioned Saunders give me leave to add for his honour what I know of him. He was cordate in his practice, and I believe never in all his life betrayed a client to court a judge, as most eminent men do. If he had any fault it was playing tricks to serve them, and rather expose himself than his clients' interest. He had no regard to fees, but did all the service he could, whether feed double or single, and though his parts were clear, his wit quaint, and his judgment profound, yet he was debonair and easy to mean capacities, and so much a well-willer to his profession, and the youth of it, that in his greatest credit he would entertain the time at the bar before the court sat with putting cases and mooting with the students that sat on and before the crickets, and that with such complaisance to their capacities, and aim to instruct them, that I admired his humanity more than his skill, and that was greater worth than the other. He raised himself from a very low estate, being a poor boy in the Inns of Chancery who by service to clerks there was allowed a hole upon an upper stairs, where he sat and taught himself to write, and by that means got hackney employment, and so lived; but, passing on in the same way of industry, he went from writing to drawing of pleadings, and mixed reading with his work, which at length made him an exquisite pleader, and that was his intromission to the King's Bench practice, until he was one of the prime. He was born but not bred a gentleman, for his mind had an extraordinary candour, but his low and precarious beginnings led him into a sordid way of living; for he fell into the conversation of a tradesman's wife, which was great scandal upon him, and it was believed he had children by her. But notwithstanding all he might be innocent and she only his nurse. For either by constitution, or using a sedentary life, drinking much ale, without

exercise, he was extremely corpulent and diseased. It is
certain he lived in the family, maintained them out of his
plenty, and all in peace and friendship with husband as
well as wife, so that if the horns were in the case they
were well gilded. He addicted himself to little ingenuities,
as playing on the virginals, plantings, and knick-knacks in
his chamber. He took a house at Parson's Green, where
he bestowed much on the gardens and fruits. He would
stamp the name of every plant in lead and make it fast to
the stem. And in short he had as active a soul in as
unactive a body as ever met. He would cover his infirmities with jesting, and never expostulate with those he
offended in anger, but always droll. And how touchy
soever we were that stood in the very great stench of his
carcase at the bar, we could not be heartily angry, because
he would so ply the jests and droll upon us and himself
that reconciled us to patience. His first employment from
the court was the drawing pleadings upon *quo warrantos*
against corporations, which was his original study and
practice. This he performed with so much zeal (for he
was ever very earnest for his client) and slight of reward,
that King Charles II. was much pleased with him, and
often sent him good round fees out of his own cabinet.
And these he accepted with so much modest gratitude in
the manner as obliged as much as was possible. At length,
upon [1] [the dismissal of Sir Francis Pemberton] he was
made Chief Justice of the King's Bench. But the preferment was an honour fatal to him; for from great labour,
sweat, toil, and vulgar diet, he came to ease, plenty, and
of the best, which he could not forbear, being luxurious in
eating and drinking. So in a short time, for want of his
ordinary exercises and evacuations, he fell into a sort of
apoplexy, which ceased with an hemiplegia, and in a short
time after he died. But he acted as Chief Justice during
that weakness on one side, and it was pity to see a mind
conscious of its own strength labour under the load of a
disease, and strive with an unapt instrument,—a broken
body,—to act its part with but sorry success compared
with former passages of his life. *Quantum mutatus ab illo.*

[1] A space has been left in the MS., and evidently left designedly.

Thus much I thought fit to say of him, because, being of no known family or kindred, there is now already no more mention of him than if he had .lived in the days of Fortescue. And he was a person of an extraordinary character, and in the main worthy of his honour. His vices at worst were but sensual; his soul or better part was candid and free from malice, ambition, and backbiting inclinations; he supplanted none, and carried no offence about him but what he could not shake off. He did good to all where he might, and himself chiefly, as he thought; he hated faction and turbulent persons, and sincerely wrought to enervate their practices. He was rather a Bacchus than a Momus, peace and the butt were his delight. And so we leave him, subjoining only his apothegm of Jeffries', who was his coutemporary and fellow practiser. At the great trial touching spirits perfectly made, whether brandy were excisable as such or not, specimens of the several sorts of spirits were brought, some by the Commissioners of the Excise and others by the distillers. When the Act was made spirits were not potable without drawing them over a second time, which they called dulcifying, and these they said were perfectly made; but spirits at one operation were fiery, and would not last, therefore such had a lower excise. And brandy of late came to be made all at one distilling fit for use, and so was of the latter sort. The specimens were handed about, and the judges tasted, the jury tasted, and Saunders seeing the phials moving, took one and set it to his mouth and drank it all off. The court observing a pause and some merriment at the bar about Mr. Saunders, called to Jeffries to go on with his evidence. "My Lord," said he, "we are at a full stop, and can go no further." "What's the matter?" said the Chief. Jeffries replied, "Mr. Saunders has drunk up all our evidence." Which jest made no little diversion at the time.

122. I had an advantage of improving myself at the 'King's Bench, for that Hales[1] was Chief Justice there when I attended the court as a student, and after when I practised. He was a very able lawyer, and in indifferent

---

[1] Roger North always spells Sir Matthew Hale's name with a final " s."

cases a very exquisite judge. But as all mortals have their infirmities he had great ones, which centred in popularity. Whether the source of his bias that way was fear or affection I cannot determine, but am inclined to think it was fear or pusillanimity. This censure of his is different from the common opinion, for he was looked upon as an extraordinary stout man in resisting the monarchy. But he was so wise as to know the monarchy could hurt him no farther than by taking away his preferments, and his philosophy was such to resolve him that more or less money was not the measure of happiness, but sufficient with security, and that he could not want if confined to his chamber practice. But the people are violent, and know no moderation in mischief when they undertake it. He believed the monarchy was declining, and that the people would pluck it up by the roots, and that no man could be safe that was considerable in the interests of it, and perhaps was of a plebeian spirit, and inclined rather to advance a sour popular government than an illustrious monarchy, which commonly was vicious and disorderly in morals, and protected such from the course of law and justice. It is most certain he was so prejudiced that way that the very aspect of a person corrupted him. A greasy cap had always the better of a modish peruke, and he could scarce believe the latter honest and the other a knave. And a precise pretension to religion frequently caught him, as I shall shew in a relation I am about to give of the cause between Cutts and Pickering. It is said that one doubting that he had a prejudice to his cause because he belonged to the court, the day before his trial got one to go from the king to speak for his adversary, and so gained his point. I make this distinction between Saunders and him: the former was of a clear and good-natured spirit, and encouraged easiness, pleasure, and debonairtie; but Hales was sour, magisterial, precise, and adverse to all the delights that youth is apt to pursue. Then all the vices of Saunders were in the way of sensual luxury, as eating, drinking, and as most thought lechery. But Hales professed the contrary of that, hated a feast, affected to eat upon a stool, and never came to an excess of either eating or drinking. The one had no vice in his mind; but all of his sense and appetite; the other had (as seemed) a very sour disposition and no indulgence in his mind, but otherwise extraordinarily virtuous. Hales had his inclination to women, but gave no scandal by it, unless by his second match, which was with his servant maid, but that was no breach of virtue or morality, and evil only from the arbitrary injunctions of custom and vulgar expectation.

123. That which I liked worst in Hales was an insuperable pride and vanity. This in great measure proceeded from the retiredness of his life, for every man is partial to himself, and if he dwells too much upon that subject shall create impressions and habits of valuing himself that shall expose him to great censure abroad. His abilities were extraordinary, being of an indefatigable industry, ready apprehension, and wonderful memory; and having bent all his force to the study of the law, English history, and records, was arrived to the highest degree of learning that any age hath known in that profession. And towards his latter time, when he had spent all his material of study in the way he professed, and had nothing but incident practice, and when advanced to the bench, causes depending to employ his thoughts, his readiness was such that this did not fill his time, which in his retired way of living was plentiful to him. This made him deviate to other studies, for the activity of his mind would not let him be at ease, without being supplied with subjects to work upon; and hence sprang another misfortune to his reputation. If he had held himself to the law and not discovered his popular disposition, he had been chief in fame and honour as he was in station and preferment, but warping to plebeianism and valuing himself in other learning in which he was not adept, stained the purity of his fame. The first of these I have touched, I will give the most genuine account I can of the other.

124. This good man, by a long transcendence in practice and judgment upon the bench, had found a true scale of his own capacity and the defects of those that negociated with or under him, and must needs observe the advanced degree of his own above theirs. For I am of opinion that if a man can judge-truly of anything it is of himself, and we are not to wonder, if under this course, he contracted

an opinion of himself accordingly, and that by time grew up into an habit, and under age (when the mind as well as the body is less pliant, and flexible to abject occasions), extended itself not only in the law, where there was reason, but all other matters he undertook, where the like reason was absent. As from the maxim premised, " My understanding is above others," it easily follows, by way of inference or conclusion, that it is so in any particular matter to which self-flattery (natural to mankind) will apply it. If that principle be denied, the law proves it; if in that, then in all. This is a false reasoning, but such as willing human nature will easily swallow.

125. I grant this infirmity may receive a check from the opposition of more learned men, for contradiction and opposition only regulates men's understandings, and makes them hunt for objections, put themselves in the places of opponents, and so at length determine, and in such manner as may be defended if opposition should come. But without such regard to opposition we are captivated with the seeming justness of our thoughts, and prosecute consequences upon them into miz-mase of error. There is another use of opposition, or rather the history of any subject a man lends his thoughts to, which is had from books, but better by conversation with the prime professors. And this is the driving a man out of beaten trite paths, and preventing his arrogating to himself inventions which he was not author of, but have been common before. Nothing is more ridiculous than for an author to send forth a bundle of discoveries, with the ostentation which usually attends the publication of new inventions, when the whole matter was vulgar before. And this is usually the failing of illiterate men, who without much aid of books or conversation, undertake sciences upon the force of their natural abilities; and those may be very good, but uncultivated, are little to be esteemed, and stalking abroad without the breeding of books or men, are but phantasms to be laughed at.

126. The person I am discoursing of wanted this sort of check to regulate his active mind. The company which came to him were either his inferiors or flatterers, inferiors were of course so; and one gentleman in particular I well

knew young, applied himself to him in such a manner as would have tried the spirit of the most stout champion against flattery. It was Mr. Thomas Read, a twin-brother of Sir Charles Read of Suffolk. He was designed for the law, and obtained to be brought to Chief Justice Hales, when he professed to adore him, and begged he might have leave to write when he was in his company. This the old man gave way to, for it is a pain to resist the propensities of nature, and many will surrender to indecencies rather than do it. He encouraged and gratified the young man in his way, but he died immaturely, so the fruit of this advantage never appeared, but this shews how exposed the good man was to flattery. Then he was used to dictate upon the bench, and most men deferred to him there and in his chamber as to an oracle, especially lawyers and attorneys, and students, whose behaviour was all adoration, and in all state and popular matters his opinion had the common voice as from a tripos.

127. Those who came to him on account of conversation, or consultations relating to the public, which were either clergymen or the factious drivers against the government, all agreed in one harmonious voice to persuade him he was the most learned man in the world, and I have known him laughed into a good opinion of the worst of men by mere flattery. None ever gained so much upon him as Jeffries, and had his ear so much as he had in Guildhall at Nisi Prius, although he was the most rude, indecent, and impetuous practiser that ever was; and all by little accommodations administer to him in his own house after his own humour, as a small dinner, it may be a partridge or two upon a plate, and a pipe after, and in the meantime diverting him with satirical tales and reflections upon those who bore a name and figure about town. And he hated a truly learned man that did not subscribe to or concur with him in his tendency to popular authority; a Monarchist he hated as a villain and parricide. I remember a remarkable trial upon Sir John Cutts' will. An estate was given to Mrs. Do[rothy] Weld, then married to Pickering, for eighty years, if she lived so long. It was thought Pickering razed out the limitation to get the estate to himself absolutely for eighty years. It is certain there was such

erasure. And an eminent counsel, but a Monarchist, found it out, and by his skill and speedy directions about collecting the evidence made it very clear the erasure was since the death. An issue was directed out of Chancery to try the matter, and it came to the King's Bench bar before him to be tried. I never saw a judge so prejudiced against an allegation as he was. Pickering was a formal man, and used to pretend piety, and wrote sermons at the Rolls in his hat as not to be seen. The discoverer, main counsel, chief witness, and chief of the jury were of the Church and Crown party, and he did believe that the godly man was innocent, and that these men sought to impose a false charge upon him. So the trial went on wonderful hard upon them, till by a foolish slip of a witness for Pickering the matter was cleared. Then he knocked his staff, and said, " Well, gentlemen of the jury, you hear the case, find as you think upon the evidence, which I will not repeat." And in this manner delivered up a cause he had been supporting through the whole trial, knowing there was no need of his harangue to the jury on that side. I mention this only as an instance of his frailty in the way of prejudice and flattery, but there were many others, which some know to their cost.

128. He being thus besieged with a great opinion of his understanding, thought it worth his while to correct the common opinions that went abroad, though in trifling matters, such as natural philosophy. And the first piece he put out was a small essay to prove the non-gravitation of fluids upon immersed bodies, which was against manifest truth. The next he called *Difficiles Nugæ*, and it was to oppose the then cleared solution of the Torricellian experiment, or baroscope, by the spring of the air made or bent by the weight of it; and to give his own solution, or that which of all the several opinions he liked best. It is strange to observe with what exact method and expression, and with how much spirit those two pieces were wrote to maintain childish errors and prejudices; for, first, fluids weigh, but the force is dispersed on all parts of the body immersed, which makes it not perceived as a solid weight incumbent on one part only ; secondly, the mercury in the baroscope is by the air-pump demonstrated to be crowded

and upheld by the air without pressing on the stagnum; but he thought otherwise, and as many lines as he wrote so many errors appear. But in his *Difficiles Nugœ* he had very ill luck, for of all the accounts that had been given to solve the experiment he patronized the worst, which is that of Linus, who supposeth a cord extracted from the quicksilver by the weight descending to a certain degree, which tied it up to the top. Now, this is not only the silliest of all, but a mere banter of Mr. Hobbs, for he published that notion under the name of Linus as lawyers' Latin for a line, which afterwards he called funiculus or cord, not as his opinion, but to shew what silly things might be imposed upon the world in the way of natural philosophy.[1]

129. He was a great, and, as I verily believe, a true professor of piety, and according to the precise way he sequestered Sunday to pious meditation and writing. And there is a volume or two published of his meditations which are very good in their kind; for a man of wit and style as he was, well inclined and in earnest, cannot but perform considerable things in the devotionary way, which require perfection of fancy and words as well as sound reason, but the former chiefly, because the subject is above reason. He added to many of them verses and pious hymns, which had better been left out, for he had not a poetic style, which is artificial, and to be made by practice upon the models of antiquity with a natural propensity attending, all which were wanting to him, so that his verses were but as prose with syllables told out, and without feet to run smooth upon.

130. His only finished work was that called the *Origination of Mankind*. In that he seemed to collect all human learning into one heap and digest it. But the matter is very short of the design. For he spins fine and dwells upon subjects that had been worn threadbare by the learned before, and reduced by dispute to agreed notions, that lie in a few words. But he spreads all out again into large refinements, as for instance, the notion of infinity, which is reduced to this, that it is only ignorance of limits, or as

---

[1] Compare *Life of the Lord Keeper Guilford*, § 83.

Mr. Descartes expresses it, indefinite. But Hales had so many nice cases upon it, as adding, subtracting, multiplying, and dividing of infinites, that one is tired of it, and would not be bound to go through, but as a lawyer studies his case for his fee when an important trial is to follow. And the rest is of the same kind, so that although the work be pompous, well digested and penned, yet for the exility of the matter few have bought and much fewer read it.

131. This good man had much the same exit as the other whom I collated with him; for after a great sickness he was extremely changed, from a mild, patient, and for the most part very indifferent judge, to a touchy, passionate, and prejudiced one; which was to be ascribed to his disease and the weakness of his body, and not to himself, who in all his life, which ended, in truth, at this sickness, had, and well deserved a better character.

132. He was a known contemner of money, and I believe out of a right understanding and principle, for he could not know but money is the snare of life. He was sure of enough, and courting great acquests would expose him to danger and infamy, both which he declined, and with all the passion that stirred within him. He had a timorousness which is natural and incident to some as form and colour is, and therefore is not imputable as vice, but on the contrary excuseth many failings derived from it. This made him take the rabble's part against the Crown, and he believed the violence and impetuosity of the former would prevail. A beast that hath been tamed may be reconciled by courtship, but a wild one will not so yield, but bear all down before it. The House of Commons he knew would be obeyed, right or wrong, and the Crown must truckle to it for the sake of the purse, therefore that side was safest. And further, glory lay among the people also, which led him further into the engagement. It is a hard case upon poor weak mortal understanding to be attacked by fear and pride continually: there is no need of covetousness to assist. He had studied to avoid that, but at length it gained ground upon him, and in his old age he was sharper upon profits and readier to accept presents than in his youth and middle age. And that

change is to be ascribed to his remitting the reins of reason for his ease, and so letting inclination, or rather the product of his natural infirmity, fear, get ground upon him. But in the main he was a most excellent person, and in the way of English justice an incomparable magistrate. Insomuch as I have heard the greatest of his observers say that in the Exchequer, where he was Chief Baron for divers years, his learning, and knowledge of the records and proceedings of that court obliged him, though against his bias and inclination, to do the Crown, as he did, more right in point of prerogative, than the most willing and obsequious judges that ever sat there, because they, out of ignorance, dare not do what was right and justifiable by the laws of the court, and he never would judge against the Crown against his knowledge, and precedent was much for the advantage of the prerogative.

133. It is a strange infelicity to the world that men should value their judgment in things less known than when they are truly critical. The reason is that in the latter they see their danger of erring, but in the other, where they see little, they think they know all. This good man's writings relating to the law were all admirable in their kind, witness the little table to the Crown Law, which to one read is a memorial he need not go from in his whole life, for it comprehends all that is to be found in all the printed books, and more of his own besides. Then he hath some small tracts about the poor, registers, sheriffs' accounts, and some arguments which go about, in manuscript, all exceeding good. But what is beyond all is his *Historic Discourse of the Crown Law at large* and his *Commonplaces* and other tracts, which in the abundance of his diffidence he would not trust the world with, but packed them up in Lincoln's Inn library with an injunction not to be made public in fifteen years. He published an Abridgment or Commonplace of Rolls with a preface to it, which preface is most worth reading, because it gives a history of the changes of the law. And that is a subject that startles all men that think. " For," say they, " does the law change? then it is arbitrary." But the world is variable, and laws have not their patent of exemption: they belong to men and their ways, which always are

innovating. And fashion will take place with the one as well as with the other. So I leave the discourse of this great man, wishing I may be so happy to live to see such another, with all his faults.

134. It now occurs to me that he was a great admirer of Pomponius Atticus, and aimed to be like him, that is, esteemed of all parties, bountiful to all, and engaged upon hazard with none, but to lead a philosophical life, quiet in the most turbulent of times.

135. Gilbert Burnet has pretended to write his life, but wanted both information and understanding for such an undertaking. Nay that which he intended chiefly, to touch the people with a panegyric, he was not fit for, because he knew not the virtues he had fit to be praised, and I should recommend to him the lives of Jack Cade, Wat Tyler, or Cromwell, as characters fitter for his learning and pen to work upon than him.

CHAPTER IX.

THE BEGINNINGS OF SUCCESS.

DURING my practice under Hales at the King's Bench I was raw, and not at all quaint and forward as some are, so that I did but learn experience and discover my own defects, which were very great. I was a plant of a slow growth, and when mature but slight wood, and of a flashy fruit. But my profession obliged me to go on, which I resolved to do against all my private discouragements, and whatever absurdities and errors I committed in public I would not desist, but forget them as fast as I could, and take more care another time. My comfort was, if some, all did not see my failings, and those upon whom I depended, the attorneys and suitors, might think the pert and confident forwardness I put on, might produce somewhat of use to them. And I durst not undertake a solemn argument in the King's Bench, which is the way for young men to get credit, because they have time to study and compose it, and if they have matter in them on such occasions they may shew it. I went often to the Chancery, where in small motions I passed well enough, but I could scarce master to open a long bill or answer to my content, and I took little comfort besides the fees in all my business of this kind. I went often to the Exchequer too, and in all places I had great countenance and was readily and well heard, and not only so but with extraordinary respect and civility, for my brother was all that while a rising man and in growing credit, not only in Westminster Hall and the Court, but all over the nation, where he was exceeding popular with the best of the people. This gave me great advantage of practice in all courts, for my quality was one thing which made me respected, and I was sober and seemed diligent and wholly resigned to practice, and the business of my profession, being indefatigable, and running up and down in every corner where profit called, affable and easy to all, rather impertinent by overmuch talk than otherwise, which in youth is dispensed with, as an excess which time and experience will reduce into the compass of discretion and substance; but, as I said, my chief *appui* was my brother's character, fame, and interest, which made me the most general favourite that ever dealt in Westminster Hall.

137. All this while I had not the advantage of some, because the Court of Common Pleas was not accessible but to the serjeants, and I had a place only at Nisi Prius, and in the circuits, on account of favour; but the judges meeting in the Treasury before the Court sat, where they used to hear attorneys or clients upon ordinary matters of practice, I sometimes came and made a small motion for my fee, which I am persuaded was not above twice or thrice in a term. But the serjeants, who are an order of persons full of avarice, and deal in small profits, all which depend on their monopoly of the Common Pleas bar, took offence at these small essays of mine in the Treasury, where other barristers as well as myself often came, and one day agreed together not to move, as children, who for want of their wills will not eat. It was a strange scene when the court was sat, the Chief as the use is, spoke to a serjeant, " Move, brother." A reverent bow—he moved nothing. So seven or eight more. And though some attorneys stepped forward and called on them to move the business retained and instructed for, not a word could the whole bar afford. The judges thought the whole court bewitched, and rose, not imagining the cause; but, coming out of the court, some told the judges it was a discontent because they heard motions in the Treasury. My brother said if he had known it in court they would have heard attorneys' parties, or any counsel who had offered them-selves, and resolved so to do the next day, which had dis-solved the privilege of the serjeants. This exploit of the coif was known abroad, and began to be laughed at uni-versally; and at dinner they understood the judges thought themselves affronted, and had resolved to let in the bar-risters upon them the next day. The serjeants were sensible of their folly in the afternoon, and went in a body to my brother to own their error and beg pardon. But he would

not receive their recantation and humiliation there, for the affront was not to him alone, but the court, and let them there set themselves right if they could. A public affront must have a public satisfaction. So when the court was set, and a great crowd of lawyers got together, one of them begins the recantation, owning the fault and begging the court's pardon, and then my brother took up the matter and made a short discourse in the way of sharp reprehension of them for carrying themselves so, having had the civility of the court shewed to them as they had. Which done, he said to the senior (whose head with the rest was hung down) "Move, brother." Then he raised it up a little, and begun his motion in a crying tone, which made a sort of a general laugh or smile. And so ended the adventure called among the attorneys the "Dumb Day." [1]

138. This being an odd passage happening in Westminster Hall, puts me in mind of another, but of a different nature, which fell out when I was a student. It was when Bridgman sat in the Chancery and Hales in the King's Bench. I sat (by privilege) next Livesay, the secondary in the king's reporting, and on a sudden a strange noise was made in the hall (which was very full). I started up upon the table, and saw the folk divide as if the whole crowd had been split in strange haste to either side of the hall, leaving the middle void, and then scouring up the stairs, as if the whole roof were seen to be manifestly falling. This hubbub, not in the least understood where we were, ceased awhile, and the folk were gathered promiscuously again, and in an instant cleft again to either side. I never saw an odder object in my life. Upon the appeasing of this second disorder it began to be known what was the cause, and it appeared to be only a steer, incensed by the blood of the slaughter-house, broke loose in King Street, and being near or just within the Palace gate, chased by butchers, the rabble in the yard took fright, and running towards the hall frightened them in good earnest. This verifies an old observation, that a multitude is sooner frightened than a single person ; for they fright

---

[1] This story is told in the *Life of the Lord Keeper Guilford*, § 150, p. 209, but with some characteristic variations. It has therefore been considered advisable to leave it here as it stands.

one another, and when some discover fear, others, ignorant of the cause, fancy it more than it is, and run still propagating the fear, which is ever greatest when none knows why. And the judges, who are generally old and timorous, were under as bad fears as any, and testified it by the pallor of their countenances, though they were not so nimble to take their heels. Yet it was said some serjeants were so active as to curvet over the bar into the court, which, after all, was more honourable than to be made to curvet over the bar out of it.

139. During the latter time of my being a student, and the beginning of my practice, I applied myself to court keeping.[1] This employ was recommended to me [by my

[1] The expression in the text—court keeping—which is dwelt on so curiously in this paragraph, carries us back to a state of things which has now passed away, and seems to require a few words of elucidation.

(1) Every *manor* was governed, as far as the tenure, succession, and disposition of lands, and the rights, obligations, and services of its tenants were concerned, by its own customs, which were administered in its own *court*, called the *court baron*, sometimes, as in the text, called the *copyhold court*, and sometimes the *manor court*. This court, in theory, presided over by the lord of the manor, was in practice presided over by " Mr. Steward," *i.e.*, the lord's deputy or steward of the manor. The business of such courts was, practically, confined to questions of succession of property, titles, leases, conveyances of land, &c., and actions for debt under 40*s*. The court had no jurisdiction outside the limits of the manor. " The business of court keeping," even in the *manor court*, North says, had its use in familiarising one with the " process," the mode in which the court was held, as to evidence, swearing the jury, &c.

(2) Outside of the manor court, and exercising a jurisdiction over an area which in some instances included a district comprehending many manors that at one time had all been the property of a single lord, the *court leet* took cognizance of matters with which the *manor court* was not competent to deal. It adjudicated on criminal matters, assault, slander, larceny, and the like, and in some instances it had jurisdiction in civil actions. In the *court leet* " the crown law " (*i.e.*, the common and statute law), modified however in certain cases by special custom, was administered. There were, however, offences, such as treason and murder, which the *court leet* was not competent to punish; it enquired into the facts, and *recorded* its finding upon the evidence, presenting its verdict—" the view of a small ville "—to a higher court, originally the court of *Justices Itinerant* or *Justices in Eyre*.

(3) The jurisdiction of the Justices in Eyre had originally overlapped and supplemented that of the *court leet ;* the *ancient eyre*, or *iter*, of the King's Justices exercising an authority over a still wider area—" a *view* of a larger extent, as of a whole county or forest."

brother] as a very proper introduction to business ; for the gains, though small, gave a taste of the fruits of diligence. He used to remember a saying, often repeated by a grave old steward of my grandfather's, " be long getting little, and you will soon get much," meaning that all things must begin low. He found his words true, for few ever took more pains for less, and at length gat more in a few years honestly than he did. Besides this employ shews a young man how to transact with mankind in the way of business, how subtle plain men will be to shark and cheat for small matters, and what effect small authority gravely managed hath. And likewise all the business of court keeping depends on the fundamental institution of our laws. As the crown law [holds] in the court leet, which is a sort of eyre, and as that eyre is a view of a small ville, [so] the ancient eyre was a view of a larger extent, as of a whole country or forest. The nature and distinction of the court, and suitors, which was the original of trials by jury,—the county being drawn into small inquests, who in the ancient eyres attended in a body, and answered for all facts in the country. So in the franchise of the leet the court is informed by the suitors, which to them is the country, and then the court judges and inflicts the penalties according to law. Then the nature of inquests and offices, the tenderness in capital cases, in which the suitors and court are but an inquest to certify but not try. And this small and despised, or rather antiquated jurisdiction of the leet, gives any student a handle to inform himself of the ancient constitution and nature of the English government and jurisdictions. The Copyhold Court, which is called the Court Baron, instructs him in titles, and the way of examining them, through all the mutations, and to see if they cohere, and to spy out defects and cure them. And also to accommodate the business for poor men, who are governed by Mr. Steward. He will have the mortgaging and discharging mortgages ; entailing and barring entails ; settling jointures, and examining feme-coverts who join to convey, all which is working in the porch of the law, in order to be fit to enter the sacred temple of it, where the works are of greater moment and profit. The Court Baron, in the genuine sense, is the court of lords' jurisdiction in his manor, and holds plea of all land held of the manor, and in debt under 40*s.*, and may be held from three weeks to three weeks, wherein the process is after the model of the ancient common law, and the knowledge how to conduct such a court fits a man to be a practiser even at the Common Pleas bar. For all which reasons, and more, it is most advisable to put a young man destined for the law upon court keeping, and fill him with this sort of business as much as may be.

140. I entered young upon my father's courts, and kept them as long as he and my mother lived, and my brother recommended me to my Lord Grey of Werke [1] for keeping of his courts at Epping by the Forest, in Essex. This court was very considerable to me, for it was held upon Thursday in Whitsun-week every year. I went in the morning early, and returned at night with seven, eight, or nine pounds clear profit. There was a three-weeks' Court Baron which I held by deputy, but very inconsiderable to him, much less to me. Upon this Thursday Greengoose Fair at Bow is always held, and I had for divers years the diversion in my journey to see the preparation and conclusion. In the morning the country carts came in dressed up with boughs, and benched up for carrying and recarrying the rabble. At night they were drunk, and commonly as I came by at nine at night, they were upon the march to London, but with much variety of humour and noise, some quarrelling, others jesting, but in the way of rabble and obscenity. All which was tolerable, but if it happened to be a dry time the dust they made was prodigious; it is scarce credible that man or horse could live in it, if one had stood aloof and observed the thickness of the continual cloud that reached from Bow to Whitechapel. I sought once a back way by Hackney to avoid this nuisance, but was so intrigued that for the future I resolved to endure the dust, *nova non vetus orbita fallit*. But that which crowned my endeavours in the way of court keeping, and the more advanced steps of my profession, with more

---

[1] FORDE GREY, third Baron Grey of Werke, created Viscount Gendale and Earl of Tankerville, 11 June, 1695. He succeeded his father Ralph, second Baron, in 1675, and died in 1701, when the viscounty and earldom became extinct.

honour than by any other character than fidelity I could
pretend to, was the promotion to the office of Temporal
Steward to the See of Canterbury, which I hold still, and
will not part with (in right and title) so long as I am
capable to retain it, although by the inclemency of the
times I am forced to quit the possessions to usurpers.

141. This office hath three patents. First, Judge of the
Palace Court of Canterbury. This court is like to the
Court of the King's Household called the Marshalsea, and
hath jurisdiction in all personal actions of any value arising
within the liberty, that is in any of the towns whereof the
church of Canterbury had the seignioralty, which is a large
circuit in the county of Kent. For although there were no
demesnes, yet the services and other incidents of dominion
in old time were considerable. This court hath a prison
and a bailiff or gaoler, who executes all processes and is
minister curiæ, as the sheriff in the county at large under
the courts at Westminster. The court is constantly [held]
by a deputy, who paid me £30 per annum, not by articles,
which would have made the office void by the statute, but
by private understanding between us. Second, the office of
Keeper of the Liberties in the county of Kent, that is
coroner and admiral within the liberty, and to collect the
green wax profits upon the totted schedules out of the
Exchequer, and to act as minister in all the business of the
liberty, which might be upon return and execution of process or otherwise. And the sheriffs were commonly so just
[as] to send their *mandata ballivo*, according to right, and
then the bailiff of the court executed the process. This
was delegated to the same deputy. And once a year he
sued out the escheats from the Exchequer, and accounted
to me for the levies, one half whereof were the archbishop's
and the other half my own, and usually amounted to £25,
£30, or £40 per annum. This office was of great profit
before the Court of Wards was taken away, for all ward-
ships and liveries within the liberty belonged to the archbishop, and the steward of the liberty had the benefit of
them in half. The third patent was the Stewardship of
the Manors, and Keeper of the Liberties in the county of
Surrey. This carried a salary of £4 per annum for the
two courts of the manors of Croydon and Lambeth. But

the liberty profits came to nothing, being not worth the
charge of totting in the Exchequer, and therefore in these
manors, though the right was the same as in Kent, save
only the Palace Court, the liberty was not exerted. But
once a year I kept the two courts, which yielded me about
£18 or £20, so that in the whole this office was worth to
me about £60 per annum, sometimes more, and often less.
My predecessor, Phillips, came into a moiety of a fine of
£500, set in the King's Bench upon Sir Peter Temple for
corruption as a justice of the peace, but the pleading the
patent devoured most of the profit.

142. My immediate predecessor was Dolben, brother of
the Archbishop of York, Recorder of London, and afterwards a judge of the King's Bench.[1] He was a man of
good parts, bred under a clerk of assize, and executed the
office of associate of the Crown side, which gave him the
habit of a loud voice, though he was but of a small person.
He was of a humour retired, morose, and very insolent.
His servants and nephews who depended on him had much
ado to comport with his expectations, or rather exactions
from them, and, being a judge, proved an arrant peevish
old snarler; and though he looked up to the court as to a
fruit tree, expecting to be fed with preferment to fall from
it, yet would be secretly busy to undermine it. He used
to declare for the populace, of late called mob, from Horace,
mobile vulgus, and that they could not err. This is the
ordinary republican principle, but utterly fails; for the
people left to themselves never did right, and never failed
to destroy each other. Nor is it any sort of reason takes
place with them, but they are a mere mechanic engine,
wrought by pestilent knaves within, who actuate it although
not seen. When the judgment was given in the King's
Bench against the Charter of London, Dolben declined
giving any opinion, pretending not to be satisfied, which
passage came into song, and from thence into proverb, " I
doubt it, quoth Dolben."

143. This gentleman came into the office I spoke of

---

[1] Sir William Dolben, of the Inner Temple; called to the Bar
1653, Recorder of London 1676, when he was knighted. He became a
judge of the King's Bench, Oct. 1678: died 1694. Foss says he was
son of John Dolben, Archbishop of York, which is certainly wrong.

under Sheldon, archbishop, for his brother the clergyman married Sheldon's sister. In the time of my most honoured lord and patron, Sancroft, he had a great mind to recommend a nephew, and so to surrender it to a friend, which the archbishop would not allow, but if he would leave it fairly he might. That he would not do until he was promoted to be a judge of the King's Bench, and then no gramercy, for the office of steward or judge of the Palace Court became incompatible, because writs of error lay of judgments below returnable in the court of King's Bench, so he was to correct his own errors. Upon this he declared that he would hold the office no longer.

144. I know not what good angel minded the archbishop of me, for I was neither eminent so as to be picked out by so great a man, as likely to be useful to him, as the stewards of the liberties are ordinarily to the archbishops, having the conduct of all his law businesses, and is his standing counsel on whom he leans in all matters of law, which in his post are many, frequent, and of great importance, as well to the public as his private concerns. I am not conscious of any merit or reason to be so honoured by him, but from the felicity of being his countryman,[1] to whom he was always kind, and the fair character his private friend Dr. Paman[2] might give of me to him. In short, without my thoughts of any such advantage, he sent for me, and declared me his steward in the place of Dolben, and I had my patents confirmed by the dean and chapter for my life, which are still in force. All that he stipulated with me was, to make up the court-rolls in parchment. The former stewards used to enter in paper books only. I caused to be transcribed the rolls from the Restoration down to my time, and continued them so on until the enemy came, and removed me and commanded the rolls from me, which I delivered up not to the usurper, but to the Treasurer and receiver, Mr. Snow,[3] who was an undoubted minister of the

---

[1] That is born in the same *county*. ARCHBISHOP SANCROFT was born at Fressingfield in Suffolk, and there he died in 1693.

[2] HENRY PAMAN, M.D., Fellow of St. John's College, Cambridge, Public Orator at the University, 1672, and subsequently Professor of Physic in Gresham College. See *Life of the Lord Keeper Guilford*, § 121.

[3] Apparently in July, 1691.—*Luttrell's Diary*, vol. ii. p. 266.

see in those offices for his life, by patent from Sheldon, and
to whom it belonged to take up the rolls and records of the
manors as they were finished and dispatched by the
steward.

145. And, considering I am not restrained to any order
of time in these discourses, I may now relate what happened with respect to me upon the deprivation of my
noble lord and patron. The pretended Parliament gave
six months' time between the suspension and deprivation,
upon failure to take the oaths.[1] Many stood the suspension, but would not bear the deprivation. My archbishop
was firm in both. The law is that upon a vacancy of the
archiepiscopal see the revenues are in the king's hands
without office. However, for reasons of their own, the
governors let about a year pass before they constituted a
receiver, and put the profits in charge in the Exchequer.
My resolution was to stick to my right as long as I could.
And after the deprivation I kept the courts, and made out
my copies in the name of the archbishop, as if nothing [had
happened.] Which some, with regard to the unreasonable
impetuousness of the times, said was a daring action, and
I believe it was by most esteemed fool-hardy enough ; but
I, being no dangerous person whom the Government feared
for any notable practices of any sort, might escape, that
was no thought of mine. But I had another defence on
which I relied if they attacked me. I was an officer,
whether deprived or not turned on the fact of swearing or
not, which I had no warrant to determine, nor could I
justify any neglect of my duty by an officious notice of a
supposed deprivation. And I ought not to act without
authority, which I had by my patent, nor to desist without
warrant, which I had not from public favour or my own
private knowledge, without a regular warrant to produce.
This I was prepared to defend with if I had been troubled,

[1] " . . . . On the very day on which that House voted without a
division the address requesting the King to summon the Convocation.
a clause was proposed and carried which required every person who
held any ecclesiastical or academical preferment, to take oath by the
first of August, 1689, *on pain of suspension.* Six months, to be reckoned
from that day, were allowed to the non-juror for reconsideration. If,
on the first of February, 1690, he still continued obstinate, he was to be
finally deprived."—Macaulay, chap. xi.

and the wise council of the enemy knew it well enough,
though the matter fell not under the caps of the generality.
Afterwards, when a seizure came upon the revenues, I made
a kinsman my deputy, who kept the courts one year. And
when a pseudo archbishop was set up [1] I yielded not, and
would not so much as go see him, although I claimed the
office for life. And if he had not put me out I was resolved
to act not in person but by deputy. It was expected that
I should, as lawyers use, creep after my profit, and wait on
his pretended Grace to compliment him on his promotion,
and so have put myself in a way to be wheedled and wire-
drawn into an oath. . . . .
and therefore some time passed before a new officer was
made in my room. And in the interim I was told that
it was expected that I should go see the archbishop, or the
omission would be taken ill. I answered I did not believe
it would be ill taken. For if the archbishop was a good
man and a wise man (which was readily accorded) then he
would have the better opinion of and value me for not
coming near him ; because, if I did wait on him, I must
say what was proper, that I was glad of his promotion, and
declare my readiness to serve him ; or else I affronted him,
and he might reasonably ask what made me there ? If I
did say so, he must needs know I lied, which was a reason
to make him despise and hate me for a false lying flatterer
in hopes of a little gain. Therefore, being a wise and a good
man, as they said, he must needs value me for not coming
in his way. But about half-a-year after his promotion I
heard he had mentioned me with this, that he believed I
had not taken the oaths because he had not seen me. And
then I had a letter by his secretary to let me know that my
office was void for not swearing, and he had constituted
one Baber in my room, and that I should deliver the rolls
to him, for which that was my warrant. I told his secre-
taryship that I took my office not to be void for any such
cause or otherwise, and insisted upon my right, and hoped
his lord would not take from me what was my right. To
which he answered in common form and parted. I sent
the rolls to the treasurer, and keep the paper books and

[1] Tillotson was not consecrated till 31 May, 1691.

originals by me, and am not without hopes of being restored by some good Providence which takes care of the world ; if not I conclude it is so best for me and am contented.

146. It may not be amiss here to discourse a little of my comportment under the favour of the good archbishop whom I had the honour to serve. He immediately took me into the participation of his councils with respect to law businesses, wherein I served him with all the diligence and integrity possible. And I had no capacity beyond what I employed in his service, wherein I was encouraged by his most obliging acceptance, seeing, as I doubt not but he did, through my juvenile and imperfect performances, a sincere and willing mind, which I have reason to think he valued more than strong parts and acquired learning. For honesty is distinct from strength of mind, and though it is said honesty is the best policy, and truly, yet it is not found that cunning men are so. Many wise men, judging by worldly skill, miscarry for want of honesty, and many weak men succeed, are safe, and thrive, by mere honesty, for that keeps them in plain known paths, whilst wit leads men into unhappy puzzles and losses. But, as I said, I have reason to think the archbishop valued me for my fidelity, which he, being a most sagacious judge of persons, could not but discern, and dispensed with my other defects as not in our power always to correct.

147. The first thing he concerned me in was a visitation of Dulwich College, which is a lay hospital founded by one Allen for support of his kindred and name. We found that which was impossible to correct, an invincible humour of quarrelling among themselves. The master and brothers, sometimes the one and sometimes the other were predominant ; the business of the college, as the making leases, and dispensing the revenues (which was like interest in the world abroad, the true *boute-feu*) managed accordingly, and often the neighbours troubled with their differences, and forced to come in aid of peace to prevent worse inconveniences than scolding and railing, which was the daily conversation. We found ever since the foundation it had been so, and saw no cause to think it would ever be otherwise. Whereupon the matter fell, and nothing could be

done unless the nature of the men could be altered. This shews what an unruly animal mankind is, and how much we are mistaken in our ways of doing one another good. Certainly a traveller through our world would, being told it, think that such poor needy men, having habitation and all necessaries of life provided for them, and no labour or duty required, but to live at ease and enjoy their lives in their own hearts' desire, were happy. And yet in truth it were better for these men to work hard for their daily bread, and have nothing but from the sweat of their brows, for then their work entertains their minds, they have an end to pursue, the providing sustenance for themselves and families, and means for attaining it, daily labour. And the passing the time thus with pursuing and obtaining, supplies them with a reasonable content of mind, and keeps them in peace. But take away this entertainment of their thoughts and employment of their bodies, and put them to live together in a cloister as here, and as it is found in other countries where cloisters are more in request, although no sort of want afflicts them, they shall be perpetually afflicting each other with opposition and quarrel. And as in splenetic persons the malady being not in notorious places, but secret, and known only by a pain in general, it is not the subject of complaint, but offence, and charged upon some object not concerned in it, as religion, fear of want, oppression, and the like. So human nature, being an uneasy state, if there be not a daily employment to divert the sense of the general uneasiness, it is resented as proceeding from outward objects, and men think their neighbours' actions hurt them, so mutually they fall to quarrel and litigate, as if the whole society were bewitched. And it is a mistaken charity which hath prevailed, to bestow a collegiate life on mankind, to the end they may live in piety and mutual charity. For, as I said, the effect is clean contrary: if you would regulate their minds, give them business, and make their bodies work. And the things of this world may possibly hinder contemplation, but nothing else produceth humility, charity, and peace in depraved mankind. And surely that is of more use and pleasing to God than any speculations in theology or prayer itself. "I will have mercy and not sacrifice." His Grace used all the means and authority he had to coerce the contentious humour of this college, but did not proceed to any legal executions upon them, nor had he, though visitor by the statutes, sufficient power to make an effectual reform of them.

148. Another matter he employed me in was, to consult touching his power to rescind the trade of bribery and simony which was the daily practice in All Souls' College in Oxford, where he was visitor. The court was upon, or the day before, the election day, which was fixed by their statutes; the market opened, and the folk went to buying and selling of fellowships. And although former visitors had provided oaths formed with all imaginable force of words to hinder this simoniac practice there, it was in vain. Under pretence of selling the key of the door, or some such flam, they satisfied their corrupt consciences, or rather evaded as they thought the imputation. The good archbishop had his eye always on his charge, and never saw a fault but he endeavoured to amend it. We looked on his powers over the college, and found he might not only visit, but make and alter the statutes of the foundation as he from time to time should think fit. There could not be a greater power, and he exerted it effectually, but met with all the opposition that corruption could raise to preserve itself, and vice will leave no stone unturned rather than give way. He got the better of them by policy as much as by authority, for by one wise constitution the reformation was completed. He did not omit to make their oaths more categorically opposite to their practice, but that would not have done the work. He sent them a statute that no election should be made into any fellowship unless the same had been void at least about thirty days. Here lay the policy of this constitution. If one surrendered for money he would receive it upon the surrender, the other that gave would not pay till he was elected. And when this was all to be done in one hour's time the market was made, surrender, election, and payment, *quasi uno flatu*, and there was little or no trust in the case. But if the vacancy stood thirty days, *multa cadunt inter*, the purchaser could have no security to be chosen, and who would trust a pack of fellows? And without the money no surrender.

149. Thus was this trade diverted, and now the college enjoys the benefit of it, and men are promoted by fair and gratuitous choice, without money. The corrupt part of these fellows carried it so high against the archbishop that some being deprived for non-obedience to his statutes brought a mandamus to be restored. To that we made a return of the power of the visitor, who by the statutes was local judge of all matters arising there, and this return, when Pemberton was Chief Justice of the King's Bench,[1] was allowed, and so the matter rested.

150. It would make one a sceptic in charity and believe all men hypocrites and liars, to observe how strict the laws of Church and State are against simony, and what penned oaths are taken upon all promotions to benefices ; and yet there is never a living to be sold but a chapman is ready. We agree the laity to be corrupt enough to sell, but it is strange the clergy should generally be so profligate to buy. And if there could be a scrutiny of all the presentations that are made, how few are pure of this stain I verily believe it would amaze one. It is not therefore to be thought strange that when a substantial trial falls upon any order of men, clergy not excepted, there shall not be found above one in two hundred whose conscience and virtue is above gain. Men are sent to the University with admonition to study and become learned able preachers, for thence you must expect your preferment as well as future subsistence. And parents inculcate the charges they are at to bring them up to divinity (as they call it) for their good, and that they may be amply provided for, and that the youths should be careful that all this cost be not thrown away. What is this but sending youth to learn the art or trade of preaching for gain or preferment, not otherwise than as they are bound out apprentices to trade whereby to live, and having success to become rich and great ? It is not a call to the ministry that breeds up such youth, as having a disposition that way, upon finding themselves studious, and willing to take great pains for the good of mankind and not gain, who are rather willing to lay down what they have rather than take up in order to be resigned to the duties of

---

[1] SIR FRANCIS PEMBERTON was Chief Justice of the King's Bench from 11 April, 1681, till 22 January, 1683.

preachers. But their eye is upon preferment, and if an ambitious active spirit rules in them they dream of nothing but prelacy and pomp, and have no better opinion of their religion and performance of priestly duties in it than a merchant hath of his trade and accounts, that they are the means of his worldly subsistence and increase. Thus we may lament our unhappiness without power to reform, or expectation that time will ever produce a better economy of either Church or State. And what is it to us? We have only ourselves and our own actions to answer for, and how easy is it to govern them in a plain rule of living without such enormous faults?

151. Another good work the archbishop employed me in, which he executed, but hath not the effect due to his just intentions, for might will be too hard for right. Shirley,[1] the ancestor of Lord Shirley, being a Papist, was converted to the Protestant Church by Dr. Gunning, but retaining an opinion that monastery lands ought not to be appropriated to luxury, but charity, as they had been devoted. Therefore by lease and release he conveyed all the lands he had, which formerly belonged to pious uses, (in such general terms) to trustees, to be employed to like uses as his trustees should think fit. This trust devolved upon the good archbishop. And about the time of his leaving Lambeth he resolved to expect no longer, but to execute all the power he had to settle this charity. It seems that the family of the Shirleys have been long uneasy under this cloud over their estate; for it was hard to say what was not Church lands. Therefore, to clear it, there had been prosecutions in Chancery, a certificate by Sir William Dugdale, &c. Referees of the court, and a decree for the lands by them certified, to be employed by the trustees, and that the rest of the estate should be finally discharged of this charge further, which decree was obtained through

---

[1] SIR ROBERT SHIRLEY, second son of Sir Henry Shirley, Bart., by Dorothy Devereux, sister of Robert, Earl of Essex, the Parliamentary General. Among other acts of munificence he settled an annuity upon Dr. Gunning in 1656. He was thrown into the Tower by Oliver Cromwell for his fidelity to Charles I., and died there in 1657. His son, Sir Robert, whom North calls Lord Shirley, was born while his father was incarcerated in the Tower, and became in 1677 Lord Ferrars of Chartley.

two or three infancies in the family, and was a great security and relief to the estate, which in all probability in-
cludes thrice as much as Dugdale certified, who went upon
demonstrable evidence in writing. All that the archbishop
desired was that the curates on the Lord Shirley's own
estate, whose maintenance was short, might enjoy their
profits in augmentation of their subsistence, and wrote to
my Lord Shirley, who did not answer to his content.
Thereupon he made all his queries, which I answered.
Then he distributed the profits among the said curates, and
I made instruments of appointment to each of them accordingly, grounded on the trust and the decree. And
this being done, I made a conveyance of the lands by lease
and release to new trustees named by the archbishop, which
he also sealed, by virtue whereof the legal estate is gone
over charged with the trust as settled by those appointments. The archbishop sent these instruments to each of
the persons concerned, and an account at large to Lord
Shirley of what he had done, requiring him to comply with
it, but had no contentful answer but hard usage from his
discourse with others. The archbishop, for perpetual
memory of the thing, and his own justification, caused the
whole proceeding, and the correspondence about it, which
he drew up himself with his usual care and exactness, to
be registered at Doctors' Commons, where they who please
may see and peruse it. My Lord Shirley hath not allowed
the profits to be employed according to these appointments,
but hath treated us all hardly in his language who were
concerned in it, which made me desire to speak with him;
for I thought I could convince him that it was very much
his interest to hold hard upon this decree, and not to im-
peach it himself by opposing the execution of it, for it
cleared the title to all the rest of his estate, which might,
for ought otherwise appears, be tainted with this charity,
and then he could neither buy nor sell. And if the trustees
or the Attorney General (as in some future time might be
done) should question this decree as collusive, (which it
was in great measure as I believe) or build upon his waiving of it, and by an information demand a new discovery,
in what a case were his estates! I hinted by some of the
concerned persons that I would willingly wait on his lord-

ship in this matter, but he refused to admit me, which shewed him resolved.

152. There were many other affairs which he was minded to settle and put in order, for the most part in the way of reformation and charity. I settled some augmentations on vicarages and chapelries in Lancashire or Cheshire. I prepared an endowment for a school at Fressingfield, but I do not know that he had time to perfect that;[1] and divers other matters of that kind, in all which he was so kind and tender to me, dispensing with my defects and accepting my good will, that I contracted a great fondness and devotion to his service. I could know his griefs by his discourse, as when he was attacked from the Court, which began about the time of Monmouth's defeat. The dispensing power then beginning to be ventilated,[2] I studied the point, collected all the law I could find about it, found seasonable distinctions to reconcile the umbrages some passages in the law books had given to it, all which I presented to him, which he took very kindly, and perceiving it to be crude and ill penned, he gave it me again and desired I would perfect it, as I had designed, which soft reprehension was very obliging. And then I went it over again and left it with him, as it is among my papers. I likewise gave him a paper or discourse upon the high commission soon after issued which deprived the Bishop of London.[3] This good man escaped the storm because he was provided, but not to do as the bishop did, plead to the jurisdiction, and being overruled plead over not guilty, and go to fending and proving, and at length receive their judgment. But he was resolved, if he had been cited, to have brought his protestation (which he kept ready drawn by him) and delivered it to them and went his way, and never obeyed any sentence, but to defend himself at common law upon the nullity of their court. This was known, and for that reason he was not cited. The other way was to deliver up the cause. For it was not to be doubted they would judge for their own jurisdiction, and the defending after was owning

---

[1] The archbishop's intention was not carried out.

[2] See Macaulay's *History of England*, chap. vi.

[3] BISHOP COMPTON was not *deprived*, though suspended from all spiritual functions. See Macaulay, chap. vi.

it as much as before. And the like was at Magdalen College: they should not have appeared further than to protest.[1] The common law and juries would have defended their freeholds. And such mistaken proceedings as these were a means to mislead the king; whereas a stout regular opposition such as the archbishop intended would probably have stopped the commissioners.

153. After this the archbishop was threatened with a *præmunire* if he did not confirm bishops without taking the test. I gave him a discourse of *præmunire*, so full and particular, with the very forms at length, that he thanked me for it, and said that he found by the manner, that it was done with a particular good will to him and to instruct him for his safety. Then upon his pretended deprivation I studied the law of the Exchequer as to charges there, and presented him with the papers, but those are crude and wanted experience of intrusions and such memoranda of the court before the deprivation. I considered the law with respect to duty under usurping superiors such as we call lords *pro tempore*, and titled the discourse *Respective Allegiance*, that he might judge how far the law would give way to the owning powers without title. He told me he could by no means allow the distinction in our law of *de facto* and *de jure*: a lord *de facto* and not *de jure* was no lord, and applied it higher (to the Dutch usurper) and was very solemn upon the subject, whence I perceived he did not like it. After his retirement from Lambeth into the Palsgrave Court he was threatened to be tendered the oaths. I consulted the matter and found it a vain pretence, and that persons deprived were not subject to the spite, and gave him a paper. It was to me a wonder to observe the industry of that man. If any person presented him, as many did, with discourses upon business impending, he would register them in his own books with his own hand, using his exquisite orthography and abbreviations, and mending the English and periodising in all places as ought to be done. And he did me the honour to do the like with all he received from me. After his retirement to Fressing-

---

[1] See the extremely interesting volume issued by the Oxford Historical Society, *Magdalen College and King James II.*, by Dr. Bloxam, 1886.

field I constantly visited him, at least once in every year; and it was my good fortune to come to him when he was near his end, and under great trouble how to settle his affairs to his mind. He would not make a will to be proved in his pretended successor's courts, but desired to provide in several particulars of charity. The divines, physicians, and attorneys had distracted him with different fancies, and puzzling contrivances. For he and his nephews had consulted several of them they could confide in. The poor man in few words, being under great weakness and difficulty of utterance, told me his pain, and I immediately chalked out a way to his content, which was to make a deed of gift to his two nephews of all that he had in the world, and by the same deed, or another, declare that to be in trust for himself during his life, and after for such uses as he had a mind should be known, and the rest to them their executors, administrators, and assigns absolutely. And he could give them those directions, either orally or by letter, wherein he intended absolutely to trust them. This was no will but had the same effect, and though there might be an administration taken out it would signify nothing, because there was no estate to be divided, the grant *in vita* having bound it all. This scheme pleased him entirely, and he begged (such was his humility) that I would assist him in the form. I took pen, and immediately made drafts, with directions in writing for the filling of blanks, and took his blessing and departed after about an hour's stay. This form was perused and his mind took effect as he desired. It touched my spirit extremely to see the low estate of this poor old saint, and with what wonderful regard and humility he treated those that visited him, who were not worthy to serve him, and particularly myself. But humility hath its periods which none can escape. Good and bad are chained to corruptible flesh, while it lasts, and by the rotting of the plant the fruit falls, to rise again in a new life, the soul in another world, happy or otherwise, as infinite justice and mercy shall determine. I must leave this subject, as being too melancholy to give me that ease in writing I usually have, and lest I drop more than ink, which my recording thus the loss of this most reverend prelate and saint (with whose service and favour my life is adorned) ought to extort from those eyes which sympathise in uncontrollable sorrow.

154. I received much of his bounty, but as he was moderate in all things he did not exceed in that; however, what he did was with so much sweetness and obligation it surmounted the more profuse gratifications of others. But I was particularly honoured by him in a present he made me at his leaving Lambeth, of his bass viol, which he had at Cambridge, and kept all his life after till he gave it me, and was at the charge of fitting it up for use. I keep it as a sacred relic of his memory. And when he left the world he had me in his prayers and thoughts; for he ordered his nephews to make me a present of a ring, value £20, for memory of him, which they told me of, desiring if I thought anything else more conducing I would take the money and employ it. At that time I had almost finished my library at Rougham, and thought a memorial of him there would be more lasting of him than a ring. And I bought a set of law books, had them bound up after his manner, and wrote in them thus :—

Hunc cum aliis ejusdem naturæ et argumenti libris, ad valorem viginti librarum honorifici legavit Reverendissimus in Christo pater Willielmus nuper Archiepiscopus Cant. Cui dum in vivis esset, me fidelissimum filium et addictissimum servum in perpetuum jure profitebar. Cujus adhuc piam memoriam studiosissime recolo.

CHAPTER X.

PROFESSIONAL REMINISCENCES.

NOW, to return to my profession, wherein I had acquired somewhat of maturity, for I came to it very raw. My brother was always careful of me, and sought to improve me by putting me upon the practice of things I was little fit for; but he knew if the business had no profit by me I should profit by that. To encourage me in conveyancing, which is a nice art, he gave me the bundles of his former clerk's precedents or paper books, by which he engrossed the conveyances of his settling. I read these all over, numbered them on the outside, and wrote the effect of them, and made a table referring to those numbers. This did not only give me a ready recourse to any precedent I had occasion to draw by, but impressed a style and form, and also the true notion of the substance of most conveyances, and the nicety of the words appertaining to each sort, as a feoffment, an attornement, use of a fine or recovery, covenant to stand seised, lease and release, and divers others. This was as great a benefit to me as any reading or study I ever used, nay, it interpreted and confirmed all my reading about conveyances. This happened accidentally to me, and few that apply to the practice of the law are so fortunate in a friend to administer such helps as I had: others, I am sensible, would have made better use of it, I am well *that* my brother aimed I should be, and that is enough. For the most part young men do not study the form of a conveyance, which is the reason they come so late to it. They only as occasion presents peruse the deeds that friends ask them about, and perhaps they run to the material part. Nay, clerks without study have more skill, and are forwarder in this art than good students and many practisers, and for want of a formal reading and noting the substance of the divers sorts of deeds of use in the law. It is the like for records and drawing pleadings, which I never applied much to, being taken up into a higher form ; and for that reason a youth bred a clerk and then brought to study doth better than a student first and then formalising after. For the pre-science of forms interprets the law books and makes study easy, and ignorance of forms is a great obstruction of study, and makes it dark and unpleasant, and it will be very long before a good style in matter of form will be acquired by practice.

156. Some time before the Chancellor Finch died [1] my brother got me made of the King's Counsel, which let me in to advanced fees, and a more considerable post in prac-tice, especially in the Chancery, when I came to settle there. It was a good method for my profit, but not proper for a mastery of the business of that court. I came raw, with only a superficial knowledge of the practice of the court and the front of the business, and had the leading part ofttimes, being unfit for it; but more of this afterwards. My brother ordered the matter so that I was ordered to attend the Attorney General [2] upon all capital and other cases of State, to consult with and assist Mr. Attorney, for the more steady conduct of the king's law business. This was an admirable method, for an Attorney General hath too much upon him to answer for all such matters, and it is most reasonable to allow him assistants as he shall choose of the king's counsel that he shall think faithful and cordate, and this regulates his own judgment, gives him not only a courage when he hath an unfirm opinion of his side, but a screen in case of sinister success, and all will not fall out as he, they, and perhaps twenty more shall prejudge. It hath been and is the way of Attorney Generals to arrogate the direction of all matters to them-selves, and to take no advice or assistance, with a hang-dog treasurer for a solicitor, who is perhaps more than one-half suborner, to prosecute and devise against those that are questioned; and then they must suffer, because Mr. Attorney is engaged, and hath perhaps given a rash, indiscreet opinion. I was frequently at these consults with Mr. Attorney. My

[1] FINCH (Lord Nottingham) died 16 December, 1682. Mr. North was called to the Bench of the Middle Temple, 27 October, 1682, about which time therefore he must have been made King's Counsel.

[2] SIR ROBERT SAWYER.

contemporaries were Holt, Lutwyche, Finch (the Solicitor), Jones, and some others.[1] Sir Robert Sawyer[2] was the Attorney General, to whom I being related was an advantage, for he was very friendly and civil to me. Graham and Burton[3] were the Solicitors. Mr. Attorney was a person not void of learning, but had not so much as his person and assurance promised. He was bred at the University into the degree of Master of Arts, and performed exercises and commonplaces, which gave the varnish of a scholar to his actions. But he was proud, affected, and poor-spirited, and had his eye upon prosperity and success more than the intrinsic justice and decorum of proceedings. But to say truth of him, being bred in the Exchequer practice, and loyal in his principles, he was a good Attorney General, and with his person and assurance graced his office well enough. Of the two solicitors to the Exchequer, Burton was an arrant knave; but Graham, who had been an attorney of value, and employed in the business of the Burlington family, and by the Hydes brought into the Duke of York's business, was a fair-conditioned man, who regretted his being joined with such a knave, and bating a little north-country flattery, and desire to oblige all he could, was very fit for his place; and if he went too far in anything it was not out of a bad principle, but obedience and complaisance. Upon the Revolution these two men were frighted and persuaded to run away, with Jenner[4] the judge, and were taken and brought back, with no other crime upon them, and kept in custody at great charge and trouble till acquitted by law without prosecution. This error (and all that proceeds from fear is so for the most

---

[1] Sir John Holt, Chief Justice of the King's Bench, 1682 to 1710. Edward Lutwyche, Judge of the Common Pleas, 1686 till the accession of William and Mary. Hon. Heneage Finch, son of the Lord Chancellor, Solicitor General from February, 1685, till April, 1686, when he was removed by James II. and never reinstated. Queen Anne raised him to the peerage as Lord Guernsey in 1703. Thomas Jones, Chief Justice of the Common Pleas, 1683 till 1686, when he was dismissed from his office by James II. (16 April.)

[2] Sir Robert Sawyer, Attorney General 1681 to 1687. See *Life of the Lord Keeper*, § 408.

[3] Graham and Burton. See *Examen*, p. 114.

[4] Thomas Jenner, whom Evelyn calls an obscure lawyer, made a Baron of the Exchequer, 1686, but lost his post at the Revolution.

part) troubled the mind of poor Graham so that he never joyed after, but languished in his mind till he died. Therefore let it be known that an honest man hath no game but to look powers in the face and defy them, as a brother and friend of mine did.

157. At these meetings we adjusted the methods of proceeding against the plotters in King Charles the Second's time, whereupon Lord Russell and others were convicted, and being executed have been since miscalled murders, and as far as unreasonable fury, violence, and noise could prevail, made so; but the adversaries wanting ability, truth stands. I will be bold to say, that if ever trials in England were fair, both in the private and public conduct of them, those were. And in the Lord Russell's case especially, where the court and jury were inclined for his quality to acquit him, was not the evidence plain against him? This must be referred to the public trial, which is in print, with this note, that in that time the judges and counsel desired trials might be printed, that the truth of the proceeding might not be detracted by lying; but now the public will not suffer such trials to come abroad, lest their actions should suffer in the opinions of the generality, from the truth which would appear thereby. So observe the difference. I can answer at all my attendances the questions were considered sincerely upon the law and nature of the evidence. We never agreed to advance anything but what we were satisfied was true, and would be proved, and that done, was criminal according to the charge. We did not send our solicitors about to hunt for evidence, nor take evidence as they would, and have since used pragmatically, state it, perhaps out of their own instruction of the witnesses. But the examinations were all taken by the Secretaries of State, some of the Privy Council, justices of peace, or other sworn magistrates, and being transmitted to us we went upon them as a text, and considered whether they were sufficient to bear indictments or not. Mr. Attorney reported to the Council the results, being his and our opinions. If we differed, as sometimes would happen, he would represent it accordingly, and take directions, which during all King Charles' reign was never to proceed unless the case were clear. This I know to be true, and there-

fore can confidently affirm it; and which is more, and few will believe, we never took fees in any capital case, either to consult or plead. I affirm it in my own case, and that I believe it in the rest. My reason is that the solicitors did not give any, and to excuse themselves, as if it were expected, have said they did not leave fees in those cases. This was not only just but extraordinary, because the like methods have not been used before nor since as I verily believe. And where the prisoner hath no counsel we ought not to be engaged by fees to press beyond justice, and although we stand in the place of advocates, yet we are in such cases ministers of justice, to put forward the charge (leaving the defence to the court and the prisoner) according to our consciences of right and truth. But at all attendances upon cases of misdemeanour and trials we had our fees, and met with counsel to defend against us for the prisoner, or defendant, which was *durus cum duro*, and bore no hardship or inequality. We in our patents of King's Counsel had a pension of £40 per annum granted, but not paid, and in consideration of that the solicitors had orders to give us fees as business required, which they liked better, because it swelled their belts, and that was *ora pro nobis*. I do affirm I never went as counsel against any person to be tried for his life, unless commanded from the king to attend, nor ever took any fee in such cases, save one only, which was in my first entrance of practice, before I understood my duty, and it was for the murder of Mr. Masters of Lincoln's Inn, by one Captain Butler. The prosecution was by his brothers and his friends, who engaged me to go and to take a fee, of which I repented, and do of both the one and the other still repent.

158. I do not believe in any age there hath been such integrity of proceeding on the part of the Government against treason and treasonable practices as was at that time; for look into the trial of Sir Thos. Wyat, and Sir Thos. Overbury's case, Sir Walter Raleigh's case, Sir Wm. Jones' management of Oates' plot, and others more ancient and worse, and compare them, nay, those since this Revolution with them, and you will see the candour of them. And yet all those pass without censure, or at least the censure is forgot, but these are declaimed against as

butchery, murder, and illegal, nay, prosecuted, inquisited, and the persons merely formally concerned therein marked as enemies to be spited and maligned perpetually. Let but this go as a remark against the injustice and nonsense of the world, which never did nor will understand its own good, and neither reward, encourage, nor endure its true patriots and friends.

159. During the time my brother was Chief Justice I had the advantage of Nisi Prius practice, both at Westminster and Guildhall, in term time, and in the circuits in the vacations, and from a most entire rawness I grew up by degrees into a good assurance, and the business being generally ordinary in defending and attending upon batteries, words, &c., the practice was light. And when there came any stress of title or points of law, others had the ascendant, and neither my parts, learning, or assurance would engage in the front of the battle. But it is most certain that living thus in the perpetual agitation of business I acquired most knowledge in the law, and I believe it was more profitable to me than books, for I took and observed better so than by reading. And although in vulgar esteem it was not so useful knowledge as books, by enabling me to cite cases, as lawyers use and affect, which illustrates their practice, yet my judgment was better formed and less pedantic than it would have been by books, and I was from thence much more competent to advise and give measures of success.

160. I had one further advantage from the circuits, and that was a sort of travel and the breeding that is sought from it. For I was in the places of resort of all the gentry at the assize towns, and consequently conversed with them, and was let in to know their characters, and country intrigues. I went but three circuits, the west, north, and the Norfolk, the two last but once, so that in the west we were as at home; for lodgings, acquaintance, and all incidents, were by our frequent coming there, so established, that we had no trouble or uncertainty about our accommodations. And entering into the world, or acquaintance with the gentry there, I was, as I thought myself, adopted of the country, where I had more acquaintance and friendships than in my own.

III.   K

161. The counties near London, as Hampshire and part of Wiltshire [*sic*], have little singular to be noted, either of strangeness of situation or character of the people, more than ordinary; but coming into Dorsetshire, the country grows new, and things looked a little strange; the people spoke oddly, and the women wore white mantles which they call whittells. And the houses were of stone and slate; and what we call gentility of everything began to wear off. It may not be amiss to set down the gross difference I observed in the speech of several counties, by which they may be known.

162. In the west the word *them* is sunk into *'n*, as *heard 'n, gave 'n, beat 'n.* In the north the word *them* is spoken without any diminution at all, but at the full length, as *gave them;* and the word *us* is pronounced *huz.* In the east, that is towards Norfolk, the word *them* is not sounded, as in the north nor west, but middling; for they give a vowel more than the west, and say *heard 'em, gave 'em, beat 'em;* and instead of the *'n*, put *'em.* In Norfolk, for *notice* they will say *notedge;* and always instead of *ready* they say *fit,* as *fit to fall down, money fit to be paid.* There are many other varieties of words and manner of pronunciation which I observed, but these are the chief, and I do not descend to any farther nicety.

163. I shall not take upon me to give the characters of the people, or description of any odd places as I saw, but leave them to travellers as I was, and only observe a few passages which recur to my memory besides the ordinary. One was a trial of witches at Exeter. The women were very old, decrepit, and impotent, and were brought to the assizes with as much noise and fury of the rabble against them as could be shewed on any occasion. The stories of their acts were in everyone's mouth, and they were not content to belie them in the country, but even in the city where they were to be tried miracles were fathered upon them, as that the judges' coach was fixed upon the castle bridge, and the like. All which the country believed, and accordingly persecuted the wretched old creatures. A less zeal in a city or kingdom hath been the overture of defection and revolution, and if these women had been acquitted, it was thought that the country people would have com-

mitted some disorder. The trial was before Judge Raymond, a mild, passive man, who had neither dexterity nor spirit to oppose a popular rage, and so they were convict and died. The evidence was only their own confession, the rest of the stuff was mere matter of fancy, as pigs dying, and the like. I happened to take into my hand the file of informations taken by the justices, and there saw one to this effect, that about twilight the informant saw a cat leap in at one of their windows, "and this informant further sayeth that he verily believeth the said cat to be the devil." [1] And the confession of the women was mean and ignorant, the proceed of poverty and melancholy, and in the style of the vulgar traditions of sucking teats, &c. It is not strange that persons of depauperated spirits should be distract in their minds, and come to a faith of mere dream and delusion. What hath been the discourse of the sleepy chimney, with silent dull thinking, takes place as if the stories were realities, and then pride and self-conceit translates all to their own persons.

164. Another instance of this sort happened in Somersetshire, before my brother, which was not the result of error and ignorance, as this, but of mere malice. A young woman was indicted for being a witch, and bewitching a child. The evidence was the child's fits upon the witch's approach, as commonly the case is, and the child or girl of about twelve years of age that was bewitched spat up pins in her fits, but straight, and not, as usually, crooked pins. It hath been the common contrivance to crook the pins to be spat up, that they might not accidentally hurt the person, and also sound very terribly. Therefore it was thought a very strange imposture to change the form and introduce a new precedent of witchcraft, by spitting straight pins. Here was a great cry and fury too, but not equal to the other, and the evidence was pressed with very positive swearing, and yet both the judge and better audience thought it an imposture. The danger was with the jury, who were ordinary men, who, if they find an opinion against the being of witches, are very apt to sacrifice a life to prove the contrary; therefore the judge did not

---

[1] See *Life of the Lord Keeper*, § 192.

exaggerate, but let time pass, and examined with great temper and moderation, which at length resolved all the doubts, but only that of spitting straight pins; for none could imagine how the child could get them. At last the judge spoke to the justice that examined the matter at first, to say what he thought upon his view of the fact. He said that he verily believed that they were stuck right down in the top of her stomacher, and that in her convulsive strains, which were not extending, but bringing down her head to her breast, she took them out with her mouth and spit them into folks' hands, and then pretended to ease. This account was so facile of belief that it took, and cleared the poor young woman. When the judge went down, a wretched old hag, the mother of this wench, cried, "God bless your worship! They would have made me a witch twenty years ago."[1] Thus fond are the common people of traditional miracles, that they will not receive conviction by any reason, but retain them with an inveterate obstinacy, and so much the fiercer as their superiors endeavour to rectify them, even to turn the opposite opinions into heresy and incredulity. And for this reason the popish impostures fill them with legends of their saints' miracles, and the sectarian impostures cultivate the credulity as to witches, and both triumph over Satan in their several ways of exorcitation, and in the meantime hold the people deceived when only they will work zealously to their corrupt and ambitious ends. Would it were not true that the people must be deceived. But since it is so, let them bless those times when they fall into the hands of honest and good-natured deceivers, who seek the common good and not private interest, and when they are used as pretty children are by their nurses and mothers, kept in awe with a course of never-ceasing lying, but all for their good.

*   *   *   *   *   *

*   *   *   *   *

165. It is well known how busy the faction against the monarchy were in the times when my brother was Chief Justice. And their way being to wheedle and deceive, and

---

[1] For another version of this story, cf. *Life of the Lord Keeper*, § 194.

to make men, believing them, act as fools and lose their own honour and reputation if they will not be thorough converts, they plied my brother for three years together in the circuits. And upon fanatic causes contrived to tease him both by their factious counsel at the bar and factious gentlemen in his chamber. His way was to be civil to all, and patient in hearing, but never failed to pinch in the right place; and at last they gave him over. The last experiment upon him was in Somersetshire, and that was pushed in public. Jones, that went as judge with my brother, fell sick of the gout at Wells in the summer circuit, 1680, and my brother did all the business as well Nisi Prius as the Crown side, which latter was in course the turn of Jones.[1] The faction caused to be printed in their newspapers that the Lord Chief Justice North, in the place of Jones, had in his charges declared that the King was for the future determined to grant liberty to tender consciences, and that for the future the laws against dissenters should not be put in execution, or to that effect. This happened when the reform was made in the council, and the factions' heads came in by twos: as two barons, two judges, and two commoners, &c. Then Shaftesbury seemed to carry all before him, and Sunderland was Secretary. My brother, by what means he knew not, was then one of the two judges, and thought that such a lie published of him being a privy councillor was both in the King's disservice and his own dishonour if not contradicted. Therefore he wrote a short declaration of the passage and the falsity of it, his brother Jones desiring to be concerned and joined in it, and caused it to be published in the *Gazette*, which was such a stab to the design as made the faction very angry with him and resolve his ruin if ever it fell in their power.

166. In short we were very welcome in the west, and my brother was extremely caressed in all places, because he was the first clear loyalist of a judge that had come amongst them since the wars; which puts me in mind of a passage in Devonshire merry enough. There was one Duke, that had a good estate and a seat in the east part of

---

[1] See *Examen*, p. 252. This is Sir Thomas Jones, about whom see Macaulay, *Hist. of England*, chap. vi. vol. ii. p. 337, ed. 1847.

the country near the sea, but a most busy driver in the
wheel of faction, which made some call him Spirit Po! as
at everyone's service, in short a rigid Presbyterian. He
prevailed on my brother to pass by his house and to lie a
night, which we did, and were well entertained. But there
was no chaplain, and the family prayers were performed
by Mr. D. himself, who in that way performed evening
service, reading a chapter or two and some long formal
prayers. When we came to Exeter we were rallied that
we should be all presented by the grand jury for being at
a conventicle.[1]

167. It happened in Dorsetshire once that the High
Sheriff[2] had ten sons carried halberds, and wore his livery,
and his eldest was the captain of his band. Great notice
was taken of this, and being complimented by the judges
upon it, said if they were too good to serve the King and
their father they were no sons of his, and he would disown
them.

168. It was ordinary for pickpockets to travel the circuits; nay, I mean not the lawyers, but literally such.
These use to ply at giving the charge, and it was seldom
any charge held out without the outcries of some sufferers.[3]
This we understood by one caught in the fact at Launceston
in Cornwall, who confessed all, but was tried and hanged.

169. 'Size sermons used to entertain the company, for
seldom any was without somewhat so remarkable as to be

---

[1] *Life of the Lord Keeper*, § 171.

[2] The gentleman referred to was Thomas Gollop of North Bowood
and Strode, Esq. He was of the Middle Temple, and was Coroner of
the county of Dorset. He served the office of High Sheriff in the 27th
year of Charles II. [1670], and while discharging his duties he was
attended by ten of his eleven sons as javelin men, who were led by their
uncle, the High Sheriff's younger brother.—Hutchin's *History of Dorset*,
vol. i. p. 263 (ed. 1774).

[3] In reply to an enquiry which I addressed to a very learned legal
antiquary, asking for some explanation of this passage, he writes as
follows: "I am quite unable to explain *ply at giving the charge*.
'Giving the charge' would naturally apply to the judge's charge to the
grand jury, though why the pickpockets should find that a specially
good time I cannot conceive. Unless indeed this, that the barristers do
not come into court until the charge has been delivered, and formerly
(before libraries and robing rooms were provided) they were accustomed
to loiter about the doors of the court while the charge was being delivered, and so afforded an easy prey for pickpockets."

discoursed of either to the advantage or disadvantage of the preacher. The parsons on those occasions think they must harangue judge, juries, officers, and all orders of men. Once the Doctor had finished his catalogue, and at last looked about and said, "But now, as to the lawyers. Stay, I think there is none of them here." And so went on to other matters.

170. I was very hard, as to fatigue, in those days, riding for the most part a trotting mare, and ever esteemed my horse the easiest time I passed. It was observable that horses that had gone once or twice came to understand their trade, and to know the trumpets sounded their ease and accommodation, and at the first clangours of them the horses would always brisk up as at good news. I observed also my horse would not, though a year after, forget a by-lane by which he had passed to a gentleman's house, but would make his proffer to go that way. The cathedral towns were our greatest refreshment, for there were good company, and the clergy were our friends, besides, we made Sundays there if possible, because of the music and the pleasure of the cathedral. After business was over we usually hunted the ladies, who seldom failed to be jugged together at some ball or good house or other. And we were not without our evening frolics till almost morning, but it was more humour than vice on my part; but I had this notion, that women are never so little dangerous to play with as when one foot is in the stirrup. If we must stay, they extend their web, but if we are pulled away we break all.

171. We went the Northern Circuit once, and once the Norfolk, but since I mean neither topography nor chorography, and nothing very remarkable otherwise happened to us in either, I shall not dwell on this matter longer, only let me note a failing or two of my own, which I cannot but remember. Once in the west a perverse fellow was prosecuted for sedition and traversed. I was attended to be of counsel for him, which I should not have been but I knew not the nature of the business beforehand. After, I perceived the loyal gentlemen all engaged against him, and much displeased with me for appearing as his counsel; but now I suppose I am excused, since those very men went in

to the Prince and I do not swear. Another was that in Westmoreland a great feud was depending among the gentry, which had troubled Whitehall, and was recommended to my brother to compose, and upon their attendance I was of counsel on the wrong side. I was also innocent of the meaning of the business, for the pretence was the keeping sessions at one place or other, but the substance pique and spite at one another. And I knew not but counsel would have been on the other side, but none was, which put me out of countenance. The spite was at Sir Philip Musgrave, than whom a worthier Englishman was not found. Against him was myself, and Sir John Lowther of Lowther, and divers others; Sir Philip, with the assistance of his son, now Sir Christopher, bore the brunt and answered bravely. My brother gave both sides content by an expedient, which was to hold the sessions on both sides of the county by adjournment, as is done in Suffolk and other large counties. But then they were so weak to hold double sessions, independent of each other, which is not legal, because the quarterly sessions is defined by statute, and can be but one.[1]

172. If I should go about to observe all my indiscretions which were incidental in these and other transient businesses, I should have work enough. It was my comfort and affliction that I was sensible of them either immediately or soon after, and not only so but of my incapacity of being much wiser. This was the affliction; the comfort was, that being thus sensible argued me not a senseless sot, but one that was not wise in my own eyes, therefore within the pale of hope.

---

[1] This occurred in 1676. See *Life of the Lord Keeper*, § 209.

CHAPTER XI.

EXPERIENCE AS KING'S COUNSEL.

THIS is all that I think material enough to note relating to my practice, while I was a plain barrister, and
that state I terminate in my being made of the King's
Council. This I fix as another *epocha* or degree of advance of my life, which let me into affairs of an higher
nature, and these shall be the subject of what follows.
And first—

An account of my patents of preferment and the times.

24 Feb. 1679.   The patents of the Archbishop's Offices.
26 Oct. 1682.   The first patent to be of the King's
                   Council.
10 Jany. 1684.   The commission to be the Duke of York's
                   Solicitor General.
9 Feb. 1685.   The second patent of King's Council under
                   Jac. II.
19 Jany. 168[6].   The patent to be the Queen's Attorney
                   General, with a salary of £50 per
                   annum.

Memorandum.

At Easter I was made of their council with a pension
of £3. 16s. 4d., which is still paid.

And I had a patent from King's College to be of their
council, with a pension of £5 per annum for ten years, but
they continue it to me though the time be expired.

174. It was not long before the death of my Lord Nottingham [1] that I was constituted of the King's Council
extraordinary; but it happened well for me, because when

[1] Lord Nottingham died 18 December, 1682.

my brother had the Great Seal I came into a very honourable post, and that which gave me the fortune I now lean
upon.   This order of King's Counsel under the coif was
not very frequent in former times, and there was none since
the Restoration till my brother was made, as I have given
an account in his life.   Therefore it was a greater honour
to him than us, for of late it hath been more frequent, and
out of favour more than merit in the profession as his
was.   There used to be two serjeants, called the King's
Serjeants, for long time past, and these had greater
dignity and authority than the Attorney General; they
hold the precedence still, but have little authority and no
business but as Mr. Attorney call them.   This is the reason
that in proclamations for discharge of prisoners in cases of
no prosecution, the King's Serjeant is named before the
Attorney General, which makes me think that of old time
the King's Attorney was like a common attorney, and not
a pleader, and the serjeants pleaded, and the attorney prosecuted.   And in after times when the Chancery grew into
business, and the Attorney General grew more considerable,
there was an under officer who was to take the soliciting
part and Mr. Attorney pleaded.   This was called the
Solicitor General.   Now this officer is grown high, and
almost a peer to the Attorney, and is come to be wholly a
pleader, and still new under officers are made, as the
Solicitor of the Exchequer, who was a runner up and down
to call for process about the king's debts and dispatch
them, is a sort of mechanic Attorney General, and doth
in effect more, as to the prosecuting and soliciting part,
than attorney and solicitor put together.   This employment was first conspicuous under Jones, who prosecuted
the popish plot; after came to Graham and Burton, and
since to Whitmore and Aaron Smith; [1] but the latter engrosseth all, and by his management ought to be the
honourable beginning of a new style of officer, that is
Suborner General.   But to let him pass.   The Attorney
General in the King's Bench is an officer by the Constitution, and hath a place under the Chief Justice when he sits,
and puts on a round cap like the prothonotary and chief

[1] Some account of this worthy may be found in the *Examen*.

clerk of the Crown, but profit calls him away, and to take place of a pleader within the bar. In the Common Pleas the Attorney General may come into and sit in the court, and appear to speak in the king's business, for he hath power *ad perdendum et lucrandum pro rege*, but he cannot take the place of a serjeant at the bar. This I allege to shew that the Attorney General, whatever his station is now, was anciently little more than a sort of Aaron Smith in the law.

175. This, by a sort of analogy, shews how the attorneys are grown upon the lawyers in general; for anciently, as I have been informed, all conveyancing, court keeping, and even the making of breviats at the assizes was done by the lawyers. Now the attorneys have the greatest share, and the young practisers, I might say old ones too, truckle to them, and men of law expect business to come from their hand, and the attorneys depend little on the others. The truth is, the gentlemen of the law, having left the mechanic part of their practice, that is to speak with the client at the first instance to state his business and to advise the action, and not griping for fees at first, but making their conversation easy to the suitor, hath been the cause that the attorneys carry all from them; for the first undertaker in business doth all, and he must go through in the cause; he is instructed, and can instruct others; he is resorted to on all occasions; he (perhaps) disburseth money, and is easy to let himself into the business; and if young gentlemen will ever think to secure a practice to themselves, they must set pen to paper and be mechanics and operators in the law as well as students and pleaders. Mere speculative law will help very few into the world, and if a man have not extraordinary felicities he shall not succeed that way; the other can scarcely fail.

176. My brother being of the Privy Council, and of chief authority in matters of law, I had frequent occasions to attend upon hearings there, which made me personally known to the King and great men; but I cannot say much to my advantage, because I wanted those abilities that prevail in great men's esteem, that is confidence and put-forwardness, as well as a contracted sense materially and

shortly delivered.   Modesty and good meaning are not coin
current there.

177. About this time, and before as well as after, my
brother Dudley was a Commissioner of the Customs, and
that brought me into much business concerning the Customs, and I may say scarce any part in the circuit where I
was, or in Westminster Hall, where I might attend, but I
was at the end of it.   This let me into a knowledge of the
court of the Exchequer, which I should not have so well
attained without it, and that court is so mysterious that
a man must be not only a practiser but an officer, or of
an industry and curiosity equivalent to obtain the true
knowledge of it, but that was too profound for me.

178. I have had occasion to wonder at several things,
one is, that insurers of ships have a sort of obloquy, which
either chance or custom hath given them, and they come
not to the law without prejudice, such as extortioners,
usurers, or pawnbrokers usually meet with, and the insured
is favoured, and all presumptions taken on his part.
Whereas the insurer cannot be a cheat, but is very often
cheated by the insured; for the falsities come on their
side, who know their own motives, which are secrets to
the insurers.

179. Another strange thing is, that although it is very
much for the interest of the public that trade should be
equal, and that all pay custom alike, and so it not be possible that some should undersell others, as they may if the
customs be not duly collected, but unfair merchants smuggle
goods ashore custom free, which the fair merchant will not
do.   And thereby they are at a great disadvantage, for the
uncustomed goods, having less cost upon them, may be sold
cheaper, and so may bring down the price below common
profit.   Wherefore one would think that custom-house
prosecutions should be favoured; but it is so far otherwise
that wrong-doers are favoured, and every prosecution out
of the custom-house is looked upon as a tyrannical way of
proceeding, little less than an invasion of property, and by
the Exchequer juries and judges the poor merchants are
the favourites—that is the false traders and not the honest
merchants.   And although it is well known that for one
discovery there are hundreds of escapes, and it is very

difficult to trap a fraud in the customs, and proof can scarce be other than circumstantial, but such as to a right understanding is more cogent than any positive swearing, yet the prosecutors of frauds are battered and held to strict proof, circumstances (which are indeed the best) slighted, and a perjured rogue who will swear flat and right down, carries it.

180. There are many more of this sort which failings seem to be in the way of mercy, as if the English nation were less cruel than other nations, and so they colour it in their abominable favour of some sort of criminals. Whereas *re verâ* the reason is, they intend to be or think they may be criminal in the like kind themselves, so they do to others as they would have others do for them. And this is the wonderful pitiful nature of the English nation. As in cases of sedition, stealing custom, customary forswearing of themselves, which have so much countenance, not out of tender-heartedness, but secret wickedness, supposing at one time or other to be guilty themselves.

181. Upon my being made of the King's Council[1] I began to keep a chariot, as was fitting in the state or order I was in, but did it at more ease than any other, because I only bought the chariot, my brother let me have the use of a pair of his horses; so I preferred my footman to be coachman and took another footman. And all this while I lived with my brother at his house, only lodged at the Temple, and was one of his family, without paying anything, which was a very great advantage to me, and I have reason to remember his goodness with gratitude and honour.

182. I think our way of living was extraordinary happy. My brother was the bond to the fagot: he kept us together and was as a common father to us.[2] When he first married

---

[1] Pat. 26 October, 34 Charles II. 1682.

[2] This paragraph is a good instance of the author's strange disregard of chronological sequence in his writing. Sir Francis North, then Solicitor General, married Lady Frances, third daughter of Thomas, third Earl of Downe, on the 5th March, 1672. Her Ladyship's sister, Lady Finetta, married Robert Hyde, son of Alexander Hyde, Bishop of Salisbury, on the 4th May, 1674. All that is related in this paragraph obviously happened in the course of the two years between these two dates.—See *Life of Lord Keeper North,* and *Collins' Peerage,* vol. iv. 474 (ed. 1812).

he used lodgings in Lincoln's Inn Fields, and soon removed to Chancery Lane, which lay convenient for his
business, especially after he was Chief Justice [1675], for
there he had a back way to his lodgings in Serjeants'
Inn. He was extremely kind to his lady's relations, and
often entertained the Countess of Downe and her daughter,
the Lady Finetta, for three months together, and we sometimes went to Wroxton and stayed a month with the
Countess. It was thought that I might have taken this
opportunity to have gained upon that lady, who was a great
fortune, but had some personal disadvantages. I cannot
deny but there was a great aspect by her demeanour in
public that such a point might be gained ; but I that had
a nicer observation found it was not the same in private,
which made me conclude that the procedure was politic,
whereby she might be invited to London for further opportunity, which I discovered to my brothers, and till then
they believed I had a fair game, but from that carriage and
other circumstances collated they at last were of my
opinion, and approved my not prosecuting the matter. But
I went farther, and by an opportune slight put upon her,
which was too rough and plain to be mentioned, I think
I cancelled the debt charged by practising to make me a
property.

183. Our conversation was much upon music and philosophy. Our brother John, who was a Cantabrigian and
very ingenious as well as learned, gave much life to our
entertainments ; for he was excellent at sparring doubts,
and reserved himself to be moderator of our disputes, which
would be sometimes very warm. I remember once we had
a hot dispute about the barometer, and the reasons of its
keeping time with the weather, and agreed to put our
sentiments in writing and send them to Oldenburg of the
Royal Society [2] to be printed, and he returned them all,
which made my brother Francis laugh and say his fared ill
for being in such company. I thought then, and do still,
that I was in the right, and have set forth the matter at
large in my discourse on the barometer, which had its
start from this controversy. My brother Francis went on

---

[1] HENRY OLDENBURG, for some time Secretary of the Royal Society,
died in August, 1678.

the common notion of vapours, but made them heavier when low and ready to rain than when high, as all gravity is less far from than near the surface of the earth. I battled these vapours, and persisted that the common air was water or vapour, and that heats and colds intermixing swelled or shrunk the atmosphere by producing the effects of fair weather or rain, and that influenced the mercury; but of this I think I have spoke, and is found at large in my discourse. In short, nothing ingenious was stirring but we had it, which was very diverting and profitable.

184. When my Lady Frances began to want health my brother took a house at Hammersmith, and there his family was all day, and we used to come there after eight at night and return in the morning, which was a very pleasant variety.[1] It happened that one morning I had occasion to ride two or three times between London and that place when the weather was extreme hot, and I perceived, watering at my Lord Finch's spring-cistern, a sudden heat almost insupportable, which was not so either at any time before or after. When I was come to Hammersmith and lighted I found myself very weary, but made no complaint, and at dinner had no stomach, but I could drink. At night I went to London, and was ill in the night. Next day company was at Hammersmith, and healths went round. I join in all to a wonder (being used to shirk) but eat nothing. I continued ill, and at nights worse and worse. I was extreme thirsty in the day and hot and sweaty at night. I went to a dairy-house and swigged of the milk and water, but little better. I gat gruel at night, and was then not able to conceal my illness longer, but was so bad that my brother sent me a visit in the morning (after three or four of these nights), and I, being engaged at my Lord Chancellor's,[2] would not be absent, but waited in the cause-room dejected and ready to die, till I could hold out no longer. I gave away my brief, and I think my fee, and came home and sat down so ill all over that I knew not what I ailed, but

---

[1] Her Ladyship died 15 November, 1678.

[2] SIR HENEAGE FINCH was made Lord Keeper of the Great Seal 6 November, 1673, but he was not constituted *Lord Chancellor* till 19 December, 1675.

had a mind to go to bed. I remember I asked my brother what it was that could affect me all over so that I could not find one point about me that I could say was easy. He gave a doctoral reason, such as they sputter when asked such questions, knowing as he did that it was all nonsense, and he used to tell it as a story, what a ready account he gave me of that image of universal illness which I had, and that I was very well satisfied. When I was laid Dr. Masters[1] came and pronounced me seized with an acute fever, prescribed juleps, interdicted flesh, discharged much of the bed-clothes, and in that course I recovered. The fever abated immediately upon my submitting and lying down. And to say truth, I had almost spent the increase of it before I truckled, for I perceived myself delirious; that is, sitting in the company, I should perceive a plain expergiscence, though I had no sense of drowsiness or sign of it, but I should on a sudden perceive the company and their discourse as waking, without any connection with what preceded or memory of it, when it was plain to me and the company that I did not sleep. This was a sort of delirancy. The greatest trouble I had before I lay down was pain in my stomach. I gat some fantastical bandages of dimity made, with hooks and eyes, and had a disposition perpetually to eruct. This I strove so much in when I was alone, thinking if I could raise the wind (as it seemed to be) I should be well. And by a perpetual striving to eruct, I have fixed on myself an eructation, which is but a convulsion of the œsophagus, which I shall never quite wear off, and was plainly at first derived from this error of conduct; but it grows less, and I hope will become inconsiderable or nothing. It is with many as I found it to be with me, that a disorder or convulsive motion of the fibres of the stomach, or mouth of it, is believed to be wind, and medicines go accordingly, as ginger and warm drugs ; whereas it is not so, but plain convulsion. In my sickness, when the fever began to wear off, in sleeping I had an image of thought, as if a small point or seed within me grew and swelled as if it would

[1] Probably JOHN MASTER, M.D., of Christ Church, Oxford, admitted an Honorary Fellow of the College of Physicians 30 September, 1680. —*Munk*.

have blown me up. This came two or three times, and was great pain, and caused the doctor to be sent for, who with a cordial kept down the evil. And I conceive it was but a general convulsion of the stomach, from want of spirits or good order of them; but these sick images are strange things, and few that are sick observe them, but think the reality is according to their sense.

185. Another great trouble in my sickness was that I should not be well time enough to go out with my brother into the Norfolk Circuit. And in this the doctor was the prætor to edict or interdict my journey. I pressed him, but he answered that my tongue was not yet clean, and he must not send me into the circuit with a foul tongue. His jest was not amiss. I passed my time after I got up in riding little journeys about London, and found myself mend more by that than anything else. I was very uneasy after this fever, having little or no appetite or taste, and weak, which was a comfortless state to me, who could not endure tenderness. At last I resolved to venture into the circuit, and in two days reached Huntingdon, and thence went through. I remember I sweat in all places most immoderately, which was a remedy beyond all the power of physic. This and the travelling was a complete purgation of the fœci which sticks upon a patient after a fever; but I was not wholly free till, being at Stourbridge at a sister's the same summer,[1] I lay over a kitchen where a fire was all night, and the heat of that was co-operative with a disposition, and I sweat with such profusion that I never was sensible of the like. It was very uneasy, but salutary. I thought all the fevers in nature were taking possession again, and had no ease in my mind till in the morning I began to look, and found it was all vented in a deluge of sweat. This was the *ultimum vale* of all the feverish indisposition, and neither since nor for a long time before had I any sickness, unless in the year '84, a spring tertian, which was kind and beneficial.

186. Many thought my proceeding at the beginning of

---

[1] The sister was the Hon. Ann North, married to Robert Foley, Esq., of Stourbridge, Worcestershire, a younger brother of Thomas Foley from whom the present Baron Foley is lineally descended.

this fever desperate, for wine and milk are both pernicious; but I believe my want of appetite and eating no flesh was that which prevented the others doing me much harm. For, although they do ascend, yet they, being liquids, pass off soon, but flesh lies in a man's body, and the digestive and expulsive faculties failing, as in fevers, it corrupts and heats like a dunghill, and nature cannot shake it off. I believe that I had this advantage by my pertinacity, that the bed when I took it was more refreshing than it would have been if I had submitted at first; for being extraordinarily tired it came to a pleasure, but if I had taken that ease at first, when the fever had grown high, I should have nauseated it and pined to be up. So ended this sickness, and it may give me an opportunity to speak shortly of my regimen of health, for I have been often asked concerning it, because, seeming of a good constitution, others think conduct did conduce to it.

187. Once in the company of old Doctor Denton[1] I was fleering at the infinite scrupulosity Mr. Boyle used about preserving his health, for he would speak with no physician unless he declared, *in verbo medici*, that he had seen none with the smallpox in so long time; and had chemical cordials calculated to the nature of all vapours that the several winds bring; and used to observe his ceiling compass every morning that he might know how the wind was, and meet the malignity it brought by a proper antidotal cordial.[2] So that if the wind shifted often he was in danger of being drunk. But Mr. Boyle had such a party, that all he did was wise and ingenious, and the doctor took his part and defended his regimen. A lady in the company, observing the dispute, asked me what course I took to be so well. I answered that I had no thought or regard to my health in anything I did. "Truly," said the doctor, "and you are not much out of the way neither." So truth will sometimes make an

---

[1] WILLIAM DENTON, M.D., Physician to Charles I. and Charles II. He died March, 1691, in his 86th year.—See Munk's short account of him, *Roll of the Royal College of Physicians*, vol. i. 306.

[2] The story is given in Birch's *Life of Robert Boyle*, quoted in the *Dictionary of National Biography*, *sub nomine*.

eruption, though against the weight of interest, which ordinarily keeps it down.

188. It is a common proceeding to make known all fears and apprehensions about health by telling of catching cold, and headache, gripes. . . . . All which I have thought an impotence to be mastered if possible; for how importunate is it to say, I intend to put on a waistcoat or leave off one, to take physic, that last night his sleep was bad, he has no stomach, and asking advice on these matters. I have considered the true reason of this infirmity, and I find it comes all out of fear and pusillanimity. It is natural for all people to think (or rather without thinking they take it for granted) that what is important to them is so to everyone else, and in the same degree, and being under a melancholy fear about some circumstance of health would have others condole with them, *solamen miseris socios habuisse dolorum.* And it may be observed, that if there be any interested in the person's life, who will resent such complaints, as wives, children, and friends, they shall be sure to have them amply displayed, and with a ridiculous seriousness. So take it for a principle, that woes will make themselves known, and I think much more constantly than felicities. Now all timorous people fear to die, and in that species mankind itself may be justly esteemed timorous, though some less than others, and the least have a great degree, but such as prudence and consideration may conquer. Others that have a greater share are transported, and abandon all discretion and decorum to the will of fear, which bears down all before it.

189. When fear takes place the concerned does as much regard the circumstances and the perils, not considering or weighing so much the odds as the main chance. As if they have a great dread of mortality, sickness is the mean, and preservation of health the opposite, which consists in many various cares, in all which the end seizeth the thought, and that raiseth a passion, and passion knows no discretion, but indulgeth itself whatever befalls in consequence. And thus, in each circumstance relating to health, or which they think doth so, the persons shall be as concerned and serious as if they were

at point of death; for the fear skips to the end, and there's the fright.

190. Having this notion of the timorous complaints about health, which most indulge, it may be easily believed that I was not much apt to complain. And this I carried so far as to pass into a humour or unjustifiable obstinacy. For as I have perceived in myself an inclination to be concerned and to talk of sweats, colds, and stools, as others do, so I have endeavoured to keep down the effect of it, and say nothing, which hath made me pass as of a much better constitution than I really have, though I do think many have not so good.

191. I must needs say, that although I do not argue that I did right, yet I have found it very successful to me. For when I have been very ill, and with the symptoms of want of good temper, which makes folk run to doctors, as in or fearing a fever, I have let all pass, and eat and drank with my friends as usual, though uneasy and improper, being disposed to endure anything rather than submit and own myself sick that brought upon me the ordinary importunity of catechization, how I did, and this and the other medicine. When I have been forced to own an indisposition I have retreated all diet into water gruel, and not a little, but a very great quantity, which I thought would clear me, and I have ever found my distempers wear off of themselves. I never took preventive physic, nor let blood. About the time of the death of Charles II. it grew a fashion to let blood frequently, out of an opinion it would have saved his life if done in time. And being reduced to water gruel once, I was very much pressed by a near relation to a degree to make me angry. I answered, if she had a mind to a porringer of blood for her breakfast I had it at her service. This conceit, more rude than reasonable, eased me as much of trouble as breathing a vein in a plethora. And as to matter of complaining, I ever declined it in other matters of fortune and success as much as in the concern of health. It was a sort of *braveur*, but with this reason too, that I did not see any good of it. And I had a contempt for the complaints of others, as at cards some will not be contented unless you grant them that none had ever such ill-luck as they. And in business

that which we call fretting, which is the same thing as complaining, only doth not always burst out, I have laboured to conquer it, and believe I have brought myself to as much apathy as to good or ill success as any have, and I own it partly to temper, which hath much of passion, but is not easily excited. And as fretting or being afflicted at successes is all error, I would as little endure it as I could. And this is to be opposed to the excess of the other extreme, which is more vain and more offensive, I mean ostentation. For complaint calls for help, but ostentation does no good, and reacheth at none, but vexeth others with envy, and against fretting and grief at ill-success, which is inward, set pride and joy, both impertinent extremes. To conclude this matter touching my regimen, or rather no regimen of health, I never was perfectly at ease till I had fixed in my mind two grand points of philosophy. First, that labour and pain was not an evil beyond the necessity we have of enduring; but life itself and the greatest ease of it is actual pain; and that labour as commonly understood with regard to a man's strength and spirits takes off the tedium of life, which compensates and overpays all the trouble of it, and then with the ease and refreshment that follows it brings an actual pleasure. And when pleasure is sought by adding to life, as the philosophers intend by the pleasures of sense; by heaping of objects of taste, ease, and venery, they waste the spirits, bring diseases, and lose their force; but labour is natural and nourisheth the body, keeps it sound, and giveth vigour to the pleasures of sense. Second, the other is, that it is in all cases and circumstances better to die than to live, and that it is all weakness and infirmity that makes us desire to live, and therefore the weaker the body and judgment the stronger is the desire of life, which we see eminently in very old and sick persons; wherefore, in sound and happy state of mind we have the greatest indifferency of life, and can put on the firmest resolution to die. We argue for life from the generality of the desire, as when we affirm the pain of even living. Yet say others, we all desire it, as if the desire of life were by divine impress, whereas it is the result of fear, weakness, and pusillanimity. This opinion frees us from the greatest

solicitude of life, the vast care and passionate concern of
health, which afflicts the most vegete and athletic con-
stitutions, and it frees us from fear of pain, because death
easeth us, and indeed from all other cares and solicitudes
of life, which were insupportable were there not a certain
conclusion by death. What care could set us at ease
under all the revolving mischiefs and disorders of powers,
and accidents of fire, robberies, and injustices? If a man
were sure to live five hundred years what could secure him
that that long thread was not to be spun out in pain,
want, misery, contempt, and sorrow? No, let my retreat
be secure, death in due time, and I defy the world. But
what is due time? When living neither is nor can be
tolerable. I grant much pain will be reasonably sustained
in prospect of mending life and the restoring it to ease,
such as is commonly called so, as setting broken bones,
and other hard cures, not to omit instancing the pox,
which many improvidently, and some ignorantly, get; and
being a disease if neglected certainly mortal, and undertaken in time certainly cured, but with great and long
torment, we will excuse the weakness of human nature so
far as to endure more pain than death usually brings to
save life, and not to relieve nature in such cases by accelerating death. What I say of corporal afflictions and
pains may as well be applied to mental, which grow out of
the diseases of a man's estate or fortune; that will have
wounds by hopes and casualties, as well as errors and bad
conduct, and I blame not men who slave themselves (as
the word is) to repair it. Nay, when either from spirit or
education, the increase of what is provided becomes needful, to make it adequate to the ambition of the person, for
the pleasure of hoping, or expectation of good is greater
than any enjoyment.

192. These are pleasures that are in our nature, thinking
we shall be happy we are happy in the thought and the
pursuit, which is not from reason but weakness, yet scarce
to be mastered, though in some philosophy and strong
thinking will go far. And I cannot but, as I said, indulge
this weakness that men not desperate in health or fortune
desire to live. But when the contrary happens, as not
seldom, as in case of wretched old age, or chronical, in-

curable, and tormenting diseases; and some come to a crisis so that death is certain, but the time uncertain, only the acute pains and comfortless condition in the interim infallible, or when either by great losses, especially proceeding from vice or folly, the remorse whereof is very oppressing, the necessary support of life in such a manner as spirit and ambition hath made essential to ease is lost, and there is no hope of retrieve, but misery and the gaol are to follow, I admire that any man in such condition should desire to live, or indeed should not court death, I was going to say wilfully procure it, but that with a little more deliberation.

193. Now to debate this grand controversy, whether it be lawful for a man to shorten his life in a desperate case or not? I am of opinion, and always was, that it is lawful, and done iu a right mind, without conscience of fault in so doing, is no sin. I grant, as an erroneous conscience justifies *coram deo*, so here a conscience convinced that it is unlawful makes it so, whether in itself it be unlawful or not. And a clear persuasion that it is lawful doth the same, though in truth it be unlawful. Therefore these points of the case made upon conscience are beside the question, and to be laid aside with this, that if a man cannot bring his mind to a clear settlement either way, but doubts remain, it is good to take the safe way and endure, rather than hazard dying in a sin which, being the last act of life, can hardly be repented of, and we come back to the point whether lawful or not.

194. This consists of two parts—first, positive command; second, the reason of the thing. First: there is no positive command against my position, for the Decalogue, "Thou shalt not kill," was a law only to the Jewish nation and not to the whole world; and if this article were apposite it extendeth not to us, no more than that of the Sabbath doth, further than the morality of it. And if it did extend to us, it is not against self-killing, because it regards our neighbour, as our Catechism teacheth, and so toucheth not our own case, for *volenti non fit injuria*.

195. Second: as to the reason of the thing, I think it is highly on my side, for the whole force of the objection is,

that we must submit to Providence and bear all that God thinks fit to lay upon us; which I grant is true as to patience, submission, and not cursing and blasphemy, as men in torment and despair are apt to do. But to deprive us of using the most rational and innocent means for relief and ending torment, I think none can justly extend the doctrine. I see not how to distinguish the case of life from other cases that touch our well-being or the contrary. If we must submit to Providence, and not help ourselves when we may, why do we seek by labour to accumulate wealth for our own and family support, and settle it through ages and generations? or why do we take physic and call in the mortal help of doctors, apothecaries, and nurses? When we are sick we are visited by Providence, and we strive against it. Is it not because the same Providence that sends the disease sends the expedient or cure, if any be: if none, it sends the means of ending the pain all at once? The truth is, this using of special Providence in every occasion of argument is the wielding a weapon we understand not. Who will say that a miracle is wrought for this or that, or indeed any circumstance of everyone's life, as must be if such arguments as these hold? No, surely the common laws that God hath given to the world govern ordinarily, and effects answer them, and we have senses to observe, memory, and the art of reasoning, which enable us to determine our will in the use of them accordingly. And what special law or Providence is there which forbids us to use our reason in making ourselves happy without injury or malice to any, or where we are our own governors and proprietors, to determine desperate pains and torture by means inoffensive to all? Some say we must by our example of patience and long-suffering do good to others, and the more we endure the stronger the force of the example is. I know it is ordinarily held that everyone is bound to do as much good as they can; but I allow not that rule, at least in the extent it is taken. For I say it is enough not to do evil, which takes in the omission of the necessary duties of charity, devotion, &c.; for the doing of what is forbidden, or not doing what is commanded, are equally positive transgressions; but to say that I must do all the good that is in my power, and that it is a duty the breach whereof is sin, were to make mankind mad, and therefore is impracticable and cannot be law.

196. For if I must do all the good I can, I must deliberate in every emergence, great or small, what is best, and so spend all my time in weighing scruples of good and evil, and never do anything. For it is scarce possible to have a criterion of good and evil, so as to give one a reasonable satisfaction in the comparison of things. Then the degrees of comparison can scarce ever be fulfilled, for when you go upon one thing somewhat else will occur that may be better, and then another, and so we shall snatch ourselves every way according to these occurrences like madmen or irresolute fools. Then again, be we bound to do most good. This takes in ourselves, with the custody of whom we are intrusted, and we are bound to do ourselves good before any others. Charity begins at home. So that to hurt ourselves to do others good is out of the rule and reason of charity. When we relieve them we become thereby objects for the charity of others, and mankind in the general no gainer by the good we do. Wherefore charity and goodness to others ought to consist with charity and goodness to ourselves. And if we are miserable to the ultimate degree in which (in mercy) we would kill a beast, why not ourselves as a charity which takes place of all others?

197. Some will say we have time to repent, and the sharper our affliction is, and the longer, the more sincere and confirmed is our repentance. I grant affliction opens men's eyes and makes them see the evil of their ways, which were hid by their passions, ignorance, and the deceitful pleasures of the world, the great enemies and obstructions of thinking. What then? What is to be expected more from affliction than a true repentance? And what is true repentance but a clear understanding of the evil, full resolution to do well for the future, and beginning with restitution for the wrongs already done? After this, would you have pain continue for pain's sake? No, God hath no pleasure in any evil, nor in the evil of pain in anything, and however pain is permitted for deep reasons, there are also remedies in many cases laid before

us, and it is not only lawful to use them, but folly or a sin not to do it. We count it a sin to wound or afflict ourselves or others unreasonably. Why? Because God wills the good of all creatures, and pain is evil. Then is it not a sin, when a cure of otherwise incurable evil is laid before us and put in our power, not to use it?

198. Lastly, some will say affliction is a pathetic opportunity of praising God. It were well if there were not more danger of raving, cursing, and blaspheming; for acute pains are too apt to provoke such exorbitances of mind and expressions, and it is most safe in all respects for avoiding scandal and the handle atheistical people might take, that men in pain kept their complaints to themselves, and have their misery ended rather than suffered to speak out in the voice of pangs and groans such things as reason can have little to do with.

199. These inducements have settled my thoughts in this great and consequential matter, but not so far as to make any resolutions, but only that I might not be put to deliberate when my reason is not capable, and so as I may determine freely in all emergencies to do as the present occasion shall require. And if I never act otherwise than those who are of the contrary opinion, as I believe I shall not; yet I have this advantage, that I have ease and repose in my mind so as if ever I am overwhelmed in irremediable calamity and pain, I may, if I find I cannot bear them, put a period to free myself, and in this thought I have great comfort, and have had and shall continue to have all my life long.

200. Now, to return to our way of living between London and Hammersmith. We had, as I said, our brother the divine much with us, and once we heard that he was much indisposed at Cambridge, and apt to great defluxions of rheum, which made his uvula swell; and he being one of very intense and searching thought, could never keep his mind from being led in a series to the extremes of all evils, as if the worst that could be would certainly arrive to him. Therefore he concluded that this swelling would grow and at last his uvula must be cut off. This process of fear and despair sent him to the doctors, who always are free to venture their skill whatever the

patient ventures. They advised the taking away the cause by cathartics to purify the blood, and to defeat it another way than by that of spitting. This course of physic brought him low and dispirited him, and much more because he had a restless discontented spirit, which made me often think his body in some respect or other did not fit it so well as to sit easy upon him, and that it was defective in some considerable organ of vital continuance. We invited him to come to London to us, and we found him the most changed that ever was—tender, sickly, low-spirited—as if age had surprised him. Our hours abroad were after sunset; he would not be persuaded to be abroad at the time. We used a glass of wine; he would scarce drink at all, because drink promoted rheum. He had amber to smoke in pipes to dry his uvula, which I heard a physician say would put a well man into convulsions. He had astringent powders to blow up into his throat; would eat nuts, but not touch a grape or anything humid. Our way of talk used to bear hard upon doctors of physic, because we were more disposed to demonstration than authority, and accordingly used to rally this brother of ours upon the subject of his rules and practices upon himself, till at last we routed his cap and puritan handkerchief from his neck, brought him to walk, and drink a glass with us, and at last almost converted him, and sent him down hale and well to his college. There he fell again to his austerities, rising at five, studying all the morning and afternoon, no refreshment but a dish of coffee, and very anxious about college business, his throat troubling him, physic dispiriting him, the vent of humours that nature had found at his throat stopped, and forced to break open a new channel, whereupon, once in a passion with some disorderly scholar which touched the trigger and made the eruption, the humour broke out upon his brain, and he fell down in an apoplexy, which turned to an hemiplegia, in which state he lived miserably three or four years, his condition being fitter for oblivion than history.[1] We had the mortification of his company some-

[1] The dreadful sufferings which Dr. John North endured at the hands of his physicians may be read more at large in the *Life of Dr. John North*, § 91. The account there given leaves an impression of

times, but without hope or comfort. My brother used to leave his lady then when he went the circuits and return to her when he came back.

astonishment and horror at the empirical character of medical science at the time, and the unsparing cruelty of the experiments resorted to by physicians even of repute and some intelligence.

CHAPTER XII.

THE CASE OF STEPHEN COLLEDGE.

IT was the last circuit we went in the west save one, when the Plot had grown rank, when the Lord Chief Justice was attempted at Bristol. I intend to touch that and other matters of his conduct in his troubles more largely in my history of his life, if I am so happy to compass it, but I having had a share in the conversation and soliciting part throughout, I cannot forbear a short mention of them. From the first he thought the plot an imposture, and I was not a pretender to differ in opinion in politics, whatever I did, and he indulged me to vary from him and dispute in philosophy; so I was of the same opinion. He was attacked twice by the House of Commons publicly, and often by private stratagem. The first attack in the House was the cause of Bernardiston and Soam, supposing the judgment was given by his solicitation.[1] There we had friends, and I was a solicitor, and we carried our points by party which were principally our western men. The second was for the proclamation against petitioning for the Parliament, which was called abhorring.[2] Then we had no friends, but the King stood firm, which gave all a courage, and we defied them. Here we had no solicitation. By this time the plot was turned upon the Church of England men. There was a great desire to ruin or remove the Lord Chief Justice, who was an incurable *remora* in their way.

202. Once concluding at Bristol, we were told Bedloe was in town, and was burdened in his conscience with somewhat which concerned the nation, and had a mind to ease himself by revealing it to the judge. He concluded by all the marks it was a cheat and a trepan, and walked

---

[1] This was in 1679. There is a full account of the business in the *Examen*, p. 516 *et seq.*, though no date is given.

[2] See *Examen*, p. 546 *et seq.*

cautiously. He took me, the minister that preached, the sheriff, and his clerk with him, and proceeded as is mentioned elsewhere. Afterwards, when the matter came before the House of Commons, that he might not appear to conceal anything, he made me give him an account in writing of what I observed, and so made a relation in writing, which was presented to the House, and afterwards cried about town by the name of "My Lord Chief Justice North's Narrative."[1] This caution was a means that Bedloe could not say anything considerable nor pretend anything was said more than was exposed, and thereby the trepan prevented which was to have the Lord Chief Justice accused of stifling the plot. However, it came that this fellow died of his sickness. I am sure he did not expect it; for one of his chief points was that the Chief Justice should make his case known to the King, and intercede for money. His errand was so important that he came down post, and overheated his obscene lewd carcase, which occasioned his death. But if I ever saw an impostor, or have any guess at one from the air of his procedure, this was a rank one.

203. Another notable scene we had of Colledge's trial.[2] That fellow was deep in the practice part of overturning the Government, and actuated by Shaftesbury and other the grandees, he was bold and presuming, and being a joiner, had a sort of *mobile* attending him. His employment was the handing libellous matter to the people, being taken as a medium or instrument between the politicians and them, and acted his part so well as to be honoured with the style of "the Protestant Joiner." In those days all that was good was "Protestant," and "true Protestant," and all else was reprobated as "Popish." So even Protestants not approved were Papists, which made the distinction of true Protestant. And the ignorant *mobile* had the word Protestant so much in use, and all the distinction of good and evil was resolved into Protestant and Papist. The faction had, by the election of

---

[1] The document is to be found in *The Life of the Lord Keeper*, § 180, and in Howell's *State Trials*, vii. 1493.

[2] See *Examen*, p. 585 *et seq.*; *State Trials*, viii. p. 570; Burnet's *Own Times*, vol. ii. p. 283.

sheriffs, gat London into their hands, so that all treason in London became dispunishable; because packed juries would not convict, and even grand juries refused to find bills, which stigmatised these with the note of "Ignoramus Juries." Colledge acted chiefly here, but the Parliament being appointed to be held at Oxford, it was necessary for the factious party to go down there, because corrupting the Parliament (which to say truth was ripe enough without their help) was a great point however the countenance of the Parliament was to consecrate their actions, and whatever was done was to be under them, either directly or obliquely. And great matters were intended to be executed here, by force if they could compass it no other way, and it was a great mortification at the time to want the London rabble, who were to have lifted at the whole fabric. Colledge, among the rest, went down here, and had the part of dispersing libellous pictures and libels, together with prating against popery and slavery. Ribbons were made with "No Popery," "No Slavery," woven in the stuff, and those were worn in hats, and being invented at a treasonous club at the King's Head Tavern, over against the Inner Temple Gate, where other like stuff was hammered and dispersed, they were called the Green Ribbon Club. There was a picture graven making the King with a raree-show-box at his back. which was a type of the Parliament, and this raree-show with his box was to be pulled into the ditch and be drowned. Another had the Church of England, with several men booted and spurred riding in the rigging, which were the Tories and tantivies riding the Church to Rome. And the Duke was made half Irishman and half devil, the latter part setting fire to London; and apt songs were fitted to these exquisite pieces of wit which this sanctified crew used over their cups (for drinking was so much a fashion no business could be done popularly without it) to troll in scurvy tunes, and all come in at the chorus.

204. This puts me on a reflection of a matter very strange. It is that the reformers of this age were the most vicious, lewd, and scandalous of all mankind, and the sober and judicious part were those borne hard upon. I need not name persons, for it is invidious to friends and

families, but I speak it of my own knowledge who lived in the observation and censure of them.· And for whoring, drunkenness, and professed atheism, they had not their fellows. Impetuous, injurious, and cruel, and yet the cause of religion and property was in their hands, and supported by them as they had the good or ill luck to persuade the world. In Cromwell's rebellion the cause was managed by whining hypocrites, and no wonder if they cheated ; but these fellows never thought fit to hypocritize in the matter. A strange mystery, of which I can give no other resolution than this, that the age generally was debauched in their principles, and in truth had no religion nor morality. It was interest, either real or supposed, which was the true motive of all things. When the faction had once put fears and jealousies into men's heads that their estates were not safe, the wiser (I should say the cunninger) sort were glad others would act, and be in the front to receive the shot from the Government, and succession, which they were taught to fear. So looking upon them as men engaged in their own cause, abetted them in their insolencies and clamours, which all harped upon religion.

*   *   *   *   *   *

*   *   *   *   *

205. Now to return to Colledge, the Protestant joiner.[1] Divers of those miscreant wretches who wrought in the plot under Oates, finding the spirit of it gone, and gain to cease that way, took in with Graham and Burton,[2] and laid open all this trade. Thereupon searching, Colledge was taken, and whole editions of libels and prints found

---

[1] ROUSE and COLLEDGE were apprehended on Wednesday, the 29th June, 1681, and committed to the Tower on a charge of high treason, by Mr. Secretary Jenkins. He was indicted at the Old Bailey on the 8th July, the jury returning the bill with the finding *ignoramus*. Next week a bill was preferred against Colledge at the assizes at Oxford for high treason, and the grand jury found it *billa vera*. He was put upon his trial on the 17th August. He was found guilty, and hung at Oxford on the 31st.—*State Trials*, vii. 570 *et seq. ; Luttrell's Diary*, vol. i. 117, 120; *Burnet*, vol. ii. p. 283.

[2] GRAHAM and BURTON were solicitors for the King : "fitter men," says Burnet, "to have served in a court of inquisition than a legal government."

in his house, so that besides the witnesses there was *testimonium rei* against him. He was indicted at the Old Bailey and ignoramused. Then it was considered that as in Oxfordshire a Parliament had sat and so had been a scene of treason, and great part lay there,—he was indicted in Oxfordshire and the bill found. Then for his trial a special commission issued to the Lord Norris (since Abingdon), the Lord Lieutenant, my brother, Jones, Levinz, and I think Raymond. The sessions were appointed so that we came from the circuit in the west to Oxford, where I was of counsel, with others that came down. And after a long trial of near twelve hours he was found guilty of high treason, and in due time executed. There was obloquy upon this trial, as is always when faction is not pleased; but the print shews how little cause there was for it. The only thing harped on with colour was out of the trial, viz., that his papers, which should have been his defence, were taken from him. I was a witness of the matter. Notice was given that papers were sent privately to him, and they were sent for and looked on. The greatest part were not concerning the fact or challenges, but harangues to the country, going from the matter to libel the Government, and in a most scandalous invective manner. These were detained, and such as were material to his defence given him. And surely that which the court ought not to have heard him read were well taken from him and none else, so that there was not ever a fairer trial than he had.

206. It was remarkable to see what a congregation of the faction's solicitors here were to fetch off their friend Colledge, if possible, as West, Whitacre, Aaron Smith, &c., whose faces were well known to us. And I believe no stone was left unturned towards gaining their point. They tried to intimidate the Chief Justice, my brother, and accordingly at his arrival a letter was delivered to him, in an assumed hand, containing only these words, " You are the Rogue who are pitcht upon to draw the first blood." He was above taking notice of such stuff, but kept it to himself, making only us of his confidence acquainted with it, and did his duty. And Aaron Smith was so impudent to say in court, " Have we not reason when our lives and

liberties are beset here?" He was not aware of the immediate conviction he was liable to. For the Chief Justice ordered the clerk to record the words, which had been a conviction on which he might be fined and imprisoned. Then he recanted and said he did not speak such words, but others, and without the word "here." Whereupon, lest rigour against him should breed an ill opinion of the trial, this passage was let slip. The chief entertainment was to see the plot witnesses fall out and swear each other to be arrant rogues. Oates himself came in on Colledge's side; and in his testimony, that he might *impune* blaspheme in public, charged one of the other side, formerly his fellow evidence, to have said "God damn the Gospel!"

207. This trial lasted from nine in the morning till two the next morning, and wearied us to death, but it ended in a conviction. I may perhaps speak more of it in my account of my brother's life;[1] let this suffice here.

[1] The trial is lightly touched upon in the *Life of the Lord Keeper*, § 216, but related more at large in the *Examen*, p. 585 *et seq.*

CHAPTER XIII.

PERSONAL EXPERIENCES WHILE SIR FRANCIS NORTH WAS LORD KEEPER.

THIS was the last of our going the Western Circuit, for the Lord Nottingham, then Keeper of the Great Seal, declined very much, and at the last died. My brother, then Chief Justice, was the person on whom all eyes were fixed for a successor; but he continually groaned at the too great certainty of it. He would sometimes in heat vow he would refuse it if offered, and rather retire than accept. I ever told him it could not be refused, as it would sully all the honour of his life if he did, and all tolerable pretence was wanting. He was hale, vigorous, and very much honoured for his quality, joined with so great knowledge of the law and felicity in dispatch of business, not to mention loyalty to the Crown, and obliging to all mankind but the utter enemies of the Crown. And there was not a person whom (laying him aside, who was fortified with so much reputation) the age would bear: so that the force and call was too strong for his easy and affable nature to resist. And it so fell out, that after the death of Nottingham [18 Dec. 1682] he came home one evening with his load in the coach—the Great Seal. And after the stir was over, and we came to ourselves, and fell to discourse as usual, I perceived him full of passion up to the brim, to a degree as to hinder even his utterance, and at last to fly out in terms of passion and concern, that men should think him worthy that charge and withal so weak as to be imposed upon as they attempted to do. When a man's heart is full a small thing will heat and inflame it. The *crepa cuore* was, to be removed from a quiet honourable station in the law, which was a. b. c. to him, with profit enough, to a post of first ministry in the State, full of trouble, form, noise, and danger; in no sort agreeable with his temper, nor very profitable. But the circumstance was they endeavoured to engage him without a pension, and at last wrought him to accept £2000 per annum, half what his predecessor had. So it was, and however little patience he brought home he was forced at length to resume his temper, and discover no more resentment after than he had done before; whilst no one could discern him displeased until he first let fly in my company, *solus cum solo.* I wish this unfortunate place had not been his lot, for he never (as poor folks say) joyed after it, and he hath often vowed to me that he had not known a peaceful minute since he touched that cursed Seal.[1] But it was an happiness to me, who took the station of his friend in the Court of Chancery, and was immediately filled with retainers, and came into capital business, with great increase, (indeed the opportunity of getting that small estate I am master of) in the time he sat in Chancery. I felt not his cares, and had a great share in the harvest. I mention this as an happiness, and truly it was a great one, such as few meet with in their lives, to raise an estate by a clown, and without pretence from abilities of my own, to take that post in the Court of Chancery as I had. An happiness I say, but with regard only to the immediate gain. For with respect to the future conduct of my life it was an unhappiness, at least to come to it so soon, raw as I was. It was beginning at the wrong end. The method of acquiring masteries and predominances in all sorts of public performances is to begin at units, or the least items of the business, and to grow up gradually and to fall into stations upon the removes of others, till one with the chief is had. Thus a man builds on a sure foundation. But I that came into the front of Chancery business *per saltum,* all at once, wanted the skill of an underpuller, as they call the drawer of pleadings, and therefore without some extraordinary felicities to recommend, which I had not, I must needs, as I did, seem less or unequal to the post I was in, and, consequently when my bladders that held me up were gone, sink down into a place fitter for me, and that with disadvantage more than falls

---

[1] The story of all this business is told in the *Life of the Lord Keeper,* § 290. In Lord Campbell's venomous *Life of the Lord Keeper,* extraordinary ingenuity is shewn in an attempt to disparage the motives and conduct of the object of his rancour.

to the share of a fresh young beginner, whose face is to
the sunshine advancing, and mine would be from it declining. I never was so elated with my prosperity but I
considered this fully, and accordingly made the best of my
way, honestly, to gain what I could by my practice. I do
not know the hour or moment that I was out of the way
when the course of attending business made it my interest.
I stuck to my chambers in the Temple, where I lay, and
was stirring always very early; my meals, company, and
pleasure, as well as my business, were at my brother's
house. When he was Chief Justice I usually went to
Westminster in the coach with him, but not after he had
the Seal; but it was well known he had scarce a retired
minute without me. I never left him but in bed, and
commonly he would unbend himself with a song to my
thorough bass before he went into his chamber; and I was
with him in all his removes and pastimes, and am a
thorough witness of his conversation to be always upright,
harmless, and pleasant, and above all his mind to be ever
bent in contriving to do his duty and benefit mankind.
And I have scarce patience to think of the effrontery of
many since his death, who have impiously aimed to sully
his memory; but more of this in his life, if mine may have
the honour to conduce to the presenting it to the world.

209. My whole study was in being instructed in causes
and motions. At first it was very tedious and painful to
me. As a country gentleman set to read and give an
account of a marriage settlement hath ten times the labour
of one who passeth recitals and parcel, and runs instantly
to the *habendum* and uses, which he cannot do, so I was
forced to read over all the papers brought to me. And
this I could not do in the client's company. But my way
was to hear from the solicitor an account of the cause, and
write on the back of a sheet upon the breviate short notes
of all the matter as he stated it, then I read the brief with
more content and ease, for I knew the drift and where the
question lay. I was not able to do, as Sir Wm. Jones was
wont, to find some counsel on his side and take an oral
account of the cause, and then by opening of the pleadings
be instructed to appear in the front. And if I could have
done so I think I should not; for I made it a rule and

obliged myself strictly to read my breviate if it were
possible for me so to do, which made my brother say, as
he did often, that I was always well instructed. I did not
pretend to much cunning, as that court hath encouraged,
by vacillating in opinion, and being steered by counsel,
sometimes a bar and a half too short and at other times
beyond the right; for my brother was so acute he was not
to be imposed upon, so to inform him was the great use
of counsel, their art and oratory signified little. And as
my qualifications were but moderate in themselves, but far
short of the old stagers of the court, yet neither my failings nor theirs, however less frequent, (for all have some)
hurt not our clients. And I believe my brother had that
friendship for me, as well as justice for men's causes, that
he neither triumphed over any slips of mine, as most
judges do when they can trap a counsel in error, even to
hurt justice by a vain and elated pride, in ostentation of
their own abilities, nor was he wanting to pick out the
best sense that my expressions bore, and to cover them as
might be done with justice to all sides. He used to say
that a favourite was but a ceremony, and a judge ought to
regard application to him but as a common respect, as
when one says " your Lordship's humble servant," and to
be no more obliged by it. But a total slight of a favourite,
while it is the use to have young counsel in causes to open
pleadings, and to encourage them as the only decent means
of educating them in practice, is as much the contrary as
if they said "I care not for your Lordship;" but neither
the one nor the other to have any weight upon the bench
but elsewhere only as civilities or incivilities are reasonably
resented.

210. I must confess the beginning of my practice was
very surprising, because the multitude of old and opulent
causes came to be re-heard, for *dernier* experiment, supposing they might obtain better decrees than before,
ordinarily the case of a new Keeper. And this brought in
retainers and breviates extraordinarily thick, so that in
one year I believe I was a clear gainer of above £4,000,
and the next near as much, but the third year less, because
the business of the court was well dispatched, and the new
not so opulent as the collection of re-hearings was. And

not being acquainted with such great fees as are ordinarily
given, I was so silly at first, to scruple them, lest they
might be understood as bribes; but my fellow practisers'
conversation soon cured me of that nicety, who informed
me it was usual so to do in great causes. The greatest fee
I ever had was twenty guineas, in the cause of Mr. Frederick
against David, wherein Paul Joddrell was solicitor, who I
believe wondered at my declining to take so much. Once
I had a new year's present of the six clerks of one hundred
guineas, which are the only sums out of the common
hackney road of fees I ever had. Otherwise in very great
causes ten guineas with a huge breviate was extraordinary,
and five in the better sort of causes; but two and three in
ordinary ones, and one for motions and defences were the
gage of my practice.

211. I had heard of some of my worthy predecessors
(not Finch) who were famous, or rather infamous, for
undertaking in causes, viz., "Give me so much, and you
shall be at no further trouble, the cause shall come to a
hearing in ―― time." And one merry story we had of
one whom the wags, then the top practisers, had made
merry at a tavern, and persuaded that he had a right of
precedence to Mr. Attorney General, and if he would insist
upon it, it would bring him in God knows what. This
gentleman was no fool, whatever else, yet he was so blind
as to credit this, and next day so impudent as to desire
Mr. Attorney (publicly) to sit down and speak in his turn,
and insisted till the court bade him go on, as he did,
wondering at the man's impudence, and thinking him the
better half mad. But in the meantime the wags had
diversion enough, and lay sneering at one another, which
the judge, as one would guess, took very ill of them, and
might be one cause why he made, as he did, open war
against the bar, but they despised his infirmity; for
although he had much wit he could not make an order that
would hold water without their help, until at last they
brought him to truckle, and then no man ever courted the
bar as he did. I had at the beginning of my practice
some offers or approaches of this kind. As for instance I
have it said to me by a client, alone by himself, that he
wanted some one counsel that would take the conduct of

his whole cause. He was weary of the solicitor and so many as he had, who were so full that they could not undertake the direction of his, and in order to it possess themselves with his entire matter, and then what would I advise? Such beginnings as these I always scented and rejected, so that in a short time my practice grew clear from all such smut, and if less profitable yet more easy and to my content.

212. I had frequent engagements to attend the council board, and once in the House of Lords, but the practice there was too nice and exquisite for me to meddle with. I was always careful not to say much, which conformed with the expectation that I believe was had, that I should say but little. And I had often in my mind a passage my brother sometimes related, that when he was a beginner my father asked " And what good did you do, Frank?" He answered, he had enough in doing no hurt; which made the old man merry enough that he should breed his son to a trade of being paid for doing no hurt.

213. It seems that it was advantage enough to get an estate; but I have higher thoughts, and even then, and ever since, valued the opportunities I had by living so high upon the rising ground, in a general prospect of human actions joined with the conversation of the most subtle and prudent men of the age, beyond my profit. It hath cured me of all pining after courts, and their deceitful preferments; I have learnt that there is no condition like the private. I can take wrong with patience, and think I know the value of remedy as well as disease, and rather take the former, when it is the lesser evil. I know the vanity and error of news and of vulgar opinion of things; I have no thirst after it. When I knew the greatest secrets of State, as soon as it was lawful to be acquainted with them, and at the same time the ordinary sentiments of men upon such affairs, nay, even gazettes, as well as other prints, all the latter were mere error and mist, from whence I conclude all news do but taint, not help a judgment which never can act but upon true facts, else it is not judgment, but illusion. I have learnt the monk's rule, and found it to be profound wisdom: "*Sinere mundum vadere sicut vult (quia vult vadere sicut vult) nunquam*

contradicere priori, et dicere officium taliter qualiter." I have learnt the folly of projects, the danger and the countenance of all false and treacherous plotmongers; can smell and avoid them at a distance, and not to be drawn forth by any *ignis fatuus* into danger; to do my duty in private, and not to over-value my character to think that I can avail anything in the affairs of the world to influence them one way or other. It is enough if I can govern my private economy; I am satisfied, and hope nothing will ever prevail to draw me from it. I could see the rottenness of men; those against the Government were mad, and those for it generally false. That neither one sort with their impetuosity of threats, nor the others with their authority and flattery, ought to prevail over men to leave the law and strict justice of life. That no safety lies in the contrary, and an Englishman hath nothing to lean on in public business but the law, which only can or will bear him out. And in that whatever prudence or knowledge I have, passive or active, I owe it to my experience and observation in those three years.

214. In particular, I had much conversation with Mr. Anthony Keck,[1] who was a person that had raised himself by his wits, and bating some hardnesses in his character, which might be ascribed to his disease, the gout, he was a man of a polite merry genius. He used to argue much for a republic, or, which was the same thing, a king always in check, so that there should be a magistrate so named, but to have no power without the consent of a council to do anything in the State. And he would ask seriously if I did not think that better than to be ordered by any one person, whose humour and genius might contradict the true policy of the nation. At least, no one course of policy could be continued as is needful, neither in his own time, nor through any succession. I said I thought so too; but still could not consent to such change, because the speculation and practice would vary. And I asked him whether he did not think his council, whenever a number of men should on such account be brought together, would not prove knaves? And unless the council were honest, a single

[1] He was one of the Commissioners of the Great Seal on the accession of William and Mary, 4 March, 1689, when he was knighted.

person with all his faults was better, and easier for the people to deal with. And he never could say to me, that he thought mankind honest enough to promise such a happiness, which was as much as to submit the cause which I believe he and many were well enough satisfied of, but not being in the air of preferment under the present, thought they might expect a gale under a change; the rather supposing themselves to be much the more deserving than such as enjoyed it. And this was all the motive, whatever else hath heen pretended, that drove men to act against the royal family, and to change the succession.

215. The preferments I had in that, or any after time, were inconsiderable. Upon the decease of Sir J. Harmer, I was made the Duke of York's counsel and solicitor, but before I acted, the King, Charles II. died. This was an honour, but no profit.

216. I was, during these three years, (in which I matter not to distingush times) invited by my countrymen in Suffolk to stand for Burgess of Dunwich ;[1] but of this more hereafter.

217. I made myself a piece of a courtier, and commonly on Sundays went to Whitehall, where the great variety of persons coming together always made a diversion ; and I could not pass my time better, because my brother attending to the chapel, we could not dine but as those hours permitted. And when the Court was at Windsor my brother usually went on Saturdays and returned on Monday mornings. And in his company, as also to Hampton Court, sometimes on Thursdays, when the public council was held; but not often, in regard my practice at home found me better diversion.

218. In long vacations we gained some small time to be with the Seal at Wroxton, where we enjoyed much of ease, but that was often invaded by great companies that came to dine with my brother. And once I remember the noble Lord Northampton[2] with near thirty gentlemen came, and as the use was healths at dinner gave me a warmth as

----

[1] He was returned for Dunwich, 28th March, 1685.

[2] GEORGE COMPTON, fourth Earl of Northampton. He was born 18th October, 1664, and therefore can have been hardly more than twenty years old at the time referred to.

much as I ever cared for ; but after dinner in came my old
acquaintance the mayor and aldermen, with the council
of the neighbour corporation of Banbury. And my brother
came out to them and received their compliment, and
having answered and drank to them retired to his better
company, and left them to me in charge to make welcome.
I thought that sack was the business and drunkenness the
end, and the sooner over the better ; so I ordered two
servants to attend us with salvers, glasses, and bottles, and
not to leave us wherever we went. Then I plied them
sitting, standing, walking, in all places with the creatures
(for I walked them all over the house to shew the rooms
and buildings, and sometimes we sat and sometimes stood)
until I had finished the work, took leave, and dismissed
them to their lodgings in ditches homeward bound. But
having had a load at dinner, which made me so valiant in
this attack, and such a surcharge after, it proved not only
a crapula but a surfeit. And I made my way like a
wounded deer to a shady moist place, and laid me down all
on fire as I thought myself upon the ground ; and there
evaporated for four or five hours, and then rose very sick,
and scarce recovered in some days.

219. I never had but once such a rush, and that was
with Mr. Chiffinch [1] at Windsor, who delighted to send his
guests away fox't ; and to finish me (who was not easily
drawn to any degree of good fellowship) he put the King's
drops (an extract of bone) in our wine. I had not very
much, but found it heavy, and that I must have some care
to carry it off steadily, as I did (I think) over the terrace
into the park, and then to the side of the cliff among the
bushes, I laid me down and lay on the ground for six hours.
If anyone saw me or not I know not. My brother jested,
and said he wished the King had walked that way and
found his learned counsel drunk in a bush. This course

---

[1] WILLIAM CHIFFINCH, Clerk of the Closet to King Charles II. The
Lord Keeper called him " Will. Chiffinch, the trusty page of the back
stairs." There is a good note upon him in the *Life of the Lord Keeper*,
§ 316. Roger North speaks there again of Chiffinch drugging his
guests, and of his putting " his master's salutiferous drops (which were
called the King's, *of the nature of Goddard's*) into the glasses." These
drops appear to have been some narcotic which had proceeded from the
laboratory of Dr. Jonathan Goddard.

of taking the ground was not wholesome, as they told
me, together with the stories of some that lost their hearing and some their lives by such frolics; but as I had and
hope to keep a very indifferent opinion of human life, I
regarded no cautions of the kind, but have held me to the
common preservation of God's creatures, appetite, and it
hath not succeeded ill.

220. This may seem trivial stuff, and indeed most is so
which I present, else I should not draw my own picture as
I intend in these papers. But seriously, being so fox't was
no jest with me, for I always hated the custom and extravagance of drinking, and avoided it sedulously. It was
a common jest in our privacies that I should be brought
out and made to do reason, for shirking was in that kind
both my profession and practice; and I had been very unhappy if my friends had lived a sottish life, as some do.
I was much more averse to wine young than elder, for it
grew up with exhaustion and decay of spirits, which youth
seldom is sensible of. And if anything did affect my
perfect ease at my brother's house it was that too much
wine was stirring. This was the age of Tory and Whig,[1]
the former were our friends, and much addicted to the
bottle, the others were not wanting in that, but much exceeded their antagonists in envy, hatred, malice, and all
uncharitableness. So that a reasonable compliance was
necessary to hold up with our party, but no pleasure, but
the contrary to me. I mention this not so much as a
virtue as a felicity; for if I had been propense, as some
are, to wine, I had been an arrant sot, and the little understanding I had would have soon been obfuscated.

221. Next to drink I declined cards and all manner of
play. This was not virtue more than the other, but inclination, for all my bent was upon books and manufactures;
yet as all men will always argue for their foible, I used to
talk in dispraise of play, and for my own habit of gim-
cracking. I grant play conduceth to form and keep steady
men's habits of foreseeing and thinking, and for that reason
is not unuseful in itself, but I used to allege that all employment which left a product of any value was more

[1] See *Life of the Lord Keeper*, § 286 n., and the references there
given.

laudable than such as spent time and nothing of any use came of it. Making of tile pins is an addition to the public of so much riches from the product of men's labours; but after twenty sets at picquet or backgammon the public hath nothing to shew for the loss of such persons' time. This aversion made me careless, and that for most part a loser, when I did join in play, which exaggerated the humour. The game I most liked was the Spanish game l'hombre, and my brother used to observe it to contain much of policy, and to be an emblem of the world.[1] The word signified the Man, supposing some one person is ever exalting himself above his neighbours, who join in opposition to this growing power, to prevent an universal monarchy, and sometimes they overturn him, which is a *qui dillio*, and sometimes he them, which is the same on his side, and often the mutual opposition hath no great effect one way or other, but the public stands in *statu quo prius*, only with some increase of wealth by peace, for which a new game is to be played, and is but the same as before, with new accidents and emergencies of the cards. For mankind is the same, they are a pack of cards, in all ages and countries, and the same or like methods are continually used in managing them, and it resolves into this, that their own errors and caprices shall be steered so as to compass their own subjection, or what men call ruin; like a great ship, whose force crusheth all direct opposition, yet shall be so wound and managed with the tender hands of men that it shall become a mere property, and endure the winds and storms and be shattered, and at length cast away for the sake of their avarice and ambition. This equality is called a repuesta or a reposit. Then the order of the cards is peculiar. The courtiers move steadiest, such are the nobility and gentry, their order is the best first, &c., but the inferior cards vary. The black, which we may call the clergy, follow the same order, so as the deuce is the least, and with the red, which are the rabble, the seven is the least, and the two next the knaves. For it matters not

---

[1] This game has been celebrated by Pope in *The Rape of the Lock*, where the poet describes the course of the game. An elaborate article on "Pope's game of Ombre" appeared in *Macmillan's Magazine* for January, 1874.

for quality with them, the pertest fellow is forwardest though the veriest scum of the company. The middle cards, ten, nine, eight, which are the common owners and tillers of land, are laid aside and put out, as not concerned in the game. The ambitious and the rabble, one subtle and undermining and the other impetuous and overbearing, are the ingredients of all changes in government. The honest husbandman may go on and drudge, he is not much regarded, as he himself regards little but his work and the success of that. Here are the characters next for the person's arms and ammunition employed. First, the sword or soldiery is the most considerable, he that hath that hath one inexpugnable card, which is spadillio, or the ace of spades. Spada in Italian and Spanish is a sword. The next to that is the favourite, and that in most instances is one raised from the dregs of the people. He that is the aggressor meditates his force and arms, and determines how to make his attack, and with what weapons. So the player names the trump, then instantly up starts the least card of that suit, two in black and seven in red, into preferment, next to spadillio, and is called mallillio, I suppose from malleus, a hammer for pounding, battering, or keeping down the enemy. The next to these is basto, the ace of clubs, or bastone, a weapon of correction, which signifies slavery and subjection, very useful to be wielded by all tyrannical governments, for it keeps the people in awe. He that hath these three cards hath the mattadores, or amazzadores, the murderers, and can very hardly be beaten. And then as many more as he hath, that win in succession, are added to the number of the mattadores and gather tribute. But one would think it strange if wives or mistresses should be excluded from this politic game, having ordinarily such considerable influence in the affairs of the world. Here it is considered that feminine influence is not constant and sometimes nothing; it is not a necessary but an accidental spring in the wheel of power, and therefore when the red suit is trump the ace comes in next to basto and is called punto, and hath the honour to be added to the mattadores. Else the red ace hath a share but in the mean between the court and the common people, for it is the best card next the knave. So much for politic l'hombre.

I knew the course of play in most games, but spent no time to master any, being, as I said, no lover, careless, and consequently for the most part a loser, and chose any entertainment, or indeed mere idleness, rather than that.

222. This course of life I led during the time my brother had the Great Seal, mostly in business, and little or no recreation without him, unless in my voyages by water, which I think I have spoken of. And we were at good ease till near the time of King Charles' death, for then the good temper of the Court began to change, and pernicious ministers to gain ground; the honest set of councillors, who laid their heads together and consulted for the establishing the regal power upon the foot of the law, was broken and shattered. This was in Secretary Jenkins' time.[1] Then I remember my brother had good heart, for he was an honest man, with whom he could be free, and it was usual to meet at his office to confer of matters depending, and which way to direct affairs to the best end, and most pure and chaste from the malicious insinuations of the Whig party (new grown into a sort of convict infamy upon those men and times), that arbitrary power was their aim, whereas in truth, their consultations were to keep down arbitrary power as well in the Crown, which was by acting all upon the foot of the law, and also in the Whig party, who aimed at nought else but to exalt themselves into it, which was to be done by a legal opposition. Thus far all was well; afterwards Secretary Jenkins' laid down, the influence of the Duke increased, which necessarily led towards the papal interest, to which my brother was *mordicitus* opposed, but not with a Whig spite to turn his opposition into sour and morose affronts, but with all possible tenderness and honour for the person of the Duke, yet without the least yielding or giving way. The passage of the motion to discharge all convictions at once I have related in his Life, as also the encroachments that Jeffries

[1] SIR LEOLINE JENKINS was made Secretary of State, 11th February, 1680, and superseded 1st May, 1684. Burnet says of him " He was a man of an exemplary life, and considerably learned : but he was dull and slow : he was suspected of leaning to popery, though very unjustly : but he was set on every punctilio of the Church of England to super-stition, and was a great asserter of the divine right of monarchy, and was for carrying the prerogative high . . . ."—vol. ii. 245.

was encouraged to make upon him, and other grievances
of that time, for Halifax, Rochester, &c., were more supple
courtiers than he was, and when the power was sufficient,
as then it appeared, to protect or maintain anything for a
time, they would not, as he did, set themselves against it.
It was time to veer when the wind began to quaver, and,
which was the worst of all, the dregs of Shaftesbury grew
a favourite again. The Lord Sd. (*sic*),[1] who seeing my
brother a rock impregnable, began to wear him out with
affronts and lies tending to vilify him, and did not stick
to say openly, as if he had been an oracle, that the Lord
Keeper was no lawyer; but these matters I omit here, belonging to another place. It is enough to observe that
the clouds began to appear, which hath brought us bad
weather, and are not cleared up yet. Thus it stood when
King Charles fell sick, and died. King James continued the same ministers, and at first gave content to
most people, and it had been well for all had he continued
so to do.

[1] ROBERT SPENCER, Lord Sunderland, one of the Lord Keeper's
most bitter opponents.

CHAPTER XIV.

THE DEATH OF CHARLES II. AND ITS EFFECT UPON THE NORTHS.

I CANNOT pass by the melancholy course of life we had during that sickness. My brother was at Court, and in council almost continually with a parcel of physicians about the regimen of the King in his sickness, and came home always heavy laden in his mind. He foresaw and knew the train of evils to come if the King did not recover, and it darkened his soul to a degree, that I verily believe his spirits took an infection and were poisoned, though not immediately appearing. I had the company of my brother Dudley, than whom a braver soul there never was. We walked about like ghosts, generally to and from Whitehall. We met few persons without passion in their eyes, as we also had. We thought of no concerns, public or private, but were contented to live and breathe as if we had nought else to do but to expect the issue of this grand crisis.

224. At last the King died, and then forthwith the succession was to be proclaimed, and when all were busy about preparing for that, we continued our sailing about Whitehall from place to place, without any conversation but our two selves, and at length we crossed up the banqueting-house stairs, got to the leads a-top, and there laid us down upon the battlements, I mean upon the flat stones over the balustres, expecting the proclamation, which then soon came out, being persons of quality and heralds mounted, who, after drums and trumpets, made the proclamation, the sergeants having performed the Oyes. And we two on the top of the balustres were the first that gave the shout, and signal with our hats for the rest to shout, which was followed sufficiently. And here I had the reflection of the fable of the fly upon the wheel,

we animalcules there fancying we raised all that noise which ascended from below.

225. Now our faces began to clear up and we thought of our affairs. The King was buried privately,[1] and from the Duke's Solicitor I was made the Queen's Solicitor, Herbert[2] being her Attorney General. After his promotion to be Chief Justice, I was made the Queen's Attorney, and sat at her board while the King stayed, and a little after. All these steps were without my making court: my brother obtained them, and I had only to kiss the King and Queen's hands. Jeffries once told me that there were endeavours to put me by, but that he stood my friend, and then ranted at the unreasonableness of the attempt. He might say true for aught I knew, but I was about that time told that he had in other places ranted against the Norths, that nothing could happen or fall but a North was presently to be considerable, as if they had a monopoly of preferment.

226. After I had this charge, and the patents of all the Queen's establishment were to be made out, that is her councillors for management of her revenue, her chancellor, treasurer, secretary, woodward, auditor, surveyor, as well as my own, and my brother the solicitor who was Mr. Oliver Mountagu, I bestirred me to get the forms of the grants, and a sight of some patents of former queens, that matters might come fairly from my hands to the Queen. Mr. Caryl,[3] her secretary, was so kind to bring me the forms, which I took as a singular favour, though I had them. He was a witty and a good man. I sent to the Heralds' Office for a draught of the Queen's achievement, and had it graved on a broad plate with mantling and decorations, and I also caused the Queen's picture to be graved by Mr. White, all which were imprinted on all the Queen's patents, and succeeded extremely well, and my Lord Rochester, her Chancellor, was surprised to see the

---

[1] 14th February, [1685.] "The King was this night very obscurely buried in a vault under Henry the Seventh's Chapel at Westminster, without any manner of pomp . ."—*Evelyn's Diary.*

[2] SIR EDWARD HERBERT. He was made Chief Justice of the King's Bench, 23rd October, 1685.

[3] JOHN CARYLL, titular Lord Caryll. See an excellent account of him in the *Dictionary of National Biography.*

patents come in so good order, without his having been previously troubled about them. The plates I have still by me, and I may keep them as a token of my office, which brought me more honour than gain, for I had but £50 for a salary, and made not above three or four leases, for the Queen's land revenue was only the manor of Dantse, and the 10,000 acres fen land; all the rest the Queen Dowager had in possession. I had an accession by acquaintance and friendship with the Queen's ministers and servants, of whom I may speak afterwards. And I went to Court often as before, but very rarely in my habit to the Queen's Court. The times began to grow sour, all favour leaned towards the Catholics and such as prostituted to that interest. We who were steady to the laws and the Church were worst looked upon, and I could perceive at the King's levee and at the Queen's Court I was looked upon with an evil discouraging eye, which made me forbear. I thought my person was no agreeable object, and it was better court to keep it away. If I had been pert and forward, as in truth I was perfectly otherwise, as being modest and diffident, I might have gone into the closet and told what opinion I had of the King's dispensing power, and have laid up a sure interest for preferment (if it had pleased), as my elder brother attorney Herbert did. But that was not my character, however clear I had been in their interests, I could not have put myself forward, which made me sensible of my incurable unfitness for a Court interest.

227. The chief occurrence in this time wherein I was concerned was the Parliament. I had the opportunity to be elected for the borough of Dunwich, to serve in the Parliament first summoned by King James after his accession to the Crown. It was the interest of the neighbouring gentlemen that chose me and not my own, who never was nor intend to be at the place. But I thought some small sums must be spent among a few poor people there. So I gave £10 at Christmas to the poor, for divers years, and even after I was discarded the Parliament. And this I thought better than to present them with a week's guzzling and drunkenness.

228. In that Parliament, as much a courtier as I was, I

joined with the Church of England, partly to maintain the laws and religion established. I voted with those who were against the Court in the article of the dispensing power. But in the matter of money, which was but a trifle—$\frac{1}{2}d$. per lb. on tobacco, and $\frac{1}{4}d$. on sugar—I was tooth and nail for the King.[1] And I was altogether against the affronting set of men, who had not much power there, but aimed to overturn the Crown, and had shewed by a series of trouble given to it, they meant nothing less, and that nothing would content them which should leave the Crown power to keep its own or peace among others. In short the Parliament, that is a great majority, was unanimous, and I was cordially with them to defend the Crown and the laws.

229. I cannot forbear remarking some things that occurred to my observation there. As how apt the gentlemen of England are to be wheedled and deceived. There was a division of the Court party: some were for all the King's purposes whatever: others were for the Crown, but the laws also. But our friends and relations out of the country look on us who were of the latter sort to be as bad as the worst, and we had no sort of credit with them. Once a motion was for leave to bring in a Bill which should oblige all foreign churches to use the Liturgy, as the French, Dutch, &c.[2] This aimed to get the King to confirm the Liturgy by Act of Parliament, though it was feared, after all, he would not do it. The arguments were

---

[1] This measure was proposed by Sir Dudley North, whom even Macaulay calls " one of the ablest men of his time."—*History of England*, chap. iv.

[2] On Wednesday, 1st July, 1685, a " Bill for a general Naturalization of all *French Protestant Strangers* now residing in England, Wales, Berwick-on-Tweed, and the isles of Guernsey and Jersey, *and such as shall come over within a limited time*, was read a second time." The committee was instructed to prepare a clause " That the Liturgy of the Church of England, now by licence translated into French, shall from henceforth be used in all French Churches and Congregations. And that it be a condition of the naturalization intended by the Bill, that, if any persons thereby naturalized, or their children, shall hereafter go to any other Congregation than where the Liturgy of the Church of England is used . . . . they be from thenceforth deemed Aliens to all intents and purposes . . ."—*Journal of the House of Commons*, vol. ix. p. 755.

plain, and spoke by Sir Thomas Meers. If you indulge one sort of dissenters, how can you blame the Crown indulging another, as Papists for instance, &c. The mere courtiers, as I may call them, all spoke against it, as H. Savill, the Lord Antrim, &c. They had travelled, and knew the Vaudois, Walloons, &c., all to be good Protestants, and so jargoned the word Protestant that the ears of the country gentlemen were tickled, and they divided with them against us; for which we rallied them sufficiently in our private recesses, when they had nothing but ignorance to extenuate the shame of such a mistake.

230. And really it appeared strange to me that the most indifferent of the English gentry were perpetually hunting projects to make their estates richer to themselves without regard to others: some to have wool dear, others corn, and the like. One cannot without the very thing imagine the business that was in all their faces. All this came from their clubs, where those of a country and interest usually met and plotted projects for their private interest. I had at the desire of my neighbours the conduct of a Bill about corn, and carried it through, but some suspecting a trick of the city of London, whose friend (or rather retainer) they took me to be, gave me trouble, which the interested soon removed. But I was so angry as almost to resolve not to meddle any more in such matters, but my friends not being spokesmen, set me upon the part as belonging to my trade. And truly it is a most useful education we have that are bred to speak in public, else we could not, as I did, being young, and bashful in nature, as well as not gifted to public oratory, instantly fall to speaking and managing in a public assembly, where is so much noise and confusion as there often will be.

231. Once upon the Money Bill I was put in the chair of the committee of the whole House.[1] Mr. Finch was absent, which made me, though a novice, called to the service. There was much noise and importunity upon the wording of the questions, which I always took as the Court party worded, and then would be the noise of a bear garden on the other side. But I carried it through, and

[1] This was on the 17th Nov. 1685, when the House " went into committee on supply."—*Commons' Journals, u.s.* p. 759.

was well backed, and though I did not this with so much
art as an old Parliament stager would, yet it pleased the
managers for the Court, who loved to see their measures
advanced, right or wrong. I was for the Bill, and sided
as much as I could with those that promoted it, and had
no ear for those that obstructed and puzzled it, which
made the Court rally and say I was the best chairman
they had, as men will always say of those who serve their
turns.

232. I opposed the Bill against hawkers and pedlars.[1]
I perceived it was brought in by men that solicited for
corporations, who would have no buying or selling out of
their shops, whereas a world of honest dealers in the
country go from house to house, especially with their own
or neighbours' manufactures, and many buy such things
when laid open, as ribbons, gloves, &c., who would not lay
out money at all if it must be sent to a market town; so
it promoted trade and helped poor people, as well buyers
as sellers, with most convenience to each other. I had a
great cry upon me from the corporation members, but that
did not discourage me, but I battled the Bill in every
instance, and at the engrossing and last reading I brought
in a clause to answer the colours of the Bill, (which were
that Scotchmen and vagrant thieves went about spying in
men's houses), that Justices at sessions might licence
housekeepers to travel and sell within ten miles; but this
would not do, my clause was rejected, reasonable as it was,
and the only argument was, this set up a shop of licences;
and Mr. Finch took my part, and rallied very handsomely

---

[1] On the 26th May, 1685, leave was given to bring in a Bill "*against
wandering Scotch pedlars,*" and (2) *another* "against hawkers, pedlars,
and petty chapmen."—*Commons' Journals, u.s.* p. 719. On the 13th
June Sir Jos. Tredenham reported that the committee, having taken
the Bill against pedlars, hawkers, and petty chapmen into consideration,
" had agreed upon several amendments to be made to the Bill; and that
a clause be left out of the Bill." The clause was left out accordingly.—
u.s. p. 731. On the 22nd June "an ingrossed Bill against pedlars,
hawkers, and petty chapmen was read the third time, and an ingrossed
proviso being presented to the House to be added to the Bill; and being
read, it was *Resolved* that the said proviso be rejected." In this form
it appears from the narrative that it was sent up to the Lords and
thrown out by them (*Lords' Journals,* pp. 57, 69) on the 11th November,
after the second reading.

on that subject. But I was not wanting to acquaint the
lords of my acquaintance, and particularly my brother, of
what was coming, who was against it, and the House of
Lords threw it out, which much angered my opponents,
who ascribed more influence in the matter to me than I
was guilty of, though I confess I did all I could within
and without the House to prevent them, and was moved
in it by pure zeal for poor men, and the benefit of ordinary
housekeepers who were to be oppressed by corporations.
But on the other side, I found solicitors for the Bill, even
members who paid fees at the office for all things, as for a
private Bill.

233. I had often been angered at the insinuations
against the lawyers, as if they had no regard to anything
but fees. It was usual for members to say, the lawyer
speaks for his fee. I have expostulated if they knew a
member that did not consider the interest of his own
estate, country, or borough, apart from the good of England. That it was so usually, witness the prohibition of
Irish cattle, and the many projects even then on foot of
like intent. I condemned with them all scent of a fee in
parliament, but it was hard to be so reflected upon at
random, when nothing appeared of it, by those who visibly
promoted their private interests every day. If a lawyer
took a fee to present a petition, it was not so bad as to
give a vote against the public for the sake of a paltry
private advantage to themselves. If the matter be well
weighed, it will be found the former is less corruption and
breach of trust than the latter. It happened that a gentleman of the long robe presented a petition thus:[1] "——
hath a considerable estate, but it is all settled for children,

---

[1] On the 27th May, 1685, on the petition of EDWARD MELLER, ESQ.,
praying leave to bring in a Bill to enable him to sell lands for payment
of his debts, the House divided, and the question being put, the petition
was rejected, the Ayes being 195, the Noes being 218.—*Commons'
Journals*, ix. 721. On the 2nd June Mr. Meller's petition was again
read, and leave was given to bring in the Bill apparently without opposition. On the 6th the Bill was read a second time and referred to a
select committee, of whom Mr. North was one. The Bill was read a
third time and passed on the 13th, and passed by the Lords without
alteration or discussion on the 19th.—*Commons' Journals, u. s.* pp. 725,
730, 735, 742.

so is not able to raise money upon his estate for payment
of his debts, and desires that a bill may be received to
enable him." " What!" said some, " are we here to give
away the children's estates to pay the father's foolish
debts?　No!" and the petition was rejected.　I knew the
person and his circumstances, but nothing of this attempt,
and out of mere respect to him endeavoured to soften the
matter, but it would not do.　Afterward the gentleman
was advised to re-offer his petition, but not by the same
hand.　He came to me and offered a fee (as I guess he had
given the other), desiring I would, having appeared for
him, present it.　I refused his fee, and undertook it with
some civil reproof for his offensive manner in coming with
a fee.　I told the House that the estate was settled upon
children by way of contingent remainder, but he had been
married many years and had no child, and now it was next
to impossible he should have any, and it was the opinion
of all friends, as well his wife's as his own, that it was the
interest of both, and the family in general, that he had
such a power if the House should think fit.　I believe the
story of the fee had been told, which made his friends give
an applause upon the motion, as the use is there, and the
leave was given and the Bill passed.

234.　I remember once a motion was for leave to bring in
a Bill to naturalize all Protestants, and I opposed it extem-
pore, which much surprised the party that set it on foot,
for they did not expect so sudden an opposition.[1]　I
thought that this was a thing of inconceivable consequence: no mortal could foresee the event of a general
naturalization, and it would be a desperate stroke to do it,
of which I saw no need.　I thought if our people were
increased from abroad by an accession of good and labo-
rious men of our own religion, it would be for the public
benefit, but this made no distinction, the scum of all
Europe might come and be officers and jurys and what
not?　If the motion had been for a court to be erected to
naturalize such foreigners as should be found conformable
to our religion and laws; or if the persons were named, so

---

[1] This appears to have been on the 15th June, 1685.　The House,
however, on a division, allowed the Bill to be brought in by 156 to 114.
—*Commons' Journals, u.s.* p. 738.

as an account or record might be of the persons to take
the benefit of the Act, I should be for it; but I did not
think it fit to give out franchises to we knew not who.
Whether this weighed or not I cannot tell; but the matter
went no further, if leave were given, which I do not remember.   I am sure no Bill to that purpose as was moved
was read while I sat.

235. I promoted a Bill for the stopping further divisions
of the fens.   It was found that the dividing the commons
depopulated the fens ; for a house was kept up for the
sake of its right of common, which as soon as an allot-
ment was made of a share to it in severalty was mortgaged,
sold, and let fall, being a charge, and the land better
manageable without it.   In the agitation of this matter
some mistakes were strangely supine.   Sir Wm. Killigrew
had a Bill for the enclosing some fens in Lincolnshire,
which had been offered every session since the restoration
of the late King Charles II., and being a project had been
always rejected, yet constantly brought in, and as an omen
of ill luck commonly towards the latter end of the session,
so it used to be jestingly said " the session is not long-
lived, for Sir Wm. Killigrew's Bill is come in."   Some
members took the Bill to be that, having heard or at least
minded only the words "fen," "inclose," " common," &c.,
and rose up upon it with such fury that we wondered
whence the opposition should come, and it cost us some
time and attention to find out the mistake, but more pains
to correct it.   So the Bill was to be heard a second time.
Then we ourselves found a danger that some persons
might be surprised who had sued decrees for inclosing,
but had them not actually signed by the commissioners,
whereby the Act referring to decrees of the commissioners
might hinder their suing out their decrees.   Wherefore a
proviso was offered to give a time for so doing.   This was
taken to be a trick, and opposed with great earnestness,
as a manifest surprise intended to be put upon those
people.   I endeavoured to satisfy them it was not so intended, but the contrary, for their very sakes, and to prevent a surprise which too large a construction of the
words of the Act might infer, but I was not so happy
to be understood.   And offering to be more explained I

was taken down to order because I had spoken before in
the debate; but Sir Joseph moved I might be heard,
which being granted, I convinced the House, and the proviso was received.[1]　These and many such blundering
passages would make one sick of public business there.
It must be a warm zeal for the common good that must
inspire a good man to act in those walls honestly.　So
many rubs, affronts, and scratches will meet with him as
shall make his heart ache.　Nay, it is strange, considering
how disorderly Bills pass, that common sense comes out.
Everyone offers his conceit for wording clauses, and many
without much attention to the connexion, and others as
supine to let it pass.　But enough of this sorrowful
reflection.

236. It was not long before the rising of the Parliament that a Bill for a register of estates was brought in.[2]
This Bill was much opposed, and particularly by the gentlemen of the gown; and to say truth none else are capable
to make objections, which makes it thought that such are
for the most part against the thing, affixing the reason as
hindering lawsuits.　I am sure I was for the thing, though
not for that Bill, which was open enough to objection, and
I spoke so long and so warm in it that the House thought
fit to order a committee to meet during the recess and to
prepare a Bill upon the debate, and recommended it to
me to take care of it.　I shall not here deliver my model
and reasons, because it is done in part by a late pamphlet
I published upon the subject, and intend more largely to
treat the subject.　But as to the proceeding upon this
order I was sincere, and drew the Bill, prepared abstracts
for my committee; I caused accounts to be sent me from
Holland, Scotland, and France; I had an account of the
registration in our fens, that I might be instructed in all
the models of that kind considerable in Europe.　Towards
the meeting of the Parliament the second time I had my

---

[1] The allusion is probably to a Bill for repealing a clause in an Act
for draining the Bedford Level.　The Bill was passed 15th June, 1685.
It was resolved that the Title of the Bill should be "An Act for repealing a Clause for dividing of Commons," &c.—*Commons' Journals,*
u.s. p. 737.

[2] *Commons' Journals, u.s.* p. 752.

tackling all ready, and met my committee, who were all able Parliament men and very affectionate, as I thought, to the cause. But (oh wonder!) not one would meddle with the matter: they would not hear the Bill read, nor look upon an abstract, but were all full of fears and jealousies of I knew not what. So that I could not then imagine what had fixed my committee; but I put up my papers and drank my glass, and so we parted. Afterwards I was told the secret, that they had it insinuated amongst them that the King must name the officers, who would be popishly affected (at least), and so the Papists would have an account of all the estates of England. This poisoned the best design that ever was advanced for the establishment of English titles, and so fare it well. I did my best, and hope I shall never want the aid of such law, and let posterity reflect what advantage might have been to them from it if their predecessors would have suffered it to pass. I am sure they owe little to them for letting the motion fall upon an imaginary, and that but temporary, and (as I say and affirm) vainly supposed evil consequence.[1]

237. I think it was during this recess that the coronation of the King was, and that (to me) fatal sickness of my brother happened. It was told me one morning that he was dangerously ill, so I went immediately to see him. As soon as I came he asked what I thought now, if he were sick or not? For I used to rally his complaints, he being much solicitous and full of fancies about his health, and I that had a better constitution used to make slight of them; but this it seems was in earnest. His head was wounded, or rather worn out by care and thinking, and there lay his pain. I was too full to speak. Words are like crowds that too much hinders the issue of any, *ingentes stupent.* So I sat upon his bed. He had an honest faithful physician, Dr. Masters, bred under Willis, but not so happy as to be a favourite of the town. He was a plain man nurse, and that is all I care for in a physician. He had the most friendly phrase of a doctor: " Stay, let us see how it will work. So did no great matter, only

---

[1] On this subject see *Life of the Lord Keeper,* § 160.

brought Mr. Wiseman to let him blood, which did not amiss. His illness continuing, Sir Wm. Soames brought in Dr. Short, saying it was not fit to trust a person of this consequence with one physician, and he said it was not fit to trust him with a fever. So the cortex was administered, and that took him out of his bed, and he seemed in a way of recovery ; and if he had thrown off the cursed Seal it might have proceeded. He sent about it, but Lord Rochester overruled him, and made him keep it. His ardour to his duty was such that he would go out to the Court of Claims, and to the Parliament afterwards, though he looked like death, and was wonderfully dispirited. At nights he used to drink strong ale and wine, thinking to repair his spirits that way. But it did but exasperate a lurking ember or seminal of a fever he had in him. The cortex had suppressed the ferment but not overcome the venom at last that grew up and was too strong for it. And no means the doctors could use would touch his distemper in the least, when and no sooner they advised his recess into the country to try the waters. He concluded he went to his grave, and had scarce hopes of life. He often lamented his load, the Seal, and declared he had never kept it so long but for the sake of his friends. I begged of him not to consider me, who had the greatest share, but to throw it from him. I had enough to live better than ever I hoped, or had reason to pretend to. I shall dwell no longer upon this dreary history, having enlarged it in proper place. In short, at Wroxtou my brother died, and with him all my life, hope, and joys. Only some share was left to keep me from despair in the remainder of my brother Dudley, who was a most incomparable friend and companion, with him I grew into close alliance and friendship, which continued untainted to his death.

238. My brother the Keeper, in his sickness at Wroxton, took his will into his thoughts, which he had by him, and no wise man can be without one ; but he was of opinion it was not so well united and compact as became him to leave, for it consisted of a will and three or four codicils, therefore he gave them all to me with charge to compose them all into one body, and to make up an orderly will

containing the sense of them, which I did, and prepared it with my own hand for his sealing. But finding him weak, I thought the sheets were too many, and retired with my brother Dudley, who reading, I transcribed it in a shorter time than I could have imagined, and so with much ado he subscribed and published it.

CHAPTER XV.

THE AFFAIRS OF SIR PETER LELY.[1]

IT was during my brother's life that I had devolved upon me a trust and executorship of Sir Peter Lely. It seems my brother and he were great friends, and fell into a way of commuting faculties, whereupon my brother advised him about his estate and settlements, and he made pictures for my brother gratis, of which my own and my uncle Jno. North's I still have are two, and I think valuable as any he left. I will not change for some I had seen of Vandyke, no, barring relation. It was happy for Sir Peter's son that this acquaintance was, for Sir Peter was averse to business, and loathly drawn to do anything but paint. I was ever his counsel at sealing the writings of his purchase of Dallyton, which (as usual) was a tedious attendance, and many emerging scruples must be considered and appeased, all which to him was a torture, and he came to me and said "For God's sake let me be cheated so I am but cheated quickly."

240. This makes me reflect how arts and business are like contraries, and will not consist *in eodem subjecto.* An art fills a man's life and thought, and he can no more endure business than a man of business can endure the minute phantasms of an artist. Therefore we are to blame when we expect artists should be adroit in the affairs of the world at large, that a scholar should be well bred, and many other such expectations, be they what they pretend; in all things else ignorance is their foil and becomes them.

241. Sir Peter Lely married his wife after her children were born, so although legitimate by the canon law were not so by the law of England, whereby all his estate, real and personal, without settlement were made, devolved to

[1] Sir Peter Lely's Will is to be found in the Collection of Wills published by the Camden Soc., 1863.

the Crown, and had been a prey of the courtiers. This I found would have happened, for one small estate he left which was copyhold of the manor of Richmond at Kew Green. This did not fall under his settlement, and Sir A. Apsley begged it of the Duke of York. Although I was his solicitor and my brother Keeper of the Great Seal, we had both much ado to get the Duke's grant of this, and at last he gave it me as a boon from him, and I might have kept it to myself, but I always intended it, and so gave it to his son Mr. Lely, who at this day enjoys and lives in it.[1] Sir Peter gat his settlement perfect before he died, but not long. However, we were clear his will was perfect, but no codicil as was intended. We, that is myself, Dr. Stokeham, and Mr. Hugh May, were executors and guardians of his children, a son and a daughter. Those were provided by the will, and a legacy given to his relations in Holland, but all his hang-bys disappointed of their legacies, for we found the instructions or shell of a codicil my brother had given him, but none was ever made, so no small legacies went out.

242. Mr. May and Dr. Stokeham were honest, just, and friendly men, but fitter to consult and advise than to handle business effectually; that lay all upon me. For divers weeks after his death we met at his house, about disposing the estate and managing it to the best advantage. We made no secret of anything. All that had been friends to him in his lifetime had access to us whenever we met to stay or go as they pleased, and being there to advise or interpose as their conceit was, whether painters or others, we took all in good part, and were glad to hear anyone's suggestion how best to manage our affairs. For we intended nought to ourselves but to improve what we could for the heir. Our conduct was such that we had much credit from it, as Sir Peter's business and curiosities were much known and discoursed of; and whether flatteringly or not I know not, but I had been often told by Sir Peter's most considerable friends that they never heard of a trust duly executed but that. I am sure if it was not so, the fault was none of mine, for I was young and vegete,

---

[1] See more about this business in *Life of the Lord Keeper*, § 4 12.

and as such fond of business, though such as since I find
by experience more wisely declined than embraced. But here
I plunged into it and conducted it to the best of my ability
and skill for the greatest improvement it would admit.

243. The state of it was thus: there were legacies to
near £5,500, and debts of near £3,000, so that in the
whole there was near £9,000 to be raised, besides main-
taining the heir. All we had to do it with was the household stuff, pictures, drawings, and utensils of painting,
besides the house at Covent Garden, not worth above £40
per annum above rent, and the Lincolnshire estate that
yielded about £800 per annum. The pictures and curiosities were the main fund we hoped to raise money by. If
that failed, as might well happen in things of mere gaiety
and humour, we were confounded. Here was our care.
The method we took was first to have inventories of all,
and particularly the pictures. I sealed all the originals,
and the pictures of the collection, and I caused the best
artists in town to value them, such as were of his own
painting, with respect to his prices, and the defects of
finishing. We put into the house Mr. Sonnius his friend,
that knew most of his concerns, with orders to let all
comers see the pictures. And such as were finished or
unfinished might be taken away, paying the inventory
price, and discounting antecedent payments where any
were, and for ascertaining them we took affidavits, so also
for other cases of claims that had not clear evidence. As
to the drawings and prints, I sealed them up, and kept
the keys also. The collection of pictures remained in the
house, exposed to view. Thus we ordered matters while
we cleared the house of trumpery, which was the furniture. As to that, we took peoples' offers in writing, and
exposed it if none bid more in a week or fortnight. So
we got rid of the chief, and the rest Mr. Sonnius sold as
he might. As to the utensils of painting, I caused notice
to be given to all the painters and colour sellers to come
in at a time, and there set them to work among themselves, to sell all such things to the best bidder, and they
were so earnest as to give prices beyond the shops, at least
the utmost value was raised.

244. Next I entered upon consideration of the collection

of prime pictures, how to dispose of that nice and critical part of our trusted estate. I at once formed a lottery, valuing the whole at £5,000, and distributed into a thousand lots, at £5 per lot, without blanks. This would not then take (however, of late lotteries have grown into fashion), the reason given was, that they valued their choice, and cared not for anything chance should throw upon them. The missing this drove us to an outcry, for we could not stay long, for want of supplies to pay our debts and great legacies. I made the lists of the pictures, with the authors' names, and dimensions. I caused them to be sent into Holland, France, and Italy, and at Easter opened the sale, and all along made this declaration, that nothing was exposed but what Sir P. Lely left without alteration, and nothing subtracted, but the whole laid before them, and without any false bidding. We had parted out a place with chairs for quality, the rest of the ordinance was a table and forms. The managers were Sonnius, Lankrink, Walton, and Thompson the crier, and in four days we finished our work, and sold for above £6,000, which was a success to our content.

245. But to leave this discourse of trusts with one mark only, viz., that it is a pity as well as a mortification to an honest man to meddle with them. One may (nay indeed must) lose, and cannot honestly gain—gratitude at the end not to be expected, but the contrary, raking suits to be feared. And as friends to fools are hated, so trustees to their wards, if not hated yet suspected and avoided, and the debt charged on their virtue; for the good done them is an incumbrance to their minds, and a knave's flattery better music than a true good guardian's counsel. We must, as debtors to humanity, pay to allied friends, in the persons of their orphans and widows, this duty, else the world would be worse than savage, and take the reward in merit and the comfort of doing well; and surely if there be any merit to be obtained on earth, the honest and careful accomplishment of this duty is the price of it.

246. Thus far I acted in the trust during my brother's life, all which time I looked upon myself to be in my minority, having scarce a character in the world of my

own, but supposed to act wholly by my brother's measures: I might bear the censure of my failings, but I had little credit by my regular courses, because ascribed to him and not to me. But after his death I was turned up to shift in the world as well as I could; and this I make another great crisis of my life, for from henceforward all my actions were both really and in appearance my own. It is true I had the conversation and friendship of my brother Dudley, which was the comfort of my life, indeed, all I had then left, or hoped for, till my brother Montagu arrived from Turkey. But for matter of our government we advised each other, and were mutually assistant, but he knew as little of my trade as I did of his, so each answered for himself.

247. Upon the death of my brother we (being executors and guardians, but M. N.[1] absent) took order about his interment, and then posted to Windsor to the King, attended by the officers, to carry and deliver up the accursed Seal to the right owner. We arrived late at Windsor the second day, and were carried unto the King, who was in cabinet council. He seemed surprised at the death of the Lord Keeper, and took the Seal and dismissed us. And we returned back with all the speed we could to Wroxton, and there we found a letter from Mr. Jno. Cary of Stanwell[2] to his deceased friend, my brother. We opening it found the contents to be an invitation to him to send his son forthwith to be married to his niece, Mistress Willoughby. For he expected death every day, and therefore urged dispatch, little thinking his friend was gone before. This was laid by, having other affairs, and no answer was given, supposing the news of my brother's death would be an answer.

248. Now were we engulfed in a most heavy and important trust, the breeding of my Lord Guilford, his brother, and sister, all orphans; and the management of a considerable real and personal estate.[3] My brother Dudley was an ex-

---

[1] Montagu North.

[2] He was of the Falkland family, and Master of the Buckhounds under Charles II. He was the second husband of Mary, third daughter of Sir Charles Montagu, widow of Sir Edward Byshe of Stanstead, co. Essex, and sister of Anne, Lady North, mother of the Lord Keeper.

[3] LORD GUILFORD left behind him two sons and a daughter: (i)

traordinary manager and accountant, which made the business lighter upon me than otherwise it had been, and he lived to perform the most troublesome part, the beginning and methodizing the whole affair. I shall have occasion afterwards to discourse incidents in this trust, which I postpone at present, and come to my private affairs.

249. After we came to London, we were to wait on the Lord Jeffries, who had the Seal, to congratulate and offer him all the service we could do, and to receive his commands touching the house in Queen Street, where the Lord Keeper lived, and it was so proceeded that he took the house. But I had such holy water from him, such elaborate speeches of encouragement, as I never hope to, or rather hope never to hear again. There was no service he could do me but he would lose his sleep, and run at all hours to do it, I had, said he, lost a brother, but found a friend, with very much *ejusdem farinæ*. I did not much weigh nor slight his good words ; I concluded I must be no longer favourite, but stand on my own legs. I had a post of honour in the Court, Queen's Attorney, which would hold me above contempt, and in sequel I found my practice much better than I expected, which continued tolerably well for divers years. At length he began to bear so hard upon me, that it declined so much as to be scarce worth my attendance ; however, I used the Court until the Revolution, since which I have forborne. The first onset he made was a formal rating, and to a degree, as such who knew not his way, would have concluded him mad. It was less extraordinary, because my fellows round about had most of them had their turns, and the rest expected it, so we used to jest while he was rating—Now it is mine, yours will be next, and it not seldom happened so. After all the taunts he could think of to give, he concluded that I thought I had the monopoly of understanding. I never was of that opinion ; however it was not manners to contradict his lordship, but this took off my assurance ever after with him, and I was often sorry to find my clients suffer, as I thought many did for my sake, all which made me in-

Francis, born 14th December, 1673, who succeeded him in the title and estates ; (ii) Charles, who died unmarried ; (iii) Anne, who also died unmarried.

different in my practice, and almost weary of the court;
but however, as I said, I jogged on while my service
lasted.

250. It was a new thing to me to have no house to repair
to, to eat and drink and with friends to be free and merry
as formerly, but to put my servants to board wages, horses
to livery, and myself shift with or without company as
I could. And company being seldom of my strain, but
such as drank and spent high in eating. I was not cove-
tous, but so parsimonious as to think 10*d*., 12*d*., or more at a
meal extravagant, and the wine after dinner and at night
was fastidious to me. Besides I had been much worn in my
brother's time, and thought I was not so strong as formerly.
For I used to be up early and late and perpetually intent,
so that had I not used to take a refreshing nap after dinner,
I believe I could not have held out. And I thought I was
most sensibly impaired in my constitution, all which, with
the disorder of my servants and horses, made me meditate
taking a house. I thought my pocket expenses in a loose
way of living would bear, as it did, the better part of the
charge. Upon this I took into my hands Sir Peter Lely's
house in Covent Garden, and lived there by myself divers
years. Many of my friends wondered I would be at the
charge to pay a rent, &c., that had chambers in the Temple
to my own wish, and might have lived apart as others have
done with much more ease and thrift. These knew not,
and I as little cared to make known to them my reasons.
I kept myself by it in order, and had my servants all
together about me. I was of a disposition to bear my own
company, which everyone cannot. I was more happy by
myself with one dish alone than with any company except
my brother, whatever the feast was. I spent most of my
time, as well at meals as in my chamber, alone. I had no
tormenting thoughts to drive me from myself. My misfor-
tunes were past my power to foresee, prevent, or cure ; and
such never gave me a pang. I feared nothing but my own
doubts and failing and the consequences of my own actions.
Besides, I had in all the course of my life, as I think I observed, prepared myself for solitude. I was a pretender to
philosophy, music, mechanics, and study. I had a sound
head to bear long puzzling about anything, whether writing

or drawing, or ought else of minute inspection; and as for writing, I am not at more ease in any posture, nor is my mind less distract or discomposed than in the exercise of that. Whatever the subject or the occasion be, I had rather write than speak.

251. This hath made me particularly reflect on many of my friends and acquaintance to whom writing hath been the most uneasy exercise they could undertake, and although accustomed and habituated, yet they decline it. Others, as for instance my brothers, the Lord Keeper and Dudley, had a like disposition and perseverance as myself, though I think I could have tired them both. The practice of writing is extraordinary useful, for it creates a dexterity in good order and orthography, and which is more, breeds a style, it makes composition easy. These things are wonderfully hard to persons of the best will and however replete with matter, for want of exercise, that furnisheth a ready supply of expletive and connecting clauses, and makes out of scraps such as gold dust a comely and intelligible vessel. This is perceived by divers who have good sagacity in business, but can neither speak nor write. They persuade themselves with effective and sound oratory (if I may give that name to silent deliberation) who cannot persuade another, nor in any way present the reasons which guide them. Others there are who are ready at censure and repartee who cannot lay two reasons together, much less write their mind in any method or coherence. Others are used to the practique of business, and will examine, order, approve, blame, and act in multifarious negotiations that have neither gusto nor grace in speaking deliberately to a company, or writing, and yet, to give them their due, they are more fit for their business than others greater formalizers; for speaking they are understood, however vulgar their words and manner is, and in writing they keep to the business and nothing else. And that is the substantial part which outweighs all other embellishments.

252. On the other side, that which is with some a felicity, as loving to write or to speak orderly, with many proves a failing, and of a ridiculous kind that is empty wordiness. A readiness of words wheedles one to an

excess of complaisance to it, and to neglect the material part, which many look first after, for we think the jargon, when apt and clever, serves the turn, whereas the other extreme, want or difficulty of words, makes men attend the matter, and strive by quintessence of that to supply their defect of clever expression. This instance we had in the Chancellor Nottingham, who had so great a talent of speaking and expression, that however exquisite his judgment otherwise was, it had not force to contain the other within bounds; but a handsome turn of expression must out, whether material or not, which gave him a character of a trifler, that he did not so much deserve. But his failing that way had a good effect upon his son, Mr. H. Finch, whose felicity of expression was equal to, if not exceeding his father's; but he managed it with judgment, and did not shew himself an impotent slave to his fancy. But it is time to cease this subject; enough is past of writing to shew it is not uneasy, but a pleasure to sit, as I now do, passing the pen from side to side of the paper.

253. My solitude was very much increased by my being a housekeeper, for every evening I went from my chamber to my house, which was a change of scene as diverting to me as others going into company, for I had my trinkets then to play with, as for instance music, which was a very great entertainment to me, nor more by the practice than writing ever into books such as I could collect and thought good. This I did for most part in score, and constantly examined as I went along, and so both wrote true, and I also acquired the knowledge of it *au fond*, and enabled myself to play with perfect readiness and ease upon those instruments I best commanded; but also to compose with elegancy of harmony such as the best masters used, and is to be found in perfection in the Italian concertos and recitatives, and to my own thinking I had got up in this skill equal, if not superior, to most of our English masters, else I had not pretended to write so boldly as I have done on that subject.

254. This solitude also enabled me to proceed in the execution of another part of Sir Peter Lely's trust, the selling of his collection of prints and drawings, and in

order to it, I got a stamp, **P. L.**, and with a little printing ink, I stamped every individual paper, and not only that, but having digested them into books and parcels, such as we called portfolios, and marked the portfolios alphabetically, **AA., AB.**, &c., then **Aa., Ab., Cc.**, then **Ca., Cb., Cc.**, &c., so consuming four alphabets. I marked on every cartoon and drawing the letter of the book, and number of the paper in that book, so that if they had been all shuffled together, I could have separated them again into perfect order as at first; and then I made lists of each book, and described every print and drawing, with its mark and number, the particulars of all which were near ten thousand. And this I could never have done if I had not condemned myself to this solitude, in which it was so far from being a pain or labour, that it was a very great pleasure to me.

255. And having completed this work I instituted another public auction, and dispatched it in the house, when also I caused the drawings to be exposed for a fortnight. And at this sale in eight days I raised above £2,400. But then the buyers began to be clogged with the quantity, and could not well digest any more, so I interrupted the sale, intending to continue it next year for the rest, which were half, though not the better, but this wonderful Revolution came and hindered me.

256. It was wonderful to see with what earnestness people attended this sale. One would have thought bread was exposed in a famine. Those that bought laid down their guineas, which a receiver immediately fingered, ten, twenty, thirty, &c., and gat their papers up, well covered with a sort of soft paper we had in plenty for them, and put them either in their bosoms or very close and near them. I remember an Italian with whom *sangue* and *dinari* are equally sacred, seeing this, burst forth, "*Par Dio, io non so che fanno.*"

257. I made the same profession here as at the former sale, that it should be perfectly candid, without addition, subtraction, or false bidding. I remember a lord, now a duke, said, "Damn me, what care I whether the owner bids or not as long as I can tell whether I will buy, and for what." But I answered that since we had made that de-

claration I thought myself bound to hold to it. Another
lord, finding one of our managers, Mr. Sonnius, old and
touchy, took a fancy to fret him, which I did not like, because he had foreign commissions, and much depended on
him. This made me stand up and beg his Lordship to re-
prehend me if anything was amiss; for it was my doing,
and not his, that was but an agent, and followed orders. I
thought our heat would have gone on, but some more prudent interposed and turned the matter into jest. I shall
give one only instance to shew the prodigious value set
upon some of those papers. There was half a sheet that
Raphael had drawn upon with umber and white, that we
called washed and heightened: a tumult of a Roman
soldiery, and Cæsar upon a *suggestum* with officers appeasing them. This was rallied at first, and some said 6*d*.,
knowing what it would come to; but then £10, £30, £50,
and my quarrelsome lord bid £70, and Sonnius £100 for
it, and had it. The lord held up his eyes and hands to
heaven, and prayed to God he might never eat bread
cheaper. There is no play, spectacle, shew, or entertainment
that ever I saw where people's souls were so engaged in expectation and surprise as at the sale of that drawing.
Some painters said they would go a hundred miles to see
such another. Whereby one may perceive how much
opinion is predominant in the estimate of things. If all
the good and evil in the world that depend on mere fancy
and opinion were retrenched, little business would be left
for mankind to be diverted with; but Providence hath so
ordered it that as children they shall not want baubles to
pass their time innocently with. And really the comparison
is too egregious to be passed by here; I must add that in
nature there is no difference between the baubles of children, such as babies' carts, &c., and the furniture, coaches,
and habits of men and women, only the latter is tied to
usefulness. As a coach is a good thing, but whether lined
with velvet or cloth, or so fashioned or carved; and the
like of china, pictures, and a world of other gaities the
mode authenticates to be played with, are all mere human
baubles and playthings. I do not either blame or despise
this, but addict myself as much to them as anyone living,
but not in the common way. For I heed not my dress, but

love dearly a picture: I care not for a feast or for a ball, but a music meeting is a sure trap to me. I would go five hundred miles for a new discovery of nature such as the Torricellian, but I would not give sixpence to see an entry of an ambassador. And if I have any happiness I think it is that I can play and trifle away my time by self. And so for the rest of mankind, if they can be pleased with reputable baubles, and not hurt themselves, it is well; but they mostly affect knives or scissors, that will wound and make bleed their estates and families, and by so playing with edge vanities bring the harmless innocent toys of the world into discredit.

258. To give a short account of the nature of these curiosities, with half of which I raised so much money. They consisted of drawings and prints: the former were more esteemed, because there could be but one true: the prints might be many from the same plate. When painting was in its growth towards perfection, which was in the height of Rome's greatness and power, after the emperor and all earthly princes were subjugated to the spiritual dominion, then the popes, cardinals, and princes of Italy fell to building of magnificent churches, chapels, and palaces, in which they spared for no cost. And this bred an emulation among painters, everyone if possible to exceed the rest, for what industry will not encouragement raise up? And the art not being elevated to a high level, with the utmost reach of human capacity, they found they advanced, which makes endeavours much more ardent than when men with all their labour can scarce hope to arrive at the pitch of those who went before. Then they flag and sink. Despair is the death of industry, as hope and dawning of success is the life of it. Thus it fell out, as for instance when any altar was to be adorned, the painters were made acquainted with the desire of the padrone, and he that happened to please by a design had the employment. Thereupon many would make models, some more and some less perfect, and try their ideas upon paper with black or red chalk, the pencil and wash, or with the pen, and perhaps lay it by, and go another way to work, and to show his eminence there would be a perfect model, heightened and shadowed in perfection; all the rest of the papers lay by,

and whatever else he had scratched or done by way of essay or model, either for study or caprice, and sometimes perhaps half drunk; as also memorandum scratches or draughts by way of copy after some antique relievos or other admired paintings, all lay by in his boxes, not much esteemed by him or any else but scholars, who kept themselves in draught from them.

259. These drawings are observed to have more of the spirit and force of art than finished paintings, for they come from either flow of fancy or depth of study, whereas all this or great part is wiped out with the pencil, and acquires somewhat more heavy, than is in the drawings. These were not much esteemed in England until Nicholas Laniere was employed by Charles I. to go abroad and buy pictures, which he loved. He used to contract for a piece, and at same time agree to have a good parcel of waste paper drawings, that had been collected, but not much esteemed, for himself. This and the Arundel collection were the first in England, and of them Lely had a good share. The matter of prints is very nice, for such as come off the same plate shall be decuple the value of others. And this is by the earliness of the stamp before the plate is worn, for with often printing the delicacy of the graver will wear off, and the fine hatches become united by points or breaches in the white threads that part the black; but above all, a proof print is most esteemed, which is an impression before the plate is finished, done for the satisfaction of the graver, who perhaps while he is at work will often roll off a sheet to see how the draught proves, that he may mend or alter if he sees cause. And these proof prints are known by some unfinished part that appears.

260. There is a sort of antique graving which is much more esteemed than any modern, and it is of the ages contemporary with the great masters, as Buonaçono, M. Antonio, &c. These graved after Raphael and others' painting. One would think that the French graving much excelled it, for it seems neater, and the strokes pure and parallel; the others were confused. But artists say those antique stamps are correct as to the draught, and so have an unknown excellence, besides, the graving hath more of

the pencil, whereby a student is more assisted by them than any of the moderns. It is certain some of those antiques sold for £10 and £12 apiece, and all Le Brun's great stamps came not to half the money, and the finest French prints could not reach to a crown apiece.

261. There is a mystery attends all sorts of picture trade, whereby the ignorant are often surprised, and that is copying. The masters will guess it very perfectly, but it is extreme difficult for virtuosos at large to find it out. In paintings it is more discoverable, because a noble design ill performed, as when the painting and colouring is not adequate to the mastery of the draught, it is a copy. A scholar will copy good pictures and hold the design, but not reach the colouring. But a good master will hardly copy a picture not well done. But artists go farther, and by the working of the pencil or the grain and manner of laying the colour, which they call the handling, will know a copy from an original. This they have by much acquaintance with pictures. Some men's handling is so peculiar that every one knows it, as Bassano, Rubens, who for that reason are called mannerists; other are more difficult, as Titian, Paulo, &c. And the scratches and drawings shall be copied so wonderful exactly, that even masters shall be deceived. And this is so frequently done, that one runs a risk that buys a drawing, if he be not very careful. This aptness to be copied deprecates drawings much; but the masters will seem to be very much assured of copies and originals, and will turn up the nose at some, and say that others as originals stare you in the face. It is certain they know much in their own trade. The variety of masters, to whom drawings are ascribed, is much greater than those of pictures, as the number of drawings passing about is infinitely greater than of pictures. And considering the multitude of painters and really great masters that have been in Italy, whose names are scarce known, but probably were the authors of very many of these drawings, it is pleasant to see the confidence of the masters in christening drawings. They have a list, as Giulio, Paulo, Raphael, Titian, &c., and because the drawings of these men have been seen, all that have any resemblance with them are fathered accordingly, and a value set, as their work. One

would scarce think that prints should be copied, but it is so.
Many plates that have been lost, and the stamps from
them grown scarce, have been copied in graving other
plates very curiously, but so far short in imitation of that
kind from the original pattern, that a small acquaintance
with prints will discover it.   Another disguise prints have,
which they call touched up, and is when a plate with many
stamps is worn and its delicacy taken off, some graver will
pass his tool lightly over all the strokes, and give them a
little briskness or sharpening.   This is harder to discern,
but I found that printmongers soon discovered it.

262. I have engaged myself in the rehearsal of some passages relating to this trust of Sir Peter Lely's estate, I shall
proceed and finish all I have to remember concerning it,
which may be as material for information of others in regard
to such trusts, as I have to shew of any sort.

It consisted of two parts ; firstly, the estate ; secondly,
the son and daughter.   The latter I shall come to.
As to the estate, I have dispatched most, and it only
remains to tell that scraping all these matters together, I
had got about £5,000 together, besides all charges and
payments.   And about the time of the heir coming of
age, I thought it best not to leave a sum of money for
him to waste, but to lay it out in land.   And I did accordingly agree with one Dr. Constable, for about £300
per annum, near the estate in Lincolnshire, and settled it
according to the will, which made all just on that side, and
I applauded myself for so doing : the reason will appear
anon.

263. As for the sister, there was not much employ with
her, because Mistress May, a niece of my co-executor, Mr.
Hugh May, and married sometime since to Mr. Coel, was
pleased to let her live with her, and I paid £50 for her
board, and about as much for her clothes.   And so she
whiled away her time till she came of age, and then was
pleased to come to London and settle herself at a boarding
house, where one Mr. Frowd, a younger brother, came acquainted with her, and gained his point to marry her.   All
I desired was (for she declared against counsel in the case),
that she would give me leave to settle her own fortune for
a provision for her and her children.   And so far she com-

plied, and her principal portion, £3,000, was settled, but £500 that we had increased for her was sunk in her match. It fell out she died in childbed of her first child, and not long after the child died, so our trust settlement, money, charge, and friend, all went away *in fumo*.

264. The son was a comely boy, but much given to mean company. I introduced him at my brother's to be a companion to his son, the new Lord Guilford, and there he passed some time; but some of his bad language and habits, picked up among his poor acquaintance, made him unfit to be continued there. And we found him so extremely addicted to be wild about the streets, and to be with sad ragged youths of his acquaintance, and having no friend's house to entertain him in, we found it necessary to send him abroad. Whereupon we contracted with a governor, one Genault, a Gascon, recommended by Sir Jno. Knatchbull. He was to have £80 per annum, and not to exceed £400 per annum expenses for all charges. For this we made him article and seal, and further provided in his articles that if he exceeded it should be paid out of his own purse. This was extraordinary, but we found it useful, for however hard it were to have taken the advantage and made the governor pay, yet it kept him in awe so as they did not exceed, a thing it is scarce possible to keep young men from in travel.

265. Now I am to shew a strange sort of treachery, for from the first moment we entertained this governor he contracted with Sir Jno. Knatchbull for matching him to one of his daughters, and under this engagement he passed all the time of travel, and enjoyed the hopes of his premio, which was to be £300. But that which was most extraordinary was towards the latter end of his travel, when they were in Flanders, he brought him over into England to see his mistress, and some say married, but very probably affianced her, and took him back to Flanders, and all a secret to us that were his guardians, who knew nothing of his intrigue coming or going.

266. But such is the world, an umbrage of this had escaped either from their own or some servant's blurting out hints, so that a rumour spread itself in Flanders and Holland, and from thence came to us, that Genault was

going to marry his charge to a sooterkin, as they call
a Dutch woman, and all that wished well to Mr. Lely im-
portuned us to send and prevent it.   Upon this I sealed a
revocation of the authority he had by his articles, and
dispatched Mr. Widdrington with it to find out Mr. Lely
and bring him away, and armed him with such notarial
acts as were necessary to support him in courts of foreign
justice.   But Genault having notice of this, to prevent the
disgrace, brought him over before Widdrington found him
out, so his voyage was *incassum*.   After he came home we
took what care was fit for his expenses and to supply him
out of his moneys from time to time, all which he desired
might be sent him in gold or crown pieces ; for I charged
my man to make him tell over all he received, to give him
a notion of the quantity.   For when young men talk
of money, forty hath no more letters than twenty, but
they find telling what the money is.   Thus supine are
young men that nothing but necessity will engage them to
any exercise or practique of what is good for themselves.
His next expedition was to Bury St. Edmund's, to visit his
sister, and as the fop-way of that place is, shewed himself
in all his *beaux airs* at church, and so was the subject of all
the afternoon visits to be canvassed and read upon.   One
lady was asked her opinion of him, which she delivered
sententiously that one might just discern he had travelled.
So great judges are the belles of that place what education
and behaviour ought to be.   It might save the nation much
money by sending all the youth thither, and not to Italy
and France, if the exquisite sense and breeding of that
place were but understood.

267. After his return to London the sequel soon brought
into my cognizance what a subtle plan was composed and
to be exercised in order to bring me into this business of
the match, with a salvo for the honour of Sir John ; because it did not sound well for one of his senatorian character to appear in such a practice as this was, and to marry
his daughter to a minor without the guardians' consent.
So Mr. Lely was despatched to me, and he told me he was
desirous to marry and settle himself, and that he had
a good liking for one of Sir Jno. Knatchbull's daughters.
He said he supposed there would be a competent fortune,

though not so much as possibly he might have elsewhere ; but he liked the lady, and was contented with what she had. And he thereupon desired me to treat with Sir Jno. Knatchbull for him about the settlements. This it seems was thought more necessary to come by me, for he wanted about six months of age, and agreements would not be so firm to be made good in Chancery, without the guardians' joining. I, poor ignoramus, thought the man in earnest, and knew no harm in the thing, answered in conformity, and went about the business. I told Mr. Lely that I did not oppose his choice, nor objected to the exility of the fortune, because he might have a better, and settlements being proportionate, he liking the lady, I wished him success and joy.

268. I have often reflected on the pleasure men have in a trick, as I perceived Sir John had in finding his train take, for he put on all the show of surprise at the overture (though started by himself) as if it were news ; and much of doubt and difficulty he made concerning Mr. Lely's character and estate ; what a hazard it is to match a daughter with a person so young, &c., but knowing his governor in travel, who had given him a fair account, if his daughter liked it, and we could agree, he would not be against the match ; but for this I was forced to go twice, it was too much to come out at once.

269. Then we came to speak of fortune, £3,000 was to be the portion. What jointure ? £500 per annum. Why so ? the custom is against that measure, £100 per annum for £1,000 is the London orphan price, called a Smithfield bargain. He insisted for many flams called reasons, and some I took great offence at, being insinuations of dishonour, which he would have made up by jointure. Upon this I disagreed, and broke with him, declaring Mr. Lely might do as he pleased, he might marry, I could not hinder him, but I would never agree to such exorbitant terms as those were. I was set upon often to be wrought over, but moved not a hair. Mr. Lely himself came, it availed not : Sir John came at last to threaten, as if he would tickle me about my accounts as guardian and trustee for Mr. Lely. This I must confess provoked me, and I could hold no longer, but instantly wrote a long letter to Mr. Lely, con-

taining a deduction of what had passed, and at last declaring my positive dissent to his match during his minority in other terms than I had agreed; and withal charging him to keep that letter as the evidence of my fidelity to him, which I would adhere to, though Sir John Knatchbull endeavoured to move me from it, even by threats.

270. Such is the weakness of youth, and age too, not having discretion and experience, that, like the force of weighty bodies, they are made the engines to manage their own ruin; and are pushed upon the way, and then with a *vis impressa* they go on till they fall. So Mr. Lely entertained this advice, and instantly carried the letter to his mistress, and she to her father, and that brought him to me to deny the threatening; such ungrateful parts have false men to act.

271. At length this couple (not venturing to stay six months for his majority) married; and then so soon as time was ripe for settlements, and Mr. Lely was free to do as he pleased, they all came to me, as I beforehand expected, and desired me to take the part of a common friend, and treat and settle the jointure and security for the portion, as I did to their content, though not to my own, for Mr. Lely was easy and yielded to disadvantages in the portion, taking land for money, and at length, annuity for land for twelve years, wherein I had no authority, and having served with my open and plain representations and counsel, and then seeing executions of deeds pursuant to what Mr. Lely and his father agreed, *liberabam animam meam.* Mr. Lely was pleased to pass my accounts without exception, and made me a present of a balance of about £300 in my hands resting, and a parcel of pictures left of his father and others' doing, all which I have in my house, as well for ornament as memory of Mr. Lely's handsome acceptance of my endeavours in his service.

272. I could not prevent one unhappiness to him, though I desired it extremely,—it was the bribe to his governor for betraying him. This fellow insulted me with importunities for rewards extraordinary, which I soon blew off with indignation, knowing he had in some sense more than he deserved, and in other respects, I mean his treachery, less. But this left not Mr. Lely, who had not strength to resist

his governor, father-in-law, and wife, but poor Genault must have a reward, and the father-in-law paid it, and made his son give him his bond, and at last it was set off his portion ; such success will knavery sometimes have.

END OF THE AUTOBIOGRAPHY.

APPENDIX I.

LETTERS FROM ANNE, LADY NORTH.

Dudley (fourth Lord) failing in health—Troubles with servant maids—A mad dog—Charles II. at Newmarket— Francis North, the Lord Keeper Guilford's son—Lord North and Grey—Dr. John North's condition—The comet of 1681—Highwaymen.

[The last of these letters is dated 23rd January 1681. Lady North was buried at Kirtling on the 15th of February following. Her Ladyship writes of her eldest son, Lord North and Grey, as "my son North"; of Sir Francis as " my son Chief Justice"; of Dr. John North as " my son Doctor "; or " your brother, Dr." This was the fashion of the time.]

1.

Catlidge, [*i.e.* Kirtling] 18th June, 1677.

DEARE DAUGHTER,

I should indeed have been in great feares had I not rec^d a letter from you last week. It brought me the good news of my Son's perfect recovery and my little Garle's being so pretty a footwoman. You cannot imagine what divertizement my Lo : hath found since o^r coming hither, both in looking abroad and w^thin, he having been so long from hence that everything hath a new face ;[1] but the

[1] A short week after this letter was written Dudley, fourth Lord North, died at Kirtling, and was buried there 27th June, 1677.

park and other groundes wee had wont to ayre in are so full
of bushes and molehills that it makes it more uneasy than
pleasent, yett he is every day in the coach, and endures a
pace very well. He desires to be rem^d to you and both of
us to my Son, and my blessing . . . . .

Y^r most aff^{nate} Mother,
A. NORTH.

[The following letter is addressed to Sir Francis North,
then Lord Chief Justice of the Common Pleas. He had
been left a widower with three children in November, 1678.
They were Francis, afterwards Lord Guilford, Charles, and
Anne—the little *Misse* of these letters. On the death of
their mother the children were committod to the care of
their grandmother, with whom they remained till her death,
in February, 1681.]

2.

[Tostock] 16 March, 1678-9.

DEAR SON,

To-morrow Mrs. George intends to begin her jorney
towards London, where she hopes to be upon Tuesday
night. She had given up the children's clothes that she
had here to me, and I have sett them downe in a note to
give them in charge to Mrs. Lifford, and she hath given me
some stock of Misses and Charles, wch I have made a note
of. She saith there are some of these things at London
that she will send downe ; but there hath been some dispute wth Betty Harbert. It seemes she was promised to be
Misses maid and to have all her clothes and £4 a year
wages. Now she thinks if there be one above her that her
place will not be so good as she made acc^t of. I spoke wth
her to-day and askt her what she resolved on, for at first
she had a great picque against Mrs. Lifford (but I think
that is pretty well reconciled) but she tells me unlesse she
may have £4 a year wages and all M^{ls} clothes she will not
stay, so I promis her to write to you about it, so she should
have y^t, but I wondred she should stand upon it when Mrs.
Geo : told her before me that it was that wch my La : yor
wife never agreed with any servant for, but gave them as

she thought good, and indeed it is a captious thing and breeds nothing but contention. I tell her Frank will have breeches ere long and it will be a kind of injustice if they come to dividing the other two children's things not to lett the cheife take her choice. If I may speak my mind under the rose I fear she will be more than quartermaster of Mrs. Lifford in one week. Mrs. Geo : can give you a fuller acc^t of all but the last sentence, and saith if you speak to her of it she will tell you how it is. I prays God the children are all very well except a little sometimes Frank is out of order and not so lively nor so good a stomach, and sometimes for 3 or 4 hours in an after noone very dull and will not play ; but before night as brisk againe as may be. It hath made me suspect some kind of aguish distemper, but if it be it is so little that wee neither percieve coming nor going. I expect my son John upon Tuesday or Wednesday. I have not written to my son North this week because I would have all the timber for my Barne first. I must beg yor blessing for the little ones, and rem :

Yo^r most aff^{nate} Mother,
A. NORTH.

3.

[Tostock] 7th July, 1679.

DEAR SON ROGER,

I prayse God little Misse is pretty well againe, her fevorish distemp^r quite gone but, she is faint that if she stirr but a little it puts her into a sweat. This day she took an opening julip by the D^{rs} direction which hath wrought very well without the least disturbance to her, so I hope she will quickly be perfectly well, but I have bin and am still in sad fears for some of my family. My dog Tugg ran mad ; but my servants did not beleeve it at first, and lov'd her so well they would try severall things to her, so y^t they have all been slabered and blodied, some of them she bitt, and 2 of my little dogs she tumbled about, but whether she bitt any we kno not, but I am in great fears and care about it. I have sent this day to Cat : [Kirtling] to fetch the coach that the keeper told me stood in the Barne and was scarce worth the fetching. Nobody would give 20*s.* for it, but I fancy when I have trim'd it up and used it a little about the fields to carry the children ayring it will look more to the advantage than now it doth. I have written to my da: Wyseman [1] that if you would have the £9 for yo[r] horse and what monys else you have layd out for me that she would pay you. ·

From yo[r] most affec[nate] Mother,
A. NORTH.

My most kind love to my son Ch : Justice.

4.

FFOR THE HON[ble] M[rs] FFOLEY [2] AT STOURBRIDGE IN WOSTER : SHIRE.   THESE.

[Tostock] 5th Octo[br], '79.

DEAR DAUGHTER,
        We have had here so very wett weather that I beleev if y[r] Bro: Roger had not been engaged in his journey he would scarse have ventured at this tyme of the year, yet they say the King is so pleased at Newmarkett that he will stay a fortnight longer and the Queen at Ewston,[3] but I am so little a courtier that I see none of them. I am sorry to hear that little North is not well. You had need take heed of an ague for they are very rife everywhere. I prayse God all my little ones are very well, but some of my servants have Quartain agues. I supose yo[r] Cosen ffoley is brought a-bed that you were going thether. My most kind love to my son and blessing to the little ones.

I am y[r] most aff[nate] Mother,
A. NORTH.

[1] ELIZABETH NORTH. She married Sir Robert Wiseman, 24th September, 1672. Subsequently she married William, second Earl of Yarmouth.

[2] ANNE NORTH. She married Mr. Robert Foley in 1674.

[3] Euston, the seat of Henry Fitzroy, Duke of Grafton, a son of Charles II. by Barbara Villiers, Duchess of Cleveland.

5.

FFOR THE R^T HON^{BLE} THE LORD CHIEF JUSTICE NORTH
ATT HIS HOUSE IN CHANCERY LANE.   These.

[Tostock] 10 October, '79.

DEAR SON,

Nobody beleeved that you could make so short a stay here, so that the letters are directed hether still, and this enclosed was brought me yesterday. You cannot beleeve the great concerne that was in the whole family here last Wednesday, it being the day that the taylor was to helpe to dress little Ffrank in his breeches in order to the making an everyday suit by it. Never had any bride that was to be drest upon her weding night more hands about her, some the legs and some the armes, the taylor butt'ning and others putting on the sword, and so many lookers on that had I not had a ffinger amongst them I could not have seen him. When he was quit drest he acted his part as well as any of them, for he desired he might goe downe to inquire for the little gentleman that was there the day before in a black coat, and speak to the men to tell the gentleman when he came from school that here was a gallant with very fine cloths and a sword to have waited upou him and would come againe upon Sunday next. But this was not all, for there was great contrivings while he was dressing who should have the first salute, but he sayd if old Lane had been here she should, but he gave it me to quiett them all. They are very fitt, everything, and he looks taler and prettyer than in his coats. Little Charles reioyced as much as he did, for he jumpt all the while about him and took notice of everything. I went to Bury and bo' everything for another suitt, which will be finisht upon Saturday, so the coats are to be quite left off upon Sunday. I consider it is not yett terme time and since you could not have the pleasure of the first sight I have resolved you should have a full rela-tion from   Yo^r most aff^{nate} Mother,

A. NORTH.

When he was drest he asked Buckle whether muffs were out of fashion because they had not sent him one.

6.

For the R^t Honble the Lord Chief Justice North
att his house in Chancery Lane.　　These.

[Tostock] 12 Oct^{br}, '79.

Dear Son,

I thank you for sending me so perticular an account
of the little ones' ages, which I think as forward children
for these times as can be.　I gave you an account in my
last that this day was designed wholly to throw off the
coats and write man, and great good fortune it was to
have it a fayre day.　It was carried with a great deal of
privacy purposly to surprise Mr. Camborne, and it tooke
so well as to put him to the blush as soone as he saw him
in the church, wch pleased Frank not a little.　I perceive it
proves as I thought, that yor brother North would think I
infring'd upon his right when I presented to Drinkston.
But I wonder he should declare so much when he knows
it is my unquestionable due: it looks as if he grudg'd at
what I have, though it be but the honour and gratifying
of another, without any profitt to myselfe, and indeed I
cannot take it well of him for he layes an aspersion bothe
upon my dear Lord and myselfe, but I shall look upon it
only as selvishnes and lett him say his pleasure.　I am
really troubled to heare that my son Roger is grown so
melancholy, and wish wth all my heart you would endeavour if it be possible to find what may be the cause of
it.　I fear he may have some illnesse growing upon him
wch some little thing in tyme may help to prevent.　I am
sure you are able to doe more by way of persuasion than
anybody else, therefore I pray get him to take some little
gentle things wch may make him the fitter for business when
the Terme comes.　I cannot at all suspect anything of love.
I rather think it is the more than ordinary charge that
comes upon him upon the new building his chamber,[1] but
I hope he hath so much prudence as not to lett any such
thing goe so neer him as to endanger his health, which is

---

[1] See Chapter V. of the Autobiography.

the greatest misfortune that can happen either to him or
to his friends, amongst which I have so great a share it
may be a means sooner to hasten my short days.

I am yor most aff^{nate} Mother,

A. NORTH.

7.

FOR THE HON^{ble} Mis FOLEY.

[Tostock] 25 July, '80.

DEAR DAUGHTER,

It was a great trouble to me to think that I had
omitted giving you an acc^t of my son Dr., but really I
have scarse been I may say at home since I came hether,
for continuall company and the disorder of my things
being unsettled hath made me not know which way to
turne.   My son Dr. I expect here this week.   He saith he
is pretty well, but the truth is the doctors advise him to
gett into fresh ayre, wch is as much as to say they kno not
what to doe wth him, but I hope this place will doe him
good.   My son Dudley came hether last Munday, and I
have prevailed with him to stay all this week and I hope
as long as his busines will give him leave.[1]   I am concerned that I have not heard from you since yor being at
Stourbridge, how my son gott thether and how you found
the little ones and how . . . . . but I am in hope every
post should bring me newes from you.   I prayse God
these here are very well, but grown so wild that I know
not how to order them, and did not Frank goe every day
to school this little house would be too little for them.
My most kind love to my son and blessing to the little
ones.

I am yor most aff^{nate} Mother,

A. NORTH.

My son Dudley and Nancy[2] present their services.

[1] He had just returned from the East after an absence of nineteen
years. See the amusing account of his arrival in London.—*Life of Sir
Dudley North*, § 322.
[2] The *little Misse* of previous letters.

8.

[Tostock] 23rd Aug^r, '80.

DEAR DAUGHTER,

Yo^r bro. Dr. hath been very ill all last week, but this day he is brisk and talks as well as he can with a sore tong, wch he bitt on Saturday night in one of his fitts. He is very weak and hath almost lost the use of his right arme, for he cannot lift it to his head for a cup of drink, but makes a shift to bring his head to his hand to feed himselfe. He talks of going to Cambridge the next week, but I think it will not be either convenient or possible if he is as weak as he is now, tho' all the doctors say the more he stirrs about and 'changes places the better for him, and he must have his fancy if he sett upon anything.

I am so continually wth yor bro: that I have very little writing time, therefore must only desire my love and service to my son and blessings from

Y^r most aff^{nate} Mother,

A. NORTH.

9.

[Tostock] 6 Sp^{tbr} '80.

DEAR DAUGHTER,

It was impossible for me to persuade y^r bro. Dr. to stay any longer here, so he went to Cambridge last Thursday and endured the jorney very well, and I had a letter to-day that says he is rather better than otherwise and nothing so faint as he was. I have now a great deal of good company, 4 of y^r bros: and y^r sister North, &c., from Catlidge; but she bro^t not her dau^r Ketty but M^{ls} Gambleton in her roome, and says she will be gone againe to day. 'Twould have been a great happiness if I had had y^{rs} and my son Foley's and I would have so contrived that you should not have wanted accomoⁿ. I prayse God all my family are pretty well, but some of my neighbours sick, but it quickly goes off. Pray rem^{br} me to my son, and blessing to the little ones.

I am yor most aff^{nate} Mother,

A. NORTH.

10.

[Tostock] 2nd Jan. '80 [81].

DEAR DAUGHTER,

I beleev none of y^r letters have miscarried, tho' some of them came not in there due time, indeed the weather hath been so very ill that every body tells me they were never so bad hereabouts : for I never stirr my-selfe, my horses are so old and bad they cannot goe farr if I would. The Comett you writ of I heard of a great while ago and saw it every clear night when the other starrs appeared : it is just here as you say you saw it, wth a very extraordinary long stream from it. I am very glad my son gott so well home, for hereabouts everyone com-plains of the ways, and I fancy the weather here is colder then in other places, for I cannot keepe myselfe warme, but the children are so brisk and lively that they never complaine. Poor Goody Mason this weather pinches. She has got a third day ague and was so ill 2 or 3 nights agoe I feared she would have died. My most kind love to my son and blessing to the little ones.

I am y^r aff^{nate} Mother,
A. NORTH.

11.

[Tostock] 23rd Jan^{ry} '80 [81].

DEAR DAUGHTER,

I am very. sorry that my son's business calls him away from you, especially if it fall out so that he comes not home againe before the time that you expect your good hower ; but you are in a place where you have good neigh-bours and those that have been formerly with you and you are well acquainted with, wch no doubt will be very kind and carefull of you. I wish it were a good time of the year and I wthin a reasonable distance, I should give the venture whether I could endure the journey ; but as the times are wee dare not ventur out of dores for fear of being either rob^d or beaten, for if the theifs find no mony then they beat them. My da: Wenyeve[1] hath gott a very great cold, and the ways so ill that I cannot goe to see her. Pray rem^{br} me to my son, and tell him I wish he may meet with no good fellows in his jorney to London. My blessing to the little ones.

Y^{or} most aff^{nate} Mother,
A. NORTH.

[1] CHRISTIAN NORTH. She married Sir George Wenyeve of Bretten-ham, co. Suffolk, in 1665.

APPENDIX II.

LETTERS OF THE HON^{BLE}. ROGER NORTH.

1.

To the Honourable Mrs. Anne Foley, at her house at Stourbridge, Worcestershire.

August 3rd, 1678.

Dearest Sister,

You must needs have heard of Lady Downe's death, which I fear will hinder my waiting upon you immediately after the circuit, for my brother will go from Bristol to Wroxton, and make some stay there, to settle his concerns; and I believe my sister [1] and Lady Beata [2] will meet him there. You know, I suppose, my obligation; who must serve instead of better company. I am more concerned about the design of meeting Mr. Wrotesly, of which if there be haste, I cannot, for the reason aforesaid, partake. However, if he pleaseth to take Cambridge in his way he may have the same accommodation as if I were there. I know not whether our brother [3] will be at Trinity College or not: if he be there he will be very well pleased to

[1] Lady Frances, the Lord Chief Justice's wife. She did not long survive her mother, but died on 15th November following.

[2] Lady Beata Pope, the second daughter of Thomas, third Earl of Downe. She married in 1668, William Soames of Thurlow, in Suffolk, whom Charles II. made a Baronet in 1685. She died without issue.

[3] Dr. John North, then Master of Trinity College.

entertain the company; if not, he will have servants to wait upon you and the rest. I do intend to give him some notice by letter that such a thing may fall out. Pray present my service to Mr. Hunt, and confer with him of this. I have bought an able horse on purpose to carry a portmanteau and be a drudge at hunting, and I find he will acquit himself well, therefore prepare for the sport against you are troubled with

Your most affectionate humble Servant,

ROGER NORTH.

2.

[*Death of the Lord Keeper.*]

TO MR. ROBERT FOLEY.

Maiden Lane, 21st September, 1685.

DEAR SIR,

Beginning to look into our affairs we find that your debt hath run up an account, and as the balance has been adjusted, interest grows, but we are not sure whether we have the last account or not, or whether any payments have been made since the last account, therefore we desire you will do us the favour to state the account to the last sum paid so as we may begin the account upon a clear foundation; this I doubt not but you can soon send us, and you will oblige us accordingly. You may depend upon it that there will be a session of Parliament this winter, although no proclamation, for it was so declared at the rising, and the meaning of a proclamation was in case the exigence of the Rebellion required a session sooner. This gives us assurance of your good company.[1] Here are abundance of lies and idle reports concerning my Lord Keeper's illness,[2] and they make bold enough with the Doctor, but they do meet with such contradiction that the

---

[1] MR. ROBERT FOLEY was Member for Grampound Borough, co. Cornwall, in the Parliament 1685.

[2] The Lord Keeper died September 5th, 1685. The allusion in the text to a running account between Mr. Foley and the deceased is explained in the *Life of the Lord Keeper*, § 438.

mistake will not last long. It is concluded that my Lord Jeffries will have the Seal.[1] Some say it is declared. I hear Charles Porter is to be of the King's Council. This, I hope, will clear the account of news which we little inquire after and seldom meet with. You have servants of everybody here, especially of, &c.,

Your most affectionate humble Servant,
ROGER NORTH.

Pray let us also know what things belonging to the children are in your custody.

3.

[*Water Carriage in the Seventeenth Century.*]

TO THE SAME.

January 30th, 1685-6.

DEAREST SIR,

I ought in the first place to make an excuse for writing to you on the behalf of a gentleman that writes much better than myself, especially he sitting at my elbow. It is Mr. Edmund Chute,[2] upon whom the troubles and cares of this world, especially housekeeping, are lately descended; of whom I have a more than ordinary care and commiseration, because of my own case contains all the evil without the advantage of his circumstances. The business is factorage for cider and bottles, *simul et semel.* I tell him that he may have both together from Worcester as cheaply delivered in London, besides the advantage of that which is right and good, as he can have them in London, where it is scarce possible to get right and unsophisticated cider. He will have occasion for near one hundred dozen of bottles, and if they may be packed well

---

[1] He had the Great Seal delivered to him September 28th.—*Luttrell*, i. 359.

[2] EDMUND CHUTE, grandson of Challoner Chute, Speaker of the House of Commons during the Commonwealth. His mother was Catherine, daughter of Dorothy North, by her first husband, Lord Dacres.

at Worcester and sent down the Severn, and so to London
by sea, he will receive them and then send the cargo up
the Thames to Reading, which is within a few miles of his
house at the Vyne. At present it is only desired that you
will give yourself the trouble of a letter to me, with your
opinion of the matter, whether or not it is worth so much
contrivance for the benefit it is likely to produce, and according as you encourage so I will inform him, and I believe he will determine. I have received the £50 of Mr.
Hays, and 'he has the note. I am sorry the Parliament
doth not sit, because we shall lose the enjoyment of your
good company, but I hope time will restore it. My service
to all, and pray continue to esteem me, as

I am, your most faithful and affectionate
humble Servant,

ROGER NORTH.

4.

TO MISTRESS ANNE FOLEY, AT MR. ROBERT FOLEY'S,
STOURBRIDGE, WORCESTERSHIRE.

7th July, 1690.

DEAREST NIECE,

If the charge of the cabinet had been your own you
had fully paid it by your neat and obliging letter, at least
by your kind acceptance of my poor endeavours and appro-
bation of your choice. But seeing it is your father's, he and
I must reckon at another rate, and he must not escape so.
There will be the cage for him to pay for also, therefore
let him make the best of the doubt; and that he may not
think himself neglected by this to yourself you may tell
him that the fleet is beaten into harbour, but the army in
Ireland successful, and the King master of Dublin. Mr.
Fenton is alive and well, ready to serve any of his old
friends, and upon a letter will despatch christening stuff
what you please. Pray for me, wish your mother a good
hour, and esteem me as I most sincerely am

Your most affectionate humble Servant,

ROGER NORTH.

Lord Yarmouth is committed to the Tower for high

treason and not allowed bail.[1]   There is no charge against him, and this done for security in dangerous times.

5.

To Robert Foley, Esq., at his house at Stourbridge.

April 21st, 1691.

Sir,

I received my sister's letter, which gave the good news that you and yours were well, and also that we may hope to see you in London this spring. I desire the favour that you will send and bespeak me four Turkish bits of the short cheek, but desire him to open the ring as wide as may be, and to make it smaller, that is lighter than the others were, for some of them were too gross, and the ring would have borne being somewhat bigger, and played well enough. I desire also you will get me a very good coffee mill, and if he can contrive it to screw fast to a table board, rather than to have it the ordinary way, so that a post must be set up on purpose for it. We are shipping off my Lord Guilford, having a very good and a safe conveyance.[2] Send him a good voyage. It is said that the Parliament sitting hath been considered, but not resolved on; perhaps it may be thought they may not so readily supply the great occasions as we could wish. It is said also the Lord Preston is to suffer on Friday, but I believe nothing till I see it.[3] Reports are so uncertain.

I am, Sir, yours, &c.,
Roger North.

---

[1] This was on the 4th July.—*Luttrell's State Affairs*, ii. 68.

[2] Francis, second Lord Guilford, son of the Lord Keeper. He was now in his eighteenth year, having been born 14th December, 1673.

[3] He was reprieved on the 1st May, and subsequently pardoned.

III.   Q

6.

To the same.

3rd October, 1691.

Dear Sir,

Yours received with the enclosed touching the money business. I shall take care when I am called on by those concerned to give you an account. My Lord Guilford had the smallpox at Minden, in Germany, but is recovered, and about going forwards towards Italy. I have had the relation of the progress of his disease from time to time, from the physicians, in Latin, but I thought not fit to trouble any of his friends with the news of it till he was well, for it would have raised a concern, especially in the house, to no purpose, and some with you are for their own sakes not to be trusted with bad news. I hope I shall be informed from you of those petty matters I made a long digression of your time upon. I believe I may have need of a good parcel of nails, but as yet time enough. I am, &c.

7.

To the same.

28th October, 1691.

Dearest Sir,

I hope you and my sister have forgiven us for not waiting upon you this summer. You little imagine what persecution we have lived in, but in time you shall be merry at the history of it. I mean what tied us by the leg at Wroxton.[1] Then our rambles with the lady in company of no small importance to visit lands and tenements, messuages and houses, hurried us through divers countries and places like knights-errant. And now, though my ninety-one travels are at an end, Dudley North is about it still in the Forest of Dean to receive rent, that is

---

[1] Roger North and his brother Sir Dudley were trustees for the estate of their brother, Lord Guilford, which they were now arranging for the young lord, who was abroad. On the way in which they lived at Wroxton at this time see *Life of Sir Dudley North*, § 422, &c.

to allow the tenants their tax reckonings, and I am as solitary in London as in a wilderness, like a jackdaw among rooks. But having cast anchor in Norfolk I am one-half there, that is in thought; and chiefly to prepare for making your worships welcome when you will do me the honour of appearing there, in which laudable work as you have promised you must contribute. And know that the travelling in a stage coach long journeys in such fury as they drive be not proper for the constitution. Yet small journeys sometimes in coach and sometimes on horseback is better physic than all the colleges in Christendom can prescribe. But now to the point. The set of locks you were pleased to promise the procuring of I desire they may be ten, whereof five right-hand and five left-hand. One master key, the rest one key to open two locks, and lest a key should happen to be lost, I will be at the charge of two of each sort, so there will be as many keys as locks, and two over with the master keys. You may wonder at this humour, but I think there is reason. And the keys I would have without any finery of inward filing, but only a handsome turn or shape and clean filed, otherwise plain as a pike-staff, and I would have also ten bolt latches suitable to the locks, such as are cast, and turn with a button and bolt with a pin. You remember all these are to be lined and not rivetted to the brass, with staples as deep as the case, and if I cannot have them as cheap as you had, yet pray let them not exceed much, but be good and true work as possible. In the next place I desire you would inform yourself of carriage to Lynn, and oblige me with an account of the prices. I understand that the country trade, viz., all from manufacturers, &c., come to the market about Candlemas, and then carriage may be had and at known rates. I find perpetual use of nails in the country, and we have them at worst hand there, so I would have a good stock of them, if not now, another year. But when I know the conveniency of carriage I shall give you a particular commission, and I shall use you better than D. N., for he pretends to allow you profit in his trade, but I declare you are to get nothing at all by me. I am at present positive of one thing, viz., that you shall send me a faggot of the best steel, in bars of several sizes, between 150 and 200 weight, which some of your iron tenants may get together and bind up fast, as they do split iron. As for shop tools (for we intend to work very seriously) [1] I hope to have them at second hand, upon tolerable terms, near to us. If that opportunity fails you may perhaps hear further. The shop is to be built this spring, and I shall send directions where the thing shall be delivered in Lynn. As for news, I have none, being but a freshman in London, and neither see nor seek company. We country lawyers do but just keep terms, as old dogs go to church, for fashion's sake. Pray let us hear from you, and therein (I hope) that all with you (whose humble servant I am) are well, and thereby oblige your most affectionate, &c.

8.

[*Death of Sir Dudley North.*]

To THE SAME.

December 31st, 1691.

DEAREST SIR,

May the new year be better than the beginning ominates. My brother Dudley died last night about seven. His disease was asthma, that brought a fever and inflammation of the lungs, in spite of blooding and all extreme remedies. He had the incomparable Dr. Paman perpetually with him, and Dr. Ratcliff, who in formality was (sure) a sufficient warrant to die. He has left his wife executrix, given her all his moveables, and his young son Roger (Robert being dead about a fortnight before) £2000, whereof one is in the power of his mother, the reversion to his brothers. I suppose you will have a remembrance. It is fit you should know all this, though I could, for my sister's sake, have suppressed it till common fame had disclosed it, and make it known to her with due preface, lest she hurt herself with grieving. No loss is like mine, that am left alone, scarce able to go alone, in an afflicted

---

[1] *Life of Sir Dudley North,* § 425.

family, under burdens to oppress porters. And sometimes
I can think that sorrow hath somewhat manly in it, and
reason as well as truth itself warp that way, but upon
recollection, say, it is the women's prerogative, usurp it not.
Let not Chute's vary in habits from yours, and I see no
reason for them, since no provision being .made it is not
expected.

I am, yours, &c.

9.

[*Funeral of Sir Dudley North.*]

To the same.

7th January, 1691-2.

.Sir,

Yours of condolence came to my hands, and as to
the funeral it was from my house, with very honourable
attendance of coaches to Covent Garden Church. Hearse,
scutcheons, flambeaux, twelve peers' coaches, all mourning
attendance; from end to end, the great room in my house
was put in mourning and lined down to the outward door.
Silver sconces in the rooms, and black without, waxlights
and scutcheons; the coffin, velvet, black, with gilt nails
and handles; the body in the withdrawing-room with ell
tapers and mourners and like sconces. All this, than which
nothing could be better, without company, only the pall
carriers invited, who had rings, scarves, hat bands, and
gloves. Some few more came. You will receive a memorial token, and your wife also. His desire was, no
company. His will is mercantile, without settlement. All
moveables to his wife; the rest to his eldest son at age of
twenty-one; to Roger, £2000, of which £1000 in his
mother's power, the casualty of death before twenty-one,
to his brothers. This is all. Now to business.

As for the carriage I shall be heartily glad if I could have
it by 8th March, because I intend to buy a London carriage
and send them down by my own horses, with many other
things; but the difference between £7. 4*s.* and £8, which
is 3*s.* 6*d.* per cwt., is a bad account in merchandise, therefore pray bespeak the quantity and house then, and in a
week or a fortnight you shall hear of carriage more (if you

do not declare yourself tired with the correspondence). As
to the smith, I believe you guess right, as I thought also,
that they are all reprobate drunkards; however, if there
be a vacancy in his line I will send him over to you, and if
he do not earn his living send him back with a pass and a
whip at his tail. Let him work under common wages, but
I believe a maker of edge tools or somewhat of jackwork,
or right down farrier will be most useful to him. I have
contracted for 100,000 bricks to be made next summer,
and of all one 10,000 will not come to my share, for I do
but contrive, for the benefit of mankind, to convert rascally
clay walls that the wind blows through and through, to
brick that will keep folks warm and alive. I desire no
more for my own part, and hope to work as hard as the
best, and if you contribute to this intended charity to
mankind will oblige

　　　　　Your most affectionate humble Servant,
　　　　　　　　　　ROGER NORTH.

I find, by experience, death a terror only to the weakness
of the senses, but otherwise it is most desirable seeing that
reason and peace invites. I have done.

10.

[Preparations for Building at Rougham.]

TO THE SAME.

Braintree in Essex, March 3rd, 1691-2.

You may well wonder to be troubled from hence, but
know that I am idle, and then usually contrive mischief,
which now falls upon you. I had a letter from Montagu
North,[1] who is very well, and is very large in comforting
us upon the loss of D. N. I am going for Norfolk, and
intended to have wrote to you from London, before I
left, but one to my sister, and a world of fiddle faddle
called business, diverted at that time, now in leisure it

---

[1] At this time a prisoner at Toulon.

breaks out. Therefore, for the information of my economy take notice, I have fraught a two-wheel carriage from London, which I have bought of the remains of some colonel, with at least 1000 weight. There is good lead, a scarce commodity in the country, some nails, a vice, and [of the navy merchant], tools in abundance, boxwood, a joiner's chest, colours for painting and what not. Young beginners want many things to set up with. This goes under the conduct of wise William, with two horses, by Newmarket, while I budge with other two this way, by Brettenham, where I know the liberal Sir G [1] will pour out his one bottle to the health. I have contracted for 600,000 bricks and more, and all this more for repairs than building. We purchasers come into decayed estates, and must pay the last payment to workmen.

11.

14th April 1692, London.

Dear Sir,

I stayed at Rougham till the breach was made and the enemy entered. There I have left him. What ravage he will make I cannot forsee, but shall bear and pay. I was very much concerned that the bill of £50 was tardy and came when I was out of town, that it could not be paid at sight as I informed you and designed. But no harm is done, for one Joshua Hall hath brought it and received the money, the bill being assigned to him by Jno. Wheeler. I suppose now the time of cheap carriage is coming we shall have the merchandise sent up. You will wonder to see me at Stourbridge this summer. If at all it must be by horse, for I have left my travelling chair at Rougham, and to say truth my horses carrying lime, sand, coals, bricks, stones, whinns, timber, &c. In a bad world and growing worse, we must shift, and I having but one to please, who I think is reasonable, I shall be contented anything shall serve. I believe I shall trouble you for more locks and latches, and it may be a bale of stock-locks of the ordinary sort, the prices of which pray let me under-

---

[1] Sir George Wenyeve of Brettenham.

stand, for the smiths have, I believe, double price. And
even in nails the profit bears more than charges, though
the carriage be land, and double, but in goodness of. iron
it is very much, and for that, Sir, I must own myself
obliged to you, as for many other things always to be
owned as signal favours, by,

Sir, &c.

[William, Lord North and Grey, to whom the following
letters are addressed, was born 22nd December, 1678. His
father died in January, 1690, leaving his children to the
guardianship of Roger North and his brother Sir Dudley.]

12.

[*The Plot of a Matchmaker.*]

Rougham, March 16th, 1695-6.

My Lord,
        I received the honour of your Lordship's with the
minutes of a treaty enclosed, and those are a subject of
what follows. I must confess so advantageous a match
would be extremely pleasing to all that wish well to your
Lordship. And there shall remain no stone in *statu quo*
which my stirring will tend to compass it. I must confess
this hath a fair face, but not without symptoms that give
great suspicion, if somewhat amiss at the bottom, and
such unsound propositions are often held forth with the
most inviting circumstances, that is in matches ordinarily.
Money, which is always pronounced in a thundering sum,
it being as easy to say much as little, and few will bite
unless the bait be fair and large. If there were not false
jewels made to look as the true or better (if words will do
it) there could be no cheats, of which it is well known there
are very many *grassant* in our time, and in no trade 'so
epidemic as that of matchmaking. This in general. Next
as to this that which is the worst symptom, that the conceal-
ment of the . . . . and it seems before that be known or
demands be made for settlements, the bribe must be deposited and articles made, whereby your Lordship's estate

must be particularized, as also the lady's fortune and your Lordship's expectations.   Until this is done, *ne plus ultra.* I observe that the lady is commended by her age and her family, but not a word of a person or wit, and this must be despatched for another great fish is coming.   Now this may be sincere, but there are all the marks of a cheat, with secrecy, security, and haste.   I mentioned the person, so of that first.

I am of opinion that your Lordship sees her and she your Lordship, and you know her and her family and she you and yours before any engagement at all.   For if such articles should be made as are minuted to your Lordship, what a blind bargain would there be.   Your Lordship would be engaged to pay the bribe, and they may produce a monster, or one that neither you can love nor she your Lordship.   Whatever the fortune is, the person must not be disagreeable, if your Lordship intend to live comfortably, and I am persuaded your Lordship will think half the sum named with one your Lordship likes a better match than any fortune you cannot comport with, and this is not to be known till some interview.   But then secrecy is never without guile.   If all be sound there is no reason for a secret in the matter, and nothing is more proved by the practice of the world than that a fraud hath always a secret or somewhat dark or unintelligible in it; so that if it came only with the disadvantage of concealing the person till articles are made, I should not approve that way of proceeding, and as to the fortune, if an angel were at hand to determine I would lay a wager it is not half what is pretended.   Besides, they will (as the notes say) prove her fortune to be worth £40,000, so that there will be fending and proving about it, and a Chancery suit must settle the disputes about performance or non-performance of articles, which Mr. Scrimshire (who I think is a lawyer) will endeavour to order so as to fit what they know (but not we) will fall out.   A fortune is best proved by itself, and nothing is so ready as ready-money, and a little, with consent of friends, paid down clear, is much better than a very great sum pretended to, and to be torn with suits from I know not who.   But if we be remiss and do not go to law s . . . . . they will say we have lost the prize, it is

our fault, and they will prove that it might have been recovered. This may be a black box, plantations in America,
ships at sea, desperate debts, and what not, but they will
prove, it seems, a little clear dealing aforehand is better
than a world of proving afterwards, as a bird in the hand
is better than two in the bush. So much for secrecy.

The next thing is security. If they had proposed to
give your Lordship security for the money, it had been
well; for that we could deal with and know who was
to be bound and what land to be mortgaged. But they
will give the particulars and prove, which is no security at
all to your Lordship, that in the meantime must deposit or
secure the bribe; that shall be fast, whatever becomes of
the rest, and if you like not the lady nor her fortune
(whatever they may prove) you refuse her at the peril of
losing your money, which will never be cleared without a
Chancery suit. So this tying down of £3000 so strongly
looks as if that were the chief article in the business. If
there must be a trust off one side, one would think honour
and the engagement of parole by your Lordship's friends
(for such a sum will not be wanting if your Lordship hath
a good occasion for it) might serve.

But now the last thing I hinted is their haste. Nothing
is a better argument for phlegm on one side than extraordinary urging on the other. I do not find that your Lordship is so much considered as the £3000, and that is to be
the preliminary deposit. As I said before I may repeat, that
this may be a reality, but never cheat came without extraordinary haste, and many reasons for precipitate despatch.

There is another complexion which seems to taint the
whole business, and that is manifest treachery and corruption: in plain English, a sale of the young lady by
those who are trusted with her. Your Lordship would be
very uneasy to hear it said to you, " you bought me of my
gouvernante." I know this is the way of dealing, and I
know it is very common, so ordinary that few fortunes
match without being sold, even by parents and guardians.
No wonder if mercenary servants sell their power over
young creatures, but I cannot approve it at all the more
for the frequency, but I think all treachery reciprocal, as
well on the part of the buyer as the seller; and this stipu-

lating for £3000 is no better than buying of those who are but thieving that they sell. If service be done, let gratuities be ample, and more from honour and gratitude, and not contract. It will be said that this is an out of fashion stiffness, and may lose your Lordship an opportunity; but that is not to be charged while I only present' to your Lordship my sense, and your Lordship acts for yourself. The good and evil in consequence are yours, and I must needs say I have not known a match founded in treachery ever happy. Besides, honour is not a chimera as the loose world makes it. It will be found the greatest ingredient in a happy life and posterity, and I must, though to your Lordship, say that, by what I have observed, I am sure your Lordship is not only partial to honour, but are confirmed rather than shaken by the little regard you will continually observe it hath; and that when you consider this way of treating, you will not approve of it.

But that I may not be wanting to serve your Lordship the best I can in it, I have wrote to my lady Dacres,[1] whence the motion comes, to give me a serious and clear account of this affair, and if I find by my Lady that she knows so much to have a good opinion of it, none shall be more earnest than we shall be to serve your Lordship to the utmost. But if I find by her that is a secret, and must be so till articles are made, it shall be so still by my consent. I fear I have wrote nonsense, but I must ascribe it to haste, and beg your Lordship's pardon for it, because your Lordship commanded me to write by the next post. I shall run the venture, if your Lordship excuse, for what is amiss, rather than slip this time, in hopes of being more correct another time. I am sorry Mr. Faubert is dead.

[1] DOROTHY, LADY DACRES, was daughter of Dudley, third Lord North, therefore aunt to Roger North. She seems to have been left one of the guardians of the children of Charles, Lord North and Grey. She must have been at this time of a great age.

13.

FOR THE RIGHT HON. MY LORD NORTH AND GREY, AT M. FAUBERT'S ACADEMY,[1] IN LEICESTER STREET, LONDON.

Rougham, 18th March, 1695-6.

MY LORD,

Since making up my other letter, I recollect that I did not mention what I thought might be said to my Lady Dacres and to Mr. Scrimshire, if they come to speak more of this proposition, and to have an answer. I think it becomes your Lordship to say, that before you engage, you desire to see the lady and that she may see you; for, if you should not like her, a prior engagement, though in honour only, would be a great difficulty to your Lordship; and if she should not like you, all that her *gouvernante* could do would not make her marry. And if occasion be, to say plainly that your Lordship's uncles desire to know the person and circumstances, that they may judge of the probability of what is pretended before they engage your Lordship by their advice. If this will not be given way to there is a canker in the proposal. This may be called refusing a great advantage, but if it will not be treated fairly and openly, who can tell if any and what advantage? It is good for the main chance to see before one, or, according to the proverb, look before you leap. Your Lordship will have

---

[1] M. FAUBERT, who had come to England as a French refugee, had set up as early as 1681 an academy " for the education of youth, and to lessen the vast expense the nation is at yearly by sending children into France to be taught military exercises." He first took the Countess of Bristol's house, between Swallow Street (now Regent Street) and King Street. Next year the Council of the Royal Society favoured the scheme which Faubert had in his mind of setting up a military academy, and a subscription was set on foot " of worthy gentlemen and noblemen," for building such an academy. Evelyn in his *Diary* gives an account of an " assault at arms " held at M. Faubert's institution on the 18th December, 1685. It was evidently a favourite place of resort for the sons of the nobility who were ambitious of embracing the profession of arms. Young Lord North had already elected to seek for himself a military career. There is an interesting account of these military academies in Mr. T. W. Jackson's Preface to Part vi. of the First Series of *Collectanea* published by the Oxford Historical Society, 1885.

many overtures made to you of several sorts, and pray in all observe that a vast profit or advantage is the surest sign of a snare.

There must be some reason why strangers should be such unaccountable friends as cheats will pretend to be (I do not say this is one, unless it be on the part of the *gouvernante* that would sell her charge), and that is their own and not your interest.

Your Lordship will excuse this second trouble from, &c.

14.

To the same.

Rougham, 26th March, 1696.

My Lord,

Your Lordship's with the enclosed received; and I find the matter presseth and must have a success one way or other, and if it prove in your Lordship's favour, with a fortune of the magnitude they represent, it will be most happy. I have been very much troubled that this advanceth in our absence, because it is impossible to be transacted without the presence of some advice on which your Lordship may rely. Now I find that nothing will serve but bonds and engagements, which must be carefully done, and, as I told your Lordship, upon such advantage neither engagement nor the money, if it were required, shall be wanting. And after all the beating about, I can find only this expedient for a thorough service to your Lordship, under this difficulty of our being here. I have a very able friend, whose integrity and care, as well as ability in matters of this nature, I am security for. Besides he is qualified to inform your Lordship of the lady and her circumstance, having relations in that county. It is Mr. Longueville of the Inner Temple.[1] His chamber is in Stanfield Court, one pair of stairs on the right hand in the high building next the end of the Inner Temple Hall. I have

---

[1] Apparently WILLIAM LONGUEVILLE, an eminent conveyancer. He was made a bencher of his inn in 1677. He was of Alvescot, Oxfordshire. Cf. *Life of Lord Keeper*, § 399.

wrote to him by this post to acquaint him of the matter,
and I beg your Lordship will speak with him, and with
all the freedom that can be, and your Lordship will certainly be satisfied with his candour and friendship. He
hath been a real good friend to your name and family, and
will be such to your Lordship. As for charge, which is
usually thought of in such cases, I have taken that upon
me to do what is fit, so that is not to concern your Lordship. Mr. Longueville will treat for your Lordship with
Mr. Scrimshire, and if he settles any articles or bonds,
whatever they are, I will join in them. As to the particulars of your Lordship's estate, I can only suggest that it is
£1500 per annum, which may be said to anyone. For the
great house and homestall will supply what the rental
wants, and your Lordship hath power by settlement to
make a jointure of half, as I remember, and the estate of
the Lord Grey of Wark,[1] in Essex and the North, which
hath been called £8000 per annum, is bound to your Lordship indefeasibly upon failure of issue male of the Lord
Tankerville and Grey, Mr. Ralph Grey, and Mr. Charles
Grey, his brothers. This is what at present I can suggest
for your Lordship's service. As to the journey, I hope
your Lordship will find encouragement from the account
Mr. Longueville will give you. I must confess this secrecy,
haste, articling, and reward stick in my stomach, but yet
all may be well, as I always shall wish from whatever is to
concern your Lordship, being, &c.

15.

TO THE SAME.

Rougham, 3rd April, 1696.

MY LORD,

I have heard from my friend Mr. Longueville, who
tells me that he waited on your Lordship to Mr. Scrimshire, and that he declared no aunt or relation must be
privy to this, or be treated with, but only the gentlewoman
with whom she lives. This makes the matter stronger in

---

[1] *Cf.* note to Letter 24.

the dishonourable part, and it is certain that if all which they propose should succeed there would be so much infamy and inconvenience as would overbalance all the seeming advantage by it. And, to say truth, no man on one side or other could hold up his [head] with confidence to be looked upon by the world, who should be concerned in it. I am ready to sign any particular or value of your Lordship's estate, and to procure any sum for your service, but I must needs beg it may be in a cause that will not make us (as one side will declare) infamous. Mr. Longueville says his lady is nearly acquainted with this lady's relations, and, however otherwise he might be concerned, he desires in that respect to be excused, as being liable to more blame than any other. I did not know of this, but believed by the country [*sic*] he could inform your Lordship of the state of the lady, and her fortune, as it seems he doth. I intend to write to my Lady Dacres, to acquaint her of the matter, with my opinion of it, and that is in short that it is fit some relation of the lady be privy to the treaty, and that to deal as is proposed is very dishonourable, and I fear not safe in point of law, of which I shall consider more, and give your Lordship an account, being, my Lord, &c.

16.

For the Right Honble. my Lady Dacres at her house in Bedford Walk, near Gray's Inn, London.

Rougham, 5th April, 1696.

Madam,

I have, as well as I can by letters, advanced in the proposition of the match, which my Lord North had encouragement from your Ladyship to look after, and I find the lady every way qualified to answer his ends. But the circumstance of the affair is, in short, this: no relation of hers must be privy to the treaty, although she hath several aunts and other relations; but the person with whom she lives must only be dealt with, and that for money directly and plainly declared to be for this child, who is just capable of marriage and under age of discretion. This is neither safe in point of law nor honourable, and unless some relations are concerned, impracticable. Therefore, I humbly crave leave to represent this sense of mine, which is also my brother's, to the end that your Ladyship may not condemn us for any unreasonable aversion to so advantageous a proposition. And in truth, Madam, I have known many like, but none that did not end in lawsuits and infamy, witness Hyde and Emerson's case, which was like this, and was deemed no marriage by the supreme court of delegates. I humbly beg your Ladyship's pardon for the presumption of this trouble from,

Madam,

Your Ladyship's most dutiful and obedient
humble Servant.

17.

[Narrow Circumstances of Lord North.]

FOR THE RIGHT HONOURABLE MY LORD NORTH
AND GREY.

Middle Temple, December 15th, 1697.

MY LORD,

I received the honour of your Lordship's from Venice (I suppose, for no place or date is superscribed) and also the music and strings, which are a most welcome present to a lover, as we call ourselves, and I return your Lordship my hearty thanks. As for bugles, I have conferred with the concerned on the subject, and now they wholly decline further trouble to your Lordship in it, and beg your pardon for having already given your Lordship so much. I believe my Lord Yarmouth [1] hath set his heart on the virgin quicksilver to be sent by your Lordship, and if your Lordship can despatch it by some gentleman or governor returning, who will give it room in a valise, I think it will come best, and the charge put in your Lord-

---

[1] WILLIAM PASTON, second Earl of Yarmouth. He married (24th September, 1672) Elizabeth, sister of Roger North, widow of Sir Robert Wiseman.

ship's next bill, so as to be no loser. This brings me to the other part of your Lordship's letter, which insists upon £200 increase of allowance, at least for the next half year, your Lordship saying that the £400 per annum is not sufficient. I wish I could say that your Lordship's estate was sufficient for that character, but (without your Lordship's fault) it is not;[1] therefore necessity requires that your character in point of expense must condescend to the estate. Nor is it any dishonour, but the contrary, most honourable; for honour is the judgment of the wise, and not of youth and folly, and it is now a prime wisdom whereon all future ease and felicity depend to calculate by weight and measure expenses. It may be your Lordship doth not consider that you left your revenues anticipated, so that moneys could scarce be got to pay your arrears of trades, and we borrowed for the bills to renew again when we could. As for your last, which is still owing, your Lordship's sister[2] is a greater charge than before, and costs your Lordship near £80 per annum. She hath travelled and been sick, which hath increased the charge. Your Lordship's brother is a constant charge;[3] and all these things set off no tunes, but the estate is all sunk, and now, after peace, more heavily in probability than before. So costly is the catchery of changing. I had almost forgot the debts at interest, which eat like cankers if not kept under. It was a sacred rule with my brothers to be good husbands among strangers, and to spend what money they had among their relations and friends. If ever your Lordship can retrench, it is abroad, where most never saw you before, and seeing, mind only outside, which is the same in everyone, and expect never to see you more. Shall you not want your money ten times more at home upon your return? Is it tolerable to think that your Lordship then must tick for all your conveniences, as must be if you do not spare in travel? The word sufficient is of itself unde-

---

[1] It is pretty evident that the young lord dipped very heavily into his resources while at M. Faubert's Academy, and that he must have lost seriously at play and in other extravagances.

[2] HON. DUDLEYA NORTH.

[3] HON. CHARLES NORTH. He served in the Netherlands, and attained to the rank of Major, but died early of " a calenture."

termined, and hath no sense but comparative. If the exit do not exceed the income in all quantities the sufficiency is equal, as well in the lesser as the greater denominations. It is easy, as many have done, to make ten times your Lordship's allowance to be insufficient by wasting more. And however we may wish for an enlargement and think it were but suitable for your Lordship, yet, as the posture of the estate is with respect to the other charges, it cannot be; for after your brother, sister, interest, servants, and other incidents, as taxes, some repairs, perhaps failing of tenants in time at least, we cannot answer to have in money £600, nay scarce £500 per annum in hard money. One end of your Lordship's travelling, as hath been done by many persons of honour and quality in other times, is to gain time in the estate, by retrenchment of expenses, which may be done abroad but cannot be done at home. Here you will find your revenue at stretch will not serve, much less incumbered as your Lordship's is. What can you propose then, but if possible to get a little beforehand against your return? I say if possible, because I much doubt it, and rather as times are and are like to continue, I conclude the contrary. Could your Lordship shake off the debts and make that which seems to be, really your own, it were something. I know I argue against the grain. The impulse of the present is strong, but pray consider the future will be present, and as very a now as what you feel, and have all its cravings, only with this disadvantage, that youth bears and shifts with less than age, and then the *mancamenti* will come nearer your soul than when younger. Nothing is so dismal as when money and spirits fail together, which is the case of age following on improvident youth. Then there is an effectual *crepa cuore*. Therefore I cannot forbear urging your Lordship with all the fervour I am able, to keep to your allowance; for if it should, as your Lordship says, bring your travels to an untimely end, it will still prevent the same necessity (as your Lordship calls the circumstances of the present occasion); for if you need a crown abroad it will be one guinea here; and as for necessity you supposed, there is no room for discourse, for necessity is what will be, and therefore is always lawful, and has no law; but great occasion or strong desires,

such as I admit your Lordship's to be, are not necessity.
The word is *traducé* in that sense. And it is far from
being without law, as nothing is more governable; and
every wise man governs his occasions by the measure of
his supplies, and so your Lordship must do. I might go
further, and say a wise man, such as your Lordship gives
so great hopes of being, will govern even his desires. I
am sure your Lordship knows the doctrine of quantity,
and that a subtraction greater than the addition makes a
negative progression, seeming nonsense, but yet real and
true. When people spend more than they have, they have
less than nothing left. I would but have your Lordship
consider that all is for yourself, and then I hope you will
consider that all this moves from a sincere good will and
service to you, and be consequently excused by your Lordship, which will infinitely oblige

My Lord, your Lordship's most affectionate
humble Servant.

18.

To the same.

London, 13th January, 1697-8.

My Lord,

We have made a reform in your Lordship's business
at Catledge, which we hope and in part proved to good
effect. It is that James Taylor go over quarterly, and that
none else receive your moneys. We have got a credit for
£200, not knowing but your Lordship may expect it to
come, rather than draw yourself, as we 'thought possibly
you might. I have had an account from some travellers
that your Lordship is a manager, but this is at several
removes, though people who are no less inquisitive after
your Lordship than liberal to discourse what they hear.
Your poor sister has been very ill, but with the help of a
good nurse, her aunt,[1] is better. I was guilty of a mistake
in my letter. From Mr. Wittington I received a few
strings and some music from Italy, and I could not ima-

---

[1] Hon. Mrs. Foley.

gine from what hand, unless it were your Lordship or Mr. W. that directed them, which made me take the notice I did. Since I find it from my father-in-law, Sir Robert Gayer, so I have pardon to beg for the impertinence of my mistake, which I hope your Lordship will grant, as for all other troubles, from

My Lord, your Lordship's most faithful, &c.

19.

To Hon. Mrs. Foley.

Bedford Walk, 4th January, 1697-8.

DEAREST SISTER,

It is in conformity to your demands that I trouble you at present, for really I can say only that we are in reasonable good health, colds (as all must bear with at this time of year) excepted, and the little one is very well, and grows so that I fear she will be a girl rampant. She hath no teeth yet, but wakes and cries for them. M. N. is gone to Brettenham to Christmas it there. Old Sands is dead, which I say is happy for Mrs. North, because she will now know if anything but obedience made him point at her, or if he be a man or a monster. All our hearty wishes, &c.

R[OGER] M[ARY] N[ORTH].

20.

To the same.

Middle Temple, 25th June, 1698.

DEAREST SISTER,

I believe, not hearing from me so long, you think I am lost, but I hope to make amends now by coming all at once. And first for my cousin's espinette. I have bought one costs (case and all) six pounds, and I think it is a very good one. I wish she may have a good master and a good tuner, which makes all the pleasure of the instrument. If

ever any new pins are put in, let them not be stiff and
hard, which spoils all. I have committed the case to the
youth to send it down. Next, as to the son whom you
would have a merchant.[1] The trade of staking vast sums
with youths for little expectations is at such a pass that
one would almost choose an annuity without a trade to
buy it so dear. All crowd their sons into trades, so that
the country wants and cities swarm. I have had much
talk with Montagu North, who I say (morose as he is)
ought to stir his stumps for a nephew; and for discourse
of what might possibly be done, he says that he could take
a practice, which will intitule to give out, and be free, and
then send him to Aleppo to board him with the Consul,
who is his particular friend, and pay to the young man a
sum of money, as £800 or £700 (the price of a master in
London) at Aleppo, with which he may trade and negotiate for himself, and make at least £12, £18, or £20 per
cent., and so live well, and if he acquits himself, he may
take a master there (by the Consul's care), and be left in
an house of business, to grow rich assuredly, if his own
fault and neglect hinder not. Here what is given is given
to the son, who else, besides binding, must have a sum,
£500 or £600, to set up. He is sure of the best point and
settlement abroad, and stands to no hazard but his own
life, and then what he hath will come back to his family.
All I can get out of this is, that it may be done; but besides, we have so many objections. He would with less
pain do it for a stranger than a relation. *They* think he
has some end of his own. They expect he should find
business abroad, which he is not resolved to do, or rather
resolved not to have any; and much more such stuff that
I fight against, but cannot say he is determined. One in
my hearing, when we were discoursing of such a project,
offered £200 to pay him down for it; and it is certainly
much better than a practiceship bought for £500. I could
not but acquaint you with this, that Mr. F. may ruminate
upon it; and if he and you approve we will join and attack
the fort vigorously; and whatever anyone else would give,

---

[1] This was Dudley Foley. He sailed for the East, 21st Feb. 169⅜,
and was most generously assisted by his uncles Roger and Montagu
North.

he shall take nothing and do it.　I say he shall, or a will shall fail.

Your most affectionate humble Servant,
ROGER NORTH.

My wife is yours, and we all join in services to Mr. Foley, and all with you, particularly my niece North.[1]

21.

TO THE SAME.

Rougham, 11th September, 1699.

DEAREST SISTER,

I am extreme sorry that your time in London falls without ours.　When we move it is with the whole family, and that is not till Christmas; but I have found an expedient, which I heartily wish may succeed, for bringing us together, and that is: come down to Rougham, and take Brettenham and Downham on your way, and you are not much further from Stourbridge here than at London, for, going by Wisbech, Peterborough, and Warwick, it is no long journey.　I cannot tell how you old folks (as they say) may hold out, I'm sure it will be pleasant to the young ones to travel, and it is grown much the fashion of the world to ramble, and I am sure when so near as Brettenham, nothing would be more pleasing.　I have this day wrote there to acquaint them of your purpose, and to dispose my sister to meet you, but what they will do I know not.　My Lady North[2] and M. N. will be in town.　I wish you a safe and pleasant journey, not only to London, but this way also, and should be glad to receive a word, and hope that you would do us such a favour, than which nothing could more oblige

Your most affectionate humble Servant, &c.

My wife, with the company here, all join in humble service to yourself and Mr. Foley, and all with you.

---

[1] Hon. Dudleya North.
[2] Anne, Lady North, widow of Sir Dudley North of Glemham.

22.

[*The First Steel Pen.*]

To the same.

London, March 8th, 1700-1.

. . . . . Lord North and Grey is returned a great courtier, to tell good news. We have no news, unless it be about a small concern called a Parliament, which they say is to sit next March. [Farewell Circuit.] But *where* is a question answered negatively. Not in London. You will hardly tell by what you see, that I write with a steel pen. It is a device come out of France, of which the original was very good and wrote very well, but this is but a copy ill made. When they get the knack of making them exactly, I do not doubt but the government of the goose quill is near an end, for none that can have these will use others.

I am, your most obedient Servant, &c.

23.

To ——— ———

Rougham, 6th December, 1702.

Sir,

If I am too much a trespasser on your better time, I hope you will endeavour to mend me by your reproof, which I must own to deserve for troubling you about an affair that for aught I know may be exquisitely impertinent.

This village is small, the rectory impropriate in my hands, and the vicarage so inconsiderable as commonly to have gone by sequestration, and not presentation ; but Mr. Briggs, the present vicar, hath the seal (?) and is instituted and inducted, for it is in the gift of the Crown but zero (if I may write French) in the King's Books. Perhaps with the advantages I allow the vicar may have £25 or thereabouts per annum. There is neither house nor glebe belonging to it, and I am disposed to mend it, if I could have the presentation by some way or other, making it practicable for a vicar to live in the town. It may be you or my worthy good friend Lord K. B. sometimes . . . . . . with Mr. Edwards, the Secretary of the Presentations, and can know from him if it be possible now-a-days to get the presentation to this vicarage granted me of the Crown. I have heard formerly of great difficulty in such requests, and lately that they are more easily obtained. I am sure the thing is not worth the charge of a perpetuity patent; but as I am settled here and would have the benefit of a vicar's residence in the daily service as chaplain, would also desire the choice of him. Now, if such a thing may be had, and Mr. Edwards can put me in a way as may be most likely so to obtain, he will oblige me exceedingly. And, to say truth, all must be debt on my part, for I have no merit if I keep myself free from crime, and must expect time in higher powers to enable me to null the score of obligations which, Sir, will run high in your books if you at your leisure will favour me with your opinion of this, as also your pardon for the importunity of it, as coming from, &c.

[The following pedigree will explain at a glance the difficulties in the ensuing letter.]

WILLIAM, 1ST LORD GREY of Werke, died 1674. = ANNE, daughter of Sir John Wentworth of Gosfield, co. Essex.

| THOMAS GREY, eldest son, died without issue, 1672. | RALPH, 2ND LORD GREY, died 15 June, 1675. = Catharine, da. of Sir Edward Forde. | CATHERINE = CHARLES, 5TH LORD NORTH of Kirtling, died 1690. |

| FORDE, 3RD LORD GREY, died 1701, without issue male. Created Earl of Tankerville 11 June, 1695. | RALPH, 4TH LORD GREY, died July, 1706, without issue. | CATHARINE. = Richard Nevill, Esq. | WILLIAM, LORD NORTH AND GREY, born 22 Dec. 1678, i.e. before the Chancery suit with *Forde, Lord Grey,* was commenced. |

24.

FOR THE RIGHT HONOURABLE THE LORD NORTH AND GREY, AT CATLIDGE, NEAR NEWMARKET.

To be sent from thence express.

Rougham, 23rd February, 1703-4.

MY LORD,

I am honoured with your Lordship's of the 19th instant, with the enclosed opinion, concerning which I beg leave to acquaint your Lordship, that upon your Lordship's last expedition, and the assurance of many people's discourse that your Lordship was not in the entail of Werke, so contrary to my remembrance as I have acquainted your Lordship, I made a search among all the paper I had of draughts, &c,, and found the copy by which the grand settlement of Lord William Grey was engrossed, and in the critical word an obliteration thus, whereby I saw plainly that the draught was first settled with males; in it that had brought the estate to your Lordship, but it seems they wrought on the old man to put that out, so the heir general takes. I shewed this straight to James Taylor, and I was much in doubt if I should send your Lordship word of it or your sister, but considered it would do you no service to be so forward, and determined to stay till I had a fair opportunity. I am very certain at the first the old man's mind was as the draught was made, and then altered, which did not fall in my knowledge, being then chiefly concerned in the first instructions. As to Epping, &c., I crave leave to tell your Lordship how that stands. It is the manor of Epping, and part of the great estate at Gosfield, which the family owns, settled indefeasibly on your Lordship. Epping, I account worth £1200 per annum, if not more. It is one of the best copyhold manors in England,—fines arbitrary, all the houses copyhold and perpetually changing. Gosfield I cannot give much account of, being as now it stands but a piece of a greater estate, and how that comes is history to your Lordship. Old William, Lord Grey, had two sons, Thomas, that died *sine prole*, and

Ralph, whose children were Forde late Lord Grey, the present Lord Grey, Charles (dead), and Mrs. Nevill, a daughter. Your Lordship's mother was the old Lord's only daughter. He purchased the estate of Gosfield, not all at once, but at several times, and took the conveyances of the general manor and much the better part in the name of his son Thomas, who was estated to him and his heirs, in trust for his father and his heirs. The old man used it as the rest, and there was not any knowledge of Thomas Grey being concerned, but lived and had his exhibitions, not out of that, but out of his revenue at large. So the old man settled it with Epping (called in the family the southern estate), as the settlement speaks. Nor were we that acted in doing it ever informed of other title but that William Lord Grey was seized in fee. Nor did T. Grey visibly interpose in any other character than filial regard for his father, and so all rested in peace. T. Grey died, then the old Lord; after whose death Ralph Lord Grey was advised by counsel that the estate was his (that was bought in Tom's name) as heir to his brother, and so fell not under the settlement of his father. Thereupon Ralph, the father,[1] encumbered and charged that part of Gosfield with debts and children's augmentation of portions, and then died. After his death Forde, Lord Grey, the eldest son, claimed by the settlement, and did not own his father's power; and thereupon suits began in Chancery, between him and his mother, who followed on the behalf of her younger children. The point was whether the conveyances to Tom Grey were a trust (as we who were concerned in wishes for your Lordship's family, and all the counsel for Forde, Lord Grey, thought most clear), or an advancement intended by the old man for his son; and my Lord Nottingham, then Chancellor, decreed that if a father useth his son's name in a purchase it should be construed an advancement and not a trust, so the estate went that way by decree, and since it has been tossed and tumbled between the brothers, the gold to one and other, and at last it is sold to Sir Thomas Millington, now dead. And this is the bar by which your Lordship is hindered of all

---

[1] *i.e.* Ralph, second Lord Grey.

that estate, and came in remainder only as to part. I believe Mr. Dobbins can give your Lordship the history of this case so far as it was agitated in Chancery, and it may be worth your while to ask him (if he is your counsel) concerning it, though it doth not occur to me that your Lordship hath any title, for want of the original assurances, and the decree, that is in your way. The only point in your Lordship's favour is that neither your mother that was named in remainder, nor your Lordship, that was then born, and had the remainder in suit vested, were made parties to that suit, and then why should you be concluded?—*res inter alios acta nemini nocebit*—but this is no case till it is stated upon the proceedings for having advice, unless it be whether your Lordship shall concern yourself further or not, and in order to that I take this opportunity to acquaint your Lordship thus much. Now, as to your Lordship's commands as to advice about the proposal to buy you out of Epping, &c., it is a point of prudence of which your Lordship is judge. However, I decline not to say what my sense is, which is that the contrivers on my Lord Grey's side think to take advantage of your Lordship's occasions for money, and so to have a pennyworth.

25.

For Mistress Anne Foley, at the Hon. Mrs.
Foley's house at Stourbridge.

Rougham, 8th March, 1703-4.

Dearest Niece,

Yours came to hand here, date the 3rd instant; and as to the security of your brother, to be given pursuant to his father's will, to enable him to act, he consulted me what it should be, and I could not tell what to propose better than a recognisance in Chancery, and directed him to the office where such things were done. I take this to be as good, if not better, than any mortgage, and it is such as the Masters in Chancery always take, when the court refers it to them to see a security taken. He hath not told me he hath done it, nor sent me a copy. You may

please to let him know I enquired of you and desired you
to ask him. I believe it is done, because he told me it
should be so; but it was his own business also, therefore I
doubt not of it; and if it be not (as one may show the
horse water, but not force him against his inclination to
drink) you are safe enough, for he is not accountable for
the personal estate. I assure you, you may depend on all
the aid and friendship we can give for reconciling all
things among so near and esteemed relations; and as for
your brother, I believe want of experience and earnestness
of youth may cause him to be guilty of excesses, which he
will, and I believe already doth, think both indecent and
better spared; for what should anyone make a splutter
for, that hath a plain rule to walk by. The methods of
obliging, that is doing right and readily, he will find most
profitable; and I presume his principles, and if not those,
his pride (for what is a gentleman but a little preference
to others) will make him honest; and I would be very
sorry that of all the nephew relations we have he of whom
I expect all candour and generosity should give occasion
for any contrary reflection. I have nothing more but
dearest respects to my sister, with all service to yourself
and relations with you.

We are, your most affectionate humble Servants,
MONTAGU NORTH.
ROGER NORTH.

My wife, who is at her old trade of grumbling and
groaning, with little ones, are all my sister's and your
humble servants.

26.

FOR NORTH FOLEY, ESQ.

Rougham, 20th August, 1704.

DEAR NEPHEW,

This bearer is the Vulcan of our village, and one of
the eaters of us farmers. He hath a design to buy his
goods at the fountain head in the country. If it be not
inconvenient to you I shall take it for a favour to let him

have £5 on account of the Temple, and if your plenty from the coal work be as I wish it, to lend it him, so much more. But all or part is wholly submitted to your convenience, and I do not urge it, or shall be in the least dissatisfied if you do not supply him. He is rich, and may be safely trusted for what he deals for, and I may hereafter at better time consign him what I may receive of yourself. I hope he will return with the good news of your health and prosperity, which is ever desired by your most humble and affectionate Servant.

ROGER NORTH.

27.

TO MRS. FOLEY.

Rougham, 13th February, 1705-6.

DEAREST SISTER,

I can do no less than return you many thanks for many obligations, but most of all for the kind purpose of seeing us here, which I must lay holden as an engagement, if nothing intervene unforeseen of necessity to hinder it, and my smith shall be the convoy, or I will send a servant, and I have one at my elbow that will put in his subscription. You see how I am pinned down here, that you may judge a little of the difficulty of moving. We are all very well here, only the little boy [1] had a violent access of a cold (I take it), but for fear of worse we resorted to his sheet anchor, bleeding in the jugular, which once saved his life, and perhaps has done the game, for he is much better after it, but weak, having lost at least eight ounces. I have no more but to add my wife's humble service and intense wishes that some way or other she may wait on you. In part suspended by the hopes you give of the company here, I am no less,

Dear Sister, &c.

---

[1] His son Roger, who succeeded his father at Rougham.

28.

To Mr. Philip Foley, at Peterhouse College.

Rougham, 22nd December, 1706.

Dear Nephew,

I received the favour of your book, safe and sound, with your letter, in compliment for which I return you many thanks, and for the 4*s*. 6*d*. if I have not a sooner opportunity you may account it with your brother John, if you deal by him, as I suppose you may in money matters, for he hath some small sums to receive of my brother, and that may come in with the rest.

As for the books you give me an account of, nothing of news to me is more welcome than such. I can make a shift with Horace without any comments, and if the great doctor mends the author after the critics before him, he will do wonders, for they have left nothing but wild guess to their posterity; and nothing hath ever in the world been so wit driven as the critics on the classics.[1] And his note of *ter natos* for *tornatos incudi reddere versus* hath turned my stomach, and I have no appetite to his book; for being acquainted with the European languages grown out of Latin, and most like to indicate a native sense, when the pure words are retained, I am of *tornatos* party, for *torna* and *tornare* are universal and common, signifying the forming and shaping of anything. In the French *contour* of a figure, in painting of an house, or of a verse is proper, and in Italian *contornare bene* is to design well. If one should say in Italian *conternascere* it would be pleasant; but whatever way born *sub incude* things are hammered and shaped over and over again, but not bred and born there. And as they fable bears' whelps (like the verses that are to be brought to the hammer again) are deformed

---

[1] Dr. Bentley's edition of Horace was not published till 1711, but his note on *Ars Poetica*, line 441, with the conjectural emendation of *ter natos* for *tornatos*, was published many years before, in his notes on Callimachus, which appeared in Grævius' edition, Utrecht, 1697. Though praised by Grævius it was rejected and attacked by Gronovius in his notes on Aulus Gellius, in 1706.

till licked into shape, the doctor would think one bantered that should tell him bears whelped the same cubs three or four times over, or as often as they new licked them. Mr. Newton's algebra will be very abstruse, but extraordinarily good and new, for that is his masterpiece, and if he had kept to that and mechanics, and let dabbling in physics [*sic*][1] alone, he had done no wrong to his fame, for he hath broached a sort of philosophy more occult than that of the Peripatetic school, and his aim, as I guess, is to sanctify all vulgar and natural prejudices in a philosophic dress, and to keep the world from looking further; while in geometry he is boundless and liberal.

When Dr. Whiston's book of lectures comes out[2] I shall beg your opinion whether it meets with an esteem as good to the purpose he designs them, and then I may trouble you with a commission, but I have no fancy for an Apocalyptic Geometer. And it hath often happened that explainers are confounders, for the Geometry of Cartesius is rather so served than helped by the commentator, for nothing could match his felicity in lucid expression, and his hints are clearer than the glosses of others.

I had rather receive this *petit* book from your own hand, and if you had any time to be lost at Rougham, and let me know as much, and that you were at Cambridge, I could have sent over an hack of our poor stable for you, always being most satisfied in your good company here, when you will think fit to oblige with it.

Your most affectionate, &c.

[1] But the word can hardly be what the writer intended, he must be referring to Newton's speculations on the Book of Daniel and the Revelation of St. John.

[2] Sir Isaac Newton's *Arithmetica Universalis*, comprising the illustrious author's lectures on Algebra, was published in 1707. The work was conducted through the press by Dr. Whiston, Newton's successor and for some years deputy as Lucasian Professor at Cambridge.

29.

To Mrs. Foley.

Rougham, 13th January, 1706-7.

Dearest Sister,

I am both inclined and shrewly solicited, which is a civil word for commanded, by one of no small authority here and accounts herself obliged, to return you thanks for your kind letter, and being able to do it without grunting am thought most competent. We hope you and all your family are in health, which is more than can be said of poor sister Wenyeve[1] at London, where she thought to settle herself and to enjoy her ease, and accordingly, with all her stock, hath bought an house, but hath had so severe sickness and moving, from breathing fast, that Dr. Ratcliffe is thought to have done a considerable work to recover her. So great a change from business, action, thoughts, cares, all in a good air, to perfect retiredness in one not so good, turned the case upon the constitution, and as that fared worse the other tyrannized. My mother was never well after my father died, but was gnawed with cares within when there was nothing without to employ them.

The town is a rare thing with health, money, and spirits; but really to old folks that are worn to a course of living it is a dangerous purchase, and with them, what least alters and disturbs is best. And I believe even I should now choke in London, and be ruined with colds, that here scarce remember a cold, and am seldom dry when it is abroad wet. We have your disciple here that, like a knight-errant in a desert, cannot get . . . . for his life.[2] But seriously, I never saw such a creature since I was born, so void of capacity and devious to vice, and yet he hath two legs, two eyes, ears, a mouth and nose as other human kind, and an audacity of look and speech for which I envy him; but knows nothing but the way to his mouth, but

[1] Christian Wenyeve, cf. p. 220 n.

[2] The allusion is to his nephew, Roger, second son of Dudley North. He made a disgraceful marriage, and died early.

would be as imperious as Lucifer, and sometimes practices with the servants, and is paid his swearing back with interest, but with us as tame as a lamb, and will, with our good woman above, read sermons on Sundays and give Maundy signs of penitence till the morning comes, and then the cat appears. In short, he is not fit for a civil family in any respect, but we have patience for some short time. I have nothing from hence, but to let you know your godson is a good boy, and if he have no worse quality when grown up than now, for his age, he may be as reasonable a creature as most of those that go upright on two legs. And that will be no great matter, for I think if we all relapse to go again upon four, it would as well become our calling, since little is within but beast, nor action savouring better pretension. Then why should we be such degenerous monsters, like nursling dogs and monkeys, to forsake our proper garb of all four? The fireside here is crowded, and like to be more so, but all are your most humble servants, especially dear sister,

Your most affectionate humble Servant.

30.

For North Foley, Esq., at Stourbridge in Worcestershire.

Rougham, 27th February, 1708-9.

Dearest Nephew,

I had the favour of yours some time since, but I did not think it reasonable to trouble you to know it till I could also acquaint you that the box is safe arrived, with the cargo in good order, for which I return you many thanks. And as for exceeding your commission, if I had known the box had been so large I should have contrived to fill it. My smith was soliciting for files,—now I can supply him, and break with my old customer if needs be. The next work will be to hollow some trees, to make water run from one ditch to another, which is all the aqueducts we have. If the dispensation of a good coal were as diffusive as the cold is, you would hollow the earth and let

III.   8

Netherton drop in, for sure fires were never so much in
fashion.   I wished heartily for my niece here, though she
ventured starving, for we have had a most rare harpsi-
chordian, the most exquisite teacher, player, and composer
I ever knew; but he was too big for us, and after a taste
of his skill we parted.   My nephew Philip hath promised
us a visit this spring, but I shall not put him in mind of
it till the library is tenable.   My brother writes that he
hath not paid the carriage, so please add to the bill and
put it to account to him, and excuse all troubles from
                  Your most affectionate humble Servant,
                                          ROGER NORTH.

My wife and bairns are your most humble servants.

31.

FOR MRS. FOLEY AT STOURBRIDGE.

1709 ?

Though I have been thus long in telling you, dear sister,
I received yours, yet I am truly sensible of your affliction,
and am very much concerned for it; but I do believe there
have been more people disturbed in their heads within this
two years than for an age before.   The other day we lost
a fine lady, Sir Edward Bacon's sister.   She had been mad
this twelvemonth, and at last, as it is said, took too great
a dose of opium, for she never woke after it; but seemed
to be in great pain by her groaning, though never waked.
We have received our box of glasses safe and well.   We
have lately been at Glemham, and found my brother Montagu very weak and ill.   We hear he is now much better.
Lady North had then the gout, and niece Catherine not
well.   We stayed but a fortnight, but since have received
the good news of their amendments.   I should rejoice to
hear the same from you of yours, being, dear sister,
                  Your most affectionate humble Servant,
                                          R. NORTH.

My kind service to my niece and nephew will make this
the more acceptably yours.

32.

[The Trial of Dr. Sacheverel.   The House of Lords pronounced sentence on the 21st March.]

To the Hon. Dudleya North.

Rougham, 27th March, 1710.

Dearest Niece,

I waylaid you at Catledge, expecting by your language your course had been that way ; since, I understand you are at Epping. So now I am upon the chase, and shall follow you with my thanks for your letter, which hath cheered abundance of people's hearts, in which the thoughts of the Doctor's being mortified at a parliamentary rule, had sunk deep. It is probable his counsel did much for him, but he himself more by his speech, which is read about by the common people, as if it were a catechism, but most of all, an advocate he had which argued with great force, and that was one Mr. Mob.[1] He is descended of the Stantons, and has that advantage of haranguing that he seldom comes into any house or court but says what he has to say without doors, and the voice comes in strangely, and seems to be more efficacious than at the bar. But I cannot but wonder at the fate of a Christian sermon with a text, and fraught with the same : perhaps it is to appease the manes of a certain pastoral letter which had the like fate. I am continually refreshed in the memory of the frequent instances in ancient history of the hard fate of public-spirited honest men. I do not wonder that the party of the philanthropist is so inconsiderable,   Athens used once, in one or two years, to banish some person for the security of the Republic, and this used to fall on the forward ambitious persons, and plausible as it was once, the justest, wisest, and best commonwealth's man in the city was so banished,

---

[1] " Thursday, 2 March, 1710. He (Dr. Sacheverel) was followed by a great mob, who last night attacked Mr. Burgesses meeting-house, pulling down all the pews, wainscot, &c., making a bonfire thereof in Lincoln's Inn Fields, one being killed in the tumult," &c.—See *Luttrell's Diary.*

who was called Aristides the Just.   In the story it is said
that a citizen brought his oyster shell to a friend to write
the name he would banish, and that was Aristides.   How,
said the other, he is so good a man that we call him the
Just!   Aye, said the other, for that reason I do it, it is an
ambitious title and may be dangerous to the State.   But
to leave history, or rather adjourn it to the ale and fireside
at Rougham, or wherever we shall be so happy to meet
with you, I shall trouble you only with a note. How prone
it is when a business is undertaken for passion or indirect
purposes upon an unrighteous foot, and carried on with
passion and indecent fury, and the defence is generous,
free, and approvable,—how all events will reflect to purposes of reputation as well as project directly contrary to
their designs.   *Probatum est.*

33.

For the Right Honble. the Lord North and Grey.

London, 1st May, 1712.

My Lord,
     It hath pleased God to take your Lordship's sister
out of this bad world.[1]   She made a will, of which the enclosed is a true copy, and I am here, in obedience to her
commands, to take the best care I can (your Lordship
being absent) in the performance of her will.   I cannot
give your Lordship yet any account of her affairs, being
but just arrived, and taken up with the directions of her
funeral.   Your Lordship will observe some omissions in
her will: for there is no residuum of any kind, but money
given, and her chief jewels were altered since the will. But
I suspect that the £200 designed will not clear her funeral
and bills; and not only the loose coins, if any be, but the
very pecuniary legacies will be touched to contribute, for
the rule is that pecuniary legacies go all first, and specific
legacies come not in contribution.   I purpose at present to
deliver out all those things that are given in particular, and

---

[1] The Hon. Dudleya North died on 25th April, 1712, at the house of
Lady North and Grey, in Bond Street.—*Ballard's Lives*, p. 415.

reserve other matters till your Lordship's happy arrival, which I hope will be safe and soon.   In the meantime, when I have despatched the funeral and gathered together the particulars of her concerns, your Lordship will be troubled with a particular account of every matter and circumstance from, my Lord,

Your Lordship's most faithful and obedient Servant.

34.

FOR THE RIGHT HONOURABLE THE LORD NORTH AND GREY. TO BE LEFT WITH MR. GEO. READ AT HIS HOUSE IN RED LION STREET, NEAR GREY'S INN PASSAGE, LONDON.

Rougham, 19th May, 1712.

MY LORD,

This only covers a representation I have made of the condition of your Lordship's sister's affairs, a copy of which I have left with my Lady [1] (who is in very good health at Epping), whereby your Lordship will see, with the diamond necklace, and other things that happen to be undisposed, there will be but enough to clear the account of debts, funeral, and legacies, saving only the moneys supposed to be in your Lordship's hands, which being esteemed about £58, almost balances the credit of the estate, that is £62 odd.   I have delivered out the specific legacies, and shall pay what is due for moneys borrowed, but suspend all bills till Michaelmas, time being not so material with the tradesmen as with friends that were kind in her sickness.   I ordered the funeral with all decorum and regard to her intention I could, and I must needs acquaint your Lordship that your bailiff at Catlidge was earnestly careful to pursue orders, and nothing was wanting or out of order.   As for my niece's books, I have a design upon them which your Lordship I hope will not think selfish, but much for the honourable memorial of my niece. I have had a design to build a parochial library at Rougham,

---

[1] His Lordship had married in October, 1705, Maria Margaretta, daughter of M. Van Ellemeet, Treasurer of the United Provinces of the Netherlands.

and now shall finish it this summer, and placing my niece's books there, entitule the catalogue *Ex dono, &c., e libris eruditissimæ virginis, &c.*, which will be a monument more lasting than marble. I doubt not your Lordship will concur in opinion that whatever the consequences, my niece's legacy as well as debts, &c., shall be fully paid, that no person in the world may have occasion to think of her, but with all the honour and respect possible. We are in continual expectation to hear of a holy peace,[1] which, among other felicities, will, I hope, fix your Lordship's residence on this side of the water, to continue in glory and felicity to the end of things, whereby I may have the honour of frequent opportunity to assure your Lordship

I am, &c.

35.

To the same.

Rougham, August 18th, 1712.

My Lord,

I was honoured with your Lordship's from Catledge, 7th inst., for which no less than your Lordship's and my Lady's generous acceptance of our personal tender of our services at Catledge, we return our most humble thanks. I designed to have sent your Lordship's bond by a servant that I must send over for the man we left behind us, but considering that of boys the post-boy is most trusty, especially being warranted by your Lordship's command, I have enclosed it here. By the catalogue of payments that I hope to provide for at Michaelmas, I find there will be of debts £255. There is somewhat for the account at Newmarket and Epping, which your Lordship may please to order the servant to pay, because they will be out of my line. Then the funeral is £69. 19*s.* 7*d.*, and the five legacies £100, in all £425, as I take it, or thereabouts, with some advantage if any fall by abatements, and for this I have £500 and interest of £450 of it (£50 being detached for present occasions) so that I shall have a considerable sum to be

---

[1] The Peace of Utrecht was not signed till 3rd March, 1715.

accounted for, in about £77, as I shall make plain in particulars when the payments are made, and render the
balance; I having no thought but to serve your Lordship
and your incomparable sister without any interest otherwise to taint the sincerity of my intentions. The jewels,
&c., are not here, but safe at London, to be put into your
Lordship's hands when the grand assembly of the nations
brings folks together; and I must own also the very great
favour of the books which you have been pleased to consecrate, whereof the disposition will, I hope, be to your Lordship's satisfaction when you see it. I purpose to have all
the accounts of the payments in a little book together, and
if I may presume so far I should desire your Lordship
would transmit to me Mrs. Kenedy's acquittance to accompany them, for I am at stake to all the demands, and desire to have all the acquittances for my discharge, which,
when the surplus is rendered to your Lordship, will remain
to those that come after. I was obliged, for the sake of
your Lordship's annuity, to prove the will, and it was not
provable but in my name, as the will was penned, however
it was intended, for otherwise I had saved that charge,
because probate is necessary only for suits. Mr. Read
hath paid the charge, and hath the probate, which your
Lordship will take of him. I directed him to pay the
surplus of my niece's assets to Mr. Cason, that lent my
niece . . . . . and hath her note. If that be not done he
is accountable to your Lordship for it.

After the needful (as the merchants term it) I shall
trouble your Lordship with an adventure as we came home,
which was by an accident that never happened before, and
I hope never will again; and that event might probably
have been so *funeste* as the mischief that happened is put
to account amongst our good fortunes. Within a furlong
of Hilborough, the pole of the coach splintered quite off at
the stem, and that falling down with the spring-tree bars
clattering under such a weight at the fore horses' heels
made them run. The coachman commanding back the
wheel horses, the splinters of the pole pricked them in the
haunches, and one was run in above four inches. This
made all run, and the coachman was drawn down by the
leaders (because the coach by the discharge of the pole did

not follow their motions) and laid in the midst among
them, but the wheels missed him, and he has no great
hurt ; but the run increased, and the footman, thinking to
catch a bridle, was by the coach beaten down, horse and all,
and hath a contusion at the side of his knee which makes
him lame, and that is the worst of the wounds in this
action. But the coach still running, I was impatient to be
out of action or endeavour to do somewhat towards preventing the worst of mischief, put the servant in my place
next her lady, and crept out *secundum artem*, so that I had
no hurt, but could not snatch the horses for speed, but
called, and the people in the town endeavoured to stop the
horses, but could not till in the midst of the town the
coach fell with a great *fracas*. My wife had only the
ordinary bruises on the side that fell only. Somewhat I
think the edge of a coach box in rolling met with her fore-
head, and made a cut about three inches long, from a little
within the hair to the eyebrow. As soon as my speed
brought me up, I found her and the servant cleared without more harm, and having settled her in a house, went
out and gave the necessary orders for a surgeon, &c., who
came to us at a minister's house, where we were very well
entertained. Next day we, in his coach (for ours was
fracassé) got home safe, and now have leisure to reflect—
as those in military service after an engagement do—how
strangely we escaped, this being an accident neither to be
foreseen nor prevented is the less regretted, but is put in
amongst the inevitables of life. Your Lordship may
imagine my lady's fright was prodigious, but it arose
from the magnitude to be no fright at all, for the falling
of the coach was the best thing expected, which terminated
the fright all at once. I have reason to beg pardon for this
history of a *mal-hora*, but thought it better your Lordship
should have it directly, with all the just circumstances of
it, than from report, whose *proprium quarto modo* is to
deprave truth. My wife is very well, bating some weight
and stiffness that appear now, which at first were not so
sensible. Her hurt is, as the surgeon assures, next to
nothing. She is most sensible of the honour received from
your Lordship and my Lady at Catledge, and hopes we may
have opportunity at a rustic table, like Philemon and Baucis,

to make the visage (at least) of some acknowledgments for them. In the meantime we have but to wish to your Lordship and my Lady, whose most humble servants all here are, all measure of prosperity and happiness and honour, rather of peace than of war; but in either as it happens, not less than your Lordship may justly claim, which are not ordinary and would much receive.

36.

THE HONOURABLE ANN FOLEY, AT STOURBRIDGE, WORCESTERSHIRE.

19th December, 1712.

DEAREST SISTER,

I should forfeit my place of secretary if I did not with the first acquaint yourself of the increase of our family, my wife last night being brought to bed of a huge fat boy, and in all appearance she is like to do well after it. I believe the name will be Montagu, and the gossips Mr. Dudley, Sir N. Lestrange, and Mr. Jno. Wenyeve's lady, but I hope it will prove according to the intended beginning in an unchristian age, a Christian; and for the better securing that point, my wife hath in her mind dedicated it to the priesthood, and I hope you will live to hear him preach against heresy and blasphemy, so flagrant now-a-days . . . .

37.

TO THE SAME.

Rougham, 8th March, 1715-16.

DEAREST SISTER,

When a competent time is passed, as I account it, supposing you may be diverted with hearing from your friends, then I set the quill pointing to yourself; but now we have somewhat more than ordinary to account for, which was a prodigious illumination in the sky about eight on Tuesday evening last, and it is reasonable friends should compare notes to know if the appearance was in remote parts the same. I hear it was observed at London and all along our coast, and I suppose with you. I was called out by the servants as to a wonder, which indeed it was. Very much was passed before I came out, but I saw enough of it, for the light was as of a moonlight night, though no moon could shine, and the sun was too far dipped to tinge any of the clouds; but we saw in a hazy sky a perpetual moving light. It seemed often to drive from the north and north-east, where the sky was as at break of day, and so it moved about continually in a beaming undulating manner as waves, or the convulsions in the body of a dying animal, and this to all that distance about east south-east, and over our heads, and only the west point was clear from the disorder; but very often the lights emerged in all these parts of themselves, one after another, lasting a considerable time, and wasting, and others appearing: and some began by the edge, as a cloud gilded, and so dispersed, and some from small specks dilated and diffused the waving motion of the light a great way about, and very often the light would take, as it were, a centre, and radiate itself round about as beams of the sun, and frequently as beyond the haziness of the sky lights struck, as firing of cannon one after another, which the people called lightning. It was white, and sometimes a little rainbowed while I looked on, which was about a quarter of an hour. But at the beginning they said it was more extraordinary. We expect to hear discourse as usual upon sights which are called prodigies, and it would be well if wicked people took warning at anything; but after so many warnings as flow from the common course of things, I believe, like those that would not hear Moses and the prophets, they would not be moved if even one should come from the dead. I hope this will find yours as our family is, God be thanked, at present in good health, which will always be welcome news to

Your most humble Servant.

38.

FOR MR. MONTAGU NORTH, AT MR. RUSSELL'S HOUSE
IN COLLEGE STREET, IN WESTMINSTER, LONDON.

Rougham, 27th April, 1728.

DEAR MOUNT,

I have heard from all hands that you are not negli-
gent, but apply yourself diligently to the great work of
making yourself a good scholar, which, as your case stands,
that are to make your fortunes by your learning, is not only
necessary for your provision but I hope will sprout out in
time into dignities and preferments, and terminate for the
happiness of your life, and content as well as joy to all your
friends. I know that you were kept too long back from
versifying, which, as a new thing, may be troublesome, but
use and practice will make it easy, and it is not out of the
way of understanding prose authors, but helps mainly to it.
The orators themselves studied the poets, and in their
elegancies and conciseness profited by them; therefore I
hope you will go on and prosper, and nothing needful shall
be wanting to you that can be procured by

Your most loving Father,

ROGER NORTH.

Your mother has been a long time exceeding ill, but
now is better, and far away, I hope, in a way of perfect
recovery.

39.

TO THE SAME.

Rougham, 15th March, 1729.

DEAREST MOUNT,

I am exceedingly obliged by the music book, and
desire that my thanks may be returned for it. I must own
myself not capable of profiting by such a method, for my
little skill hath proceeded from experience of concert and
my own reflections, without being ever formally instructed;.

which makes one partial to that way, and not to decline
rules is enough. This book is a long series of rules without any rationale of the subject, and seeing it harps upon
the common notions and distinctions, I am not to find any
fault with it, as of concords perfect and imperfect, the in-
troducing or preparing and resolving discords, and some
others, which may be useful grammatically, but are not in
the true theory of the subject. And it seems that here all
things are to be done by rule, which belong to the mind to
perform, as transpositions for instance. I believe I have
transposed as much to accommodate voices, both single and
concert music of three and four parts, as any one Englishman whatever, and never knew any rule but to carry in
mind the tune from one key to another, without regard to
the flats and sharps upon the lines only as the use of the
assumed key required. And I guess that by the rules
given here no man will ever be able to transpose a concert
justly. Our common failing is derived of a false method
of entrance into the science of music, which ought not to
be by rule without thought and practice, and that is to be
had by toning the gamut perfectly well. And so a learner,
seeing the notes, will know the tone in his mind as if he
sounded it. And then to understand there is but one scale
of music universally understood, and that is the gamut,
and the distinction of the flat and sharp keys is included
in that, for the note next above the key-note is always the
flat key, as if to be the scale for the gamut is always a
sharp key, A the next above is the flat key, and the use of
it doth not disturb the scale in any one tone or semitone.
And then for shifting keys, may not anyone that can tone
his gamut, if required, tone the same, beginning upon any
other note? The want of this discipline is the cause so few
sing or touch a violin in tune. And for change, is it not
enough to say that any note that sounds in the full accord
of the key will take the air without offence? though some
come on with a little preparation, as they call it, better
than without it. But as for this book, I admire the industry with which it is collected and put together, but to
a learner must needs be a discouragement,—the great
obscurity and little explication it carries. And surely
examples by lines had been better than by letters, or

rather both together had been best, but it hath filled my head so much with conundrums that to discharge some of which you have this tumultuous letter.

40.

TO THE SAME.

Rougham, August 3rd, 1729.

DEAR MONTAGU,

Mr. Vernon shewed us your letter, whereby it appears that you are like to be in a pitiful case this breaking up, and all do think it would be better to be at home. Therefore if you can so far manage for yourself as to take a place in the coach that comes out for Lynn on the Friday, which will be next to your breaking up, you may come down. I know not whether your stock will bring you down, but you will contrive it one way or other. If you can get Robert Dashwood, you two may bring the coach to Swaffham, which will be less trouble than to send to meet you at Brandon. They will not come to here without two in the company that require it. You must bring your black clothes and stockings and some linen. If you can lock up your watch, it is best not to bring it for fear of robbing. Let us hear what you can do by next post, and I suppose a letter or two may pass before the time of breaking up. You need not load yourself with books, we having some here you may make use of, which is all at present from

Your most loving Father.

[Montagu North was admitted at Jesus College, Cambridge, on 26th June, 1730. He was elected scholar of his College in the following December, took the B.A. degree in January, 173¾, proceeded to M.A. in 1737, and appears to have ceased to reside at Cambridge in the July of that year.]

41.

To the same.

Rougham, October 30th, 1730.

Dear Mount,

In view of your being Greek Professor, I am content
you should have Josephus, because they say it is dressed
without Latin sauce.   It is a heavy edition, and much of it
I believe yet doth lie in hand ; the Chancellor of Norwich[1]
offered [one] to me for 50s. and now they ask £3, but it is
the way of book sales to over price, and then a few sold is
a good market. Your tutor will please to put it in his next
quarter.   As for the camping balls, I can say nothing but
that bubble-boy hath a shop in every college in Cambridge.
I would fain know what is Mr. Bradshaw's opinion of the
Scotch music book, if he hath any taste for such refinements or troubles himself with looking into them.

I am your most loving Father.

42.

To the same [at Cambridge].

Rougham, 16th November, 1730.

Dear Montagu,

I observe you are settled in a chamber, I cannot say
too good, but much too big for you, for it held Dr. North
and myself.   My study was up a little stair by the bedside
and his by the chimney. The greatest inconvenience is the
sun's heat in summer afternoons, and then we retired into
the bed chamber.   In short, if you get to be Fellow, you
need not change your chamber, which is not the ordinary
lot of a Pensioner.   But I have a confidence that what is
preternecessary will not turn to your inconvenience, that is
pretending to entertain idle company, I mean *vino fugi* of
the *fumosum genus*, for I would be loath you should confirm
the scandal charged upon the universities of learning chiefly
to smoke and to drink. You are shipped upon a voyage of

---

[1] Thomas Tanner.   He became Bishop of St. Asaph, January, 1731.

adventure of the good or evil of your whole life, and precious now lost will never be regained. You must be very observant of your tutor, who will faithfully direct you in all concerns as well of study as course of life, and in the end be (as I am fully persuaded) a very good friend. And you have to gather, not only learning but a good character, both in your college and university. These are the elements of good fortune in the world.

I am your most loving Father.

My service to Mr. Bradshaw.

43.

To the same.

Rougham, 15th June, 1731.

Dear Mount,

I had yours, by which you intimate that the 30th inst. will be a convenient time for your horse to come to bring you home. I think that must be referred to Mr. Bradshaw, whose opinion I would have you send me by your next, and if he makes no objection I shall make none, but send the horses. Only I must tell you that I believe it is true of the Universities that is said of the Inns of Court, that if any person pretends to be a lawyer he must study there; so a scholar gains little but in the University, where learning is or should be meat, drink, and clothing, as hath been said of lawyers, that they must eat, drink, and sleep law. This is not so desperate, but much may be got by country application, and so it will be when study becomes a direct pleasure. If you have anything to come by water let Mr. Nutting's boats have your custom. I have been much obliged by him, but have had no dealings with the Lynn man. I hope Mr. Bradshaw hath received my letter and bill for the last current quarter's account. So, expecting to hear from you, I am

Your most loving Father.

I observe the music you have bought, but as to the solos they are of no use without another, therefore bring two of the . . . . . I should be glad to join.

44.

To the same.

Rougham, 29th November, 1731.

Dear Mount,

I desire if you change your college you will not take Magdalen, nor commence any degrees near the Castle Hill. It seems the sort of learning there professed requires a long, at least Doctor's standing, to be perfect, else they would not lug out and brag of their acquisitions before the mob in the kitchen, where it was known they could not maintain their question by legitimate syllogism. But I do not wonder at such extravagance when the way of the University is become so little studious and so very expensive, and the meanest lads affect to follow their superiors, which cannot be done without a certain ruin to themselves and scandal to the University that should by order suppress the impertinent extravagances of the scholars. I approve much your deal with Mr. Nutting, of whom I have received favours, and I should be glad to make though but a semblance of a return. Therefore, if you can conveniently, without offence to the method of your college, which may expect you should do as all the rest do, I shall be glad you have your coats of him, but they must be paid for, for I will have no bills in the town on any account. When *O sapientia* comes [16 Dec.] I shall send the man with horses. Pay all possible respect to your tutor and the superiors in the college. Then you shall have more from your loving Father.

Your loving Father.

45.

Rougham, 17th December, 1731.

Dear Mount,

This only covers a letter to Mr. Bradshaw, which give with my humble service. I send a guinea by Liddyman for charges, of which you must give an account. You must by no means stop at Swaffham for the man's sake, but rather take a warm at Hilborough if need be, or nearer here. The smallpox rages at Swaffham. There are to be had a sort of small iron snuffers as drawers use in taverns. I would have three or four of them. Take care to keep warm, and, if it snows, not lose your way. Which is all at present

From your most loving Father.

46.

Rougham, 17th April, 1732.

DEAR MOUNT,

I have divers of yours since my last not formerly answered, having nothing worth postage to convey. As to directions for the study of the law, which you desire, it is a copious subject, and I remember that formerly I have wrote somewhat about it, which, if I can find it, shall be committed to you, and in the meantime a little will do but little service. I have written to Mr. Pm. to make good your allowance at Lady Day and Midsummer next, and we will consider about the time of your coming home ; and you must not expect that that can be often, for it is no small charge, therefore wings in such cases are a choice convenience. I am satisfied you are so well accommodated in the college, that I could willingly, if it were proper, commute stations with you, and in lieu of cares have ease, besides the profit to be made by the employ of time. All are well that we wish so hereabouts, as I hope you are, and wish so may continue, which is all at present from

Your most loving Father.

47.

Rougham, 30th May, 1732.

DEAREST MOUNT,

I do not hear your sisters talk of writing to you, and lest want of letters should (as they say) make you hipt, and so your college be called the Hippodrome, I write, but to very little purpose, having nothing new worth noting which you have not had from them. And indeed

III.   T

here mischances are plenty. We have a family and children fallen to the town, the man (Robt. Curry) run stark mad and kept here at the charge of two men day and night, till we could get him to Norwich and stowed up in Bedlam there at more than 4*s.* 6*d.* per week charge as long as he lives. One of our best coach-horses, leaping a hedge, staked himself, and we fear we shall lose him, and so be dismounted. I shall be glad to hear how terms are to go this next half year, which is all at present from

Your most loving Father.

48.

Rougham, 2nd July, 1732.

DEAREST MOUNT,

I had yours, which presseth to come home, a matter about this time intended, but I cannot grudge the want of your company when you are at Cambridge, which, as to improvement, is to a scholar a sort of home, where everything hath a beneficial look. The *eruditæ parietes* inspire somewhat, all which here vanish. The lectures may do much, but private study much more. I hope you will copy Tully or Pliny, so that when some good body founds (as Mr. Lucas the Greek) a Latin lecture, you may have the honour, in time, to be Latin Professor. I intend (nothing intervening to hinder) to send your horse on Monday, the 10th inst. Mr. Pimlow intended you a visit on that day, unless me sending your horse diverts him. The Wenyeves have been here in full troop,[1] the Ionian and his spouse, a matched cooked up to add a tail (in remainder) to the family, with the surviving two madams, and the Gressenhalites[2] all together, which fills us top full. We make few visits but to the latter. I shall not be able to sojourn anywhere abroad. So with my service to Mr. B. concludes

Your most loving Father, &c.

---

[1] His son Roger's first wife was Mary, daughter of John Wenyeve, of Brettenham, co. Suffolk, Esq.

[2] Henry le Strange of Gressenhall, co. Norfolk, Esq., married Mary, Roger North's third daughter. He succeeded his brother as fifth Baronet in 1751, and died without issue in 1760.

49.

Rougham, November 12th, 1732.

DEAR MONTAGU,

On Saturday last your box was delivered to the boat at Lynn, directed as you left it, and I hope it is come safe to Cambridge. At the same time I ordered the cart to call at Mr. S. Browne's for the hops, which I hoped to find there according to Mr. Nutting's advice, but it was said they were not come down yet, but when they came he would take care of them. I suppose your Tiber wants water, unless the parcel is carried to some other place in Lynn. I want to know Mr. Nutting's charge that I may send him his money with thanks; you may make a gentle inquiry about it, and let me know what you hear. It is out of tenderness to the *caput priscianum* that I do not write in Latin to draw the like, but having none which doth terminate *cum dasho*, which will not parse in your regions, therefore hold me to English, as when I say I am

Your most loving Father.

50.

Rougham, February 26th, 1732-3.

DEAR MONTAGU,

I had yours wherein you hold out your wish for an allowance on account of sophistry treats. I will have nothing to do with such matters that have no bottom. I have made you an allowance for all personal charges, besides your college, and out of that you may be as noble as you please. But I have much to say on that account, with which if I had been better satisfied you had heard from me sooner; and it is that I find from Mr. Bradshaw's bill, payments to tailors and milliners and other smaller concerns of your own which must be made good to him; but I expected from you, that ought to consider justly, not to call on or trouble Mr. Bradshaw about anything that falls within your allowance. You are much mistaken if you think me capable, having so many to provide for, of being profuse, therefore you must put economy among your liberal sciences.　I might fall into particulars if such did not refer to a right judgment of things, which I hope you will not want, it being your own concern.　I have referred it for Mr. Bradshaw to determine the case of your treating (which for the future on like occasion I shall take no notice of) and what he allows shall be made good by

Your most loving Father.

51.

[University Expenses.]

Rougham, 14th March, 1732-3.

Dearest Montagu,

　　You have made a fair declamation for one side, but like a true rhetorician you should have taken the alternate and made another against it, and such are commonly found the truer.　I was told that £80 per annum was enough for a Pensioner, and your having £20 of it for personalities will, as I find, exceed that.　You pretended great fruit of your own management, if you had a certain allowance, and paid your bills yourself.　And I was willing to ease your tutor, so that he might not be troubled with them nor with your coming to him for money, but that he should pay your allowance quarterly and the college dues only, which I thought an easy expedient.　But now I find there must be both all and some, which I get by a trust reposed in you.　And if you were sensible of my straits (which I am not inclined by words to exaggerate) you would avoid all those impertinent ways that draw fruitless expense. You would think much if I should rescind your allowance and turn all into your tutor's hands, who might think of matters otherwise than as you do, that will scarce think anything that you are sure of, enough.　But at present I have acquainted Mr. Bradshaw with my sense of matters, and desired him to make good your allowance, and see that nothing that is suitably necessary be wanting.　I believe if he wondered at anything it was at the fulness of your allowance, rather than at the smallness of it. But I will not enter into particulars, desiring you will consider your own work is doing as well as that of

Your most loving Father.

You said nothing of the last bill and the application of it.

52.

Rougham, March 26th, 1733.

DEAREST MONTAGU,

I had yours desiring a recommendation for a collegiate of yours to the Lord North and Grey, a candidate for Burwell living. Upon your character I do believe him to be a very deserving person, but I do not deal in recommendations, and not having writ to his Lordship or he to me this five or six years,[1] he will look upon such a letter now as obtained by treaty, and given for a civil compliance, as upon all vacancies is usual, and accordingly looked upon as such, in common course, unless there is some strong and personal engagement to induce it, therefore I must be excused in a matter I have no title to interpose. Which is all the needful at present from

Your most loving Father.

53.

Rougham, June, 1733.

DEAREST MONTAGU,

I had yours, or rather a plurality, for according to your ordinary measure four or five in one, which is the more esteemed being a method among friends, never *satis super que*. As for your Middletons, I desire not that our library should stink of his freedoms, a foolish pride as if none thought freely but they, whereas others out of free-

---

[1] About the year 1728 Lord North had forsaken the Church of England and joined the Church of Rome. This must have caused a coolness between the uncle and nephew, as it did between Lord North and Bishop Atterbury, who refused to see his Lordship after he had deserted the Anglican communion.—See *Memoirs of Atterbury*, by G. F. Williams (1869), vol. ii. p. 310.

thinking are assured of the truth of revelation, and by that of the truth of things revealed.[1] But as for the *trans-Tiberine* doctor, I shall be glad to see anything from him. . . . . You see my hand goes from bad at best to worse, which must be excused upon weakness every way prevailing in all that belongs to

Your most loving Father,
ROGER NORTH.

54.

Rougham, 2nd June, 1733.

DEAR MONTAGU,

I had yours, by which it is understood that you are well, and that is always an epistolar sum as welcome a burden as the post can bring. But the garniture of news, as it is called, serves for diversion, such as you have store of, either of public or private squabbles, not to mention the more scholastic disputes and witticisms, or graver controversies, but you afford us but little. I am almost deserted by the ready pen I used to play with, as you may see by the grub characters I am now forced to make, but you may exercise with pleasure the *copia* of expression and order, as well as form of writing, always advancing for the better, while I must droop in everything, always tending to the worse, and be glad chiefly when I find the contrary proceed from you. I hope you have a strict care of the MSS., which I would not have miscarry in any respect, being a sort of writing slight and slovenly as it is (such a fool I am) pleaseth me to peruse better than any books, of which the best soon tire with me. You will do well to use your strength while it lasts, for you will be sensible what is the value of lost time. We are here *in statu quo*, only a wedding happening fortuitously in the family, not without untimely fruit, with which your sisters may make you merry, who will make the account and tell you how it stands. I wish you continuance of health and increase of academic wealth, being

Your most loving Father.

---

[1] Middleton's famous *Letter to Dr. Waterland* was first published in 1731, and his *Defence* and *Remarks on a Reply to the Defence* in the following year.

55.

Rougham, 12th February, 1733-4.

DEAR MONTAGU,

I am glad you have passed the pikes, and I hope strenuously, and in time your two letters will be translated, and not stand for *Artium Baccalaureus*, but A Bishop.[1] Present my best services to Mr. Bradshaw, whose care in this affair must have been great and beyond my power duly to acknowledge . . . . You see how unable I am to write, and can read only that

I am yours.

56.

[*Advice to a Young Student of the Law.*]

Rougham, March 16th, 1733-4.

DEAR MONTAGU,

Your short letter received, and as to answer to the former, I believe this met it on the road, so no more of that. But by Mr. Clark I suppose you mean the gentleman that is inclined to study the common law. I wish I could serve him with any apt instructions, but really as to any pen work I am in a disabled condition, and as to memory and judgment no better than effete. I had once made a short dissertation of that sort, but what and where it is I cannot tell.[2] I am sure among my papers I can find no footsteps of it. The ordinary books recommended to beginners are, 1, Institutionary; and 2, Precedents or Reports of Cases. And first of the first, Littleton's *Tenures* is a prime book to be read alone, and not with Coke's *Comment*, which is a common-place of difficult matters, that confound rather than explain the author, of which one excellency is, that it is as plain and will not be

---

[1] Montagu North had just taken the A.B. degree.

[2] Probably *A Discourse on the Study of the Laws, by the Hon. Roger North*. Now printed from the Original MS. in the Hargrave Collection, with Notes and Illustrations by a Member of the Inner Temple. 8vo. London, 1824.

made plainer by any comment. Other books there are, as Perkins, the *Natural Review*, Crompton's *Jurisdiction of Courts*, to which may be joined the Lord Coke of the same subject, Stamford's *Pleas of the Crown*, and Coke of the same, and some others of like kind to be found in common catalogues, and (2) for reports, Plowden is usually recommended and probably enough. If the too great tediousness did not discourage it, one of the year books . . . . then Dyer and others, not forgetting the Lord Coke's, and of this last division there is such a farrago that will tire post horses to flounce through. But more pleasant studies are to be joined, as history, records, or precedents, when to be had, and mornings are proper for law, afternoons for relaxation and discourse, the prattling of which is to be cultivated, for some have defined the law as *ars bablativa*. It is certain that putting cases is a most useful exercise, and some say there never was a good lawyer that was not a good put-case. I wish I could serve the gentleman, as I would to the best of my power any friend of yours.[1]

I am your most loving Father.

---

[1] In the *Gentleman's Magazine* for 1734, p. 164, we are informed that "Roger North of the Inner Temple, Esq., aged 90," died on the 1st of March of that year. That Mr. North was *not* aged 90 in 1734, is certain; but did he die as early as the 1st of March? If so, the foregoing letter is wrongly dated. Taken in connection with the previous letter, in which he complains of his difficulty in writing, I incline to believe that the two letters were written at no long interval from one another, and that Mr. North made a slip of the pen. In any case this was probably the last letter he ever wrote, and for that reason was preserved by his son.

SUPPLEMENTARY.

THE family of the Norths was originally seated at Wakeringham in Notts; it emerged from obscurity and insignificance when the first ROGER NORTH of whom we have any distinct knowledge settled in London and became a merchant there. By his marriage with CHRISTIAN, daughter of RICHARD WARCUP of Sconington, he became the father of a son, EDWARD, who, because he gave early indication of his great abilities, was entered at one of the Inns of Court and bred to the law. This was he whom his great-grandson calls "the common parent and raiser of our family."

2. He was born about the year 1496. His success in his profession was less conspicuous at the beginning of his career than might have been expected. Made Clerk of the Parliament in 1530, he became King's Serjeant in 1536, Chancellor of the Court of Augmentations in 1544, and a Privy Councillor in the last year of King Henry's reign. Six years before the spoliation of the monasteries he purchased his manor of Kirtling, which his descendants still enjoy; but I believe that the vast sums which he acquired by royal grants of monastic estates were all dissipated long ago. He was executor to Henry VIII.; one of the Council of Edward VI.; was raised to the peerage as Baron North of Kirtling by Queen Mary, in 1554; made Lord Lieutenant of Cambridgeshire by Queen Elizabeth, and died at the Charterhouse in London in December, 1564, leaving behind him two sons, ROGER, his heir, and SIR THOMAS NORTH, Knight, the translator of *Plutarch's Lives*, a book from whose pages Shakespeare drew some of his inspirations.

3. ROGER, SECOND BARON NORTH, was a prominent per-

sonage at the Court of Queen Elizabeth. He was Ambassador Extraordinary to the Court of Charles IX. of France, was present at the famous battle of Zutphen, in which Sir Philip Sidney fell, and displayed on that occasion conspicuous valour, wounded though he had been in a previous encounter. He became Treasurer of the Household and a Privy Councillor, died in London on the 3rd December, 1600, and was buried at Kirtling on the 12th February following.

4. He married Winifred, daughter of Robert, Lord Rich, Chancellor of England, widow of Sir Henry Dudley, son of John, Duke of Northumberland, and by her was father of Sir John North, who died during the wars in the Netherlands, on the 5th June, 1597. Sir John North took to wife Dorothy, daughter of Sir Valentine Dale, Master of the Requests, leaving behind him, among other children, Dudley, his heir, and Roger, who was one of the great seamen of his time.

5. DUDLEY, THIRD LORD NORTH, succeeded his grandfather in December, 1600, being at that time under age. In 1602 he travelled on the Continent, having previously married Frances, daughter of Sir John Brocket of Brocket Hall, Herts. He enjoyed his title and estates for the long period of sixty-six years, and during that time did much to impoverish himself and his successors. He kept up great state at the Court of James I., and on one occasion "some rough words" passed between him and Bacon, who, "coming into his house, did no reverence, as he said the custom was."[1] He seems to have received no recognition for his long service as a courtier; and when on the accession of Charles I. he saw that no Court preferment was likely to come to him, and that his resources had become seriously diminished, he retired to his estate at Kirtling, and led the curious life which his grandson in his Autobiography has given us a glimpse of. He was fond of literature, and has left us some trifles which he wrote in his retirement; was an enthusiastic musician, and "a person full of spirit and flame"; by which his grandson seems to mean that he was imperious and self-willed,

---

[1] *Court and Times of James I.*, vol. ii. p. 232.

brooking no contradiction, and exacting from all about him the utmost deference and the most prompt and un-questioning obedience. His children and grandchildren held him in great awe, and the impression which he leaves upon us as we read about him is rather terrible than pleasing. He continued to live at Kirtling for nearly forty years after his retirement from the Court, and only once took part in public business, when he served upon a commission for managing the affairs of the Admiralty, in 1645. He died in January, 1668, in the eighty-sixth year of his age.[1]

6. He was succeeded by his eldest and only surviving son, DUDLEY, FOURTH LORD NORTH, father of that remarkable brotherhood which the youngest of the band has done so much to immortalize. The fourth Lord North was made a Knight of the Bath at the creation of Charles I. as Prince of Wales, when he was a boy of fourteen. Subsequently he served under Sir Francis Vere in the Low Countries, travelled much on the Continent, and was esteemed a man of learning and many accomplishments. On the 24th April, 1632, he married ANNE, one of the daughters of Sir Charles Montagu of Cranbrook Hall in Essex, brother of the famous Henry Montagu, first Earl of Manchester, Lord Privy Seal under Charles I., of whom Clarendon has drawn one of his most favourable characters.

7. ANNE, LADY NORTH, was a worthy daughter of that illustrious house. At the time of her marriage she was in her nineteenth year, her husband being in his thirty-first. She was a lady of a right noble and loving nature—brave, practical, and sagacious—a perfect mother, and a perfect wife. She brought her husband a considerable fortune; but, during the greater part of her married life, she had a hard game to play, and a great deal to try her. The old lord insisted on his son bringing his bride to Kirtling, and making that his home; and he demanded what in those days was a very considerable annual payment for the en-forced accommodation. Even when by increase of their family it had become necessary to set up a separate estab-

---

[1] His widow—Frances, Dowager Lady North—survived him more than ten years, and was buried at Kirtling, 28th February, 1677.

lishment elsewhere, the payment was still exacted. It was assumed that their apartments were reserved for them in the great family mansion, and if they did not choose to avail themselves of their opportunities, it was their loss.

8. Lady North bore her husband no less than fourteen children, of whom ten grew up to maturity. The education and settling in life of so large a progeny were a serious drain upon the parents' resources, and necessitated a constant exercise of economy and self-denial.

9. Roger North tells us but little of his father. In one of the many fragments in the mass of his literary remains now deposited in the British Museum, he describes him as " knowing in books of all sorts, but not pedantically, so as to quote, but so as to rectify his judgment in the occurrences of his life." In the account book referred to (§ 12) almost the only entries which tell of expenses incurred in the way of luxuries are the frequent payments made for musical instruments, and books added to his library. He was one of the subscribers towards the printing of Walton's *Polyglot*, and he too was an enthusiastic musician, as his father was before him. He kept an organist in his house for many years, one Mr. Loosemore, and it was in 1660 that the famous John Jenkins (*Autobiography*, § 111 n.) took up his residence at Kirtling, and remained there till young Roger matriculated at Cambridge.

10. His Lordship appears to have taken to smoking first in 1657, and the habit grew upon him, the frequent entries for pipes and tobacco shewing that he became more and more addicted to this indulgence. Probably it afforded him some solace in the dreadful malady from which he suffered so long.

11. But it was when speaking of his mother that Roger North always expressed himself in terms of the tenderest affection and the most enthusiastic reverence and admiration. In a letter to his sister, Mrs. Foley, in 1689, he says :—

" I think there never was such an example in the world as our mother, who was no Hector, but never appeared disturbed during all her painful nursings which she had with many of us, and more with my father; so that although she was as tender as was possible, one would have thought she had an heart of brass. I have heard that, upon terrible wounds made up, after the work done she would swoon, but rubbed through the work like a lion."

12. In his latter years Mr. North contemplated, and actually began, writing a brief account of his parents, and the following is extracted from this memoir, which appears never to have been completed.

" She knew her lord to be just to the greatest rigour, than which nothing more could oblige her; and in all the extremity of the stone, with which he was most extremely afflicted, she had comfort in the good service and help she gave him, and that which would have sunk common spirits into despair stirred up her strength and vigour, being invincible in patience, indefatigable in care and watching, not only for years, but I may say her whole life, and never relented till her business was done, and then I must allow that she would surrender her spirits to a swoon, as if it were to refresh them against a new occasion . . . . . She survived her lord about three years, and lived upon her jointure comfortably and honorably, never more pleased than when her house was filled with her children, with whom she was merry and free, and encouraged them to be so too, all the while making good cheer of what her estate produced; and in that her conduct was such that there was no country curiosity wanting, and even in the greatest perfection of the kind, both of meats, bayry [*sic*], fruits, and confections, besides all made wines and cider, which she made with much curiosity. . . . . . I must not omit one extraordinary virtue and qualification of that good lady, which was keeping accounts and writing, in the midst of all her business of the family, and care of her sick and aged lord. She would write letters to all her children in remote parts, although it happened she had received none from them, or which required no answer, and this every week, to keep them to their custom of writing to her. And they, well knowing her desires, were seldom wanting, but supplied her copiously enough, she being also in that her lord's secretary, encouraging all manner of freedom of style and matter, and this correspondence was, as they declared, not the least comfort of their lives. But she not only wrote over whatever her lord had for the entertainment of his solitude composed into books, but kept strict accounts of all the household affairs and dealings whatsoever,[1] and in a large, plain, and most legible way of character, of which I have volumes to shew.

"And then she passed the tedious nights alone while her lord slept, and was ready to administer to him upon his waking what he desired, which was usually about one of the clock. And for divers years before he died she never thought of bed or repose till after that time of night."

13. Roger North was born at Tostock, in Suffolk, on the 3rd September, 1653. He passed most of his childhood at Kirtling, and at five years of age he was placed under the tuition of the clergyman of the parish, Ezekiel Catchpole by name, who, in the parish register, describes himself as Lord North's *Chaplain and Curate*. This is the worthy man of whom his pupil gives so attractive a picture in the second chapter of his autobiography, and it is of Kirtling that he is speaking when he describes the daily life of "the town [which] was then my grandfather's." For teaching the brothers Montagu and Roger, Mr. Catchpole received seven shillings a week, and for their music lessons Mr. Jenkins was paid one pound a quarter. The two boys were sent to Thetford School in 1663, where Mr. Keen was the master; and here the cost of their education, including everything, never amounted to forty guineas a year for the two. Before Roger North was ten years old, his four elder brothers had all left the nest, and were making their several ways in the world.

14. CHARLES, the heir, was one of those who sailed in the fleet to welcome Charles II. at the Restoration; and he made a very favourable impression upon Pepys, who describes him as "a fine gentleman," and was much struck by his skill as a musician, for "at night he did play his part exceeding well at first sight." He married early, Catherine, daughter of William, Lord Grey of Werke, widow of Sir Edward Moseley, a Lancashire Baronet, and

---

[1] See Note A.

with her obtained a large estate. Between him and his brothers there was little cordiality.

15. FRANCIS, the second son, and eventually Lord Keeper of the Great Seal, was called to the Bar in 1661, and that same year DUDLEY, the third son, left England to seek his fortune in foreign lands.

16. JOHN, the fourth son, was living the life of a retired student at Cambridge, precocious and very learned, a bookworm who was to succeed Dr. Isaac Barrow as Master of Trinity in his thirty-second year, and to become Clerk of the Closet to the King by and by.

17. There was not a single son or daughter of this household whose abilities were not of a very high order. Sir Francis became Solicitor General at thirty-three, Chief Justice of the Common Pleas at thirty-seven, and Keeper of the Great Seal at forty-four. It was an age of immeasurable rancour and party bitterness, when any man of force and genius who occupied a prominent position was denounced by his political opponents with a ferocious malignity of slander such as to us is almost unintelligible; but no one, even in that age of unexampled scurrility, ventured to disparage the intellect of the Lord Keeper, or to hint that he was other than one of the greatest lawyers of his generation. It was reserved for a writer of the nineteenth century to suggest that he was not only wicked as a man, but lacking even in legal acumen. Of Sir Dudley North, the third son, Macaulay, who certainly did not love the Norths, pronounces that he was "one of the ablest men of his time." John, the fourth son, was elected to the Professorship of Greek in the University of Cambridge in his twenty-eighth year. When, three years afterwards, he preached before the King at Whitehall, Evelyn, who seems to have been much struck by the performance, wrote of him that he was "a very young but learned and excellent person," and when he made his acquaintance at dinner some months afterwards, he describes him as "a most hopeful young man." Montagu, the fifth son, was less fortunate than his brothers, though only less successful as a London merchant than Dudley North himself had been, because he had the ill luck to be thrown into prison while passing through France on his way to Constantinople; and his

three years' detention in the castle of Toulon happened just at a time when his absence entailed very serious loss.

18. The daughters of the family were no less gifted, and hardly less highly cultured than their brothers. With Anne, who married Mr. Robert Foley of Stourbridge, Roger North kept up a brisk correspondence till her death ; a large number of the letters have been preserved, and they indicate that the lady was a person of alert intellect and well-furnished mind. But of all the sisters, Mary, the eldest, who married Sir William Spring of Pakenham, in Suffolk, was by far the most brilliant—a woman of real genius—who died in childbed in her twenty-fourth year. "I do just remember so much of her," says her brother in his Life of the Lord Keeper, " (for I was very young when she married) that, for hours and hours together, she diverted her sisters and all the female society at work together (as the use of that family was) with rehearsing by heart prolix romances, with the substance of speeches and letters, as well as passages; and this with little or no hesitation, but in a continual series of discourse, the very memory of which is to me, at this day, very wonderful. She instituted a sort of order of the wits of her time and acquaintance, whereof the symbol was a sun with a circle touching the rays, and, upon that, in a blue ground, were wrote $αὐτάρκης$ in the proper Greek characters, which her father suggested. Divers of these were made in silver and enamel, but in embroidery plenty, which were dispersed to those wittified ladies who were willing to come into their order; and for a while they were formally worn, till the foundress fell under the government of another, and then it was left off."

19. How many of the Knights and Dames of the Primrose League have any suspicion that the details of their own organization in some of its most characteristic arrangements were anticipated two centuries ago? The Order founded by Mary North in the seventeenth century, however, was started upon another basis than that of community in political sentiment; it was an Order of Intellect, and its badge the symbol of a community of taste and interest in literature, science, and art.

20. Though Sir Dudley and his lady, as has been said, would have preferred to live in a house of their own, and did at last establish themselves upon the estate they had bought at Tostock, the old lord loved their company and that of his grandchildren too well to allow them to spend more than a portion of their time away from him. Kirtling was during his lifetime much more than any other residence the home of the North family. It was a magnificent mansion, and in Roger North's boyhood perhaps the most magnificent country house in the Eastern Counties. It had been erected by Edward, the first Lord North, upon the site of a much older manorial residence, placed upon one of those artificial quadrangular islands which are so common in Norfolk and Suffolk, and whose history for the most part has been lost in the distant past. The island at Kirtling was originally a rectangle of about seven acres in extent, surrounded by an enormous moat of great depth, and fifty yards wide. This moat was supplied with water by tapping the springs in the green-sand below the chalk of the district round. The remains of extensive earthworks towards the east clearly indicate that at whatever time the moat was excavated it must have involved a prodigious expenditure of organized labour, and that the island was intended to serve as a place of defence and security. It is evident, too, from the position of the Norman church, that we are face to face with a stronghold that existed long before the Conquest. If the chalk and earth dug out from the moat had been heaped up upon the island enclosed, it would have gone far to raise the level to a not inconsiderable height above the surrounding ground; but as it was necessary to construct a huge dam to resist the pressure of the water on the east, the material taken out of the moat was utilized for this purpose, and no more than sufficient earth was available to raise a plateau on which the house itself was built, the island probably never having stood more than a few feet above the water which surrounded it. This plateau was about three-quarters of an acre in extent, and on it Edward, Lord North, built his mansion. It seems that before beginning to build his new house he filled up one side of the moat—no inconsiderable undertaking—and the magnificent gateway, which was spared

III.   U

when the dismantling of the edifice was effected, occupies the place of the drawbridge and approaches of the earlier time.

21. In September, 1578, Roger, Lord North, entertained Queen Elizabeth at Kirtling for three days. The account of his expenditure on the occasion has been printed more than once, and is a record of lavish, almost barbaric hospitality. In Roger North's boyhood the Queen's room was still kept sacred, and even to the close of the last century her chair of state, the footstools on which she had reposed her royal feet, and many other reminiscences of her visit were still shewn to sight-seers.

22. Kirtling was in its glory in the days of Dudley, the third Lord. The pictures which his grandfather had removed from London, when he sold the Charterhouse to the Duke of Norfolk, still hung upon the walls. The grandson had added to them many noble portraits of the great men with whom he had associated at the Courts of Queen Elizabeth, James, and Charles I. Among them some splendid specimens from the easels of Federigo Zuccaro, Van Somer, and Cornelius Janssen; and a portrait of Vandyke, said to have been by the great artist's own hand. Roger North and his brothers, from their childhood, were educated in a school of art, the eye and ear trained from infancy. Outside the great moated house the country was then thickly wooded, the well-stocked deer park extending far away to the horizon. The old lord was as a king of the shire, keeping up constant and prodigal hospitality, insomuch that young Francis, when newly called to the Bar, his brain filled with dreams of ambition and devoted to the study of his profession, found it hard to escape from the festivities and country amusements that were always going on while he was for burying himself in his law books. But it is pretty plain that the estate was suffering severely from the wasteful expenditure. When the old lord died the house required substantial repairs, and the park was little better than a wilderness. Dudley, the fourth Lord, had not time or opportunity to carry out any great reforms; and when his son Charles died in 1690, Roger looked upon the prospects of his nephew, the young Lord, as well nigh

desperate.[1] Kirtling could never be again what it had been.

23. The Lives of his three distinguished brothers, which Roger North drew up during his retirement, need no further introduction here. They speak for themselves, and must always be regarded as works of prime importance for the historian and student of the period over which they extend. It is to be lamented that Mr. North's own Autobiography should be incomplete. It ends at what may truly be called the great crisis of his life—the death of the Lord Keeper Guilford, on the 5th September, 1685. Though he was only just thirty-two when this event happened, he had already been talked of as likely to succeed Judge Hugh Wyndham as Baron of the Exchequer the year before.[2] He was in the enjoyment of a large and lucrative practice at the Bar, and seemed on the high road to preferment. With the Revolution all his hopes of advancement were at an end. He refused to take the oath to King William III., and threw in his lot with the nonjuring party,—Archbishop Sancroft at their head—and though he accepted the condition of affairs as inevitable, in sympathy was a loyal supporter of the Stewarts. A conspirator and plotter he could never have been, whatever his sentiments. By the terms of the Lord Keeper's will, his children and the trusteeship of his estates were left to his brothers, Dudley and Roger, and in the *Life* of the former we are furnished with a highly entertaining account of the manner in which the brothers discharged their duties, and the way in which they lived at Wroxton while superintending the alterations and improvements of the mansion. These occupied all their leisure hours for years after the death of the Lord Keeper, and had reached completion when Mr. North, in the year 1690, purchased the estate of Rougham in Norfolk. It had been for nearly three hundred years the seat of the Yelvertons, and in the fifteenth century the famous Judge, Sir William Yelverton, had kept up some state here as one of the magnates of

---

[1] William, Lord North and Grey. He became later on a very rich man, when, at the death of Ralph, Lord Grey of Werke, he succeeded to that nobleman's estates.

[2] *Prideaux Letters* (Camden Society), p. 138.

East Anglia. The estate had recently passed, through a daughter of the last Yelverton, into the possession of one Yelverton Peyton, whose exigencies had compelled him to sell it. There was a large old rambling house which had been enlarged from time to time, and which must have been a gaunt and comfortless mansion.

24. A passion for building has at all times been a characteristic of the Norths. The Lord Keeper had spent large sums upon Wroxton. Sir Dudley had rebuilt the mansion at Glemham, and now it was Roger North's turn to convert an old house into a new one, or to rebuild it from the ground. He entered upon possession of the Rougham estate in the autumn of 1690, and was still residing in his house in Covent Garden when his eldest brother Charles, Lord North and Grey, died in his fifty-sixth year,[1] in January, 1691.

25. His lordship in 1673 had married Catherine, only daughter of William, Lord Grey of Werke, and he had been thereupon summoned by special writ to take his seat in the House of Lords as Lord Grey of Rolleston. At his father's death in 1677 he succeeded to the barony of North of Kirtling, and from that time he was known as Lord North and Grey. He left behind him at his decease a family of two sons and two daughters, and a widow who waited little more than three months before she married again to the Hon. Francis Russell, Governor of Barbadoes.[2] With him she left England, taking with her one of her daughters, who soon fell a victim to the West Indian climate. The other three—or at any rate the two sons— were left in England; but with the exception of William, the eldest son, who had succeeded to his father's title, and presumably to some of the settled estates, no provision for their maintenance had been made. Their father left them nothing but a legacy of five pounds a-piece. Their mother, for all that appears, turned her back upon them, crossed

---

[1] He was born at Kirtling on the 1st October, 1635.

[2] He was second son of Francis, fourth Earl of Bedford, and younger brother of William, the first Duke. Collins (*Peerage*, vol. i. p. 284) gives a wrong date for his death. Luttrell (vol. iv. p. 131) records it under the date of 27th October, 1696. It must have occurred some weeks before.

the sea, and left them behind her.   Yet they were children that any father and any mother might well have been proud of, as the sequel will shew.

26. The year closed with a very heavy blow to Mr. North. His brother, Sir Dudley, for whom he entertained an ever increasing admiration and affection, was cut off suddenly, while staying at his house in London.   It was a grievous loss and sorrow.   His only remaining brother, Montagu, was now a prisoner of war in the Castle of Toulon, and destined to remain there nearly two years longer.   Standing alone, as he did, Roger North must have been something more or less than man if he did not at this time feel keenly the responsibilities that lay upon him.   The Lord Keeper's children were absolutely orphans, the young Lord Guilford only in his eighteenth year; and the large estates which had been left to accumulate during the minority being now under Roger North's sole management.   Sir Dudley's two sons were fatherless, though their mother was a woman of good common sense, and not inclined to marry again.   She, too, leant upon her brother-in-law, and referred to him on all occasions of difficulty, with entire confidence in his judgment.   But the children of Charles, Lord North and Grey, were in a sad position indeed, and had been left without any provision for their maintenance, except the very narrow pittance which remained from the Kirtling property, after paying the extravagant jointure settled on Lady North and Grey. If her ladyship had lived to old age, instead of being cut off in middle life as she was, the young Lord, his brother Charles, and his gifted sister would have been homeless, except so far as their uncle Roger should be inclined to offer them a shelter.

27. The purchase of the Rougham Estate was completed in 1691.   Ugly and inconvenient as Rougham Hall must have been when Mr. North took possession of it, in mere size it was the largest house in that part of Norfolk, with the single exception of the house at Raynham, which Inigo Jones had designed for Sir Roger Townshend at the beginning of the century, and which the second Marquis added to so largely a hundred years after. Houghton, the ancestral seat of the Walpoles, was in the condition that Sir

Robert Walpole found it when he determined to replace it by the immense palace which still remains as a monument of the great minister's magnificence. At Holkham not a brick was laid or a tree planted. Sandringham, on the coast, was then occupied by the Hostes, who had recently acquired the estate. Hunstanton Hall, the venerable mansion of the le Stranges, lay some twenty miles off as the crow flies, and at Hillington was a house of some pretension, which had been built by the Howells sixty or seventy years before.

28. What Mr. North found on his newly-acquired property and what he built up in its place he has taken some pains to describe. When he had carried out the larger part of his designs he amused himself in writing a curious account of his proceedings.

29. The building of Rougham Hall commenced in 1692, and seems to have continued busily for three or four years. In the meantime Mr. Montagu North was released from his long imprisonment in France, and appears to have taken up his residence with his brother, spending his time partly in London, where, in Roger's chambers in the Temple, and in his house in Covent Garden, the two brothers got together a considerable collection of pictures, of which a list remains.

30. In the autumn of 1694 Lord Guilford came of age. He took his seat in the House of Lords in November, and married in the following February.[1] This terminated the trust of the Guilford estates, and released Roger North from many demands upon his time and thoughts.

31. They who make *heredity* their study may find some curious and noteworthy points in the family history of the Norths. Among them is the fact that the progeny of only one of the gifted brothers exhibited any signal proofs of great ability or genius. Lord Guilford, indeed, is always spoken of with high esteem and admiration. He was made a Privy Councillor in 1712, and the next year filled the office which we now call President of the Board of Trade. But of Sir Dudley's sons one was a cypher and the other was the only instance in the whole history of this race of

---

[1] His first wife was Elizabeth, third daughter of Fulke Greville, Lord Brooke. She died in November, 1699, leaving no issue.

any low tastes and vicious habits shewing themselves either in youth or manhood. Roger North's two sons appear to have had respectable abilities, but nothing more. The extraordinary mental activity of their father lay dormant for awhile.

32. It was far otherwise with the children of the eldest of the brothers. Charles, Lord North and Grey, is not represented to us in an attractive light. He certainly was not an amiable person; but the children whom he left behind him, whom he neglected, and for whom he cruelly made no provision, were gifted with very great abilities, though to much brilliancy of intellect and many accomplishments there was united some of the erratic temperament which often characterises genius. They were William, Lord North and Grey, born 22nd December, 1678; Charles, a year younger; and their sister, Dudleya, a year or two older than her elder brother. The three were brought up together—learnt the same lessons, read the same books, joined in the same amusements. Among the three there grew up a deep and romantic affection, the brothers almost worshipping the sister, the sister returning that love by a jealous idolatry which by its very devotion tended to make the objects of it heroic. There are a few letters of Dudleya North at Wroxton, which I have not thought it within the scope of the present work to print, but they confirm to a great extent all that her uncle has said of her; and all that I have gathered incidentally concerning her goes to shew that Dudleya North was a most noble character, besides being one of the most highly-cultured and accomplished women of her time. The two brothers (the elder being in his thirteenth year) entered at Magdalen College, Cambridge, together, on the 22nd October, 1691. Charles, the younger, continued to reside for some years at the University. He took the M.A. degree, as a nobleman's son, in 1695, and was elected to a Fellowship in his college in July, 1698. But the attraction which the hope of a soldier's career exercised, at a time when Marlborough's consummate generalship was being talked of by all Europe, was too great for him to resist. Whatever prospects he may have had of academic distinction were sacrificed to his passion for soldiering. He was unfortu-

nate in the regiment to which he was appointed and in the
posts to which he was sent.   It was not till Marlborough's
victories were all won and his work finished that Charles
North succeeded in being promoted to some command
under his brother in Holland, and he had not obtained the
desire of his heart very long before he fell a victim to the
fatigue and exposure he had gone through, and died unmarried about 1710.[1]

33. Lady North and Grey did not live long after her marriage with Colonel Russell.   She died at Barbadoes at the
end of the year 1694,[2] just at the same time that Queen
Mary died, leaving William of Orange to reign alone.   The
young lord immediately left Cambridge, and entered himself at the Military Academy which had been established
some years before in Leicester Fields, with a view to qualify
himself for the military profession.   Europe was all astir
with war and battles.   It was in the camp that a career
seemed to offer for the venturous and the able.   But
London, with its attractions and temptations, was a bad
place for a young nobleman in his eighteenth year, thrown
among companions who were inclined to all the dissipations
of the time.   It was not long before he found himself very
seriously in debt, and his estate heavily burdened.   His
uncle Roger advised foreign travel, and Lord North and
Grey, brought to his senses by the gravity of the crisis in
his affairs, left England and remained abroad till he came
of age in 1699.   He thereupon took his seat in the House
of Lords.   He had learnt the lesson which few young men
learn, however heavy the price they pay, and moreover he
was master of more than one foreign language, for he had
spent some time in Italy, Flanders, and Spain.   In March,
1702, he was made a captain of foot-guards in the new
levies.   The signing of his commission must have been
almost the last piece of business transacted by William III.[3]

34. Marlborough set out for the war in May; the cam-

---

[1] Collins (*Peerage*, vol. iv., LORD GUILFORD), and others after him,
assert that he died at the unlucky siege of Lille.   As this was in 1708,
and as a letter from his sister is before me dated July, 1710, in which,
writing to her elder brother, she sends loving messages to Charles, it is
clear that he was then alive.

[2] Luttrell, iii. 426.   [3] Ibid. v. 159.

paign of the Meuse was over by the 29th October. Venloo and Liège, in fact the whole country between the Meuse and the Rhine was in the hands of the allies. The quick eye of the great captain soon recognized in the young infantry officer a soldier of promise, and before the next year's fighting had closed Lord North and Grey found himself in command of a regiment and in constant communication with Marlborough, now raised to a Dukedom. On the 13th August, 1704, the great Battle of Blenheim was fought—"the greatest triumph achieved by an English general since the middle ages." Among the 7,500 of the wounded on the victorious side who had escaped with their lives, Lord North and Grey was one. To a soldier his was a grievous wound, for he lost his right hand. He had, however, another wherewith to do good service in the wars. When Marlborough returned to England in December, Lord North accompanied him, and in the following February he was made Brigadier-General, in his twenty-eighth year. In the campaign of 1705 he was again at Marlborough's side, and ten days before the Duke left the army (26th October) to go on his mission to Vienna, Lord North and Grey married Maria Margaretta, daughter of M. Van Ellimut, Treasurer of Holland.[1] Next year followed the victory of Ramilies (23rd May, 1706), and during the next three years he was detained for the most part in Flanders. He returned to England in 1709. In December, 1711, he became a Privy Councillor, and was made Governor of Portsmouth.[2] When Prince Eugene visited England in the spring of 1712, among those who entertained him with marked cordiality were his three companions in arms, Lord Stair, the Duke of Marlborough, and the Lord North and Grey.[3]

35. With the fall of Marlborough and the death of Queen Anne Lord North's career came virtually to an end. He and all his family were strong Jacobites in sentiment, and

---

[1] Her Ladyship was naturalised by Act of Parliament in 1706. Marlborough appears to have interested himself in the negotiations for the marriage. There are several allusions to it in the *Letters and Dispatches* published by Sir George Murray in 1845.

[2] He had been appointed Governor of Sheerness in May, 1705.

[3] Luttrell, vi. 722.

loyalty to the great captain under whom he had served may explain a personal feeling against George I. On the 28th September, 1722, he was committed to the Tower for his complicity in Bishop Atterbury's plot.[1] The Government had either not sufficient evidence, or there were reasons of State why the trial was not allowed to proceed,[2] and his Lordship retired to the Continent, where he passed the remainder of his days in aimless wandering or bootless intriguing. About 1728 he joined the Roman communion, and died a childless man and an exile at Madrid, 31st October, 1734. The title of Lord Grey expired; the Barony of North devolved upon his second cousin, Francis, third Lord Guilford, who had succeeded his father just five years before.[3] Thus, with the single exception of Lord North and Grey, who outlived his uncle seven months, leaving no offspring, Roger North survived not only all his brothers and sisters, but every one of his nephews, grandsons of Dudley, fourth Lord, by Anne Montagu; while of all the sons of that noble pair only three had any heirs male to carry on the line—Lord Guilford of Wroxton, Roger North of Rougham Hall, and Sir Dudley of Glemham.

36. When Mr. Montagu North was released from his long imprisonment he joined his brother Roger, and for some years made his home with him. The two brothers, it will be remembered, had been schoolfellows, but Montagu had spent most of his time abroad, and his long incarceration at Toulon appears to have told upon him. He is described as reserved and "morose" in manner. His niece Dudleya regarded him as wanting in courtesy and polish. Nevertheless, it was not long before much of the same cordiality and affectionate relations grew up between Roger and Montagu as had formerly characterized the intercourse between him and the Lord Keeper, and subsequently between him and Sir Dudley. So the two brothers lived

---

[1] Historic MSS. Commission, Fifth Report, p. 190.

[2] See *Parliamentary History*, viii. 203; *The Stuart Papers*, ed. by Glover, 1847; F. Williams' *Memoirs and Correspondence of Bishop Atterbury*.

[3] Francis, the Lord Keeper's son and heir, died 17th October, 1729. His son, the third Lord, was made an Earl 8th April, 1752.

together, but when the building of Rougham was approaching completion, and he was released from the management of the Guilford estates, and the young Lord had married; when, too, Rougham must have appeared a somewhat overgrown mansion for two bachelors to occupy, Roger North, now in his forty-fourth year, determined to take to himself a wife.[1]

38. There was a certain Sir Robert Gayer, a Buckinghamshire gentleman of large means, who in 1657, by the will of his elder brother, had succeeded to the Manor of Stoke Poges, and the lands thereto belonging, and who had been made a Knight of the Bath, in 1661, at the coronation of Charles II. He was a most vehement Jacobite, and a story is told of him, that shortly after he had rebuilt his house at Stoke with some splendour, William III., being in the neighbourhood, turned aside to pay the old Knight a visit. Instead of accepting the compliment "he vehemently swore that he would never permit the King to come under his roof. 'He has got possession of another man's

---

[1] In the Forster Collection at the South Kensington Museum, there is a manuscript entitled "The Domestick or Retired Life of the Hon. Roger North, Author of the 'Examen' and the 'Lives of the Lord Keeper and Sir Dudley North,'" &c. This account was drawn up by a grand-daughter of Mr. North (probably Mrs. Boydell), and is dated 6th September, 1826. It is not a very trustworthy document, and it abounds in statements which are mere matters of hearsay. Among them is the following:—"Soon after King William's accession he offered to make him (Roger North) a judge, *when* his friend John Evelyn advised him to marry, purchase an estate, and plant trees." As to the story of William III. having offered Mr. North a Judgeship, it is extremely improbable; but that Evelyn (who was the other's senior by at least thirty-three years) can have had much to do with the purchasing or the planting of the Rougham estate is scarcely credible. Certainly Evelyn must have been brought into somewhat intimate relation with Roger North during the life of the Lord Keeper, and congeniality of tastes may have attracted the younger man to the elder. Evelyn's gardens and plantations at Saye's Court may well have exercised their influence upon Mr. North, and impressed him with the conviction of how much could be done by judicious planting in thirty years. But that Evelyn himself can ever have been at Rougham is extremely unlikely: he was in his seventy-second year when the estate was acquired, and was approaching eighty before Mr. North finally took up his residence there.

An extract from the manuscript account of Mr. North's Rougham life will be found at Note C.

house already: he is a usurper: tell him to go back again!' In vain Lady Gayer interposed; but not prevailing, she fell down upon her knees, and entreated Sir Robert to let the King (who was all this time waiting in his coach at the door) see the house. But he only raved the more furiously, and declared an Englishman's house is his castle, and that he would never permit the King to come within those walls. So his Majesty went back again, and never saw Stoke Poges."[1]

39. Sir Robert had a daughter Mary, who had passed her *première jeunesse*, but who was not at all likely to prove a portionless bride.[2] The probability is that she would have married before, but that the well-known Jacobite tendencies of her father, his choleric temper, and his uncompromising aggressiveness might well make a prudent suitor hesitate before entering into an alliance with a family so pledged to opposition to the powers that be. But Roger North had nothing to hope from the Government, and was not the man to put his head in a noose for the sake of the Pretender. Sir Robert Gayer's daughter had for him some attraction, and her father had this in common with his son-in-law, that he was an enthusiastic lover of pictorial art, and had long been a collector of paintings in England and on the Continent. Negotiations were entered into for a marriage between Roger North and the old Knight's daughter; but there was a delay. In the spring of 1696 two Jacobite plots were hatching, the one known as the infamous Assassination Plot, which was confined to a handful of villains with whom no man of honour could associate; the other known as the Duke of Berwick's Plot, which had as its object the setting the Pretender upon the throne by an invasion from France and a general rising of the Jacobite party. The Duke of Berwick came to England to organise the latter conspiracy. The gentry in large numbers compromised themselves deeply—Sir Robert Gayer among them—but rise they would not until a force from the other side of the Channel should have effected a landing. From such a venture Louis XIV. shrank, and the

---

[1] Lipscomb's *Hist. of Bucks.*, vol. iv. p. 554.

[2] Her grand-daughter tells us she had a fortune of £8,000.—*Forster MSS.*, vol. xix. fol. 62.

plan of an organised rising was abandoned. The ruffians who were bent upon assassinating the King were not to be put off so easily. They were determined to earn their blood-money. Happily such infamous schemes never succeed in England, and the murderous design was betrayed and the scoundrels brought to justice. This was in March, 1696. The discovery of the wicked design roused an immense outburst of loyalty up and down the land. The Jacobites had a bad time of it. Sir Robert Gayer took the alarm, broke up his establishment at an hour's notice, and crossed to the Continent, but left his daughter behind him, after making all due arrangement for her marriage. Where it was celebrated I have not discovered, but on the 26th May, 1696, Roger North was married to Mary, daughter of Sir Robert Gayer,[1] and the newly wedded pair took up their abode at Rougham. The bride was a kindly domestic person, a good wife, and a good mother, who managed her household with a skilful oversight, and had a reputation for her jam, her home-made wines, and the mysterious remedies for divers disorders which serious housewives two hundred years ago jealously kept to themselves—family secrets to be handed down to their posterity as precious heirlooms. Next year a daughter was born, and in 1698 a second; a son, Roger, followed a year or two later.

40. Meanwhile Mr. North was going on steadily im-

---

[1] The following is Dudleya North's letter to her brother, Lord North and Grey, announcing their uncle's marriage.

June, '96.

DEAR BROTHER,— . . . . I was a little surprised at the news my cousin brought from London of my uncle Roger's marriage with Sir Robert Gayer's daughter, indeed I thought in that charity would not begin at home, but he would have served you first, but I think since that was not to be so soon, he had no reason to stay longer if he did marry at all. His wife's father is concealed, being suspected to be in the plot, for he discharged all his servants at half-an-hour's warning, and was never heard of since, but they say he left order the match (if at all) should be concluded in six weeks' time after, as it was. They say he and she is within ten mile of " The Vyne," at her uncle's. I have insisted the longer upon this because one of the servants that was discharged by Sir Rob. Gayer lives near now, so I know it to be true. They say the lady is thirty years old, and since a maid, we may guess somewhat more.

proving his estate and becoming more and more absorbed
in his literary and domestic pursuits. He kept on his
chambers in the Temple, but he almost gave up his practice
at the bar. He has left us a minute account of his planting the gardens and the park. He was always reading and
writing, first on one subject, then on another, and as the
years went by something like a revival of the old musical
entertainments which he describes at Kirtling were repeated in the Rougham household. These was much
coming and going at the house; there was a great organ
set up in the long gallery,[1] on which one member or other
of the family performed, whilst parents and children took
their part on the stringed instruments, which sons and
daughters equally were familiarized with from their earliest
childhood.[2] The produce of the land farmed by a bailiff
supplied the house plentifully with all ordinary necessaries.
Wine seems to have been drunk only on rare occasions of
festivity. The roads were so bad that the family coach
was always drawn by four horses, and these, and all the
other horses in the stable, were used sometimes for tillage,
sometimes in the hunting field.

41. As time went on Mr. North's life became more and
more retired. In 1702 he was much troubled at the de-
plorable condition of the church at Rougham. It had fallen
very much out of repair, and the services were conducted in
a slovenly way, by an old clergyman named William Briggs,
who had officiated there since 1671, and resided upon the
living of Testerton, some ten miles off. The vicarage
yielded to the incumbent a wretched pittance, and the
vicar was advanced in years.. Mr. North was disposed to
add to the value of the living if only he could get the
patronage into his own hands. He made the attempt, but
apparently with no success. Mr. Briggs lived on till 1709,
and next year the Rev. Ambrose Pimlow, a most estimable
young clergyman of very high tone and amiability of cha-

---

[1] This organ is now in the parish church of East Dereham, Norfolk.
It has been considerably enlarged and is an unusually fine instrument.

[2] In his will Mr. North leaves to his daughter Elizabeth his "great
harpsichord"; to his daughter Christian "the first base viol;" to his
son Montagu other instruments, and to all his children a power of
selecting what they pleased from his music books.

racter, accepted the cure of Rougham, which he held together with the rectory of Dunham Magna, a parish some five or six miles off. Mr. Pimlow was a clergyman after Roger North's own heart. He was a cultivated gentleman, with scholarly tastes, and much looked up to in the neighbourhood. By the occasional allusions to and mention of him in the letters which remain, it appears that he spent much of his time at Rougham, and was on terms of great intimacy with the family. He was one of the witnesses to Mr. North's will, and by a codicil received a legacy in token of friendly regard.[1]

42. Those were not the days of circulating libraries, and a man of studious habits and literary tastes, if he could not borrow books, must needs buy them. Mr. North's library grew ever larger and larger, and it was evident that it would go on growing. Such an accumulation of books in the heart of Norfolk would in those days have been a very unsaleable piece of property, and yet might prove of great utility hereafter if it were kept together for others besides the occupant of Rougham Hall to refer to and borrow from. Mr. North had not yet abandoned his hope of getting the patronage of the vicarage into his own hands. It is evident that he contemplated having a resident clergyman who should perform daily service in the church, and it would be a distinct gain if a large library were placed at the disposal of such a *chaplain* as he desired to secure. With this view he drew up a scheme whereby his large and increasing collection of books should be removed to a new depository, and instead of remaining an heirloom to descend with the estate, should be so settled as to be a parochial library, to be vested jointly in the occupant of Rougham Hall and the vicar of the parish for the time being. A new library was built as an adjunct to the north aisle of the church, and was completed some time during the year 1709. It had scarcely been finished when Mr. North's only surviving brother, Montagu, died. He had

[1] There is a very curious and characteristic entry in the Register of Dunham Magna by Mr. Pimlow, which is printed at large in Carthew's *History of Launditch*, part iii., p. 86. The worthy rector had been entrapped to celebrate a clandestine marriage; he gives an account of the circumstance, and expresses his shame and regret at some length.

never married, and had spent the last years of his life mostly at Rougham. Roger North was his sole executor and residuary legatee, and though very liberal provision was made in the will for several nephews and nieces and others who are mentioned, the residue, after all payments, constituted a handsome addition to Mr. North's fortune.

43. On the 25th April, 1712, the Hon. Dudleya North died at the house of her sister-in-law, the Lady North and Grey, in Bond Street.[1] She, too, appointed her uncle executor, and when her affairs came to be wound up, Roger North requested that the books and MSS. which his niece had collected should be added to the Rougham Library. Her brother, Lord North and Grey, at once acceded to the proposal.[2] At the close of this year a second son was born, who was baptised under the name of Montagu. The elder son, Roger, does not seem to have given any sign of particular ability or promise.[3] A year

---

[1] Ballard's *Memoirs of Celebrated Ladies.* 4to. Oxford, 1752.

[2] The following pathetic letter from Lord North and Grey, acknowledging his uncle's letter, which had announced the death of Dudleya North, will speak for itself.

From Hey, the 28 of May, 1712.

Most hon^d Uncle,—My grief was too great for me to be able to answer y^{rs} of the 1st of May before now; for tho' I might expect that loss, yet was it not the less for that, my sister having been almost a twin with me, so good a young woman, and the last remaining child of my father besides myself. As to her executorship I do accept of it, and desire you would act for me in that affair as for yourself, and if there is any assets wanting to make good the full legacies of the deceased, I do engage myself to make them good. Only I desire that a bond I gave her before my marriage to secure her a portion, whatever might happen, may be cancelled, if she has not done it already, for I find she has made no mention of it, as knowing it only a security for her maintenance or portion.

As to myself, stript as I am of my brother and sister, and without children, I cannot yet leave the camp. I have begun warfare with honour and will end it so, by God's grace. Meantime amongst my cousins I must seek for heirs, and shall not be unmindful of my godson, who I hope is well, and my aunt. We lie pretty nigh the Maréchal de Villars, and if they make not peace shall soon make war. Pray God protect the rest of the Norths, and send me the happiness to see you once more in England, to assure you how much I am your most dutiful nephew and most humble servant,

NORTH AND GREY.

[3] In 1755 he published *A Discourse of the Poor, or the Pecunious Tendency of the Laws now in force,* 8vo, London.

or two after he came into possession of the Rougham
property Roger North bought another estate in Norfolk, at Ashwicken, a parish eight miles from Rougham,
on the high road to Lynn. Mr. North became lord of the
manor and patron of the living. At Ashwicken Mr. North
spent a great deal of money in trying agricultural experiments.[1] He planted ozier beds, attempted to grow hops,
improved the farm-houses, and involved himself in a law-
suit. The temporary want of money of which he complains
in more than one of his later letters, must be set down to
the unlucky attempt to make the Ashwicken estate into a
garden of Eden, the soil and climate being against him,
and the tillers of the soil and small freeholders being by
no means favourable.

44. While Mr. North was thus living his life in retirement
as a country gentleman, very much in the same way that
his grandfather had lived before him at Kirtling, his two
great neighbours at Raynham and Houghton were rising
to the highest offices in the State. When he first settled
at Rougham Mr. Robert Walpole, father of the great
Minister, was living at Houghton, and the young Lord
Townshend, a lad of sixteen, had recently been left as his
ward. The future Sir Robert Walpole succeeded his father
in the estate at Houghton in 1700, and that same year he
married, and entered Parliament as Member for Castle
Rising. Shortly after this date a dispute arose between
Sir Robert and his mother regarding her settlement. The
affair dragged on from year to year, and the old lady
appears to have shewn herself a somewhat impracticable
person. At last both sides agreed to submit to Mr. North's
arbitration, and he drew up a deed which served as a final
settlement. This was in 1704. Next year we catch another glimpse of the great man. Some trifling disagreement had arisen about the Ashwicken estate. Lord Townshend had been made Lord Lieutenant of Norfolk, and
Roger North had gone to Raynham hoping to meet Sir
Robert Walpole there; but, he writes, "business, as I
understand, diverted, and is like to be so continued with
you, that I despair of finding you at home." A little later

---

[1] Mason's *History of Norfolk*, pt. v. p. 64.

he is brought into relations with Sir Thomas Coke, then Chamberlain of the Household, and afterwards Earl of Leicester, and with other provincial magnates, but it is always professionally and as a lawyer, whom his neighbours consulted for their own convenience. He was never put into the commission of the peace; averse though he was to anything in the shape of underhand intrigue or to joining in plots of any kind, he yet obstinately refused to take the oath of allegiance to the Hanoverian kings, and was therefore left out in the cold and occupied a position of isolation, which threw him upon his many resources at home. Sometimes a rising scholar from Cambridge came to Rougham and brought with him the last University gossip and the last new book out. Sometimes a new instrumentalist would bring an introduction and come down to Norfolk, curious to see " Roger the fiddler," as he had been dubbed by the pamphleteers of his early life. Newspapers had begun to be printed in Norwich, such as they were, and letters were arriving regularly—now from Lord North and Grey, the hero of the family, sending news from the camp in Flanders, now from Lord Guilford at the Court, or from Lady Yarmouth, who was 'the last survivor of the sisters, or from the colony in Suffolk, who were brought up to reverence the name of their uncle Roger.

45. But old age was creeping upon the retired student and *virtuoso,* as he would have called himself. His time for collecting works of art had gone by; but five miles off from him Sir Andrew Fountain,[1] who succeeded Sir Isaac Newton as Master of the Mint, was accumulating at Narford his magnificent collection of works of art; and Sir Robert Walpole, seven or eight miles in another direction, was getting together his pictures for the new mansion at Houghton, the first stone of which was laid in 1729.[2]

46. The avenues—one of them a mile long—and plantations which he had himself laid out, attained to nearly fifty

---

[1] The Christian name of one of Mr. North's grandsons (Fountain) indicates that a close intimacy existed between the families at Rougham and Narford.

[2] Holkham, the largest house in Norfolk, the seat of the Earl of Leicester, was begun in 1734, the year in which Roger North died.

years' growth under his eye. Two of his daughters had married well. His eldest son had allied himself to his cousin, one of the Wenyeves of Brettenham, and there was a grandson to carry on the name. His younger son Montagu had a respectable career at Cambridge. His wife was taken from him only when they had enjoyed together more than thirty years of wedded happiness.[1] His life had been blameless and prosperous; he had secured the respect of those about him; he had tried, and not quite in vain, to make his own little world better than he found it. In October, 1730, when he had entered upon his seventy-eighth year, he made his will; a codicil was added on the 6th January following, and another in October 1733. He takes his leave of his children in the following words:—
"I do hereby leave unto all my children my most earnest recommendation, or rather command, to persevere in the true Christian faith and practice of life according to the doctrine of the Established Church of England, and to live together, or as near as may well be, in all brotherly love, correspondence, and friendship, always inclining to condescend rather than contend, and so (with God's blessing) they may be happy, and not otherwise." He was writing to his son Montagu a year after this with no sign of any failure in his mental powers. He died on the 1st March, 1734, in his eighty-first year. The Rougham estate descended to his eldest son, Roger, from whom the present possessor has inherited it in the direct line. The Ashwicken property was divided among his other children, the advowson of the living being devised to his younger son Montagu. The estate was sold before many years had passed, and Montagu North never was presented to the living. He took Holy Orders in 1738, became Rector of Sternfield in Suffolk, and proceeded to the D.D. degree in 1767. In 1775 he was promoted to a canonry at Windsor, and he died at Sternfield, where a tablet to his memory still exists, in 1779. By his father's will he came into possession of all his father's papers, and in obedience to instructions which he had received, he published first the celebrated *Examen* in the year 1740, which was followed

---

[1] She was certainly dead when her husband made his will in October, 1730.

almost immediately by the *Lives of the Norths*. These works Roger North could not be prevailed on to print during his own lifetime,[1] but he spent extraordinary pains upon them, and the Life of the Lord Keeper he wrote and re-wrote, transcribed, altered, and added to again and again. If his Autobiography had ever been carried much further than appears by the fragment that has come down to us, the probability is that his son would have published it when the author's name was so much talked of as it was, just after the *Examen* appeared; but on the other hand there may have been persons and incidents mentioned and commented on in it whom it might be imprudent to offend at the time.

47. The following letter, addressed to Francis, first Earl Guilford, and father of the Prime Minister, Lord North, gives a sufficiently full account of Roger North's children and their alliances, and shews that only one of them had issue.

My Lord,

I received the honour of your Lordship's letter, wherein you desire a particular account of my father's marriage, descendants, &c. With regard to my father, he married Mary, the daughter of Sir Robert Gayer, Knight, of Stoke Poges in Buckinghamshire, I think, or Berkshire. He had two sons, Roger and Montagu, and five daughters, Elizabeth, Ann, Mary, Catherine, and Christian. His eldest son, Roger, married to his first wife Mary, the daughter of John Wenyeve of Brettenham in the county of Suffolk, Esquire, by whom he has one son (Charles now living): his second wife was Jane, the daughter of Mr. William Leak, merchant, of Heacham in the county of Norfolk, by whom he has two sons, Fountain and Roger, and two daughters, Jane and Airmine. His youngest son, Montagu, married Elizabeth, the daughter of the Reverend Francis Folkard, Rector of Clopton in the county of Suffolk, and has no children. His eldest daughter, Elizabeth, died

---

[1] The only work which Mr. North himself printed was the *Discourse of Fish and Fish Ponds*. This was first published in 1683. A second edition appeared in 1713, and a third in 1715: all are now rare.

single not long after her father.[1] His second daughter,
Ann, married [Oct. 1724] Thomas Wright of Downham,
Esquire, but left no children. Mary married Sir Henry
l'Estrange, Baronet, of Hunstanton in Norfolk, who died
a few years ago, without issue by her. She is still living.
Catherine and Christian died single, of the smallpox, at
York, not long after the death of their father. Mr. Long's
name is Charles. This is as particular an account of my
father and his descendants as I can recollect, and which I
hope will answer your Lordship's intentions; but if you
think of any particular which I have omitted, I will do
my endeavour to set it right upon the receipt of a line
from your Lordship. My wife joins in duty to your
Lordship and Lady Guilford

With, my Lord,
Your Lordship's
Most obedient Servant,
MONT. NORTH.

Sternfield,
    October 1st, '64.

I should prefer to say no more, but that my readers will
expect to be told what became of all this structure that
Mr. North raised in a little country village in Norfolk,
and left in so flourishing a condition nearly half a century
after it had come into his hands. The sequel is a melancholy one. Before the eighteenth century closed not one
stone was left upon another of the house which Roger
North had erected; the aisle of the church which he had
rebuilt, and the library which he had founded, had been
pulled down to the ground. The books were all dispersed,
none knew where or how, nor have I ever been able to trace
more than a single volume. At the beginning of the present
century there were stories still current of old "parchment
books" which none could decipher, and sumptuous to look
at, having found their way into the villagers' houses, and
it is just possible that these may refer to the Oriental
MSS. which Dudleya North had acquired from Con-

---

[1] In the account referred to in Note C, it is said that she "was
deformed from an accident in her youth and *died on horseback* in a fit
of coughing."

stantinople through the intervention of her uncles and their correspondents in the East; but of all not a vestige has survived. Nature has been more kind than man—she has spared some of the trees which Roger North planted, but they too, for the most part, have lived their lives, and few of them will survive the present century. Nevertheless there are here and there footprints of Mr. North's sagacious and generous activity still traceable, and not likely to be effaced for ages. What he thought least of and doubtless counted as trifles, these things remain; the schemes for securing for himself an abiding monument in the Norfolk village, and leaving to those that should come after a benefit that might last, these have come to nothing. How vain are all our efforts to achieve an immortality in things of the earth earthy—how idle the attempt to make posterity love us, honour us, fear us, or obey us!

*With the following Monumental Inscription from the
South Wall of Rougham Church this
notice may fitly close.*

Here lies interred
all that was mortal
of the Honble. M^r. Roger North
youngest son of the Right Honble.
DUDLEY LORD NORTH OF KIRTLING
in Cambridgeshire.
He was bred to the Law and admitted
of the Middle Temple
and practised under the encouragement
of his best brother
the late LORD KEEPER NORTH
But soon after the death
of his great Friend and Protector
He retired to his country seat in this Parish
where he lived many years
approving himself a sincere son
of the Church of England
By his constant attendance upon

Divine service and Sacraments
According to the rites and ceremonies of it
By doing good continually and
cheerfully communicating to all
without Fee or Reward
his great knowledge of the Law
Whereby he had formerly acquired
that moderate Fortune
he died possessed of.

Note A.—(See § 12).

" When I marryed in 1632, my lord's father gave him as his portion £4000 in money, which with what I brought was the use of it to maintain us till it could be disposed of in land to be settled for my jointure and upon the children. My lord's father obliged us to live in the country with him, & to pay £200 a year for our board, which wee did, tho' sometimes wee were not there above 7 months of the yeare. About '35 or '36 my Lady Dacre left us & went to a house of her owne. Then my lord's father thought it convenient that wee should keep a coach of our owne, & so wee bought a coach & 2 horses and had a coach man to encrease the number of the little family, & then our boord was increased to £300 a yeare.

" During these yeares many times the moneys lay dead & could not safly [be] put out to advantage, & at one time £4000 lay in hand 3 months in a readiness for a purchase.

" In the yeare '35 Saxham[1] was bought & cost £4300. About '37, as I take it, the Lincolnshire fen being declared drained, they took proportions out of every bodies' land, & my lord choose rather to buy the part of his which the undertakers had taken than to part with his land, so layed down £600, for it was at cost to enclose & lett it at a good considerable rent; but the times changing all was throwne out & that money & cost lost.

[1] Near Bury St. Edmund's.

" '36 my lord bought land in Ashley,[1] cost £220.

" '38 my uncle John North dyed, when wee came again into the country, my lord's father thought he had then an encrease of fortune & children wee had in the house, so my lord made us allow £400 a yeare for our boord.

" In '38 Tostock[2] was bought, but the certaine price I cannot as yet find, but I am sure it was above £6000.

" In 1640 my lord bought land in Ashly, cost £300.

" In '44 the troublesome times began & then wee parted familys & lived by ourselves most at London till about '49.

" In '45 my lord bought Norton Wood, cost £660.

" In '48 my lord bought land in Ashley, cost £714. 10s. 3d.

" In '49 Drinkstone[3] was bought, cost £3852. 16s.

" In '49 wee came again to Catlidge [Kirtling] at boord for £300 a yeare.

" In '50 wee removed again to Tostock, & after that time were never more in a settled way, but a year or two in one place & then in the other, which was both trouble & charge to us.

" In 60 though my lord had declaired as much as he could not to stand for Knight of the Shire yett when the time came many pressing my lord's father about it, he layd his comands upon him to stand, which cost him £240. Every on knows that there are few farms but there is ex-traordinary charges beside the purchase money, so was it with Ashley, where he was fain to build new barnes, be-sides other repayres, & so at the rest of the lands, which would not have been tenantable without some cost. And at his house at Tostock, when he saw himself as he thought settled, he was willing to fitt it, so as to be able to bid his children welcome there, so that besides what he had bestowed in repaires formerly, since '59 it cost him above £440, besides timber bought.

" About '60 he married one of his daughters.[4] His 4 daughters' marryage & his 2 sons that were got to mer-chants cost him £8000. 4 of his sons were brought up at

---

[1] In Cambridgeshire, near Newmarket.

[2] In Suffolk, six miles from Bury St. Edmund's.

[3] Two miles from Tostock.

[4] Mary, who died in childbed, 23rd October, 1662. She married Sir William Spring of Pakenham, co. Suffolk.—*Lives of the Norths, u.s.*

the University, tho' with as much providense as could be, yett in the quality of noblemen; and ever since, till his death, they have every one had some small proportion out of his estate toward their maintenance.

"At the time that wee lived borders wee found all necessarys for our selves & children, & for pant [*sic*], beds & furniture to them, & linen & washing & horse corne, till the latter years, all fruit & spice & sugar that was used in the chambers & . . . . . . never had so much as household stuff, linnen, plate, &c., as long as he lived from his father, & now at his death hath given to his son all the goods that are in Catlidge were his father's; so that I may safe take my oth, that I never had any household stuff belonging to the family except some of my lady's that he was pleased to give me.

"He gave his eldest son as a legacy by his will, besides all my lord his father's household stuff, which are not to be touched except there be not sufficient for the clearing of his debts, with that provision which he hath made, the parsonage of Kirtling in present worth & his copyhold in Emswell after my life, which is worth . . . .[1] he hath not given one foot of land from his. Only some small annuitys after my life out of my joynture to his 5 younger sons.

"Those that know all these circumstances of my dear lord's fortune (besides some that I think not fitt to comitt to paper) will not think it strange that he hath left a debt upon security of about 11 or £1200 besides some £300 other debts."

Note B.—KIRTLING.

At the time of the Great Survey, Kirtling (which appears in the Record under the form of Chertelinge) was held by Judith, the Conqueror's niece, who married the ill-fated Earl Waltheof, executed 31st May, 1076.[2] It had previously formed part of the possessions of Earl Harold,

---

[1] *Sic* in MS.
[2] Freeman's *History of the Norman Conquest*, iv., 523, 593, 603, 605.

and was then an extensive domain, with its park, *bestiarum silvaticarum*, and its fishery (which can only have been the produce of the moat), estimated at an annual yield of five thousand five hundred eels.[1]   The estate passed, by the marriage of Ralph de Toesny the younger with Judith, Earl Waltheof's daughter, into the possession of the De Toesnys, and on the death of Robert de Toesny, the last male of that race, in 1310, descended to his sister and heir, Alice, widow of Thomas de Leyburne, and subsequently wife of Guy, Earl of Warwick.[2]

The jurors describe it at this time as a *castle* inclosed by moats, with a park of wild animals as before.   The park, therefore, had been kept up for at least five centuries when Edward, Lord North, bought the estate; the "castle" had probably long been a ruin.

Cole, the Cambridge antiquary, paid a visit to Kirtling about the middle of the last century, when the house was occupied by Maria Margaretta, widow of William, sixth Lord North, who had married as her second husband, Patrick, Lord Elibank, and retained Kirtling as her dower house.   Cole spent most of his time in copying the inscriptions in the church, and had to hurry away without seeing the mansion.   "In the windows," he says, "are great numbers of coats of painted glass, which I only saw on the outside—the family being at dinner while I was there. *Great part of the structure was lately taken down*, and what remains now is very capacious . . . . . My lady sent us word by her coachman, that we were welcome to look over the house if we pleased; but we were then in too great an haste . . . . . so we made our compliments and excused ourselves."—*Cole's MSS. Add.*, 5819, fol. 113.

It must have been some twenty years after this, that Sir Egerton Brydges (or his informant) wrote the description of the house which appears in Nichols' *Progresses of Queen Elizabeth*, vol. ii. 219.   A more interesting account was drawn up about forty years ago, by an old servant of the family who had been brought up in the place from childhood, and whose memory was unusually clear and accurate.

---

[1] *Domesday Booke* [202 a.]

[2] Inq. post mortem, 3rd Edward II., No. 33, and 9th Edward II., No. 71, co. Cambridge.

This account is still preserved in manuscript, and though not always grammatical and sometimes obscure, yet affords us a pretty fair notion of the plan of the building.

The house was approached by a magnificent flight of steps, of which the remains are traceable; the visitor then entered "the entrance-hall, a large room but not lofty, wainscotted with oak seats round three sides." To right and left of this entrance hall were the kitchen and offices. Beyond it "a very small ante-room with stone seats round . . . . . from this little room you entered (by large folding doors, very thick and heavy, and about them plenty of large iron bars and bolts to secure them) a large passage under the organ gallery . . . . . from this passage was the entrance to the large baronial hall . . . . . there was an immense oak table, quite black with old age. Fifty persons could have dined at it very well. On the gallery, at the entrance, was placed the organ in the centre. On this gallery, too, were other pieces of music, such as a very large old harpsichord, and others which I cannot describe. At the far end of the hall was a raised platform, about four inches high. Here was a large open fireplace, where no doubt were burnt the large blocks of wood often spoken of in old times . . . . . From the platform was an entrance on the right to the grand staircase, and on the left to a very pretty and neat chapel." Beyond the grand staircase appears to have been the picture gallery, and communicating with it other rooms in a bewildering maze. "Looking to the south you entered the library, with bookcases and quantities of old books that I did not nor could read." All the rooms in the house, we are told, except three, "were hung with tapestry, and in their best days were no doubt considered beautiful." Of the great staircase, the writer says, that "from the top to the bottom the walls were hung with pictures."

It is only fair to add that incomparably the most attractive work of art in the whole collection—more attractive even than the portrait of William, the sixth Lord, " said to have lost his hand in battle and had one of wood, and that hand had a walking-stick screwed to it "—was "a large picture of a kitchen. Here was the *major domo* giving his orders to his maids. There was also seen plenty of everything, such as fish, flesh, and fowls of all kinds, with plenty of vegetables. This picture," says the loyal serving man, "I used to be delighted to look at when a boy." Had it also delighted the eyes of Roger North and his brothers a century or so before?

Note C. (See § 36.)—ROGER NORTH'S LIFE AT ROUGHAM.

* * * * * * By the advice of his friend Evelyn he began to plant, and planted a large grove immediately opposite his house with a half-mile avenue of limes, and carried on the next half-mile to the Grove with a double row of ash. The folks laughed, shook their heads, and called it *North's Folly*, and it still goes by that name. The lime avenue prospered wonderfully, and grew into immense trees, but to the trees he planted oaks, ashes, elms, with sweet and horse chestnuts, with willows, sallows, and poplars of all sorts, and fifty of the finest walnut trees I ever saw, an orchard of eight acres, a cherry ground of four; high hedges of crabs and wildings without end. and made enclosures as fast as he could get or raise the white-thorn plants, and forest trees in the hedgerows, and the wildings were of use in a scarce fruit year for culinary purposes, and the crabs afforded plenty of verjuice. We had a very large garden, with every kind of fruit then known; and when I was a young woman the gentlemen, who were planters, begged chestnuts and beechnuts, as those which came from abroad did not come up so well as from the native seed. The country folks changed their opinion when they saw the plantations get forward, for in a few years he had fine hedges, plenty of firewood from what he called his *weeds;* and yet found plenty of light firewood; and, in short, public opinion changed in his favour.

One day an old man of the name of Warner called to ask his advice. He was what was called an estate jobber, that is to say, would let those who had a cottage and a few acres of land have money, and after a certain time would seize their property.

"Well, your honour," addressing Roger North, "your name is up among us. You do not know what they call you?"

"No!" was the reply. "What do they call me?"

"Why, they call you Squire Solomon."

"Why do they give me that glorious name?"

"Why, because you make great woods where a stick never grew before; you found brick-earth where there was none; you have got a lime-kiln where none was ever suspected to have been in these parts."

"I shall find something as valuable as any of these."

"What! a gold mine, mayhap?"

"Yes," replied Solomon. "I expect to find marl, which will find wheat, which is gold."

"Well," said the old man, "I am following you as fast as I can, but I have a deal of trouble; I am rearing quickset hedges, and set a parcel of chattering women to weed them, and when the forewoman said 'Come, get on with your work,' to the rest, a saucy hussey called out 'I am sure master is a great rogue, for he buy up all the small farms for next to nothing!' when they all called out 'The devil will have him for that.' I, who happened to be near them, said, mind your work you idle hussies, and leave me and the devil to fight it out. When a strapping girl, fit for a grenadier said 'Poor Old Scratch will meet with his match.'"

This old man was brought up an attorney, and having nothing to do in that way turned estate jobber, cheated and oppressed the lower orders, lived to be very old, and left a good estate to his heirs.[1]

My grandfather pulled down the old house and built one too large for the estate, unfortunately. He loved and understood architecture, and drew it very well. Another of his failings, if I may term it so, was an inordinate passion for music, for in this house he built a gallery sixty feet long, to hold an organ built by old Father Smith;

---

[1] There is a good account of this Norfolk worthy (who was a notorious character in his time) in *Carthew's History of the Hundred of Launditch*, part iii., p. 120 *et seq.*

this is mentioned in Doctor Burney's *History of Music*. He had a taste for painting, was very fond of Sir Peter Lely, and was his executor; had a pretty collection of pictures, would dance when others danced, for, as he said, the benefit of his health and spirits. He kept the estate in his own hands, otherwise he could not have raised the woods in such perfection, there being now ten thousand oaks standing, of his and my father's planting, but those planted by the latter thrive best, from their being planted in rows instead of woods. He kept a very large flock of sheep, besides cows; and bred many fine horses, as he used to say, to good account. He treated with sack and his wife with tea, but the cups were not bigger than large thimbles, and it was first used by boiling in a coffee-pot. For this curious herb was given to my grandmother as a present when she married. Roger North was no sportsman, but rode out every day to see his plantations; had a good library, and read and wrote a great deal, was very fond of wit, and had a great deal himself, but could not bear it if it was sarcastic: he was very even tempered, and never known to be in passion: he seldom drank wine, but allowed himself a pint of good ale at eleven in the morning, another at dinner, and the same at supper, which was like a dinner, having heard that a shoulder of mutton, a dish of fish, and other substantial dishes were served up. He was guardian to Francis, Earl of Guilford, and his college vacations were spent at Rougham, as he has told me, very pleasantly. His fourth brother, Montagu, lived with him some years. He had been placed by his brother, Sir Dudley, at Aleppo for many years, and had the plague at Constantinople, and I have understood that he did very well in the counting-house, as he was very correct in his business as a merchant, but had not the abilities of his brothers, and he was buried at Rougham. Having had, when in Turkey, the plague, he fancied that he should be buried alive, and his will directed that after twenty-four hours apparent dissolution desired that his heart might be taken out for half-an-hour and replaced: this was done, and the old servants who were settled in the village told a dreadful tale that he certainly was not dead when his heart was taken out, for the butler who held the dish said that it jumped off, and that the mark remained upon the boards in the damask-room. I do not doubt but it was the butler being in a terrible trepidation occasioned this accident. But the greatest wonder of these people was that Mr. Montagu did not *walk*, and that he should lie so quietly in the chancel without disturbing the hall upon this occasion; as Sir John Bladwell did very often, with his hunting dogs, up the front and down the back staircase. Roger North was a chemist and had a laboratory, but I never heard that he did anything but found a method of bleaching bees' wax, from which he had candles made in the house. Lord Yarmouth, his brother in-law, swore that there was gold in the sand of a sand-pit; and they tried, but no gold was found. * * * * * *

North, Ann, d. of 4th Lord North, *v.* Foley.

—— Ann, d. of Roger North, *v.* Wright.

—— Ann, "Nancy," "little misse," d. of Lord Guildford, R. 249; R.L. 1, P.S., 7, P.S.

—— Catharine, "Ketty," d. of Lord North and Grey, P. 5; L. 9; l. 31.

—— Catharine, d. Roger North, S. 47.

—— Sir Charles, of Walkeringham, F. 427, *id. n.*

—— Charles, son of Lord North and Grey, P. 5; S. 32.

—— Charles, s. of Lord Guilford, F. 121, 122; D. 389; L. 2, 5.

—— Charles, grandson of Roger North, S. 47.

—— Christian, *née* Warcup, wife of 1st Roger, S. 1.

—— Christian, d. 1st Lord, m. Earl of Worcester, P. 6; F. 195 *n.*

—— Christian, d. 4th Lord, m. Sir G. Wenieve, P. 6; L. 11; l. 29.

—— Christian, d. Roger North, S. 47.

—— Hon. Dorothy, *v.* Dacres.

—— Dorothy, wife of Sir John, S. 4.

—— Dorothy, d. 4th Lord, P. 5.

—— Dudley, 3rd Lord, P. 3; m. Frances, d. of Sir John Brocket, a courtier, but unnoticed; retired to Kirtling and there led the life described by his grandson, P. 3, 104; F. 12; R. 94 *et seq.*; S. 5.

—— Dudley, 4th Lord, P. 3; F. 6, 428; J. 4; R. 18, 22, *id. n.* 83; R.L. 1.

—— Dudley, 3rd son of 4th Lord; his parentage and name, P. 5; D. 1; how his name came in the family, *id.*; forward and beautiful when a

child, D. 2; home, King Street, Westminster, D. 2; stolen by a beggar, D. 3; had the plague and recovered, D. 4; sent to Bury School, D. 5; a moderate scholar, D. 5; ill-used by his master, D. 5; early disposition to merchandise, D. 6; placed at a writing school, D. 7; escaped ruin there, D. 7; lover of cock-fighting, D. 8; expert swimmer, D. 9, 10; short of money, D. 11; expedients to procure it, D. 11; in debt, D. 12; recovered, D. 13; bound to a Turkey merchant, F. 37, 38; D. 14; S. 15; sent as supercargo to Archangel, D. 15; account of his voyage thither, D. 17; sufferings and sickness, D. 17, 18; birds seen on voyage, D. 21; stay at Archangel, D. 24-34; sails for Leghorn, D. 35; performs quarantine at Alicant, D. 36, 37; again at Leghorn, D. 40; stays at Leghorn, D. 41, 58; visits Pisa and Lucca, D. 50; keeps carnival, D. 54; goes to Florence, D. 59; visiting Pratoa and Pistoa, D. 68; goes to Smyrna by Flemish convoy, D. 68; variety of passengers, D. 73; settles at Smyrna, D. 85; insufficient capital at disposal, D. 85; lives thriftily, D. 86; hunts as an amusement on an ass, D. 87; bears an excellent character at Smyrna, D. 89; is thrown into contact with Mr. Broadgale, Chaplain, D. 90, 91; has Smyrna fever but recovers, D. 96; has a difference with his master and returns to England, D. 97; strange company and hardships on his voyage, D. 98; agrees with his master, D. 101; and goes back to Smyrna, D. 100; visits Venice, D. 101;

CHISWICK PRESS :—C. WHITTINGHAM AND CO., TOOKS COURT,
CHANCERY LANE.

CATALOGUE OF
BOHN'S LIBRARIES.

735 Volumes, £160 3s.

New Volumes of Standard Works in the various branches of Literature are constantly being added to this Series, which is already unsurpassed in respect to the number, variety, and cheapness of the Works contained in it. The Publishers beg to announce the following Volumes as recently issued or now in preparation :—

Cooper's Biographical Dictionary, containing Concise Notices of Eminent Persons of all ages and countries. In 2 volumes. Demy 8vo. 5s. each.
[Ready. See p. 19.

Johnson's Lives of the Poets. Edited by Mrs. Napier. 3 Vols.
[Ready. See p. 6.

The Works of Flavius Josephus. Whiston's Translation. Revised by Rev. A. R. Shilleto, M.A. With Topographical and Geographical Notes by Colonel Sir C. W. Wilson, K.C.B. 5 volumes.
[See p. 6.

North's Lives of the Norths. Edited by Rev. Dr. Jessopp. [In the press.

Goethe's Faust. With Text, Translation, and Notes. Edited by C. A. Buchheim, Ph.D., Professor of German Language and Literature at King's College, London.
[Preparing.

Arthur Young's Tour in Ireland. Edited by A. W. Hutton, Librarian, National Liberal Club.

Ricardo on the Principles of Political Economy and Taxation. Edited with Notes by E. C. K. Gonner, M.A., Lecturer, University College, Liverpool.
[In the press.

Edgeworth's Stories for Children. [In the press.

Racine's Plays. Second and Concluding Volume. Translated by R. B. Boswell. [In the press.

Hoffmann's Works. Translated by Lieut.-Colonel Ewing. Vol. II.
[In the press.

Bohn's Handbooks of Games. New enlarged edition. In 2 vols.
[Ready. See p. 21.
Vol. I.—Table Games, by Major-General Drayson, R.A., R. F. Green, and 'Berkeley.'
II.—Card Games, by Dr. W. Pole, F.R.S., R. F. Green, 'Berkeley, and Baxter-Wray.

Bohn's Handbooks of Athletic Sports. In 5 vols. [Ready. See p. 21.
By Hon. and Rev. E. Lyttelton, H. W. Wilberforce, Julian Marshall, Major Spens, Rev. J. A. Arnan Tait, W. T. Linskill, W. B. Woodgate, E. F. Knight, Martin Cobbett, Douglas Adams, Harry Vassall, C. W. Alcock, E. T. Sachs, H. H. Griffin, R. G. Allanson-Winn, Walter Armstrong, H. A. Colmore Dunn, C. Phillipps Wolley, F. S. Cresswell, A. F. Jenkin.

For recent Volumes in the SELECT LIBRARY, see p. 24.

BOHN'S LIBRARIES.

STANDARD LIBRARY.

334 Vols. at 3s. 6d. each, excepting those marked otherwise. (59*l.* 5*s.*)

ADDISON'S Works. Notes of Bishop Hurd. Short Memoir, Portrait, and 8 Plates of Medals. 6 vols.
This is the most complete edition of Addison's Works issued.

ALFIERI'S Tragedies. In English Verse. With Notes, Arguments, and Introduction, by E. A. Bowring, C.B. 2 vols.

AMERICAN POETRY. — *See Poetry of America.*

BACON'S Moral and Historical Works, including Essays, Apophthegms, Wisdom of the Ancients, New Atlantis, Henry VII., Henry VIII., Elizabeth, Henry Prince of Wales, History of Great Britain, Julius Cæsar, and Augustus Cæsar. With Critical and Biographical Introduction and Notes by J. Devey, M.A. Portrait.

—— *See also Philosophical Library.*

BALLADS AND SONGS of the Peasantry of England, from Oral Recitation, private MSS., Broadsides, &c. Edit. by R. Bell.

BEAUMONT AND FLETCHER. Selections. With Notes and Introduction by Leigh Hunt.

BECKMANN (J.) History of Inventions, Discoveries, and Origins. With Portraits of Beckmann and James Watt. 2 vols.

BELL (Robert).—*See Ballads, Chaucer, Green.*

BOSWELL'S Life of Johnson, with the TOUR in the HEBRIDES and JOHNSONIANA. New Edition, with Notes and Appendices, by the Rev. A. Napier, M.A., Trinity College, Cambridge, Vicar of Holkham, Editor of the Cambridge Edition of the 'Theological Works of Barrow.' With Frontispiece to each vol. 6 vols.

BREMER'S (Frederika) Works. Trans. by M. Howitt. Portrait. 4 vols.

BRINK (B. T.) Early English Literature (to Wiclif). By Bernhard ten Brink. Trans. by Prof. H. M. Kennedy.

BRITISH POETS, from Milton to Kirke White. Cabinet Edition. With Frontispiece. 4 vols.

BROWNE'S (Sir Thomas) Works. Edit. by S. Wilkin, with Dr. Johnson's Life of Browne. Portrait. 3 vols.

BURKE'S Works. 6 vols.

—— **Speeches on the Impeachment** of Warren Hastings; and Letters. 2 vols.

—— **Life.** By J. Prior. Portrait.

BURNS (Robert). Life of. By J. G. Lockhart, D.C.L. A new and enlarged edition. With Notes and Appendices by W. S. Douglas. Portrait.

BUTLER'S (Bp.) Analogy of Religion; Natural and Revealed, to the Constitution and Course of Nature; with Two Dissertations on Identity and Virtue, and Fifteen Sermons. With Introductions, Notes, and Memoir. Portrait.

CAMÖEN'S Lusiad, or the Discovery of India. An Epic Poem. Trans. from the Portuguese, with Dissertation, Historical Sketch, and Life, by W. J. Mickle. 5th edition.

CARAFAS (The) of Maddaloni. Naples under Spanish Dominion. Trans. by Alfred de Reumont. Portrait of Massaniello.

CARREL. The Counter-Revolution in England for the Re-establishment of Popery under Charles II. and James II., by Armand Carrel; with Fox's History of James II. and Lord Lonsdale's Memoir of James II. Portrait of Carrel.

CARRUTHERS. — *See Pope, in Illustrated Library.*

CARY'S Dante. The Vision of Hell, Purgatory, and Paradise. Trans. by Rev. H. F. Cary, M.A. With Life, Chronological View of his Age, Notes, and Index of Proper Names. Portrait.
This is the authentic edition, containing Mr. Cary's last corrections, with additional notes.

CELLINI (Benvenuto). Memoirs of, by himself. With Notes of G. P. Carpani. Trans. by T. Roscoe. Portrait.

CERVANTES' Galatea. A Pastoral Romance. Trans. by G. W. J. Gyll.

—— **Exemplary Novels.** Trans. by W. K. Kelly.

—— **Don Quixote de la Mancha.** Motteux's Translation revised. With Lockhart's Life and Notes. 2 vols.

CHAUCER'S Poetical Works. With Poems formerly attributed to him. With a Memoir, Introduction, Notes, and a Glossary, by R. Bell. Improved edition, with Preliminary Essay by Rev. W. W. Skeat, M.A. Portrait. 4 vols.

CLASSIC TALES, containing Rasselas, Vicar of Wakefield, Gulliver's Travels, and The Sentimental Journey.

COLERIDGE'S (S. T.) Friend. A Series of Essays on Morals, Politics, and Religion. Portrait.

—— **Aids to Reflection. Confessions** of an Inquiring Spirit; and Essays on Faith and the Common Prayer-book. New Edition, revised.

—— **Table-Talk and Omniana.** By T. Ashe, B.A.

—— **Lectures on Shakspere and** other Poets. Edit. by T. Ashe, B.A.
Containing the lectures taken down in 1811-12 by J. P. Collier, and those delivered at Bristol in 1813.

—— **Biographia Literaria; or, Bio**graphical Sketches of my Literary Life and Opinions; with Two Lay Sermons.

—— **Miscellanies, Æsthetic and** Literary; to which is added, THE THEORY OF LIFE. Collected and arranged by T. Ashe, B.A.

COMMINES.—*See Philip.*

CONDÉ'S History of the Dominion of the Arabs in Spain. Trans. by Mrs. Foster. Portrait of Abderahmen ben Moavia. 3 vols.

COWPER'S Complete Works, Poems, Correspondence, and Translations. Edit. with Memoir by R. Southey. 45 Engravings. 8 vols.

COXE'S Memoirs of the Duke of Marlborough. With his original Correspondence, from family records at Blenheim. Revised edition. Portraits. 3 vols.
*** An Atlas of the plans of Marlborough's campaigns, 4to. 10s. 6d.

—— **History of the House of Austria.** From the Foundation of the Monarchy by Rhodolph of Hapsburgh to the Death of Leopold II., 1218-1792. By Archdn. Coxe. With Continuation from the Accession of Francis I. to the Revolution of 1848. 4 Portraits. 4 vols.

CUNNINGHAM'S Lives of the most Eminent British Painters. With Notes and 16 fresh Lives by Mrs. Heaton. 3 vols.

DEFOE'S Novels and Miscellaneous Works. With Prefaces and Notes, including those attributed to Sir W. Scott. Portrait. 7 vols.

DE LOLME'S Constitution of England, in which it is compared both with the Republican form of Government and the other Monarchies of Europe. Edit., with Life and Notes, by J. Macgregor, M.P.

DUNLOP'S History of Fiction. With Introduction and Supplement adapting the work to present requirements. By Henry Wilson. 2 vols., 5s. each.

ELZE'S Shakespeare.—*See Shakespeare*

EMERSON'S Works. 3 vols. Most complete edition published.
Vol. I.—Essays, Lectures, and Poems.
Vol. II.—English Traits, Nature, and Conduct of Life.
Vol. III.—Society and Solitude—Letters and Social Aims—Miscellaneous Papers (hitherto uncollected)—May-Day, &c.

FOSTER'S (John) Life and Correspondence. Edit. by J. E. Ryland. Portrait. 2 vols.

—— **Lectures at Broadmead Chapel.** Edit. by J. E. Ryland. 2 vols.

—— **Critical Essays contributed to** the 'Eclectic Review.' Edit. by J. E. Ryland. 2 vols.

—— **Essays: On Decision of Charac**ter; on a Man's writing Memoirs of Himself; on the epithet Romantic; on the aversion of Men of Taste to Evangelical Religion.

—— **Essays on the Evils of Popular** Ignorance, and a Discourse on the Propagation of Christianity in India.

—— **Essay on the Improvement of** Time, with Notes of Sermons and other Pieces. *N. S.*

—— **Fosteriana:** selected from periodical papers, edit. by H. G. Bohn.

FOX (Rt. Hon. C. J.)—*See Carrel.*

GIBBON'S Decline and Fall of the Roman Empire. Complete and unabridged, with variorum Notes: including those of Guizot, Wenck, Niebuhr, Hugo, Neander, and others. 7 vols. 2 Maps and Portrait.

GOETHE'S Works. Trans. into English by E. A. Bowring, C.B., Anna Swanwick, Sir Walter Scott, &c. &c. 14 vols.
Vols. I. and II.—Autobiography and Annals. Portrait.
Vol. III.—Faust. Complete.
Vol. IV.—Novels and Tales: containing Elective Affinities, Sorrows of Werther, The German Emigrants, The Good Women, and a Nouvelette.
Vol. V.—Wilhelm Meister's Apprenticeship.
Vol. VI.—Conversations with Eckerman and Soret.
Vol. VII.—Poems and Ballads in the original Metres, including Hermann and Dorothea.
Vol. VIII.—Götz von Berlichingen, Torquato Tasso, Egmont, Iphigenia, Clavigo, Wayward Lover, and Fellow Culprits.
Vol. IX. — Wilhelm Meister's Travels. Complete Edition.
Vol. X. — Tour in Italy. Two Parts. And Second Residence in Rome.
Vol. XI.—Miscellaneous Travels, Letters from Switzerland, Campaign in France, Siege of Mainz, and Rhine Tour.
Vol. XII.—Early and Miscellaneous Letters, including Letters to his Mother, with Biography and Notes.
Vol. XIII.—Correspondence with Zelter.
Vol. XIV.— Reineke Fox, West-Eastern Divan and Achilleid. Translated in original metres by A. Rogers.

—— **Correspondence with Schiller.** 2 vols.—*See Schiller.*

GOLDSMITH'S Works. 5 vols.
Vol. I.—Life, Vicar of Wakefield, Essays, and Letters.
Vol. II.—Poems, Plays, Bee, Cock Lane Ghost.
Vol. III.—The Citizen of the World, Polite Learning in Europe.
Vol. IV.—Biographies, Criticisms, Later Essays.
Vol. V. — Prefaces, Natural History, Letters, Goody Two-Shoes, Index.

GREENE, MARLOW, and BEN JONSON (Poems of). With Notes and Memoirs by R. Bell.

GREGORY'S (Dr.) The Evidences, Doctrines, and Duties of the Christian Religion.

GRIMM'S Household Tales. With the Original Notes. Trans. by Mrs. A. Hunt. Introduction by Andrew Lang, M.A. 2 vols.

GUIZOT'S History of Representative Government in Europe. Trans. by A. R. Scoble.

—— **English Revolution of 1640.** From the Accession of Charles I. to his Death. Trans. by W. Hazlitt. Portrait.

—— **History of Civilisation.** From the Roman Empire to the French Revolution. Trans. by W. Hazlitt. Portraits. 3 vols.

HALL'S (Rev. Robert) Works and Remains. Memoir by Dr. Gregory and Essay by J. Foster. Portrait.

HAUFF'S Tales. The Caravan — The Sheikh of Alexandria — The Inn in the Spessart. Translated by Prof. S. Mendel.

HAWTHORNE'S Tales. 3 vols.
Vol. I.—Twice-told Tales, and the Snow Image.
Vol. II.—Scarlet Letter, and the House with Seven Gables.
Vol. III. — Transformation, and Blithedale Romance.

HAZLITT'S (W.) Works. 7 vols.

—— **Table-Talk.**

—— **The Literature of the Age of** Elizabeth and Characters of Shakespeare's Plays.

—— **English Poets and English Comic** Writers.

—— **The Plain Speaker.** Opinions on Books, Men, and Things.

—— **Round Table.** Conversations of James Northcote, R.A.; Characteristics.

—— **Sketches and Essays,** and Winterslow.

—— **Spirit of the Age;** or, Contemporary Portraits. New Edition, by W. Carew Hazlitt.

HEINE'S Poems. Translated in the original Metres, with Life by E. A. Bowring, C.B.

—— **Travel-Pictures.** The Tour in the Harz, Norderney, and Book of Ideas, together with the Romantic School. Trans. by F. Storr. With Maps and Appendices.

HOFFMANN'S Works. The Serapion Brethren. Vol. I. Trans. by Lt.-Col. Ewing. [*Vol. II. in the press.*

HOOPER'S (G.) Waterloo: The Downfall of the First Napoleon: a History of the Campaign of 1815. By George Hooper. With Maps and Plans. New Edition, revised.

HUGO'S (Victor) Dramatic Works:
Hernani, Ruy Blas, The King's Diversion.
Translated by Mrs. Newton Crosland and
F. L. Slous.

—— Poems, chiefly Lyrical. Collected by
H. L. Williams.

HUNGARY: its History and Revolution, with Memoir of Kossuth. Portrait.

HUTCHINSON (Colonel). Memoirs
of. By his Widow, with her Autobiography, and the Siege of Lathom House.
Portrait.

IRVING'S (Washington) Complete
Works. 15 vols.

—— Life and Letters. By his Nephew,
Pierre E. Irving. With Index and a
Portrait. 2 vols.

JAMES'S (G. P. R.) Life of Richard
Cœur de Lion. Portraits of Richard and
Philip Augustus. 2 vols.
—— Louis XIV. Portraits. 2 vols.

JAMESON (Mrs.) Shakespeare's
Heroines. Characteristics of Women. By
Mrs. Jameson.

JEAN PAUL.—See Richter.

JOHNSON'S Lives of the Poets.
Edited, with Notes, by Mrs. Alexander
Napier. And an Introduction by Pro-
fessor J. W. Hales, M.A. 3 vols.

JONSON (Ben). Poems of.—See Greene.

JOSEPHUS (Flavius), The Works of.
Whiston's Translation. Revised by Rev.
A. R. Shilleto, M.A. With Topographical
and Geographical Notes by Colonel Sir
C. W. Wilson, K.C.B. 5 vols.

JUNIUS'S Letters. With Woodfall's
Notes. An Essay on the Authorship. Fac-
similes of Handwriting. 2 vols.

LA FONTAINE'S Fables. In English
Verse, with Essay on the Fabulists. By
Elizur Wright.

LAMARTINE'S The Girondists, or
Personal Memoirs of the Patriots of the
French Revolution. Trans. by H. T.
Ryde. Portraits of Robespierre, Madame
Roland, and Charlotte Corday. 3 vols.

—— The Restoration of Monarchy
in France (a Sequel to The Girondists).
5 Portraits. 4 vols.

—— The French Revolution of 1848.
Portrait.

LAMB'S (Charles) Elia and Eliana.
Complete Edition. Portrait.

LAMB'S (Charles) Specimens of
English Dramatic Poets of the time of
Elizabeth. Notes, with the Extracts from
the Garrick Plays.

—— Talfourd's Letters of Charles
Lamb. New Edition, by W. Carew
Hazlitt. 2 vols.

LANZI'S History of Painting in
Italy, from the Period of the Revival of
the Fine Arts to the End of the 18th
Century. With Memoir of the Author.
Portraits of Raffaelle, Titian, and Cor-
reggio, after the Artists themselves. Trans.
by T. Roscoe. 3 vols.

LAPPENBERG'S England under the
Anglo-Saxon Kings. Trans. by B. Thorpe,
F.S.A. 2 vols.

LESSING'S Dramatic Works. Complete. By E. Bell, M.A. With Memoir
by H. Zimmern. Portrait. 2 vols.

—— Laokoon, Dramatic Notes and
Representation of Death by the Ancients.
Frontispiece.

LOCKE'S Philosophical Works, containing Human Understanding, with Bishop
of Worcester, Malebranche's Opinions, Natural Philosophy, Reading and Study.
With Preliminary Discourse, Analy. and
Notes, by J. A. St. John. Portrait. 2 vols.

—— Life and Letters, with Extracts from
his Common-place Books. By Lord King.

LOCKHART (J. G.)—See Burns.

LONSDALE (Lord).—See Carrel.

LUTHER'S Table-Talk. Trans. W.
Hazlitt. With Life by A. Chalmers and
Luther's Catechism. Portrait after
Cranach.

—— Autobiography.—See Michelet.

MACHIAVELLI'S History of Florence, The Prince, Savonarola, Historical
Tracts, and Memoir. Portrait.

MARLOWE. Poems of.—See Greene.

MARTINEAU'S (Harriet) History
of England (including History of the Peace)
from 1800-1846. 5 vols.

MENZEL'S History of Germany,
from the Earliest Period to the Crimean
War. Portraits. 3 vols.

MICHELET'S Autobiography of
Luther. Trans. by W. Hazlitt. With
Notes.

—— The French Revolution: the
Flight of the King in 1791. N.S.

MIGNET'S The French Revolution,
from 1789 to 1814. Portrait of Napoleon.

MILTON'S Prose Works. With Preface, Preliminary Remarks by J. A. St. John, and Index. 5 vols.

—— **Poetical Works.** With 120 Wood Engravings. 2 vols.
Vol. I.—Paradise Lost, complete, with Memoir, Notes, and Index.
Vol. II.—Paradise Regained, and other Poems. with Verbal Index to all the Poems.

MITFORD'S (Miss) Our Village. Sketches of Rural Character and Scenery. 2 Engravings. 2 vols.

MOLIÈRE'S Dramatic Works. In English Prose, by C. H. Wall. With a Life and a Portrait. 3 vols.
' It is not too much to say that we have here probably as good a translation of Molière as can be given.'—*Academy*.

MONTAGU. Letters and Works of Lady Mary Wortley Montagu. Lord Wharncliffe's Third Edition. Edited by W. Moy Thomas. With steel plates. 2 vols. 5s. each.

MONTESQUIEU'S Spirit of Laws. Revised Edition, with D'Alembert's Analysis, Notes, and Memoir. 2 vols.

NEANDER (Dr. A.) History of the Christian Religion and Church. Trans. by J. Torrey. With Short Memoir. 10 vols.

—— **Life of Jesus Christ, in its Historical Connexion and Development.**

—— **The Planting and Training of** the Christian Church by the Apostles. With the Antignosticus, or Spirit of Tertullian. Trans. by J. E. Ryland. 2 vols.

—— **Lectures on the History of** Christian Dogmas. Trans. by J. E. Ryland. 2 vols.

—— **Memorials of Christian Life in** the Early and Middle Ages; including Light in Dark Places. Trans. by J. E. Ryland.

OCKLEY (S.) History of the Saracens and their Conquests in Syria, Persia, and Egypt. Comprising the Lives of Mohammed and his Successors to the Death of Abdalmelik, the Eleventh Caliph. By Simon Ockley, B.D., Prof. of Arabic in Univ. of Cambridge. Portrait of Mohammed.

PASCAL'S Thoughts. Translated from the Text of M. Auguste Molinier by C. Kegan Paul. 3rd edition.

PERCY'S Reliques of Ancient English Poetry, consisting of Ballads, Songs, and other Pieces of our earlier Poets, with some few of later date. With Essay on Ancient Minstrels, and Glossary. 2 vols.

PHILIP DE COMMINES. Memoirs of. Containing the Histories of Louis XI. and Charles VIII., and Charles the Bold, Duke of Burgundy. With the History of Louis XI., by J. de Troyes. With a Life and Notes by A. R. Scoble. Portraits. 2 vols.

PLUTARCH'S LIVES. Newly Translated, with Notes and Life, by A Stewart, M.A., late Fellow of Trinity College, Cambridge, and G. Long, M.A. 4 vols.

POETRY OF AMERICA. Selections from One Hundred Poets, from 1776 to 1876. With Introductory Review, and Specimens of Negro Melody, by W. J. Linton. Portrait of W. Whitman.

RACINE'S (Jean) Dramatic Works. A metrical English version, with Biographical notice. By R. Bruce Boswell, M.A., Oxon. Vol. I.
Contents :—The Thebaïd —Alexander the Great—Andromache—The Litigants—Britannicus—Berenice.

RANKE (L.) History of the Popes, their Church and State, and their Conflicts with Protestantism in the 16th and 17th Centuries. Trans. by E. Foster. Portraits of Julius II. (after Raphael), Innocent X. (after Velasquez), and Clement VII. (after Titian). 3 vols.

—— **History of Servia.** Trans. by Mrs. Kerr. To which is added, The Slave Provinces of Turkey, by Cyprien Robert.

—— **History of the Latin and Teutonic** Nations. 1494-1514. Trans. by P. A. Ashworth, translator of Dr. Gneist's ' History of the English Constitution.'

REUMONT (Alfred de).—*See Carafas*.

REYNOLDS' (Sir J.) Literary Works. With Memoir and Remarks by H. W. Beechy. 2 vols.

RICHTER (Jean Paul). Levana, a Treatise on Education ; together with the Autobiography, and a short Memoir.

—— **Flower, Fruit, and Thorn Pieces,** or the Wedded Life, Death, and Marriage of Siebenkaes. Translated by Alex. Ewing. The only complete English translation.

ROSCOE'S (W.) Life of Leo X., with Notes, Historical Documents, and Dissertation on Lucretia Borgia. 3 Portraits. 2 vols.

—— **Lorenzo de' Medici,** called ' The Magnificent,' with Copyright Notes, Poems, Letters, &c. With Memoir of Roscoe and Portrait of Lorenzo.

RUSSIA, History of, from the earliest Period to the Crimean War. By W. K. Kelly. 3 Portraits. 2 vols.

SCHILLER'S Works. 7 vols.

Vol. I.—History of the Thirty Years' War. Rev. A. J. W. Morrison, M.A. Portrait.

Vol. II.—History of the Revolt in the Netherlands, the Trials of Counts Egmont and Horn, the Siege of Antwerp, and the Disturbance of France preceding the Reign of Henry IV. Translated by Rev. A. J. W. Morrison and L. Dora Schmitz.

Vol. III.—Don Carlos. R. D. Boylan —Mary Stuart. Mellish — Maid of Orleans. Anna Swanwick—Bride of Messina. A. Lodge, M.A. Together with the Use of the Chorus in Tragedy (a short Essay). Engravings.

These Dramas are all translated in metre.

Vol. IV.—Robbers—Fiesco—Love and Intrigue—Demetrius—Ghost Seer—Sport of Divinity.

The Dramas in this volume are in prose.

Vol. V.—Poems. E. A. Bowring, C.B.

Vol. VI.—Essays, Æsthetical and Philosophical, including the Dissertation on the Connexion between the Animal and Spiritual in Man.

Vol. VII. — Wallenstein's Camp. J. Churchill. — Piccolomini and Death of Wallenstein. S. T. Coleridge.—William Tell. Sir Theodore Martin, K.C.B., LL.D.

SCHILLER and GOETHE. Correspondence between, from A.D. 1794-1805. With Short Notes by L. Dora Schmitz. 2 vols.

SCHLEGEL'S (F.) Lectures on the Philosophy of Life and the Philosophy of Language. By A. J. W. Morrison.

—— **The History of Literature,** Ancient and Modern.

—— **The Philosophy of History.** With Memoir and Portrait.

—— **Modern History,** with the Lectures entitled Cæsar and Alexander, and The Beginning of our History. By L. Purcel and R. H. Whitelock.

—— **Æsthetic and Miscellaneous** Works, containing Letters on Christian Art, Essay on Gothic Architecture, Remarks on the Romance Poetry of the Middle Ages, on Shakspeare, the Limits of the Beautiful, and on the Language and Wisdom of the Indians. By E. J. Millington.

SCHLEGEL (A. W.) Dramatic Art and Literature. By J. Black. With Memoir by A. J. W. Morrison. Portrait.

SCHUMANN (Robert), His Life and Works. By A. Reissmann. Trans. by A. L. Alger.

—— **Early Letters.** Translated by May Herbert.

SHAKESPEARE'S Dramatic Art. The History and Character of Shakspeare's Plays. By Dr. H. Ulrici. Trans. by L. Dora Schmitz. 2 vols.

SHAKESPEARE (William). A Literary Biography by Karl Elze, Ph.D., LL.D. Translated by L. Dora Schmitz. 5s.

SHERIDAN'S Dramatic Works. With Memoir. Portrait (after Reynolds).

SKEAT (Rev. W. W.)—*See Chaucer.*

SISMONDI'S History of the Litera- ture of the South of Europe. With Notes and Memoir by T. Roscoe. Portraits of Sismondi and Dante. 2 vols.

The specimens of early French, Italian, Spanish, and Portugese Poetry, in English Verse, by Cary and others.

SMITH'S (Adam) The Wealth of Nations. An Inquiry into the Nature and Causes of. Reprinted from the Sixth Edition. With an Introduction by Ernest Belfort Bax. 2 vols.

SMITH'S (Adam) Theory of Moral Sentiments ; with Essay on the First Formation of Languages, and Critical Memoir by Dugald Stewart.

SMYTH'S (Professor) Lectures on Modern History ; from the Irruption of the Northern Nations to the close of the American Revolution. 2 vols.

—— **Lectures on the French Revolu-** tion. With Index. 2 vols.

SOUTHEY.—*See Cowper, Wesley, and* (*Illustrated Library*) *Nelson.*

STURM'S Morning Communings with God, or Devotional Meditations for Every Day. Trans. by W. Johnstone, M.A.

SULLY. Memoirs of the Duke of, Prime Minister to Henry the Great. With Notes and Historical Introduction. 4 Portraits. 4 vols.

TAYLOR'S (Bishop Jeremy) Holy Living and Dying, with Prayers, containing the Whole Duty of a Christian and the parts of Devotion fitted to all Occasions. Portrait.

THIERRY'S Conquest of England by the Normans ; its Causes, and its Consequences in England and the Continent. By W. Hazlitt. With short Memoir. 2 Portraits. 2 vols.

TROYE'S (Jean de). — *See Philip de Commines.*

ULRICI (Dr.)—*See Shakespeare.*

VASARI. Lives of the most Eminent Painters, Sculptors, and Architects. By Mrs. J. Foster, with selected Notes. Portrait. 6 vols., Vol. VI. being an additional Volume of Notes by J. P. Richter.

WERNER'S Templars in Cyprus. Trans. by E. A. M. Lewis.

WESLEY, the Life of, and the Rise and Progress of Methodism. By Robert Southey. Portrait. 5s.

WHEATLEY. A Rational Illustra- tion of the Book of Common Prayer, being the Substance of everything Liturgical in all former Ritualist Commentators upon the subject. Frontispiece.

YOUNG (Arthur) Travels in France. Edited by Miss Betham Edwards. With a Portrait.

HISTORICAL LIBRARY.

22 Volumes at 5s. each.   (*5l. 10s. per set.*)

EVELYN'S Diary and Correspond-
dence, with the Private Correspondence of
Charles I. and Sir Edward Nicholas, and
between Sir Edward Hyde (Earl of Clarendon) and Sir Richard Browne. Edited from
the Original MSS. by W. Bray, F.A.S.
4 vols. *N. S.* 45 Engravings (after Vandyke, Lely, Kneller, and Jamieson, &c.).

> N.B.—This edition contains 130 letters
> from Evelyn and his wife, contained in no
> other edition.

PEPYS' Diary and Correspondence.
With Life and Notes, by Lord Braybrooke.
4 vols. *N. S.* With Appendix containing
additional Letters, an Index, and 31 Engravings (after Vandyke, Sir P. Lely,
Holbein, Kneller, &c.).

JESSE'S Memoirs of the Court of
England under the Stuarts, including the
Protectorate. 3 vols. With Index and 42
Portraits (after Vandyke, Lely, &c.).

—— **Memoirs of the Pretenders and**
their Adherents. 7 Portraits.

NUGENT'S (Lord) Memorials of
Hampden, his Party and Times. With
Memoir. 12 Portraits (after Vandyke
and others).

STRICKLAND'S (Agnes) Lives of the
Queens of England from the Norman
Conquest. From authentic Documents,
public and private. 6 Portraits. 6 vols.
N. S.

—— **Life of Mary Queen of Scots.**
2 Portraits. 2 vols.

—— **Lives of the Tudor and Stuart**
Princesses. With 2 Portraits.

PHILOSOPHICAL LIBRARY.

17 Vols. at 5s. each, excepting those marked otherwise.   (*3l. 19s. per set.*)

BACON'S Novum Organum and Ad-
vancement of Learning. With Notes by
J. Devey, M.A.

BAX. A Handbook of the History
of Philosophy, for the use of Students.
By E. Belfort Bax, Editor of Kant's
'Prolegomena.' 5s.

COMTE'S Philosophy of the Sciences.
An Exposition of the Principles of the
Cours de Philosophie Positive. By G. H.
Lewes, Author of 'The Life of Goethe.'

DRAPER (Dr. J. W.) A History of
the Intellectual Development of Europe.
2 vols.

HEGEL'S Philosophy of History. By
J. Sibree, M.A.

KANT'S Critique of Pure Reason.
By J. M. D. Meiklejohn.

—— **Prolegomena and Metaphysical**
Foundations of Natural Science, with Bio-
graphy and Memoir by E. Belfort Bax.
Portrait.

LOGIC, or the Science of Inference.
A Popular Manual. By J. Devey.

MILLER (Professor). History Philo-
sophically Illustrated, from the Fall of the
Roman Empire to the French Revolution.
With Memoir. 4 vols. 3s. 6d. each.

SCHOPENHAUER on the Fourfold
Root of the Principle of Sufficient Reason,
and on the Will in Nature. Trans. from
the German.

SPINOZA'S Chief Works. Trans. with
Introduction by R. H. M. Elwes. 2 vols.

> Vol. I.—Tractatus Theologico-Politicus
> —Political Treatise.

> Vol. II.— Improvement of the Under-
> standing—Ethics—Letters.

TENNEMANN'S Manual of the His-
tory of Philosophy. Trans. by Rev. A.
Johnson, M.A.

THEOLOGICAL LIBRARY.

15 Vols. at 5s. each, excepting those marked otherwise.   (3l. 13s. 6d. per set.)

BLEEK. Introduction to the Old Testament. By Friedrich Bleek. Trans. under the supervision of Rev. E. Venables, Residentiary Canon of Lincoln. 2 vols.

CHILLINGWORTH'S Religion of Protestants. 3s. 6d.

EUSEBIUS. Ecclesiastical History of Eusebius Pamphilius, Bishop of Cæsarea. Trans. by Rev. C. F. Cruse, M.A. With Notes, Life, and Chronological Tables.

EVAGRIUS. History of the Church. —*See Theodoret.*

HARDWICK. History of the Articles of Religion ; to which is added a Series of Documents from A.D. 1536 to A.D. 1615. Ed. by Rev. F. Proctor.

HENRY'S (Matthew) Exposition of the Book of Psalms. Numerous Woodcuts.

PEARSON (John, D.D.) Exposition of the Creed. Edit. by E. Walford, M.A. With Notes, Analysis, and Indexes.

PHILO-JUDÆUS, Works of. The Contemporary of Josephus. Trans. by C. D. Yonge. 4 vols.

PHILOSTORGIUS. Ecclesiastical History of.—*See Sozomen.*

SOCRATES' Ecclesiastical History. Comprising a History of the Church from Constantine, A.D. 305, to the 38th year of Theodosius II. With Short Account of the Author, and selected Notes.

SOZOMEN'S Ecclesiastical History. A.D. 324-440. With Notes, Prefatory Remarks by Valesius, and Short Memoir. Together with the ECCLESIASTICAL HISTORY OF PHILOSTORGIUS, as epitomised by Photius. Trans. by Rev. E. Walford, M.A. With Notes and brief Life.

THEODORET and EVAGRIUS. Histories of the Church from A.D. 332 to the Death of Theodore of Mopsuestia, A.D. 427 ; and from A.D. 431 to A.D. 544. With Memoirs.

WIESELER'S (Karl) Chronological Synopsis of the Four Gospels. Trans. by Rev. Canon Venables.

ANTIQUARIAN LIBRARY.

35 Vols. at 5s. each.   (8l. 15s. per set.)

ANGLO-SAXON CHRONICLE. — *See Bede.*

ASSER'S Life of Alfred.—*See Six O. E. Chronicles.*

BEDE'S (Venerable) Ecclesiastical History of England. Together with the ANGLO-SAXON CHRONICLE. With Notes, Short Life, Analysis, and Map. Edit. by J. A. Giles, D.C.L.

BOETHIUS'S Consolation of Philo- sophy. King Alfred's Anglo-Saxon Version of. With an English Translation on opposite pages, Notes, Introduction, and Glossary, by Rev. S. Fox, M.A. To which is added the Anglo-Saxon Version of the METRES OF BOETHIUS, with a free Translation by Martin F. Tupper, D.C.L.

BRAND'S Popular Antiquities of England, Scotland, and Ireland. Illustrating the Origin of our Vulgar and Provincial Customs, Ceremonies, and Superstitions. By Sir Henry Ellis, K.H., F.R.S. Frontispiece. 3 vols.

CHRONICLES of the CRUSADES. Contemporary Narratives of Richard Cœur de Lion, by Richard of Devizes and Geoffrey de Vinsauf ; and of the Crusade at Saint Louis, by Lord John de Joinville. With Short Notes. Illuminated Frontispiece from an old MS.

DYER'S (T. F. T.) British Popular Customs, Present and Past. An Account of the various Games and Customs associated with different Days of the Year in the British Isles, arranged according to the Calendar. By the Rev. T. F. Thiselton Dyer, M.A.

EARLY TRAVELS IN PALESTINE. Comprising the Narratives of Arculf, Willibald, Bernard, Sæwulf, Sigurd, Benjamin of Tudela, Sir John Maundeville, De la Brocquière, and Maundrell ; all unabridged. With Introduction and Notes by Thomas Wright. Map of Jerusalem.

ELLIS (G.) Specimens of Early English Metrical Romances, relating to Arthur, Merlin, Guy of Warwick, Richard Cœur de Lion, Charlemagne, Roland, &c. &c. With Historical Introduction by J. O. Halliwell, F.R.S. Illuminated Frontispiece from an old MS.

ETHELWERD. Chronicle of.—*See Six O. E. Chronicles.*

FLORENCE OF WORCESTER'S Chronicle, with the Two Continuations : comprising Annals of English History from the Departure of the Romans to the Reign of Edward I. Trans., with Notes, by Thomas Forester, M.A.

GEOFFREY OF MONMOUTH. Chronicle of.—*See Six O. E. Chronicles.*

GESTA ROMANORUM, or Enter- taining Moral Stories invented by the Monks. Trans. with Notes by the Rev. Charles Swan. Edit. by W. Hooper, M.A.

GILDAS. Chronicle of.—*See Six O. E. Chronicles.*

GIRALDUS CAMBRENSIS' Histori- cal Works. Containing Topography of Ireland, and History of the Conquest of Ireland, by Th. Forester, M.A. Itinerary through Wales, and Description of Wales, by Sir R. Colt Hoare.

HENRY OF HUNTINGDON'S His- tory of the English, from the Roman Invasion to the Accession of Henry II.; with the Acts of King Stephen, and the Letter to Walter. By T. Forester, M.A. Frontispiece from an old MS.

INGULPH'S Chronicles of the Abbey of Croyland, with the CONTINUATION by Peter of Blois and others. Trans. with Notes by H. T. Riley, B.A.

KEIGHTLEY'S (Thomas) Fairy My- thology, illustrative of the Romance and Superstition of Various Countries. Frontispiece by Cruikshank.

LEPSIUS'S Letters from Egypt, Ethiopia, and the Peninsula of Sinai ; to which are added, Extracts from his Chronology of the Egyptians, with reference to the Exodus of the Israelites. By L. and J. B. Horner. Maps and Coloured View of Mount Barkal.

MALLET'S Northern Antiquities, or an Historical Account of the Manners, Customs, Religions, and Literature of the Ancient Scandinavians. Trans. by Bishop Percy. With Translation of the PROSE EDDA, and Notes by J. A. Blackwell. Also an Abstract of the 'Eyrbyggia Saga' by Sir Walter Scott. With Glossary and Coloured Frontispiece.

MARCO POLO'S Travels ; with Notes and Introduction. Edit. by T. Wright.

MATTHEW PARIS'S English His- tory, from 1235 to 1273. By Rev. J. A. Giles, D.C.L. With Frontispiece. 3 vols.— *See also Roger of Wendover.*

MATTHEW OF WESTMINSTER'S Flowers of History, especially such as relate to the affairs of Britain, from the beginning of the World to A.D. 1307. By C. D. Yonge. 2 vols.

NENNIUS. Chronicle of.—*See Six O. E. Chronicles.*

ORDERICUS VITALIS' Ecclesiastical History of England and Normandy. With Notes, Introduction of Guizot, and the Critical Notice of M. Delille, by T. Forester, M.A. To which is added the CHRONICLE OF St. EVROULT. With General and Chronological Indexes. 4 vols.

PAULI'S (Dr. R.) Life of Alfred the Great. To which is appended Alfred's ANGLO-SAXON VERSION OF OROSIUS. With literal Translation interpaged, Notes, and an ANGLO-SAXON GRAMMAR and Glossary, by B. Thorpe, Esq. Frontispiece.

RICHARD OF CIRENCESTER. Chronicle of.—*See Six O. E. Chronicles.*

ROGER DE HOVEDEN'S Annals of English History, comprising the History of England and of other Countries of Europe from A.D. 732 to A.D. 1201. With Notes by H. T. Riley, B.A. 2 vols.

ROGER OF WENDOVER'S Flowers of History, comprising the History of England from the Descent of the Saxons to A.D. 1235, formerly ascribed to Matthew Paris. With Notes and Index by J. A. Giles, D.C.L. 2 vols.

SIX OLD ENGLISH CHRONICLES : viz., Asser's Life of Alfred and the Chronicles of Ethelwerd, Gildas, Nennius, Geoffrey of Monmouth, and Richard of Cirencester. Edit., with Notes, by J. A. Giles, D.C.L. Portrait of Alfred.

WILLIAM OF MALMESBURY'S Chronicle of the Kings of England, from the Earliest Period to King Stephen. By Rev. J. Sharpe. With Notes by J. A. Giles, D.C.L. Frontispiece.

YULE-TIDE STORIES. A Collection of Scandinavian and North-German Popular Tales and Traditions, from the Swedish, Danish, and German. Edit. by B. Thorpe.

ILLUSTRATED LIBRARY.

83 Vols. at 5s. each, excepting those marked otherwise.   (20*l.* 13*s.* 6*d.* *per set.*)

.LLEN'S (Joseph, R.N.) Battles of the British Navy. Revised edition, with Indexes of Names and Events, and 57 Portraits and Plans. 2 vols.

.NDERSEN'S Danish Fairy Tales. By Caroline Peachey. With Short Life and 120 Wood Engravings.

.RIOSTO'S Orlando Furioso. In English Verse by W. S. Rose. With Notes and Short Memoir. Portrait after Titian, and 24 Steel Engravings. 2 vols.

ECHSTEIN'S Cage and Chamber Birds : their Natural History, Habits, &c. Together with SWEET'S BRITISH WARBLERS. 43 Coloured Plates and Woodcuts.

ONOMI'S Nineveh and its Palaces. The Discoveries of Botta and Layard applied to the Elucidation of Holy Writ. 7 Plates and 294 Woodcuts.

UTLER'S Hudibras, with Variorum Notes and Biography. Portrait and 28 Illustrations.

ATTERMOLE'S Evenings at Haddon Hall. Romantic Tales of the Olden Times. With 24 Steel Engravings after Cattermole.

HINA, Pictorial, Descriptive, and Historical, with some account of Ava and the Burmese, Siam, and Anam. Map, and nearly 100 Illustrations.

RAIK'S (G. L.) Pursuit of Knowledge under Difficulties. Illustrated by Anecdotes and Memoirs. Numerous Woodcut Portraits.

RUIKSHANK'S Three Courses and a Dessert ; comprising three Sets of Tales, West Country, Irish, and Legal ; and a Mélange. With 50 Illustrations by Cruikshank.

—— **Punch and Judy.** The Dialogue of the Puppet Show ; an Account of its Origin, &c. 24 Illustrations and Coloured Plates by Cruikshank.

IDRON'S Christian Iconography ; a History of Christian Art in the Middle Ages. By the late A. N. Didron. Trans. by E. J. Millington, and completed, with Additions and Appendices, by Margaret Stokes. 2 vols. With numerous Illustrations.

    Vol. I. The History of the Nimbus, the Aureole, and the Glory ; Representations of the Persons of the Trinity.

    Vol. II. The Trinity ; Angels ; Devils ; The Soul ; The Christian Scheme. Appendices.

DANTE, in English Verse, by I. C. Wright, M.A. With Introduction and Memoir. Portrait and 34 Steel Engravings after Flaxman.

DYER (Dr. T. H.) Pompeii : its Buildings and Antiquities. An Account of the City, with full Description of the Remains and Recent Excavations, and an Itinerary for Visitors. By T. H. Dyer, LL.D. Nearly 300 Wood Engravings, Map, and Plan. 7*s.* 6*d.*

—— **Rome :** History of the City, with Introduction on recent Excavations. 8 Engravings, Frontispiece, and 2 Maps.

GIL BLAS. The Adventures of. From the French of Lesage by Smollett. 24 Engravings after Smirke, and 10 Etchings by Cruikshank. 612 pages. 6*s.*

GRIMM'S Gammer Grethel ; or, German Fairy Tales and Popular Stories, containing 42 Fairy Tales. By Edgar Taylor. Numerous Woodcuts after Cruikshank and Ludwig Grimm. 3*s.* 6*d.*

HOLBEIN'S Dance of Death and Bible Cuts. Upwards of 150 Subjects, engraved in facsimile, with Introduction and Descriptions by the late Francis Douce and Dr. Dibdin.

INDIA, Pictorial, Descriptive, and Historical, from the Earliest Times. 100 Engravings on Wood and Map.

JESSE'S Anecdotes of Dogs. With 40 Woodcuts after Harvey, Bewick, and others ; and 34 Steel Engravings after Cooper and Landseer.

KING'S (C. W.) Natural History of Gems or Decorative Stones. Illustrations. 6*s.*

—— **Natural History of Precious** Stones and Metals. Illustrations. 6*s.*

KITTO'S Scripture Lands. Described in a series of Historical, Geographical, and Topographical Sketches. 42 coloured Maps.

KRUMMACHER'S Parables. 40 Illustrations.

LINDSAY'S (Lord) Letters on Egypt, Edom, and the Holy Land. 36 Wood Engravings and 2 Maps.

LODGE'S Portraits of Illustrious Personages of Great Britain, with Biographical and Historical Memoirs. 240 Portraits engraved on Steel, with the respective Biographies unabridged. Complete in 8 vols.

LONGFELLOW'S Poetical Works, including his Translations and Notes. 24 full-page Woodcuts by Birket Foster and others, and a Portrait.

—— Without the Illustrations, 3s. 6d.

—— **Prose Works.** With 16 full-page Woodcuts by Birket Foster and others.

LOUDON'S (Mrs.) Entertaining Naturalist. Popular Descriptions, Tales, and Anecdotes, of more than 500 Animals. Numerous Woodcuts.

MARRYAT'S (Capt., R.N.) Masterman Ready; or, the Wreck of the *Pacific.* (Written for Young People.) With 93 Woodcuts. 3s. 6d.

—— **Mission; or, Scenes in Africa.** (Written for Young People.) Illustrated by Gilbert and Dalziel. 3s. 6d.

—— **Pirate and Three Cutters.** (Written for Young People.) With a Memoir. 8 Steel Engravings after Clarkson Stanfield, R.A. 3s. 6d.

—— **Privateersman.** Adventures by Sea and Land One Hundred Years Ago. (Written for Young People.) 8 Steel Engravings. 3s. 6d.

—— **Settlers in Canada.** (Written for Young People.) 10 Engravings by Gilbert and Dalziel. 3s. 6d.

—— **Poor Jack.** (Written for Young People.) With 16 Illustrations after Clarkson Stanfield, R.A. 3s. 6d.

—— **Midshipman Easy.** With 8 full-page Illustrations. Small post 8vo. 3s. 6d.

—— **Peter Simple.** With 8 full-page Illustrations. Small post 8vo. 3s. 6d.

MAXWELL'S Victories of Wellington and the British Armies. Frontispiece and 4 Portraits.

MICHAEL ANGELO and RAPHAEL, Their Lives and Works. By Duppa and Quatremère de Quincy. Portraits and Engravings, including the Last Judgment, and Cartoons.

MILLER'S History of the Anglo-Saxons, from the Earliest Period to the Norman Conquest. Portrait of Alfred, Map of Saxon Britain, and 12 Steel Engravings.

MUDIE'S History of British Birds. Revised by W. C. L. Martin. 52 Figures of Birds and 7 coloured Plates of Eggs. 2 vols.

NAVAL and MILITARY HEROof Great Britain; a Record of Brit Valour on every Day in the year, fr William the Conqueror to the Battle Inkermann. By Major Johns, R.M., Lieut. P. H. Nicolas, R.M. Indexes. Portraits after Holbein, Reynolds, &c.

NICOLINI'S History of the Jesuitheir Origin, Progress, Doctrines, and signs. 8 Portraits.

PETRARCH'S Sonnets, Triumph and other Poems, in English Verse. W Life by Thomas Campbell. Portrait 15 Steel Engravings.

PICKERING'S History of the Raof Man, and their Geographical Distri tion; with AN ANALYTICAL SYNOPSIS THE NATURAL HISTORY OF MAN. By Hall. Map of the World and 12 colou Plates

PICTORIAL HANDBOOK Modern Geography en a Popular Pl Compiled from the best Authorities, Engl and Foreign, by H. G. Bohn. 150 Wo cuts and 51 coloured Maps.

—— Without the Maps, 3s. 6d.

POPE'S Poetical Works, includ Translations. Edit., with Notes, by Carruthers. 2 vols.

—— **Homer's Iliad,** with Introduct and Notes by Rev. J. S. Watson, M With Flaxman's Designs.

—— **Homer's Odyssey,** with the BATT OF FROGS AND MICE, Hymns, &c., other translators including Chapman. troduction and Notes by J. S. Wats M.A. With Flaxman's Designs.

—— **Life,** including many of his Lett By R. Carruthers. Numerous Illustratio

POTTERY AND PORCELAIN, other objects of Vertu. Comprising Illustrated Catalogue of the Bernal C lection, with the prices and names of Possessors. Also an Introductory Lect on Pottery and Porcelain, and an Engra List of all Marks and Monograms. H. G. Bohn. Numerous Woodcuts.

—— With coloured Illustrations, 10s. 6d.

PROUT'S (Father) Reliques. Edit by Rev. F. Mahony. Copyright editi with the Author's last corrections a additions. 21 Etchings by D. Macli R.A. Nearly 600 pages.

RECREATIONS IN SHOOTING. W some Account of the Game found in t British Isles, and Directions for the Manag ment of Dog and Gun. By 'Craven.' Woodcuts and 9 Steel Engravings af A. Cooper, R.A.

RENNIE. Insect Architecture. Revised by Rev. J. G. Wood, M.A. 186 Woodcuts.

ROBINSON CRUSOE. With Memoir of Defoe, 12 Steel Engravings and 74 Woodcuts after Stothard and Harvey.

—— Without the Engravings, 3s. 6d.

ROME IN THE NINETEENTH CENTURY. An Account in 1817 of the Ruins of the Ancient City, and Monuments of Modern Times. By C. A. Eaton. 34 Steel Engravings. 2 vols.

SHARPE (S.) The History of Egypt, from the Earliest Times till the Conquest by the Arabs, A.D. 640. 2 Maps and upwards of 400 Woodcuts. 2 vols.

SOUTHEY'S Life of Nelson. With Additional Notes, Facsimiles of Nelson's Writing, Portraits, Plans, and 50 Engravings, after Birket Foster, &c.

STARLING'S (Miss) Noble Deeds of Women; or, Examples of Female Courage, Fortitude, and Virtue. With 14 Steel Portraits.

STUART and REVETT'S Antiquities of Athens, and other Monuments of Greece; with Glossary of Terms used in Grecian Architecture. 71 Steel Plates and numerous Woodcuts.

SWEET'S British Warblers. 5s.—*See Bechstein.*

TALES OF THE GENII; or, the Delightful Lessons of Horam, the Son of Asmar. Trans. by Sir C. Morrell. Numerous Woodcuts.

TASSO'S Jerusalem Delivered. In English Spenserian Verse, with Life, by J. H. Wiffen. With 8 Engravings and 24 Woodcuts.

WALKER'S Manly Exercises; containing Skating, Riding, Driving, Hunting, Shooting, Sailing, Rowing, Swimming, &c. 44 Engravings and numerous Woodcuts.

WALTON'S Complete Angler, or the Contemplative Man's Recreation, by Izaak Walton and Charles Cotton. With Memoirs and Notes by E. Jesse. Also an Account of Fishing Stations, Tackle, &c., by H. G. Bohn. Portrait and 203 Woodcuts, and 26 Engravings on Steel.

—— **Lives of Donne, Wotton, Hooker,** &c., with Notes. A New Edition, revised by A. H. Bullen, with a Memoir of Izaak Walton by William Dowling. 6 Portraits, 6 Autograph Signatures, &c.

WELLINGTON, Life of. From the Materials of Maxwell. 18 Steel Engravings.

—— **Victories of.**—*See Maxwell.*

WESTROPP (H. M.) A Handbook of Archæology, Egyptian, Greek, Etruscan, Roman. By H. M. Westropp. Numerous Illustrations.

WHITE'S Natural History of Selborne, with Observations on various Parts of Nature, and the Naturalists' Calendar. Sir W. Jardine. Edit., with Notes and Memoir, by E. Jesse. 40 Portraits and coloured Plates.

CLASSICAL LIBRARY.

TRANSLATIONS FROM THE GREEK AND LATIN.

103 *Vols. at 5s. each, excepting those marked otherwise.* (25l. 4s. 6d. *per set.*)

ÆSCHYLUS, The Dramas of. In English Verse by Anna Swanwick. 4th edition.

—— **The Tragedies of.** In Prose, with Notes and Introduction, by T. A. Buckley, B.A. Portrait. 3s. 6d.

AMMIANUS MARCELLINUS. History of Rome during the Reigns of Constantius, Julian, Jovianus, Valentinian, and Valens, by C. D. Yonge, B.A. Double volume. 7s. 6d.

ANTONINUS (M. Aurelius), The Thoughts of. Translated literally, with Notes, Biographical Sketch, and Essay on the Philosophy, by George Long, M.A. 3s. 6d.

APOLLONIUS RHODIUS. 'The Argonautica.' Translated by E. P. Coleridge.

APULEIUS, The Works of. Comprising the Golden Ass, God of Socrates, Florida, and Discourse of Magic. With a Metrical Version of Cupid and Psyche, and Mrs. Tighe's Psyche. Frontispiece.

ARISTOPHANES' Comedies. Trans., with Notes and Extracts from Frere's and other Metrical Versions, by W. J. Hickie. Portrait. 2 vols.

ARISTOTLE'S Nicomachean Ethics. Trans., with Notes, Analytical Introduction, and Questions for Students, by Ven. Archdn. Browne.

—— **Politics and Economics.** Trans., with Notes, Analyses, and Index, by E. Walford, M.A., and an Essay and Life by Dr. Gillies.

—— **Metaphysics.** Trans., with Notes, Analysis, and Examination Questions, by Rev. John H. M'Mahon, M.A.

—— **History of Animals.** In Ten Books. Trans., with Notes and Index, by R. Cresswell, M.A.

—— **Organon;** or, Logical Treatises, and the Introduction of Porphyry. With Notes, Analysis, and Introduction, by Rev. O. F. Owen, M.A. 2 vols. 3s. 6d. each.

—— **Rhetoric and Poetics.** Trans., with Hobbes' Analysis, Exam. Questions, and Notes, by T. Buckley, B.A. Portrait.

ATHENÆUS. The Deipnosophists; or, the Banquet of the Learned. By C. D. Yonge, B.A. With an Appendix of Poetical Fragments. 3 vols.

ATLAS of Classical Geography. 22 large Coloured Maps. With a complete Index. Imp. 8vo. 7s. 6d.

BION.—*See Theocritus.*

CÆSAR. Commentaries on the Gallic and Civil Wars, with the Supplementary Books attributed to Hirtius, including the complete Alexandrian, African, and Spanish Wars. Trans. with Notes. Portrait.

CATULLUS, Tibullus, and the Vigil of Venus. Trans. with Notes and Biographical Introduction. To which are added, Metrical Versions by Lamb, Grainger, and others. Frontispiece.

CICERO'S Orations. Trans. by C. D. Yonge, B.A. 4 vols.

—— **On Oratory and Orators.** With Letters to Quintus and Brutus. Trans., with Notes, by Rev. J. S. Watson, M.A.

—— **On the Nature of the Gods,** Divination, Fate, Laws, a Republic, Consulship. Trans., with Notes, by C. D. Yonge, B.A.

—— **Academics,** De Finibus, and Tusculan Questions. By C. D. Yonge, B.A. With Sketch of the Greek Philosophers mentioned by Cicero.

CICERO'S Orations.—*Continued.*
—— **Offices;** or, Moral Duties. C Major, an Essay on Old Age; Lælius, Essay on Friendship; Scipio's Drea Paradoxes; Letter to Quintus on Ma trates. Trans., with Notes, by C. R. monds. Portrait. 3s. 6d.

DEMOSTHENES' Orations. Tra with Notes, Arguments, a Chronolog Abstract, and Appendices, by C. R Kennedy. 5 vols.

DICTIONARY of LATIN and GRE Quotations; including Proverbs, Maxi Mottoes, Law Terms and Phrases. W the Quantities marked, and English Tr lations. With Index Verborum (622 pag

—— Index Verborum to the above, with *Quantities* and Accents marked (56 pag limp cloth. 1s.

DIOGENES LAERTIUS. Lives Opinions of the Ancient Philosoph Trans., with Notes, by C. D. Yonge, B

EPICTETUS. The Discourses With the Encheiridion and Fragme With Notes, Life, and View of his Ph sophy, by George Long, M.A.

EURIPIDES. Trans., with Notes and troduction, by T. A. Buckley, B.A. 1 trait. 2 vols.

GREEK ANTHOLOGY. In Eng Prose by G. Burges, M.A. With Met Versions by Bland, Merivale, Lord I man, &c.

GREEK ROMANCES of Heliodor Longus, and Achilles Tatius; viz., Adventures of Theagenes and Charic Amours of Daphnis and Chloe; and Le of Clitopho and Leucippe. Trans., Notes, by Rev. R. Smith, M.A.

HERODOTUS. Literally trans. by I Henry Cary, M.A. Portrait.

HESIOD, CALLIMACHUS, (Theognis. In Prose, with Notes Biographical Notices by Rev. J. Ba M.A. Together with the Metrical sions of Hesiod, by Elton; Callimac by Tytler; and Theognis, by Frere.

HOMER'S Iliad. In English Prose, Notes by T. A. Buckley, B.A. Portr

—— **Odyssey,** Hymns, Epigrams, Battle of the Frogs and Mice. In En Prose, with Notes and Memoir by T Buckley, B.A.

HORACE. In Prose by Smart, with N selected by T. A. Buckley, B.A. trait. 3s. 6d.

JULIAN THE EMPEROR. By Rev. C. W. King, M.A.

USTIN, CORNELIUS NEPOS, and Eutropius. Trans., with Notes, by Rev. J. S. Watson, M.A.

UVENAL, PERSIUS, SULPICIA, and Lucilius. In Prose, with Notes, Chronological Tables, Arguments, by L. Evans, M.A. To which is added the Metrical Version of Juvenal and Persius by Gifford. Frontispiece.

IVY. The History of Rome. Trans. by Dr. Spillan and others. 4 vols. Portrait.

UCAN'S Pharsalia. In Prose, with Notes by H. T. Riley.

UCIAN'S Dialogues of the Gods, of the Sea Gods, and of the Dead. Trans. by Howard Williams, M.A.

UCRETIUS. In Prose, with Notes and Biographical Introduction by Rev. J. S. Watson, M.A. To which is added the Metrical Version by J. M. Good.

IARTIAL'S Epigrams, complete. In Prose, with Verse Translations selected from English Poets, and other sources. Dble. vol. (670 pages). 7s. 6d.

IOSCHUS.—See Theocritus.

VID'S Works, complete. In Prose, with Notes and Introduction. 3 vols.

AUSANIAS' Description of Greece. Translated into English, with Notes and Index. By Arthur Richard Shilleto, M.A., sometime Scholar of Trinity College, Cambridge. 2 vols.

HALARIS. Bentley's Dissertations upon the Epistles of Phalaris, Themistocles, Socrates, Euripides, and the Fables of Æsop. With Introduction and Notes by Prof. W. Wagner, Ph.D.

INDAR. In Prose, with Introduction and Notes by Dawson W. Turner. Together with the Metrical Version by Abraham Moore. Portrait.

LATO'S Works. Trans., with Introduction and Notes. 6 vols.

— Dialogues. A Summary and Analysis of. With Analytical Index to the Greek text of modern editions and to the above translations, by A. Day, LL.D.

LAUTUS'S Comedies. In Prose, with Notes and Index by H. T. Riley, B.A. 2 vols.

LINY'S Natural History. Trans., with Notes, by J. Bostock, M.D., F.R.S., and H. T. Riley, B.A. 6 vols.

LINY. The Letters of Pliny the Younger. Melmoth's Translation, revised, with Notes and short Life, by Rev. F. C. T. Bosanquet, M.A.

PLUTARCH'S Morals. Theosophical Essays. Trans. by C. W. King, M.A.

—— Ethical Essays. Trans. by A. R. Shilleto, M.A.

—— Lives. See page 7.

PROPERTIUS, The Elegies of. With Notes, Literally translated by the Rev. P. J. F. Gantillon, M.A., with metrical versions of Select Elegies by Nott and Elton. 3s. 6d.

QUINTILIAN'S Institutes of Oratory. Trans., with Notes and Biographical Notice, by Rev. J. S. Watson, M.A. 2 vols.

SALLUST, FLORUS, and VELLEIUS Paterculus. Trans., with Notes and Biographical Notices, by J. S. Watson, M.A.

SENECA DE BENEFICIIS. Newly translated by Aubrey Stewart, M.A. 3s. 6d.

SENECA'S Minor Essays. Translated by A. Stewart, M.A.

SOPHOCLES. The Tragedies of. In Prose, with Notes, Arguments, and Introduction. Portrait.

STRABO'S Geography. Trans., with Notes, by W. Falconer, M.A., and H. C. Hamilton. Copious Index, giving Ancient and Modern Names. 3 vols.

SUETONIUS' Lives of the Twelve Cæsars and Lives of the Grammarians. The Translation of Thomson, revised, with Notes, by T. Forester.

TACITUS. The Works of. Trans., with Notes. 2 vols.

TERENCE and PHÆDRUS. In English Prose, with Notes and Arguments, by H. T. Riley, B.A. To which is added Smart's Metrical Version of Phædrus. With Frontispiece.

THEOCRITUS, BION, MOSCHUS, and Tyrtæus. In Prose, with Notes and Arguments, by Rev. J. Banks, M.A. To which are appended the METRICAL VERSIONS of Chapman. Portrait of Theocritus.

THUCYDIDES. The Peloponnesian War. Trans., with Notes, by Rev. H. Dale. Portrait. 2 vols. 3s. 6d. each.

TYRTÆUS.—See Theocritus.

VIRGIL. The Works of. In Prose, with Notes by Davidson. Revised, with additional Notes and Biographical Notice, by T. A. Buckley, B.A. Portrait. 3s. 6d.

XENOPHON'S Works. Trans., with Notes, by J. S. Watson, M.A., and others. Portrait. In 3 vols.

COLLEGIATE SERIES.

10 Vols. at 5s. each. (*2l. 10s. per set.*)

DANTE. The Inferno. Prose Trans., with the Text of the Original on the same page, and Explanatory Notes, by John A. Carlyle, M.D. Portrait.

—— **The Purgatorio.** Prose Trans., with the Original on the same page, and Explanatory Notes, by W. S. Dugdale.

NEW TESTAMENT (The) in Greek. Griesbach's Text, with the Readings of Mill and Scholz at the foot of the page, and Parallel References in the margin. Also a Critical Introduction and Chronological Tables. Two Fac-similes of Greek Manuscripts. 650 pages. 3s. 6d.

—— or bound up with a Greek and English Lexicon to the New Testament (250 pages additional, making in all 900). 5s.

The Lexicon may be had separately, price 2s.

DOBREE'S Adversaria. (Notes on the Greek and Latin Classics.) Edited by the late Prof. Wagner. 2 vols.

DONALDSON (Dr.) The Theatre the Greeks. With Supplementary Treat on the Language, Metres, and Prosody the Greek Dramatists. Numerous Il trations and 3 Plans. By J. W. Dona son, D.D.

KEIGHTLEY'S (Thomas) Mytholo of Ancient Greece and Italy. Revised Leonhard Schmitz, Ph.D., LL.D. Plates.

HERODOTUS, Notes on. Origin and Selected from the best Commentato By D. W. Turner, M.A. Coloured Ma

—— **Analysis and Summary of,** w a Synchronistical Table of Events—Tab of Weights, Measures, Money, and I tances — an Outline of the History Geography—and the Dates completed fr Gaisford, Baehr, &c. By J. T. Wheele

THUCYDIDES. An Analysis a Summary of. With Chronological Ta of Events, &c., by J. T. Wheeler.

SCIENTIFIC LIBRARY.

51 Vols. at 5s. each, excepting those marked otherwise. (*13l. 9s. 6d. per set.*

AGASSIZ and GOULD. Outline of Comparative Physiology touching the Structure and Development of the Races of Animals living and extinct. For Schools and Colleges. Enlarged by Dr. Wright. With Index and 300 Illustrative Woodcuts.

BOLLEY'S Manual of Technical Analysis; a Guide for the Testing and Valuation of the various Natural and Artificial Substances employed in the Arts and Domestic Economy, founded on the work of Dr. Bolley. Edit. by Dr. Paul. 100 Woodcuts.

BRIDGEWATER TREATISES.

—— **Bell (Sir Charles) on the Hand;** its Mechanism and Vital Endowments, as evincing Design. Preceded by an Account of the Author's Discoveries in the Nervous System by A. Shaw. Numerous Woodcuts.

—— **Kirby on the History, Habits,** and Instincts of Animals. With Notes by T. Rymer Jones. 100 Woodcuts. 2 vols.

—— **Whewell's Astronomy and** General Physics, considered with reference to Natural Theology. Portrait of the Earl of Bridgewater. 3s. 6d.

BRIDGEWATER TREATISES
Continued.

—— **Chalmers on the Adaptation** External Nature to the Moral and Int lectual Constitution of Man. With Mem by Rev. Dr. Cumming. Portrait.

—— **Prout's Treatise on Chemistr** Meteorology, and the Function of Dig tion, with reference to Natural Theolo Edit. by Dr. J. W. Griffith. 2 Maps.

—— **Buckland's Geology and Min** alogy. With Additions by Prof. Ow Prof. Phillips, and R. Brown. Memoir Buckland. Portrait. 2 vols. 15s. Vol Text. Vol. II. 90 large plates with lett press.

—— **Roget's Animal and Vegetal** Physiology. 463 Woodcuts. 2 vols. each.

—— **Kidd on the Adaptation of E** ternal Nature to the Physical Condition Man. 3s. 6d.

CARPENTER'S (Dr. W. B.) Zoolo A Systematic View of the Structure, I bits, Instincts, and Uses of the princi Families of the Animal Kingdom, and the chief Forms of Fossil Remains. vised by W. S. Dallas, F.L.S. Numer Woodcuts. 2 vols. 6s. each.

ARPENTER'S Works.—*Continued.*
— **Mechanical Philosophy, Astronomy, and Horology.** A Popular Exposition. 181 Woodcuts.
— **Vegetable Physiology and Systematic Botany.** A complete Introduction to the Knowledge of Plants. Revised by E. Lankester, M.D., &c. Numerous Woodcuts. 6s.
— **Animal Physiology.** Revised Edition. 300 Woodcuts. 6s.

HEVREUL on Colour. Containing the Principles of Harmony and Contrast of Colours, and their Application to the Arts; including Painting, Decoration, Tapestries, Carpets, Mosaics, Glazing, Staining, Calico Printing, Letterpress Printing, Map Colouring, Dress, Landscape and Flower Gardening, &c. Trans. by C. Martel. Several Plates.
— With an additional series of 16 Plates in Colours, 7s. 6d.

NNEMOSER'S History of Magic. Trans. by W. Howitt. With an Appendix of the most remarkable and best authenticated Stories of Apparitions, Dreams, Second Sight, Table-Turning, and Spirit-Rapping, &c. 2 vols.

IND'S Introduction to Astronomy. With Vocabulary of the Terms in present use. Numerous Woodcuts. 3s. 6d.

OGG'S (Jabez) Elements of Experimental and Natural Philosophy. Being an Easy Introduction to the Study of Mechanics, Pneumatics, Hydrostatics, Hydraulics, Acoustics, Optics, Caloric, Electricity, Voltaism, and Magnetism. 400 Woodcuts.

UMBOLDT'S Cosmos; or, Sketch of a Physical Description of the Universe. Trans. by E. C. Otté, B. H. Paul, and W. S. Dallas, F.L.S. Portrait. 5 vols. 3s. 6d. each, excepting vol. v., 5s.
— Personal Narrative of his Travels in America during the years 1799-1804. Trans., with Notes, by T. Ross. 3 vols.
— Views of Nature; or, Contemplations of the Sublime Phenomena of Creation, with Scientific Illustrations. Trans. by E. C. Otté.

UNT'S (Robert) Poetry of Science; or, Studies of the Physical Phenomena of Nature. By Robert Hunt, Professor at the School of Mines.

OYCE'S Scientific Dialogues. A Familiar Introduction to the Arts and Sciences. For Schools and Young People. Numerous Woodcuts.

OYCE'S Introduction to the Arts and Sciences, for Schools and Young People. Divided into Lessons with Examination Questions. Woodcuts. 3s. 6d.

JUKES-BROWNE'S Student's Handbook of Physical Geology. By A. J. Jukes-Browne, of the Geological Survey of England. With numerous Diagrams and Illustrations, 6s.
—— The Student's Handbook of Historical Geology. By A. J. Jukes-Brown, B.A., F.G.S., of the Geological Survey of England and Wales. With numerous Diagrams and Illustrations. 6s.
—— The Building of the British Islands. A Study in Geographical Evolution. By A. J. Jukes-Browne, F.G.S. 7s. 6d.

KNIGHT'S (Charles) Knowledge is Power. A Popular Manual of Political Economy.

LILLY. Introduction to Astrology. With a Grammar of Astrology and Tables for calculating Nativities, by Zadkiel.

MANTELL'S (Dr.) Geological Excursions through the Isle of Wight and along the Dorset Coast. Numerous Woodcuts and Geological Map.
—— Petrifactions and their Teachings. Handbook to the Organic Remains in the British Museum. Numerous Woodcuts. 6s.
—— Wonders of Geology; or, a Familiar Exposition of Geological Phenomena. A coloured Geological Map of England, Plates, and 200 Woodcuts. 2 vols. 7s. 6d. each.

SCHOUW'S Earth, Plants, and Man. Popular Pictures of Nature. And Kobell's Sketches from the Mineral Kingdom. Trans. by A. Henfrey, F.R.S. Coloured Map of the Geography of Plants.

SMITH'S (Pye) Geology and Scripture; or, the Relation between the Scriptures and Geological Science. With Memoir.

STANLEY'S Classified Synopsis of the Principal Painters of the Dutch and Flemish Schools, including an Account of some of the early German Masters. By George Stanley.

STAUNTON'S Chess Works. — *See page 21.*

STOCKHARDT'S Experimental Chemistry. A Handbook for the Study of the Science by simple Experiments. Edit. by C. W. Heaton, F.C.S. Numerous Woodcuts.

URE'S (Dr. A.) Cotton Manufacture of Great Britain, systematically investigated; with an Introductory View of its Comparative State in Foreign Countries. Revised by P. L. Simmonds. 150 Illustrations. 2 vols.
—— Philosophy of Manufactures, or an Exposition of the Scientific, Moral, and Commercial Economy of the Factory System of Great Britain. Revised by P. L. Simmonds. Numerous Figures. 800 pages. 7s. 6d.

ECONOMICS AND FINANCE.

GILBART'S History, Principles, and Practice of Banking. R
A. S. Michie, of the Royal Bank of Scotland. Portrait of Gilbart. 2 v(

REFERENCE LIBRARY.

30 *Volumes at Various Prices.* (9*l.* 5*s. per set.*)

BLAIR'S Chronological Tables. Comprehending the Chronology and History of the World, from the Earliest Times to the Russian Treaty of Peace, April 1856. By J. W. Rosse. 800 pages. 10*s.*

—— **Index of Dates.** Comprehending the principal Facts in the Chronology and History of the World, from the Earliest to the Present, alphabetically arranged; being a complete Index to the foregoing. By J. W. Rosse. 2 vols. 5*s.* each.

BOHN'S Dictionary of Quotations from the English Poets. 4th and cheaper Edition. 6*s.*

BOND'S Handy-book of Rules and Tables for Verifying Dates with the Christian Era. 4th Edition.

BUCHANAN'S Dictionary of Science and Technical Terms used in Philosophy, Literature, Professions, Commerce, Arts, and Trades. By W. H. Buchanan, with Supplement. Edited by Jas. A. Smith. 6*s.*

CHRONICLES OF THE TOMBS. A Select Collection of Epitaphs, with Essay on Epitaphs and Observations on Sepulchral Antiquities. By T. J. Pettigrew, F.R.S., F.S.A. 5*s.*

CLARK'S (Hugh) Introduction to Heraldry. Revised by J. R. Planché. 5*s.* 950 Illustrations.

—— *With the Illustrations coloured,* 15*s.*

COINS, Manual of.—*See Humphreys.*

COOPER'S Biographical Dictionary, Containing concise notices of upwards of 15,000 eminent persons of all ages and countries. 2 vols. 5*s.* each.

DATES, Index of.—*See Blair.*

DICTIONARY of Obsolete and Provincial English. Containing Words from English Writers previous to the 19th Century. By Thomas Wright, M.A., F.S.A., &c. 2 vols. 5*s.* each.

EPIGRAMMATISTS (The). A Selection from the Epigrammatic Literature of Ancient, Mediæval, and Modern Times. With Introduction, Notes, Observations, Illustrations, an Appendix on Works connected with Epigrammatic Literature, by Rev. H. Dodd, M.A. 6*s.*

GAMES, Handbook Treatises on above 40 G Skill, and Manua. De Whist, Billiards, &c. E Bohn. Numerous Diag

HENFREY'S Guid Coins. Revised Edition M.A., F.S.A. With an duction. 6*s.*

HUMPHREYS' Co Manual. An Historica Progress of Coinage fr Time, by H. N. Hump trations. 2 vols. 5*s.* eacl

LOWNDES' Bibliogra of English Literature. (count of Rare and Cu lished in or relating to (Ireland, from the Inver with Biographical Not by W. T. Lowndes. Pa 3*s.* 6*d.* each. Part XI. 5*s.* Or the 11 parts morocco, 2*l.* 2*s.*

MEDICINE, Handboo Popularly Arranged. B 700 pages. 5*s.*

NOTED NAMES C Dictionary of. Includi Pseudonyms, Surnames nent Men, &c. By W. A.

POLITICAL CYCl Dictionary of Political Statistical, and Foren forming a Work of Refe of Civil Administration, I Finance, Commerce, I Relations. 4 vols. 3*s.* 6(

PROVERBS, Handb(taining an entire Repul Collection, with Additi Languages and Say Maxims, and Phrases.

—— **A Polyglot of :** prising French, Italian, Spanish, Portuguese, a English Translations. :

SYNONYMS and AI Kindred Words and th(lected and Contrasted Smith, M.A. 5*s.*

WRIGHT (Th.)—*See 1*

NOVELISTS' LIBRARY.

1 3 Volumes at 3s. 6d. each, excepting those marked otherwise. (2l. 8s. 6d. per set.)

BJÖRNSON'S Arne and the Fisher
Lassie. Translated from the Norse with
an Introduction by W. H. Low, M.A.

BURNEY'S Evelina; or, a Young
Lady's Entrance into the World. By F.
Burney (Mme. D'Arblay). With Introduction and Notes by A. R. Ellis, Author
of 'Sylvestra,' &c.

—— **Cecilia.** With Introduction and
Notes by A. R. Ellis. 2 vols.

DE STAËL. Corinne or Italy.
By Madame de Staël. Translated by
Emily Baldwin and Paulina Driver.

EBERS' Egyptian Princess. Trans.
by Emma Buchheim.

FIELDING'S Joseph Andrews and
his Friend Mr. Abraham Adams. With
Roscoe's Biography. *Cruikshank's Illustrations.*

—— **Amelia.** Roscoe's Edition, revised.
Cruikshank's Illustrations. 5s.

—— **History of Tom Jones, a Found-**
ling. Roscoe's Edition. *Cruikshank's
Illustrations.* 2 vols.

GROSSI'S Marco Visconti. Trans.
by A. F. D.

MANZONI. The Betrothed: being
a Translation of 'I Promessi Sposi.'
Numerous Woodcuts. 1 vol. 5s.

STOWE (Mrs. H. B.) Uncle Tom's
Cabin; or, Life among the Lowly. 8 full-
page Illustrations.

ARTISTS' LIBRARY.

9 Volumes at Various Prices. (2l. 8s. 6d. per set.)

BELL (Sir Charles). The Anatomy
and Philosophy of Expression, as Connected with the Fine Arts. 5s.

DEMMIN. History of Arms and
Armour from the Earliest Period. By
Auguste Demmin. Trans. by C. C.
Black, M.A., Assistant Keeper, S. K.
Museum. 1900 Illustrations. 7s. 6d.

FAIRHOLT'S Costume in England.
Third Edition. Enlarged and Revised by
the Hon. H. A. Dillon, F.S.A. With
more than 700 Engravings. 2 vols. 5s.
each.
     Vol. I. History. Vol. II. Glossary.

FLAXMAN. Lectures on Sculpture.
With Three Addresses to the R.A. by Sir
R. Westmacott, R.A., and Memoir of
Flaxman. Portrait and 53 Plates. 6s. *N.S.*

HEATON'S Concise History of
Painting. New Edition, revised by
W. Cosmo Monkhouse. 5s.

LECTURES ON PAINTING by the
Royal Academicians, Barry, Opie, Fuseli.
With Introductory Essay and Notes by
R. Wornum. Portrait of Fuseli.

LEONARDO DA VINCI'S Treatise
on Painting. Trans. by J. F. Rigaud, R.A.
With a Life and an Account of his Works
by J. W. Brown. Numerous Plates. 5s.

PLANCHÉ'S History of British
Costume, from the Earliest Time to the
10th Century. By J. R. Planché. 400
Illustrations. 5s.

LIBRARY OF SPORTS AND GAMES.

10 Volumes at 5s. each. (2l. 10s. per set.)

BOHN'S Handbooks of Athletic Sports. In 5 vols.

Vol. I.—Cricket, by Hon. and Rev. E. Lyttelton; Lawn Tennis, by H. W. Wilberforce; Tennis, Rackets, and Fives, by Julian Marshall, Major Spens, and J. A. Tait; Golf, by W. T. Linskill; Hockey, by F. S. Cresswell. *[Ready.*

Vol. II.—Rowing and Sculling, by W. B. Woodgate; Sailing, by E. F. Knight; Swimming, by M. and J. R. Cobbett. *[Ready.*

Vol. III.—Boxing, by R. G. Allanson-Winn; Single Stick and Sword Exercise, by R. G. Allanson-Winn and C. Phillipps Wolley; Wrestling, by Walter Armstrong; Fencing, by H. A. Colmore Dunn. *[In the press.*

Vol. IV.—Cycling, by H. H. Griffin; Rugby Football, by Harry Vassall; Association Football, by C. W. Alcock; Skating, by Douglas Adams. *[In the press.*

Vol. V.—Gymnastics, by A. F. Jenkin; Clubs and Dumb-bells. *[In the press.*

BOHN'S Handbooks of Games. New Edition. 2 volumes.

Vol. I. TABLE GAMES.

Contents:—Billiards, with Pool, Pyramids, and Snooker, by Major-Gen. A. W. Drayson, F.R.A.S., with a preface by W. J. Peall—Bagatelle, by 'Berkeley'—Chess, by R. F. Green—Draughts, Backgammon, Dominoes, Solitaire, Reversi, Go Bang, Rouge et noir, Roulette, E.O., Hazard, Faro, by 'Berkeley.'

Vol. II. CARD GAMES.

Contents:—Whist, by Dr. William Pole, F.R.S., Author of 'The Philosophy of Whist, &c.'—Solo Whist, by R. F. Green; Piquet, Ecarté, Euchre, by 'Berkeley;' Poker, Loo, Vingt-et-un, Napoleon, Newmarket, Rouge et Noir, Pope Joan, Speculation, &c. &c., by Baxter-Wray.

CHESS CONGRESS of 1862. A collection of the games played. Edited by J. Löwenthal. New edition, 5s.

MORPHY'S Games of Chess, being the Matches and best Games played by the American Champion, with explanatory and analytical Notes by J. Löwenthal. With short Memoir and Portrait of Morphy.

STAUNTON'S Chess-Player's Handbook. A Popular and Scientific Introduction to the Game, with numerous Diagrams and Coloured Frontispiece.

—— **Chess Praxis.** A Supplement to the Chess-player's Handbook. Containing the most important modern Improvements in the Openings; Code of Chess Laws; and a Selection of Morphy's Games. Annotated. 636 pages. Diagrams.

—— **Chess-Player's Companion.** Comprising a Treatise on Odds, Collection of Match Games, including the French Match with M. St. Amant, and a Selection of Original Problems. Diagrams and Coloured Frontispiece.

—— **Chess Tournament of 1851.** A Collection of Games played at this celebrated assemblage. With Introduction and Notes. Numerous Diagrams.

BOHN'S CHEAP SERIES.

Price 1s. each.

A Series of Complete Stories or Essays, mostly reprinted from Vols. in Bohn's Libraries, and neatly bound in stiff paper cover, with cut edges, suitable for Railway Reading.

ASCHAM (Roger). Scholemaster. By Professor Mayor.

CARPENTER (Dr. W. B.). Physiology of Temperance and Total Abstinence.

EMERSON. England and English Characteristics. Lectures on the Race, Ability, Manners, Truth, Character, Wealth, Religion. &c. &c.

—— Nature: An Essay. To which are added Orations, Lectures, and Addresses.

—— Representative Men: Seven Lectures on PLATO, SWEDENBORG, MONTAIGNE, SHAKESPEARE, NAPOLEON, and GOETHE.

—— Twenty Essays on Various Subjects.

—— The Conduct of Life.

FRANKLIN (Benjamin). Autobiography. Edited by J. Sparks.

HAWTHORNE (Nathaniel). Twice-told Tales. Two Vols. in One.

—— Snow Image, and Other Tales.

—— Scarlet Letter.

—— House with the Seven Gables.

—— Transformation; or the Marble Fawn. Two Parts.

HAZLITT (W.). Table-talk: Essays on Men and Manners. Three Parts.

—— Plain Speaker: Opinions on Books, Men, and Things. Three Parts.

—— Lectures on the English Comic Writers.

—— Lectures on the English Poets.

—— Lectures on the Characters of Shakespeare's Plays.

—— Lectures on the Literature of the Age of Elizabeth, chiefly Dramatic.

IRVING (Washington). Lives of Successors of Mohammed.

—— Life of Goldsmith.

—— Sketch-book.

—— Tales of a Traveller.

—— Tour on the Prairies.

—— Conquests of Granada and Spain. Two Parts.

—— Life and Voyages of Columbus. Two Parts.

—— Companions of Columbus: Their Voyages and Discoveries.

—— Adventures of Captain Bonneville in the Rocky Mountains and the Far West.

—— Knickerbocker's History of New York, from the beginning of the World to the End of the Dutch Dynasty.

—— Tales of the Alhambra.

—— Conquest of Florida under Hernando de Soto.

—— Abbotsford & Newstead Abbey.

—— Salmagundi; or, The Whim-Whams and Opinions of LAUNCELOT LANGSTAFF, Esq.

—— Bracebridge Hall; or, The Humourists.

—— Astoria; or, Anecdotes of an Enterprise beyond the Rocky Mountains.

—— Wolfert's Roost, and other Tales.

LAMB (Charles). Essays of Elia. With a Portrait.

—— Last Essays of Elia.

—— Eliana. With Biographical Sketch.

MARRYAT (Captain). Pirate and the Three Cutters. With a Memoir of the Author.

The only authorised Edition; no others published in England contain the Derivations and Etymological Notes of Dr. Mahn, who devoted several years to this portion of the Work.

WEBSTER'S DICTIONARY
OF THE ENGLISH LANGUAGE.

Thoroughly revised and improved by CHAUNCEY A. GOODRICH, D.D., LL.D., and NOAH PORTER, D.D., of Yale College.

THE GUINEA DICTIONARY.

New Edition [1880], with a Supplement of upwards of 4600 New Words and Meanings.

1628 Pages. 3000 Illustrations.

The features of this volume, which render it perhaps the most useful Dictionary for general reference extant, as it is undoubtedly one of the cheapest books ever published, are as follows :—

1. COMPLETENESS.—It contains 114,000 words.
2. ACCURACY OF DEFINITION.
3. SCIENTIFIC AND TECHNICAL TERMS.
4. ETYMOLOGY.
5. THE ORTHOGRAPHY is based, as far as possible, on Fixed Principles.
6. PRONUNCIATION.
7. THE ILLUSTRATIVE CITATIONS.
8. THE SYNONYMS.
9. THE ILLUSTRATIONS, which exceed 3000.

Cloth, 21*s.* ; half-bound in calf, 30*s.* ; calf or half russia, 31*s.* 6*d.*; russia, 2*l.*

With New Biographical Appendix, containing over 9700 Names.

THE COMPLETE DICTIONARY

Contains, in addition to the above matter, several valuable Literary Appendices, and **70 extra pages** of Illustrations, grouped and classified.

1 vol. 1919 pages, cloth, 31*s.* 6*d.*

'Certainly the best practical English Dictionary extant.'—*Quarterly Review*, 1873.

Prospectuses, with Specimen Pages, sent post free on application.

*** *To be obtained through all Booksellers.*

Bohn's Select Library of Standard Works.

Price 1s. in paper covers, and 1s. 6d. in cloth.

1. BACON'S ESSAYS. With Introduction and Notes.
2. LESSING'S LAOKOON. Beasley's Translation, revised, with Introduction, Notes, &c., by Edward Bell, M.A.
3. DANTE'S INFERNO. Translated, with Notes, by Rev. H. F. Cary.
4. GOETHE'S FAUST. Part I. Translated, with Introduction, by Anna Swanwick.
5. GOETHE'S BOYHOOD. Being Part I. of the Autobiography. Translated by J. Oxenford.
6. SCHILLER'S MARY STUART and THE MAID OF ORLEANS. Translated by J. Mellish and Anna Swanwick.
7. THE QUEEN'S ENGLISH. By the late Dean Alford.
8. LIFE AND LABOURS OF THE LATE THOMAS BRASSEY. By Sir A. Helps, K.C.B.
9. PLATO'S DIALOGUES: The Apology—Crito—Phaedo—Protagoras. With Introductions.
10. MOLIÈRE'S PLAYS: The Miser—Tartuffe—The Shopkeeper turned Gentleman. With brief Memoir.
11. GOETHE'S REINEKE FOX, in English Hexameters. By A. Rogers.
12. OLIVER GOLDSMITH'S PLAYS.
13. LESSING'S PLAYS: Nathan the Wise—Minna von Barnhelm.
14. PLAUTUS'S COMEDIES: Trinummus — Menaechmi — Aulularia — Captivi.
15. WATERLOO DAYS. By C. A. Eaton. With Preface and Notes by Edward Bell.
16. DEMOSTHENES—ON THE CROWN. Translated by C. Rann Kennedy.
17. THE VICAR OF WAKEFIELD.
18. OLIVER CROMWELL. By Dr. Reinhold Pauli.
19. THE PERFECT LIFE. By Dr. Channing. Edited by his nephew, Rev. W. H. Channing.
20. LADIES IN PARLIAMENT, HORACE AT ATHENS and other pieces, by Sir George Otto Trevelyan, Bart.
21. DEFOE'S THE PLAGUE IN LONDON.
22. IRVING'S LIFE OF MAHOMET.
23. HORACE'S ODES, by various hands. [*Out of print.*
24. BURKE'S ESSAY ON 'THE SUBLIME AND BEAUTIFUL.' With Short Memoir.
25. HAUFF'S CARAVAN.
26. SHERIDAN'S PLAYS.
27. DANTE'S PURGATORIO. Translated by Cary.
28. HARVEY'S TREATISE ON THE CIRCULATION OF THE BLOOD
29. CICERO'S FRIENDSHIP AND OLD AGE.
30. DANTE'S PARADISO. Translated by Cary.

LONDON: GEORGE BELL AND SONS.

London: Printed by STRANGEWAYS & SONS, Tower Street, Cambridge Circus, W